His forehead beaded with sweat.

Jon silently prayed to God not to be right, not to let the suspicions that had been gathering around him like dark clouds be confirmed.

Feeling like a thief, he hurried to David's study, flicking through the keys Tiggy had handed him until he found the one for the desk. The drawers were a jumble of unanswered mail and unfiled correspondence all thrown haphazardly on top of one another. He could see the familiar buff edge of the file poking out from underneath a thick, untidy wad of bank statements. His heart started to beat very fast.

He had just removed the file when the study door opened. He froze as he heard Olivia exclaiming, "Tiggy… Oh, Uncle Jon, it's you."

Penny Jordan's novels "…touch every emotion."

—*Romantic Times*

PENNY JORDAN

A Perfect Family

MIRA

ISBN 1-55166-414-3

A PERFECT FAMILY

Copyright © 1997 by Penny Jordan.

MIRA and the star colophon are registered trademarks of MIRA Books.

Printed in U.S.A.

The Crighton Family

BEN CRIGHTON: Strong-minded, proud patriarch, he's determined to see his dynasty thrive and prosper.

RUTH CRIGHTON: Ben's sister who, after a tragic wartime love affair, has devoted herself to the family.

DAVID CRIGHTON: Twin brother of Jon, and favorite son of Ben. Charming and selfish, he doesn't deserve his status as heir to the family fortune....

TIGGY CRIGHTON: Beautiful but fragile wife of David. An ex-model desperate for attention, she flirts with all men.

OLIVIA CRIGHTON: Daughter of David and Tiggy, she wants to break from the family and go to America with her lover, Caspar. In defiance, Livvy has become a talented lawyer outside the family firm.

CASPAR JOHNSON: An American law tutor brought into the Crighton family by Olivia, he is concerned by the family's influence over her.

JON CRIGHTON: Younger twin of David, he carries the burden of responsibility in the family law firm.

JENNY CRIGHTON: Warmhearted and practical wife of Jon. She's a partner in an antiques business and a role model for her niece, Livvy.

MAX CRIGHTON: Son of Jon and Jenny, a ruthlessly ambitious lawyer prepared to do anything to climb the career ladder.

LOUISE and KATE: Spirited twin teenage daughters of Jon and Jenny, who are determined to go their own way.

JOSS: Charming eight-year-old son of Jon and Jenny.

SAUL CRIGHTON: A caring man the family had once hoped would marry Olivia. He is now married to an American, but their relationship is on shaky ground.

The Crighton Family

Haslewich branch of the family

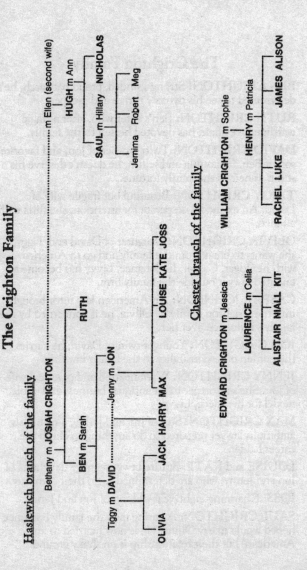

Bethany m JOSIAH CRIGHTON .... m Ellen (second wife)

BEN m Sarah   RUTH   HUGH m Ann   NICHOLAS

Tiggy m DAVID   Jenny m JON   SAUL m Hillary

Jemima   Robert   Meg

OLIVIA   JACK HARRY MAX   LOUISE KATE JOSS

Chester branch of the family

EDWARD CRIGHTON m Jessica   WILLIAM CRIGHTON m Sophie

LAURENCE m Celia   HENRY m Patricia

ALISTAIR NIALL KIT   RACHEL LUKE   JAMES ALISON

Prologue

1917

It had been a cold, wet spring followed by an even wetter summer, and the crops lay flattened and battered beneath the relentlessly driving rain.

As Josiah Crighton wiped the condensation away from the railway carriage window to look outside he paused, turning instead to study the pale, set face of the girl seated beside him.

The girl...his wife, soon to be the mother of his child. His jaw tightened as he remembered his father's fury when he learned what had happened.

'For God's sake, if you had to behave so...so stupidly, why the hell didn't you do it outside your own backyard? Oxford...or the Inns of Court...surely you had ample opportunity there to—'

His father had broken off, drumming angrily on his desk whilst he surveyed him.

'Well, there's no help for it now. The girl will have to be found a suitable husband and as for you—'

'She already has a husband,' he had told his father quietly.

Just for a moment he saw that his father had misunderstood him, noting the relief expelling the impatient anger from his eyes as he exclaimed, 'She's married...then why the hell didn't you say so...?'

His expression began changing as Josiah continued to look steadily at him and quietly explained, 'We're married, Father... Bethany and I...'

He had of course already anticipated the uproar that would follow his announcement and their mutual banishment from the lives of both their families. Hers had been no more pleased than his had been. Bethany was a yeoman farmer's daughter who had been working up at the big house. He had bumped into her when he had gone there with some papers his father had instructed him to take to Lord Haver. They had recognised each other immediately from shared summer childhoods playing forbidden games on the muddy banks of the Dee.

One thing had led to another and the inevitable had happened. As soon as she had come to him with her news, ashen-faced and frightened, he had done what he had convinced himself was the only honourable thing he could do; never mind the fact that it was virtually an accepted thing within his family that one day he would cement the ties that kept the family together and, following its long-established tradition, marry his second cousin.

Bethany, too, had been destined for a family-arranged marriage to a distant relation, a widower with some well-stocked farmlands on the Welsh side of the city and two half-grown children in need of a mother's care.

Refused the support of both families and the place that had been promised to him in the family firm of solicitors, Josiah had had no other course open to him but to find some alternative way of providing for his new wife and the child they were soon to have. And so he had taken a small set of rooms in the tiny market town of Haslewich, hoping that the business from the townspeople and the local rural community would be enough to sustain himself and his new family.

'Do you really love me, Josiah?' his new bride had asked him miserably, clinging tearfully to him on the day of their hurried and secret wedding.

He had held her tightly in his arms, unable to answer her honestly and unwilling to lie to her. The past and the comfortable security it had contained were now lost to him. The future stretched ahead as bleak and unwelcoming as the rain-lashed countryside. Turning his attention back to the scene beyond the railway carriage window, he tried not to contrast the life he had left to the one he was heading towards.

In Chester, his father's secretary would just be bringing in afternoon tea. A fire would be burning warmly in the grate of his father's panelled office. As the senior partner in Chester's most prestigious firm of solicitors, his father was held very much in awe by those who worked for him and most especially Miss Berry, who guarded his privacy as jealously as any guard dog, even keeping a watchful eye on Josiah's elder brothers who were also partners in the family firm.

The handsome silver teapot from which his father would take his afternoon tea had been a gift from a wealthy client, the china likewise, a particularly attractive and rare Sèvres teaset that had come to his father by way of a bequest.

In the bare spare rooms that were all Josiah could

afford to rent and that must serve as his home as well
as his place of business, he would be lucky if he managed the luxury of afternoon tea at all. There would
certainly be no silver teapot from which to pour it and
no Sèvres cup from which to drink it.

As he stared out of the window, his expression
started to harden. The youngest of his father's three
sons, he had known even before his father had announced his rejection from the family that he was the
least valuable of his father's many assets. With his
sons, Edward and William, already in the family business, a brother and a sister and countless numbers of
nieces, nephews and other familial connections, his father could quite easily afford to dispense with one dis-
obedient and disgraced son.

He would never treat his child, his own son, as his
father had treated him, Josiah decided passionately,
and he would, furthermore, ensure that his son would
inherit a tradition every bit as proud and respected as
the one that had been denied him. More so...much
more so. As he glanced at the face of his now-sleeping
wife, Josiah determined to found a dynasty that
would one day rival that of his father and brothers.
Rival it and outmatch it.

1969

As they drove north, the top down on the bright red
sports car David Crighton had persuaded his father to
buy him as a reward for obtaining his degree—not a
first but at least he had passed—he turned his head to
look at the girl in the passenger seat beside him, a feeling of fierce exultation running through him.

He had snatched her, virtually stolen her away, from under the nose of one of his friends, another member of the pop group that four of them had formed in their final year at college.

For a few months they had enjoyed a spell of dizzying success; a small fat man with a shiny bald head and even shinier suit, smoking a fat cigar, had come backstage after one of their gigs and offered to help them get a contract with one of the major recording studios.

It had been at a time when young unknowns were becoming overnight millionaires, their names whispered breathlessly and then screamed at in orgasmic frenzy by thousands of teenage girls throughout the land, and there had been no reason to doubt that the same thing could happen to them. Only the small fat man had turned out to be rather shrewder than they had realised, and whilst they had ridiculed his attempts to become one of them, he had been quietly skimming off most of their earnings.

All they had been left with were the remaindered copies of a record that had never made it out of the bottom fifty of the hit parade and a very large bill from the tax authorities.

His grandfather, Josiah, had paid off his share of it, angrily telling him that he was only doing so to save the family name from being disgraced. David hadn't cared what had motivated him. Smiling genially at the older man in a marijuana-induced haze of goodwill, he had carelessly listened to the lecture he was being given and then as quickly as he could escaped back to London and his friends and the lifestyle he loved so much.

That had been over two years ago. Then he had laughed at his twin brother for wanting nothing more than to settle down in Cheshire and take his place in the family business. Now though...

Now though, things were different. He glanced again at the girl sleeping so peacefully beside him. They had been married at Caxton Hall three days ago. She had been wearing the tiniest minidress there had ever been, revealing yards of lovely, luscious legs, and smiling Bambi-eyed from between straight, glossy curtains of ash blonde hair. She was eighteen years old, just...and a model. The most sought-after, the most swingiest...the most wanted and lusted-after model there was on the London scene and now she was all his. She was also pregnant.

'But how *can* I be?' she had wailed in squeaky-voiced protest after the doctor had given them the results. 'I'm on the pill....'

'Obviously it doesn't work when you go to bed with a man as sexy as me,' David had told her, grinning.

She had refused to share his amusement, pouting sulkily at him as she reminded him of her modelling commitments.

And so here they were married and on their way to make a new life for themselves in Cheshire, and not just because Tiggy was pregnant. David frowned but there was no point in brooding on that other unfortunate matter. He had made a mistake and been found out, and as he had already defensively told his father, others did the same and got away with it. It wasn't his fault that the senior partner in his set of chambers should be so ridiculously stuffy. After all, he had done nothing legally wrong.

* * *

1996

'So tell me again about this family of yours and the birthday we're going to help celebrate.'

Even now after six months together, the lazy, trans-atlantic drawl of Caspar Johnson's voice still had almost as much power to stir her senses as his powerful six-foot-odd and very masculine body, Olivia acknowledged as she turned to smile at him.

'Watch the road,' Caspar warned her, adding softly, 'and don't look at me like that, otherwise...'

His openly and frequently expressed sexual desire for her was just one of the things that made him so different from any of the other men she had known, Olivia owned as she refocused her attention on the heavy north-flowing motorway traffic and answered his initial question.

'Birthdays,' she reminded him, adding, 'and I've already told you umpteen times.'

'I know,' Caspar agreed, 'but I like hearing it and I like even more watching your face when you talk about them. Just as well you decided against a career as a trial judge,' he teased her. 'Your expression, especially your eyes, would have given you away every time. They can be very revealing.'

Olivia Crighton grimaced but she knew he was right. They had met whilst she had been taking a post-graduate course in American law. Caspar had been her tutor and, like her, come from a legal background and also like her had chosen not to go into the family partnership but to make his own way in the world. Chosen... Caspar might have had a choice but she...

There were other reasons why the two of them

made such a perfect couple, she told herself hastily, abandoning her earlier and far too dangerous train of thought—this was meant to be a happy family visit, not a means of resurrecting old problems—reasons that had nothing to do with their shared legal background, reasons of a very much more personal nature. Instinctively, as she dwelt on those reasons, her stomach muscles clenched, her toes curling into her shoes, her face flushing slightly as she mentally relived the previous evening's blissful lovemaking.

It was just over two months now since she and Caspar had taken the decision to move in together and it had been a decision that neither of them regretted—far from it. She had not yet told her family about their plans for their shared future or her decision to go with Caspar when he returned to America and make her life there with him. Not that she expected them to have any objections; after all, as a female member of the family, she was easily expendable, neither wanted nor needed in the family partnership unlike its males. Their role was decided upon and planned for almost from the moment of their conception.

Caspar had been at first amused and then amazed at her family's history, unable to believe that such an old-fashioned family still existed. Her upbringing and the whole of her family life was so different from his own. His parents had divorced when he was six, and Olivia had sensed that he was a man who was shy of emotional commitment, which had made his openly admitted desire for her all the more precious.

She knew that he loved her as she did him, but both of them had been hurt and bruised by their childhood experiences, and because of that, both of them were wary of the intensity of the emotions they shared. Both of them in their different ways feared love, Olivia suspected in her more introspective moments, but another thing she had learned young was the folly of questioning her feelings too deeply. Painful emotions, like painful cuts and bruises, were best left unprodded and not interfered with.

They had made no long-term plans for a shared future, Olivia recognised, other than that she would go to Philadelphia with Caspar when he returned to his home country. Insofar as her career plans went, it would definitely be a lateral move as she would have to requalify, but as she and Caspar had both agreed, the way they felt about one another was too important not to be given a chance. But a chance for what? A chance to develop into something permanent or a chance to die?

Olivia wasn't sure which she actually wanted and neither, she suspected, was Caspar. Right now, the biggest commitment they could give one another was to say that they wanted to be together, that right now their relationship was of primary importance to both of them.

'Your family...?' Caspar prodded her from the passenger seat of her small, sturdy Ford—a twenty-first birthday present from her grandfather. She recalled that when Max, her cousin nearest in age to her, had turned twenty-one, Gramps had given him a sleek and dangerously fast sports car.

The family... Where should she start...? With her parents? Her grandparents? Or at the beginning with her great-grandfather, Josiah, who had initially founded the family business, breaking away from his own family in Chester to make a new life for himself and the bride his family had disdained.

'How many of you exactly will there be attending this party?' Caspar asked her, interrupting her train of thought.

'It's hard to say. It all depends on how many of the cousins and second cousins have been invited. The main family will be there, of course. Gramps, Mum and Dad, Uncle Jon and Aunt Jenny, Max, their son, and my great-aunt Ruth. Maybe some of the Chester lot.'

She glanced at the motorway sign by the side of the road. 'Only another couple of exits now,' she told him, 'then we'll be home.'

As she concentrated on the traffic, she didn't notice his small frown as he heard her say the word 'home.' To him, home was wherever he happened to be living at the time. But to her...

She had come to mean a lot to him, this pretty, clever Englishwoman, who in some ways seemed so much younger than her American contemporaries and in others so much more mature. Unlike them, she seemed instinctively to put him first and that was very important to him—a legacy from all the years as a child when he had felt more like an unwanted parcel being passed from one parent to the other than a loved and wanted child.

Families—he was instinctively suspicious of them, but thankfully this visit would only be a short one and then he and Olivia would be leaving for America and their own life together—just the two of them.

1

'Do you think the weather will stay fine? It will be awful if it doesn't, everywhere muddy and wet, and with a marquee out in the rain.'

Jenny Crighton looked up from the guest list she had been checking to smile at her sister-in-law.

'With any luck the weather should stay fine, Tiggy,' she reassured her. 'But even if it doesn't, the marquee will be heated and—'

'Yes, but people will have to walk across the lawn and—'

'The marquee people are putting a walkway down from the house to the marquee. It will be covered and quite dry,' she promised her patiently as though this had not been a subject they had discussed many times before.

It had come as no surprise to her to discover that although Tiggy had spent a good deal of time on the telephone talking about what hard work organising the joint fiftieth birthday celebration for their husbands had been, it was she, Jenny, who had been left to do the actual work. But then, that was their relationship all over, she acknowledged wryly. Tiggy had always been the glamorous one of the two of them whilst she was the more homey, hard-working one.

People made allowances for Tiggy and for her vul-

nerabilities; men were bedazzled by her even now
when both of them were in their forties, and Tiggy, because she was Tiggy, could never quite resist her need
to respond to their admiration and soak it up and feed
on it. She meant no harm, of course. She adored
David, everyone knew that, and he clearly wor-
shipped her.

Jenny could still remember the look of pride and
dazed awe in his eyes that summer he had brought
Tiggy, his bride, back home and introduced her to
them all. David—how everyone loved him—his father, the clients, his friends, the children, everyone,
but no one so fiercely nor so determinedly as her own
husband, Jonathon, his twin brother.

It had been Jonathon's idea that they should have
this double birthday celebration and combine it with a
grand family reunion.

'Dad would love it. You know how much the family
means to him,' he had told Jenny when they were discussing it.

'He may well *love* it, but he will carp like mad about
the cost,' Jenny had warned him dryly, 'and it *will* be
expensive if we are to do it properly.'

'Of course we are and Dad won't mind...not if it's
for David.'

'No,' Jenny had agreed, but she had had to turn her
face away so that Jonathon wouldn't see her expression.

She knew, of course, why so much family emphasis
was placed upon David; why her father-in-law was so
determined that these twins of his should be so close,
so supportive of one another, or rather that Jonathon
should be so supportive of his brother.

Ben himself had been a twin but his brother had died at birth, and that loss had marked and scarred virtually the whole of his life.

Jonathon had been brought up knowing that in his father's eyes he should consider himself most fortunate to have such a twin there in life beside him.

Only once had Jenny seen the fierce pride in Ben's eyes turn to disappointment and that had been when David had left the set of chambers where he had been in training for the Bar, following a career pattern that had been laid out for him from the first moment of his birth.

'Well, I hope you're right about the weather,' Tiggy was saying fretfully now. 'My shoes still haven't arrived, you know, and they promised that they would be here. It's far too late to get another pair made and dyed and—'

'They'll be here. There's still plenty of time,' Jenny soothed her.

Tiggy had been a model in the sixties and she still had the same haunting, high-cheeked beauty she had possessed then, although the years of dieting and worrying about her weight had, in Jenny's opinion, left her too thin. Her almost waiflike appearance, so appealing in a young, immature girl, somehow, to Jenny at least, seemed oddly jarring in a woman of forty-five.

Not that Jenny would ever voice such views. She was well aware of how others judged her and her relationship with Tiggy, and those, apart from her closest friends, could interpret it as envy, as those same critics judged Jonathon as being jealous of David.

Her normally mild brown eyes showed a brief flash of emotion before she controlled it and turned her attention back to the large area of lawn in front of them. It had taken quite a bit of diplomatic manoeuvring to get her father-in-law, Ben, to agree that the birthday festivities could be held here.

He had grumbled as Jenny had known he would about the cost and the inconvenience, but of course, when the time came he would rise to the occasion as the convivial patriarchal host, accepting the admiration and praise of their guests without a flicker of conscience.

There had been battles over each and every stage of the preparations for the weekend's celebrations, which was no more and no less than Jenny had anticipated, but the irony of it was that Ben would be the first to complain if even the slightest detail fell short of his exacting standards—a fact that he was as well aware of as she was herself, Jenny acknowledged.

Of course, she had had to use diversionary and indeed, at times, almost underhanded tactics to get her own way on some points. A reminder that at his own insistence, members of the Chester side of the family had been invited to the event and had to be impressed had proved a handy tool for digging out his deepest-rooted objections about cost and one that Jenny admitted she had wielded shamefully at times.

Not that she minded; indeed, she positively enjoyed the challenge of doing battle with her formidable father-in-law. Conversely, she knew that whilst in public he paid lip-service to the conventional view that Tiggy, on account of her looks, must take precedence in his affections and approval, privately, she was the one who had his respect.

Oh yes, men respected her, liked her, trusted her, turned to her for advice and comfort, but they did not flirt with her or see her as a desirable, sexual woman, a situation easy enough to smile over now, but not so easy when younger.

Jenny could still remember how she had felt the first time she had met Tiggy. She and Jon had been married for four or five years at that time and had been trying for a baby without success for the last two. The sight of Tiggy blooming with David's love, basking in both that and her discreetly evident pregnancy had caused Jenny more than one pang of pain and self-pity. She had hardly been able to bring herself to look at Jon, and when she had, the withdrawn look in his eyes as he deliberately avoided looking at Tiggy's pregnant body had made her bite her lip in a mixture of guilt and despair.

Jenny's heart had sunk when they had received the telephone call summoning them to Queensmead to meet David's new bride officially. It had been one of those sticky hot summer days when even the air they breathed had seemed heavy and tainted and somehow lacking in life-giving oxygen.

The partnership had been going through a rather lean time and Jon had quietly accepted his father's decision that he should draw only a very small salary. David's allowance was a large drain on the partnership's profits but Jenny knew that Jon didn't begrudge it any more than his father did. Luckily she was a careful housewife, scrupulously saving money where she could, especially when it came to spending money on herself, and she certainly had nothing in her wardrobe remotely suitable for the garden party-cum-belated wedding breakfast Ben was insisting on throwing for the newly married couple. In the end, having stubbornly refused Jon's tentative suggestion they use some of their savings to buy her a new dress, she decided to make her own.

'Get yourself something pretty,' Jon had tried to coax her, but she had shaken her head, stubbornly folding her lips into a tight line, which he had interpreted as disapproval but which, in fact, had been her defence strategy against the tears she had been fighting not to let fall as she reacted to the unsubtle message his suggestion had concealed—that she was so plain that she needed to wear something eye-catching enough to draw attention away from that plainness and, even worse, that Jon was embarrassed by it.

She felt she was letting him down not just by her homely appearance but by the fact that she had not conceived another child. After all, she had fallen pregnant easily enough to David but that was something she refused to allow herself to think about even in her most private thoughts and it was certainly not something she could ever say to Jon. How could she? It would look as though she was comparing the two of them and finding Jon wanting. It didn't need much intelligence to know that in the eyes of Jon's family, and she suspected almost everyone else, David and Tiggy would be very much the golden couple whilst she and Jon were very much the dull also-rans.

Both of them had already been treated to a lengthy outpouring of praise from Ben about Tiggy's exceptional beauty. So it had been with a feeling of tense trepidation plus the disadvantage of a bad tension headache and the disaster that was the home-made dress she had run up herself from a piece of fabric she had bought in the market that she had reluctantly pinned an unconvincing smile on her face and tried not to look as though she minded when she was finally confronted with Tiggy's breathtakingly leggy, lithe and oh so slim reality.

Tiggy herself hadn't quite been able to stop herself from betraying what Jenny had known humiliatingly was likely to be everyone else's reaction to the difference between them, and her eyes widened just a little before she looked guiltily away from Jenny, obviously unable to meet her gaze as David introduced them.

David, too, managed to avoid meeting her gaze. David was clearly bursting with pride over the reaction Tiggy was causing amongst the male guests. They milled enthusiastically around her and barely had time to do much more than say a very brief hello not just to her but to Jon, his twin, before Tiggy caught hold of his arm and demanded to be told the names of all the men who were so eager to talk with her.

As she reached out to David, she had tilted her face up towards him, throwing her head back and laughing. The sun gleamed richly in the heavy thickness of her glossy hair, and the bones in her shoulders revealed by the cutaway neckline of her brief cotton minidress seemed as fragile and delicate as those of a bird. Jenny had watched her, mute with misery, contrasting her own flushed, shiny, wholesomely plain face with the fine-boned, high-cheeked beauty of Tiggy's.

Everything about David's new wife, from the polished tips of her fingernails to the artfully applied fake eyelashes—which, unlike her, Jenny was absolutely sure that Tiggy had little need of—spoke of someone who took it for granted that she was loved and desired. And why shouldn't she? David was so obviously besotted with her, so completely in love, he couldn't bear even to let go of her hand, never mind leave her side.

Jenny had felt her eyes start to well up with betraying and self-pitying tears as she watched them. Even Jon, quiet, slightly shy Jon, was watching Tiggy with a bemused and indulgent smile on his normally serious face.

'Jenny, could you come and give me a hand with the food?'

Reluctantly Jenny had dragged her attention away from the group of enthusiastic admirers thronging round Tiggy and turned to look at Jon's Aunt Ruth, answering automatically, 'Yes, of course...'

'Tiggy is very pretty, isn't she?' she had commented quietly to Ruth as they walked across the lawn together. Jon hadn't even noticed her leaving. He was standing next to David but slightly behind him, slightly in his shadow. Was he wishing that like David he had married someone beautiful and lively, someone who was fun to be with, someone who other men envied him being married to and not...? Her throat, already uncomfortably dry, had become even drier as she added, 'She and David look so right together and they're obviously very deeply in love.'

'Indeed they are,' Ruth had agreed, but her voice had been wry rather than warm, carrying more of a hint of cynicism than the outright approval that Jenny had been expecting. When Jenny had looked uncertainly at her, Ruth had explained lightly, 'David and Tiggy are in love, Jenny, but I suspect that both of them are rather more in love with themselves than they could ever be with anyone else. Perhaps I'm wrong...I certainly hope so.'

Jenny and Jon had left Queensmead and gone home shortly afterwards. She hadn't been feeling very well, the oppressive heat making her feel sick, and she had felt guilty about dragging Jon away especially when she had seen the look of pity that Tiggy had given them both as they said their goodbyes.

As they walked away, she had heard Tiggy saying to David, 'I can't believe that you and Jon are twins. He looks older than you but then I suppose that's because his wife is so frumpy and plain.'

Frumpy and plain. Tiggy hadn't meant to be unkind, of course; she hadn't even realised that Jenny had overheard her....

'I think I'd better go and ring them again, just to check that they *have* sent my shoes. It will be a complete disaster if they don't arrive.'

'Mmm?' Jenny murmured, coming back to the present.

'My shoes, Jenny,' Tiggy repeated irritably. Heavens, Jenny could be so dull and boring at times. She hadn't even mentioned what she was going to wear for the ball. Tiggy had offered to go shopping with her, help her choose something suitable, but predictably Jenny had shaken her head and said that she was too busy...that she would find 'something'.

Tiggy just hoped that the 'something', whatever it

was, wouldn't prove to be too horrendous. Her own dress, of course, was a dream by one of her favourite designers. David had baulked a little at the cost but she had soon talked him round.

The cream of Cheshire society had been invited after all. David's people, through the Chester side, were extremely well-connected and when one included some of their long-standing county clients...

It was a pity that the house didn't have its own ballroom...a marquee was all very well in its way but... She had been a little bit cross when Jenny had refused to agree with her that a black-and-white theme would be marvellously chic. As well as setting off her own colouring, black always looked good on blondes.

'It's too restricting, too dramatic, Tiggy,' Jenny had argued in that quiet, calm voice of hers. 'Not everyone will want to keep to the theme and wear black or white. We must be practical.'

Typical of Jenny, practical should have been her middle name. She was a dear, of course, frightfully worthy and good-natured and, oddly enough, she was more attractive now than she had been when she was younger. She had kept her figure, even if she was a good size twelve compared with her own delicate size eight and her hair was still a rich, glossy brown and naturally curly, even if it could do with a proper styling.

Tiggy had seen the way Jonathon looked at the two of them sometimes, no doubt comparing her elegance and Jenny's lack of fashion sense. Jenny really ought to take a bit more trouble with her appearance. Jonathon was a very attractive man, though not quite as startlingly good-looking as David. The wheat blond of David's hair was slightly less extravagantly film starrish in Jonathon. His was tinged with a soft caramel brown, but the twins shared the same impressive height and the same broad shoulders. Curiously it was Jonathon's slightly more spare frame that seemed to carry the years well now; David had begun to develop a paunch, although he denied it vigorously and loathed any reference to it.

'Ah, there you are....'

Jenny smiled as she saw their mutual father-in-law approaching them. He was in his seventies now, a widower, and he walked with a slight limp, the legacy of a bad fall three winters ago when he had dislocated his hip and broken his leg.

'Have a few things I want to talk to you about,' he announced as he reached them.

'Father, you look wonderful,' Tiggy told him, darting forward to give him a quick hug and to kiss him delicately on the cheek. Even with her father-in-law she still could not resist the impulse to flirt, Jenny realised.

No, not to flirt, she amended mentally. What Tiggy did, what she wanted, was to reassure herself that she was still desirable, still wanted. Poor Tiggy. Jenny wondered briefly what it must feel like to have one's whole self-worth invested in the frightening transitoriness of one's physical features. No wonder at times Tiggy seemed so brittle, so insecure.

'Tania, I—'

'Darling, I must fly. There's so much I have to do....'

Their father-in-law was one of the few people who used Tiggy's proper name and Jenny hid another wry smile as she watched Tiggy detach herself from him.

She knew quite well why Tiggy wanted to avoid being questioned by Ben.

'She does too much,' Ben commented as they both watched Tiggy hurry round the side of the house to where her car was parked. 'She's never been very strong. Ellie tells me these marquee people are due to start work tomorrow.'

'Yes, that's right,' Jenny agreed. Ellie was Ben's housekeeper. 'They're due to arrive about lunch-time and most of the work should be completed by early evening.'

'Mmm... Well, let's just hope they don't make too much of a damn mess of the lawn. Ruth tells me she's doing the flowers,' he added, referring to his unmarried sister. 'Should have thought you'd have got somebody professional in to do that.'

'Aunt Ruth is better than a professional,' Jenny told him calmly. 'When she does the church flowers—'

'The church flowers,' Ben interrupted, snorting dismissively, then shaking his head when he realised that Jenny wasn't going to allow him to agitate her but instead was simply listening serenely.

That was the trouble with Jenny; she was *too* damn serene at times and too damn clever.

'Young Olivia's coming home, I hear, and bringing some American or other with her.'

'Of course she's coming home,' Jenny agreed. 'After all, she is David's daughter—and Tiggy's.' But it was Jenny, her aunt, whom she had telephoned to tell her in the strictest confidence that she had decided to move in with Caspar, and Jenny whom she had contacted to sound her out about the wisdom of bringing Caspar home with her.

'Exactly who is he, then, this American?' Ben demanded, changing tack, having recognised that Jenny wasn't going to rise to the bait he had originally been dangling and rush to defend his sister. They were having a particularly hot summer and since his accident the heat bothered him. It got into his broken joints and made them ache so much that the pain made him irritable.

'He's Livvy's boyfriend,' Jenny returned.

'Boyfriend.' Ben frowned at her under his heavy silver eyebrows. Like his sons he, too, had a good thick head of hair, although where theirs was still blond, his was now silver. 'According to David he's in his thirties—hardly a boy. Serious between them, is it?' he demanded, shooting her a penetrating look.

'That's something you must ask Livvy,' Jenny told him.

It was certainly serious enough for Olivia to tell her mother that the two of them would be sharing a room even though David apparently had put his foot down and said no.

'David's right, of course,' Tiggy had told Jenny when relating the details of their conversation to her. 'Father would not approve at all and we'd never hear the end of it for allowing it and really, it will only be for a few days....'

'Mmm...at that age a few days can seem an awfully long time. What does Livvy say?'

'We haven't told her yet. David said it was best not to until she arrived. You know what she can be like. She's so strong-willed at times....' Tiggy pulled a small face. 'You remember what it was like when she decided she wanted to study law. Of course, we all knew it was only because David and her grandfather had both told her that they really didn't think it was a good idea and after all, she is—'

'Female,' Jenny had supplied dryly.

Personally she thought the views of the males of the Crighton family were decades out of date and that it was high time that someone challenged them. Olivia might be the first female of the family to do so, but she wasn't going to be the only one.

Jenny knew that her own Katie already, at sixteen, had very strong views as to where her future lay. It was to be the Bar or nothing, she had told her parents emphatically. Louise, her twin, was less single-minded; she still hadn't totally given up all hopes of becoming a film star. Failing that, she might well opt to study law, she had said judiciously.

'But I wouldn't want to stay here,' she had told her parents.

'No, neither do I,' Katie had agreed. She was always the one who took control, and Louise, like her father before her, seemed quite happy to good-naturedly let her do so.

Jenny, however, had been determined from the moment they were born that there was not going to be a favoured child and a second best; that both of them were going to grow up knowing they were of equal importance, equal value.

'I know,' she had told Louise. 'We'll go to Strasbourg. That's where all the important legal decisions are made on human rights....'

'Does your father know that?' Jenny had murmured *sotto voce* to her husband. 'I sometimes think he has a hard time grudgingly acknowledging that even

Chester has more impact on the legal world than Haslewich.'

'Mmm... Dad is fiercely parochial,' Jonathon agreed. 'He inherited that from his own father, of course. Aunt Ruth says that their father, Josiah, never really got over being sent away from Chester in disgrace and that he always remained bitter about the way his family treated him.'

'Well, your father certainly believes in keeping the old rivalries going,' Jenny had agreed. 'I was quite surprised when he insisted on inviting the Chester side of the family to your birthday do.'

'Oh, that's just because he wants to impress them and—'

'Just like Max wants to impress Grandad and Uncle David,' Katie had interrupted scathingly, tossing her sixteen-year-old head in sisterly contempt of her elder brother.

Over that head Jenny had looked warily at her husband. It was no secret that Max was very much the apple of his grandfather's eye and that of his uncle David's.

'That boy should have been David's son, not yours,' Ben had once infamously remarked at a family gathering.

Jenny had never forgotten hearing him say it. Neither, unfortunately it seemed, had Max.

Much as it pained Jenny to admit it, her son had a streak of vanity and, yes, weakness in him that she felt had been exacerbated by his grandfather's indulgence.

'Max will never be called to the Bar,' Katie had announced scathingly the day of Max's twenty-first when their grandfather had beamingly made the announcement of his grandson's career intentions and presented him with the keys to a Porsche Carrera that both Jonathon and Jenny had pleaded with Ben not to give him.

Max had finished his pupillage the previous year when he was twenty-three but so far had been unable to find a place as a junior in a set of chambers in London.

It would be left no doubt to Joss, their youngest child, to take his father's place in the family business in due time, just as his cousin Jack would take David's, but that lay well into the future. Jack was only ten and Joss an even younger eight.

As she walked back with her father-in-law across the lawn, Jenny paused to admire the outline of the house.

Originally a large farmhouse, it was built in a traditional hall house shape with the main central block from which two wings projected one at either end.

The rear of the property they were facing was the older portion built in the traditional Cheshire farmhouse style of huge oak beams infilled with wattle-and-daub panels. The front was a more modern seventeenth century instead of fifteenth in softly tinted locally quarried stone.

There had been those who had raised their eyebrows a little when Ben's father had moved into the large farmhouse, wondering how on earth he had come to inherit such a valuable property. Valuable not so much because of the house, but rather because of the fertile Cheshire farmlands that went with it. And it had belonged to a lonely widow, as well.

One day, following the rules of primogeniture to which they all knew Ben intended to rigidly adhere, David, simply by virtue of the fact he had arrived into the world ten minutes ahead of Jon, would inherit Queensmead, but Jenny didn't envy the inheritance. She was perfectly happy with their own much smaller house on the other side of town. Georgian in origin, it had once belonged to the church and Jenny particularly loved its walled garden and its proximity to the river that flowed through the paddock at the bottom of the garden.

She might not envy David and Tiggy their ultimate ownership of Queensmead but there was no doubt that it was the perfect setting for a large family gathering, she acknowledged.

In all, over two hundred and fifty people would be attending and over a hundred of them were in one way or another, however loosely, connected 'family'. The rest were either friends, colleagues, clients or, in some cases, all three. Working out the table plans alone had taken Jenny the best part of a fortnight of winter evenings at her desk.

Fortunately Guy Cooke, her business partner, had been wonderfully understanding and accommodating.

Her work was still a source of acrimony between Jenny and her father-in-law. It had infuriated her that instead of taking the matter up with her, Ben had manipulatively attempted to dictate what she should do by objecting to Jonathon that he didn't think it was a good thing for the family that she should be involved in a local business.

It was true that financially she didn't need to earn

her own living, but the business had brought her something she believed was equally vital to her: her own feelings of self-worth and self-justification. Her need to be something other than Jonathon's wife, the plain one...

The plain one... How those words had once hurt. And still did?

No, not any more. In fact, if anything, she was grateful for the truth of them because they had forced her to fight against them, to look within herself, to find something there that she could hold on to and value.

She glanced at her watch. Jon wouldn't be home yet and Joss was going straight from school to have tea with a friend. Katie and Louise had after-school tennis practice. She had a couple of hours in hand and her conscience had been pricking her for days about Guy and their business.

Being a partner in an antique shop and repairers might not have Ben's approval but she enjoyed it. Even more she enjoyed the actual renovation and restoration side of the business, something that Guy freely admitted she had a definite talent for. Her career plans had been shelved when her mother had fallen ill within weeks of her sitting her A levels.

Her illness had mercifully been as swift as it was relentless. Within a few short weeks she was dead, but by then it was too late for Jenny to pick up the threads she had dropped and reapply for a course she had hoped to take—in more ways than one.

She and Jonathon had been married very quietly a matter of months after her mother's death.

As she reached the main road, she paused and then turned right instead of left, heading for Haslewich instead of home. Guy had said he had picked up some silver he wanted her to see.

Tiggy exhaled in relief as she saw that the forecourt in front of the Dower House was empty. Good. David wasn't home yet. She had stayed longer in Chester than she had planned. Guiltily she opened the boot of her car and removed the glossy carrier bags, grimacing as she stepped onto the gravel and felt it grate against her delicately pale high heels.

She would have preferred to have the forecourt paved, but since they merely leased the Dower House from Sir Richard Furness and since he was fiercely opposed to any kind of change, she knew that she had scant chance of doing away with the annoyance of the gravel.

Initially when, after their marriage, David had announced that they would be living in the Dower House, she had thought that he was joking. 'But what's the point when we'll be going back to London?' she had protested.

David had looked uncomfortable and then defensive as he told her that there was no way he could afford to live in London now, that they would have to live in Cheshire where he, at least, had the security of a partnership in the family business, which included a generous additional allowance to cover the cost of the lease on the Dower House.

She hadn't minded too much at the time. She was a new bride, pretty and young, and everyone made a huge fuss over her. It was only sometime afterwards that she began to feel stifled, bored with life as a country solicitor's wife and then later again that boredom had turned to...

Quickly she unlocked the front door and hurried into the house, going directly upstairs and into the privacy of her bathroom. She shuddered, her fingers trembling slightly as she unfastened the buttons of her silk shirt, then hastily bundled it into the linen basket along with the brief and very expensive silk bra she had been wearing underneath it.

Her skirt could only be dry-cleaned and she grimaced slightly in distaste as she saw the small mark on the creased cream fabric.

Cream was one of her favourite colours. She wore it a lot. It suited her, drew attention to her fragile bone structure and pale, carefully highlighted hair.

She stepped into the shower. She much preferred the pampering luxury of a bath but today she just didn't have time. She and David were due to go out to dinner and she would have to wash her hair and do her nails. She had noticed as she parked the car that one of them was chipped. She had no idea how on earth Jenny could bear to leave hers unmanicured the way she did.

As she stepped out of the shower and reached for a towel, Tiggy studied her reflection in the bathroom's full-length mirrors. Her breasts were still as high and firm as they had always been, her stomach as flat, her skin as silken, but for how much longer?

She was forty-five now and already she was beginning to discern a certain betraying slackness in the flesh of her face and those tell-tale lines around her eyes. She had had a discreet eye tuck the year she was forty, but that wouldn't last for ever.

Tiggy dreaded the thought of growing old or not being beautiful and desirable any more. David laughed at her, but then he didn't understand. How could he? Wrapped in her towel, she walked into their bedroom. A copy of the new edition of *Vogue* lay on the bed. She picked it up, studying the model on the cover.

She had been a fool to give up her own career when she had, but at the time... David had seemed so glamorous, so exciting...so sexy...so different from all those paunchy, middle-aged men she kept being introduced to by the agency. Men who looked at her with hot, avaricious eyes and wanted to touch her with even hotter and more avaricious hands.

Knowing how much David had wanted her, how much he'd desired and loved her, had thrilled her, but that thrill hadn't lasted. It never did.

She wondered what time Olivia would arrive and what this boyfriend she was bringing with her would be like. Not too American, she hoped. Ben was bound to disapprove. Given the quite small age gap between them, it was odd that she and Olivia weren't closer. People often commented that they looked more like sisters than mother and daughter. It had shocked Tiggy when Olivia had announced that she wanted to train for the law. Somehow she had expected that she would follow in her own footsteps and go into modelling or something similar, but then in many ways Olivia really was such an odd girl. Tiggy put it down to the fact that Olivia had spent so much time with Jenny when she was growing up.

Jack would be home tomorrow, as well. Tiggy knew that Ben hadn't approved of their sending him to boarding school. Jack, like his father and all the male members of the Crighton family had attended the King's School in Chester. But unlike them, Jack boarded there on a weekly basis.

Jenny, of course, being Jenny, would make nothing of driving first Max and now Joss there day in and day out—and had even offered to pick Jack up and take him with them but Tiggy had her own reasons for preferring to have her son out of the way on occasion.

She glanced impatiently at her nails. She was booked in tomorrow for a manicure at the beauty salon in the exclusive country club close to Chester, which she and David had joined shortly after it had opened. David didn't use the facilities very often; he preferred playing golf at the same club where his father and brother were members.

Now, what was she going to wear tonight? The Buckletons were members of an old Cheshire family and well-connected; they lived in a huge, draughty, rambling Victorian house just outside Chester. In addition to the couple's being clients of David's, Ann Buckleton was a local JP. Tiggy suspected that Ann Buckleton didn't particularly approve of her and would have preferred Jenny's company, but David was the firm's senior partner and as such it was David whom they invited to dinner.

Jenny parked her car in the large municipal car park just outside the town. The town itself was old; the Romans had mined salt in the area and so had others both before and after them.

The town had literally been built on salt and now there was concern that parts of it could be subject to

subsidence because of the now-disused and extensive
salt workings on its outskirts.

To Jenny, Haslewich was everything that a small rural English town should be—a neat, compact and har-
monious blending of buildings actually built in some
cases on top of one another, absurd Georgian growths
sprouting from Tudor roots, handsome stone struc-
tures jostling for space with others made from brick.
Some of the more flamboyant stone ones sported their
purloined masonry without any hint of shame or sub-
tlety.

During the Civil War, so much damage had been
done to the town's surrounding stone wall by the at-
tacking Roundhead troops that after the war the stone
had been used, in some cases, to repair the homes of
the townspeople, and the only part of the original wall
that now remained was the section that ran between
the town and the river. The local council was presently
running a campaign to raise money to have it restored.
So far, the townspeople appeared stoically determined to leave their wall as it was and in many ways
Jenny didn't blame them.

The antique shop was in a small, narrow alley just
off the town square, a pretty, double-fronted Tudor
building with an upper storey that overhung the alley-
way.

Guy Cooke was rearranging some delicate
Staffordshire figurines when she walked in. He looked
up and saw her, immediately stopping what he was
doing to come over and greet her with a warm smile.

He was at least fifteen years younger than Jonathon
and physically completely different. Where Jon was
tall and blond with long arms and legs, Guy was

shorter, broader, his hair pitch-dark and his colouring just short of swarthy.

He had once told Jenny that there was supposed to be gypsy blood in his family somewhere, and looking at him Jenny could well believe it. They had been partners for seven years and friends for much longer. Guy's family had lived in the town for generations and his parents had run a pub several doors away from the shop before they retired and moved. He had sisters, brothers, cousins, aunts and uncles all living within a stone's throw of one another and all virtually united in their disapproval of Guy and what he was doing.

Guy had always been 'arty' as he had wryly described himself once to Jenny. Of course, his parents had tried their best to smother such an undesirable trait, which would have been bad enough in a daughter, but was totally unacceptable in a son....

The Cookes as a clan were notoriously macho; the thickset, dark-haired, very male men knew their place in life and what being a man and, more importantly, being a Cooke were all about.

Not so Guy. He had wanted something different out of life. He *was* something different.

'I'm sorry I haven't been much in evidence lately,' Jenny apologised, shaking her head when Guy offered her a cup of tea.

'Mmm. How are things going?' he asked her.

'All right—I think,' Jenny said, laughing. 'Tiggy and I were up at Queensmead this morning just checking on the final details—'

'You mean *you* were checking on the final details,' Guy corrected her.

Jenny frowned. It was no secret to her that Guy didn't particularly like her sister-in-law, which was quite odd really when one thought about how he felt about anything that was beautiful, and Tiggy was certainly that.

Tiggy didn't like him, either. In fact, she had, on occasion, been uncharacteristically vindictive about him, making waspish comments about the fact that he wasn't married.

Jenny had started to laugh. She could think of few men who were more masculinely heterosexual than Guy—not that it made any difference what his sexual preference was—and the only reason he hadn't married was because he hadn't wanted to tie himself down to one woman. In his sexuality at least, he was very much a member of the Cooke clan who had, to a man, what was tacitly understood to be a weakness for the female sex.

'What about this silver you wanted me to look at?' she reminded him.

'Oh, yes. I think it's Queen Anne but you're the silver expert. I've got it in the safe.'

It was over an hour before Jenny finally left the shop. Like Guy, she was convinced that the silver was genuine although, as she had pointed out to him, the lack of any identifying marks could mean that it might have been stolen at some point in time.

'It's too good not to have had proper markings,' she had observed. 'I suppose the best thing we can do is to check with the police.'

After she left the shop, she crossed the square. She just had enough time left to call on Ruth; her husband's aunt lived in a narrow, elegant Georgian town house on Church Walk, which she rented from the church commissioners. To get to it, Jenny made a small detour through the churchyard itself, pausing as she walked past the Crighton family plot to stop and bend down towards a small single headstone carved with laughing, naughty-looking cherubs. The epitaph read:

'HARRY CRIGHTON

JUNE 19TH 1965–JUNE 20TH 1965.'

He had lived such a heartbreakingly short time, this first child of hers, and a part of her still mourned for him and always would. Time had eased the piercing sharpness of her initial grief, but she could never forget him, nor would she want to. Before she stood up, she touched the headstone, stroking it, caressing it almost, as she said his name.

Ruth was waiting for her with the front door open as she walked up the path. 'I saw you in the churchyard,' she told Jenny. 'He would have been thirty-one this year if he'd lived.'

'I know.' For a moment both women were quiet. If having Ben as a father-in-law weighed heavily at times in the negative balance sheet of her marriage to Jonathon, then having Ruth in the family certainly added balance to the positive side of the equation, Jenny acknowledged.

'Have you got time for a cup of tea?' Ruth asked her.

'No,' Jenny told her ruefully, 'but I'd still love one.'

'Come on in, then,' Ruth invited her, and as Jenny followed her into the pretty sitting room at the front of the house, she paused to admire the huge profusion of flowers decorating the empty fireplace.

Ruth had a gift, not just for arranging flowers artistically, but for growing them, as well.

'Pieter is coming with the flowers on the day of the party,' she told Jenny, following the direction of her glance. 'He's catching the first ferry over that morning. The flowers will all be freshly picked and he knows exactly what we want.'

Ruth bought her flowers directly from a Dutch supplier whose younger son crossed the North Sea to Hull once a week delivering flowers to his regular customers but, for this weekend's celebration, Pieter had agreed to make a special trip bringing only the flowers that Ruth had ordered especially for the event.

'I imagine Ben's driving you crazy, isn't he?' she asked now.

'Just a little bit,' Jenny agreed. 'His hip bothers him at times although he won't admit it....'

Half an hour later when Jenny left, Ruth watched her walk back across the churchyard and pause a second time for a few moments in front of the grave of her first-born son.

She sensed what Jenny was feeling. Some pains never ever faded; some things could never ever be forgotten, and it wasn't always true that with time they eased.

2

'Jon, have you got a minute?'

Jonathon looked up from his desk as his twin walked into his office, then frowned slightly as he saw the way that David was massaging his shoulder. 'Something wrong?' he asked him.

'Not really, just a bit of an ache. I must have pulled something playing golf on Sunday, which reminds me, we're both down to play in the Captain's Cup next month but Tiggy is getting a bit agitated about our getting away so I might have to pull out. Look, I'm going to get off early. We're having dinner with the Buckletons tonight and there's nothing pressing here.'

No, there probably wasn't, not once you discounted the two wills waiting to be redrafted, the conveyancing for Hawkins Farm and a whole host of other complicated and fiddly commissions that increasingly recently seemed to find their way from David's desk to his own because his brother couldn't find the time to deal with them.

It had never really been intended that the two of them would go into the family business; David had been earmarked to become a member of a much more elevated rank of their profession—a barrister—and long before they had both even left school, their father was already talking about the time when David would be a QC.

All that had changed, though, the summer David had returned to Haslewich with Tiggy to tell the family that they were married and that Tiggy was expecting his child. No one had mentioned David's failure to fulfil his father's hopes for him by not qualifying for the Bar, just as no one had mentioned the debts David had run up whilst living in London or the distinctive and tell-tale, sickly sweet smell that emanated from the room that David and Tiggy were sharing at Queensmead until a new home was found for them.

Arrangements were very quickly made for David to join the partnership, but not as a practising solicitor because, of course, he wasn't qualified, but Jon doubted that anyone remembered that these days. As the favoured brother, David was automatically assumed to be the firm's senior partner and Jonathon, because he was Jonathon, had never done anything to dispel this myth. Equally David, because he was David, hadn't, either.

Now as Jonathon looked at his twin and saw the signs of weakness that age was making increasingly plain in his features, the faint coarsening of the once healthily tanned taut flesh of his face, the inability of his gaze to hold Jon's own, the fleshiness on a body that used to be as firmly muscular as Jon's still was, these vulnerabilities if anything only made him love his brother more and not less. Jon loved him with a fiercely protective, unvocalised love so intense that sometimes it physically hurt him. He would never have dreamed of telling his twin or anyone else how he thought and knew instinctively that David did not have the same intensity of feeling for him.

Watching David massaging the shoulder he complained had been aching, Jon found he was automatically copying the movement even though his own shoulder was completely free of pain.

'Looks like the weather is going to stay fine for the weekend,' David commented as he turned to leave. 'The girls will be pleased. By the way, young Max rang me the other night. He's driving up from London tomorrow, he says.'

'Yes,' Jon agreed. Max might be his son, but it was David whom he treated more like a father. It was David who would have preferred to be his father, Jon suspected. They shared the same extrovert, almost extravagantly outrageous personality, the same needs, the same love of ownership and glory, the same gifts—and the same weaknesses. Jon started to frown.

'Livvy's due back tonight,' David was continuing, and now he, too, was starting to frown. 'She's bringing this American with her. I'm not sure...look, I'd better go,' he told Jon hurriedly as the phone started to ring. 'I promised Tiggy I wouldn't be late and she's already in a bit of a state, something about the shoes she ordered for Saturday not arriving... You know how easily she gets upset.'

From his office window, Jon could see across the small town square with its neatly enclosed immaculate lawn and its tidy flower-beds. He could see Jenny, his wife, crossing the square on her way back to her car. She stopped to talk to David; David had obviously seen her, too, as he quickened his pace to catch up with her. Jon saw the way she smiled as she greeted his brother, the afternoon sun turning her brunette hair a nice warm chestnut. Once, a long time ago, so long ago now that most people had forgotten all about it, Jenny had been David's girlfriend.

The telephone had started to ring again. Looking away from the window, Jon reached out to answer it.

'What's for tea?'

Jenny smiled at her youngest child. At forty she had thought herself too old and too careful to have another baby, but nature had proved her wrong.

Jon had been almost shocked when she had told him and she had felt oddly, awkwardly self-conscious about delivering the news to him herself.

'You're pregnant, but how...?'

'Our wedding anniversary,' she'd reminded him, adding simply, 'We were supposed to be going out for a meal, remember, only you were delayed in court and instead we ate in and opened that wine that Uncle Hugh had given you.'

'Oh God, yes,' Jon had agreed. 'That stuff was lethal.'

'It was vintage burgundy,' Jenny chided him severely, 'and we shouldn't have opened that second bottle. It's my fault. It never occurred to me to think about taking any precautions.'

What she didn't add was that sex between them had become so rare an event that her diaphragm was something that was pushed to the back of her dressing-table drawer and largely forgotten. They had a comfortable, steady marriage and were not given to being physically affectionate with one another in public the way David and Tiggy often were and perhaps, because of the busyness of their lives, they had somehow grown out of the habit of being physically demonstrative with one another in private, as well.

However, as Jenny surveyed the result of their two bottles of vintage burgundy and her carelessness, she acknowledged that she wouldn't be without the consequences of their 'accident'.

'It's lamb and new potatoes,' she told Joss, named after his paternal great-grandfather, adding warningly, 'And Joss, don't forget—homework first.'

'When's Livvy coming back?' Joss asked her, ignoring her warning. 'She promised to come round.'

'Some time this evening,' Jenny responded, 'but remember, Joss, she's bringing a friend back with her and she won't have time to go roaming all over the countryside with you.'

'The badger cubs are coming out at night now. She'll want to see them.'

Jenny grinned to herself as she heard the conviction in her young son's voice. He was going to be a real heartbreaker when he grew up. By some magical alchemy he had managed to inherit the very best of both his father's and his uncle's genes. David's overconfidence and flamboyance were toned down and backed up by Jon's guarded personality; his nature was also enhanced by the ingredients of good humour and irrepressibility—a sense of fun, a love of life and the people around him.

'Max is due back tomorrow,' she reminded him. 'So if you haven't already removed your belongings from his room, I suggest that you do so this evening, and as long as we're on the subject, your brother's bedroom is not the place to dismantle your bike,' she remonstrated severely.

Joss looked innocently at her. 'But I had to do it there,' he told her winningly. 'There was nowhere else. There's no room in the garage and...'

And the truth was that there was nothing quite so much fun for him as testing the strength of Max's claim to seniority, Jenny knew, but Max was not like Olivia, indulgent of his sibling's youthfulness and disposed to be amused and entertained by him.

Max had been horrified when she had told him that she was pregnant, and that disgust and dislike of her pregnancy had been transferred into a disgust and dislike for his younger brother.

'It would be much better if Max went and stayed at Uncle David's and Olivia stayed here,' Joss grumbled.

Jenny gave him another warning look and reminded him sternly, 'Homework.' But she knew that there was an element of truth in what he said.

Max did prefer the company of his aunt and uncle, especially his uncle, whilst Olivia... Livvy was such a darling and so dear to her, Jenny just hoped that this young American, whoever he was, realised that he was a lucky man.

Max grimaced as the office door swung closed behind the chambers clerk. It was already gone six o'clock and now it looked as though he was going to have at least another couple of hours work ahead of him. He glanced in disgust at the papers Bob Ford had just placed on his desk.

It was no secret that he wasn't exactly one of the clerk's favourites, a legacy of the early days of Max's pupillage at the chambers when Bob had unfortunately overheard his efforts to make fun of him by imitating the slight stammer he developed whenever he was under pressure.

Max shrugged.

He had inherited his father's and his uncle's tall, muscular body frame, and the years of playing rugby first at King's School and then later at Oxford had developed the powerful physique of which he was now secretly rather proud.

He enjoyed it when he saw the sideways double take women gave him as they discreetly and sometimes not so discreetly assessed him. He liked it, as well, when he stripped off in the shower after a hard game of squash or rugby and saw the envy flare briefly in the eyes of other men. It gave him an advantage, and as Max was well aware, advantages were all plus points when it came to winning life's games. And Max intended to be a winner. He wasn't going to be like his father, content to be second best. No, Max only had to look at his Uncle David to see what he wanted to be.

He couldn't remember the first time he had realised the difference in the way people treated his father and his Uncle David but he could remember that he had decided that people would treat him the way they did his uncle and not his father.

The knowledge that he would have much preferred it if David had been his father had come later. He had enjoyed it when David had begun to treat him more like a son than a nephew and he had enjoyed even more displacing Olivia in her father's affections, had relished knowing that of the two of them he came first.

It had been David and his grandfather who had been full of praise and encouragement when he had announced his intention to train as a barrister.

'You'll need a first-class degree,' his father had warned him. 'And even then it won't be easy.'

'Stop trying to put the lad off,' his grandfather had interrupted. 'It's time we had a QC on our side of the family.'

'Well, that's certainly what I intend to aim for,' Max had agreed, taking advantage of his grandfather's good mood, 'but it isn't going to be that simple. There's no way I'm going to be able to get a part-time job whilst I'm at Oxford—not if I'm going to get a good degree,' he added virtuously, 'and as for my grant... And then I'm going to have to replace my car...' He had paused hopefully, and as he had anticipated, his grandfather hadn't disappointed him.

'Well, I'm sure we'll be able to sort something out. You've got some money coming to you eventually from your grandmother, and as for a car, haven't you got a twenty-first coming up...?'

Later on he had overheard his parents discussing the incident.

'It's David all over again,' he heard his mother saying angrily, 'and Max encourages him.'

'Yes, I know, but what could I do?' Max had heard his father responding quietly. 'You know what Dad's like.'

The trouble with his mother was that she was too moralistic, Max decided, but then he supposed she had to be something. After all, she wasn't as physically attractive as David's wife, Tiggy, the kind of woman that men stopped to stare at in the street. The kind of woman that other men envied a man for having. He could still vividly remember the thrill it had given him the year David and Tiggy had come to his school sports day instead of his parents.

Old Harris, the sports master, had gone beetroot red and behaved like an idiot when Max had introduced Tiggy to him. Max had amused himself imagining his wanking off later in the privacy of his rented rooms as he relived the occasion. Pathetic sod. Max bet he didn't know what it was like to have a woman, unlike Max himself, who had lost his virginity at fourteen with the able, the very able, help of a girl who worked behind the bar at the pub they all went into after Saturday morning sport.

Tucked away down a side street in Chester, it had possessed the kind of seediness that both excited and amused him. For a start it had so obviously been a place his respectable father would never have dreamed of going to, and as for his mother... But Max had enjoyed it. Just as he had enjoyed the slightly sweaty, earthy scent of the girl as she took him back to her room and let him kiss and grope her for several minutes before finally pushing him off and commanding him to wait whilst she stripped off her clothes.

It had been the first time he had seen a real naked female in the flesh, and she had had no inhibitions about letting him see her, even to the extent of laughing mockingly at him after she propped herself up on her pillows and spread her legs, inviting him to have a good look at what lay between them.

'Bet you haven't seen many of these before, have you?' she demanded, grinning at him as he touched the thicket of dark, rough hair and then parted the thick, fleshy lips beneath it. 'Know what this is, do you?' she asked him, commanding him to look as she revealed the small inner nub of hard flesh.

'Course I do,' Max responded swaggeringly.

'Good,' she announced, 'then you'll know what to do with it, won't you?'

Max certainly thought he did but she soon disabused him of this misapprehension.

'God, you're rough,' she complained. 'It's not your own prick you've got there, you know, and besides,' she added slyly, watching him, 'it works much better if you suck it.'

She laughed when she saw his expression.

'Never gone down on a girl before, have you? Well, now's your big chance.'

She hadn't let him put himself inside her until after she'd had her orgasm and by then... She had laughed again when he hadn't been able to hold back or control his excitement or the thick gush of semen that shot from his tensely erect cock, but she hadn't been laughing later when he had thrust into her and gone on thrusting until she was moaning and clawing at his back, urging him on and on and then screeching like the alley cat that she was as he took her through her orgasm and refused to stop until she had had another and then another. He hadn't seen her again after that—there hadn't been any need.

He could remember how shocked and disgusted he'd been when his mother had been pregnant with Joss, knowing that she and his father still did it.

He could remember her and his father attending one of his school functions and how furious and ashamed he had felt at the sight of her heavily pregnant body. She had no right, at her age... She was making a laughing-stock of herself and of him.

Max's mouth hardened as he thought of his parents; sometimes there was a look in his mother's eyes when she watched him....

His mother was crazy if she thought he was going to end up like his father, a second-rate man working for a second-rate out-of-touch family business in a second-rate county town. If it wasn't for his Uncle David and his charismatic personality, the business would have gone to the wall years ago. Just because his uncle had made one foolish mistake and...

It wasn't a mistake Max was going to repeat. Oh, he intended to enjoy his life but he also intended to make sure he didn't get caught in the same trap as his uncle.

Max had made sure that he left Oxford with a good enough degree to get him into a decent set of chambers after his Bar finals; and once there not only had he made sure that he brought himself to the attention of those who could be of benefit to his future career, but additionally he had also made sure that his life wasn't all hard work and paying lip-service to his professional ambitions. However, unlike his uncle, he had been discreet and careful.

'Still here, old boy? I thought you were intending to get off early.'

Max tensed as Roderick Hamilton walked into his office. Roderick was just over twelve months his senior. They had been at Oxford at the same time but had not mixed in the same circles; Roderick's parents were extremely wealthy and well-connected. His uncle was the present head of chambers, which was no doubt why of the two of them Roderick had been chosen to fill the vacancy for a tenancy at the end of their pupillage whilst Max had had to fall back on the ignominy of being allowed merely to stay on as a squatter. This meant, of course, that the only fee-paying work that Max could get was whatever had been passed over by the existing members of the chambers, including Roderick.

Max had never been the type to feel the need to make close friends; to Max his peers were rivals, obstacles he had to overcome, but in Roderick's case, Max actively disliked the man, as well.

'Mmm...the Wilson brief. Hard luck,' Roderick commiserated as he picked up the papers on Max's desk and glanced at them before tossing them to one side. 'Pity you're not free this weekend,' he added. 'Ma's having a "do" for my sister. She's coming out this year and Ma's asked me to round up some men.'

Max didn't take his eyes off the papers he was now pretending to study. He knew perfectly well that Roderick was trying to amuse himself at his own expense; there was no way Roderick's mother would welcome any uninvited extra guests to the extremely prestigious and carefully planned ball she was hostessing for her daughter's coming-out party.

'Out of the question, I'm afraid,' he responded without looking at Roderick. 'It's my father's fiftieth birthday this weekend.'

'Ah, you'll have heard about old Benson, I expect,' Roderick remarked, obviously getting down to the real purpose of his 'visit'.

Even though he had been expecting it, waiting for it, in actual fact Max could still feel his body fighting to betray the rage that had been boiling inside him all day.

'Yes, I've heard,' he agreed.

'Once he goes it will mean there'll be a tenancy vacancy in chambers,' Roderick told him unnecessarily.

'Yes,' Max responded neutrally, knowing that he had to make some response.

'Applying for it, are you?'

Max could feel his control starting to slip. 'I haven't made up my mind yet,' he lied.

'Well, I should do if I were you, old chap,' Roderick warned him, 'because it seems that tenancies aren't that easy to come by these days and I've heard that there's a lot of interest being shown in this one. Not, of course, that there should be any problem if you did decide to go for it. After all, you did your pupillage here and you've been squatting here for...let me think, it must be well over a year, mustn't it? God, is that the time? I'd better go...I promised Ma I'd be on hand at home this evening. Good luck with the Wilson brief,' he drawled as he walked into the corridor.

Max waited until he was quite sure that Roderick had gone before balling up the piece of paper he had been reading and hurling it across the room with all the force of his rugger training. Damn Roderick, damn him to hell and back and damn his bloody uncle, as well.

It was over eight months now since Max had heard the first whisper that Clive Benson was going to be invited to become a judge. He had heard it initially on a visit to Chester to keep up with the Chester branch of the family; after all, in this business you needed all the help you could get. And ever since then he had been doing all he could to make sure that *he* got the vacancy when it came up.

On Wednesday morning, when the clerk had told him that the senior partner wanted to have a meeting with him, Max had confidently expected to be told officially about the vacancy and to be assured that once the tenancy did fall vacant, it would be his.

Instead he had been told following much harrumphing and throat clearing that after much discussion the partners had decided it was time they observed the rules against sexual discrimination and gave consideration to taking on a female barrister. Not that that necessarily meant that they were going to do so, nor that he was being passed over, Max had been assured. All applicants would be considered on their merits, of course.

'Of course,' Max had returned through gritted teeth but he knew exactly what he was being told and, without doubt, Roderick also knew exactly what was going on. How could he not do?

It was too late now for Max to wish he had not announced privately to his grandfather the last time he had gone home that the tenancy was as good as his. Gramps was already champing at the bit about the fact that he was only working as a squatter. In his day such a situation had been inconceivable; you did your pupillage and then went on to work as a fully fledged junior barrister. But things had changed; places in chambers were hard to come by.

And just who the hell was this female anyway? No names had been mentioned and mentally Max had run through the female barristers of his acquaintance who might be considered. Sod the bloody sex discrimination laws. What about him...what about discriminating against him?

He had gone out that night in a foul mood, picked up the girl he was currently dating, a leggy, passionate redhead who had made no objection when he had cut their dinner date short and taken her home. She *had* objected later on, though, on the fifth occasion he had woken her in the night to vent his pent-up fury and resentment, filling her body with his without taking sufficient time to arouse her completely first, using her ruthlessly and emotionlessly and refusing to let her go until he had driven his body into a state of physically exhausted detachment.

She had told him in no uncertain terms that he wouldn't be seeing her again but he didn't particularly care. He had more important things to worry about. Despite all the sexual energy he had discharged, he was still furiously, bitterly angry. He was *owed* that vacancy.

He had worked his butt off this last year, letting them throw every bit of dross they had at him. Gritting his teeth, he had managed to master the sometimes almost overwhelming urge to turn round and tell them just what to do with their non-fee-paying, thanklessly unrewarding juvenile bits of work they wouldn't give a pupil to do but which they had no compunction about dumping on his desk, knowing he could not, *dared* not, object.

What had all that been for if he wasn't going to get the vacant tenancy? He might as well have gone into industry; there at least he would be earning a decent salary. But he hadn't gone into industry because as his Uncle David and his grandfather had desired, so Max wanted for himself the prestige of being a barrister, of rising to QC and ultimately being called to the Bench.

He wanted it, hungered for it, yearned for it, *ached* for it and, by God, he intended to have it, and no female, no sex discrimination law was going to stand in his way.

There was only one way to deal with the situation now and Max knew exactly what it was, but first he had to find out exactly the identity of the hopeful candidate for the vacancy. The partners would no doubt know and so, too, would the senior clerk, but Max quickly dismissed him from his calculations. He would never divulge that kind of information to him, which left only the partners and anyone who had their confidence or access to it.

Max was still mulling over what course of action he could take when he climbed into his car two hours later and headed for the North.

'Here we are, home.'

'Very impressive,' Caspar murmured as Olivia brought her car to a halt and turned round in her seat to look at him.

'Here's Tiggy,' she announced when she saw the front door open and her mother hurry towards the stationary car.

Caspar remained silent as he turned to take his first look at Olivia's mother. Her use of her mother's nickname whenever she spoke of her wasn't anything unusual in the society in which he had grown up, but a certain undertone that was always in Olivia's voice when she spoke about her mother made his study of the older woman thoughtfully assessing.

Physically, they were very alike; Olivia had inherited her mother's beauty including her high-cheeked facial features. In contrast to her mother, however, Olivia's beauty radiated from within her in a way that made it almost unimportant that she possessed the kind of looks that could take one's breath away. Beside her daughter, Tiggy seemed to be a beautiful but blank two-dimensional image.

Caspar's first feeling as he watched her was one of disappointment. Why so? he wondered as he got out of the car and waited for Olivia to introduce them. What had he expected...hoped for, if indeed he had hoped for anything? Perhaps despite that carefully neutral note he had already observed in Olivia's voice, her mother would still turn out to be more rather than less of what her daughter already was.

'Livvy darling...at last... Oh dear, look at your nails and your hair, and those jeans... Oh, darling—'

'Tiggy, this is Caspar,' Olivia interrupted her mother calmly. 'Caspar, this is my mother.'

'Tiggy, you must call me Tiggy,' Tiggy announced in the slightly breathy voice that years ago admirers had told her was so incredibly sexy. 'Come on in, both of you. I'm afraid your father and I are just on our way out,' she told Olivia as she urged them into the house. 'We're having dinner with the Buckletons....'

The front door was already open, the parquet floor gleaming richly of wax, and as he stepped inside, Caspar's initial impression was one of a room filled with soft colour and flowers. There were huge bowls filled with floral arrangements everywhere: in the fireplace, on a round polished table in the middle of the room, on a pair of small tables beneath imposing

Georgian silver-framed mirrors that faced one another across the width of the room.

'I do so think that flowers are important,' he heard Tiggy telling him as she saw him staring at his surroundings. 'They make a house come alive, turn it into a home,' she was saying quietly, then... 'Oh, Jack, no, don't you dare bring that animal in here. Use the back door. You know the rules.'

Caspar frowned as a young boy and a large, slightly overweight golden retriever walked in through the still-open front door.

'Well, if you're going out, we'd better not keep you,' he heard Olivia telling her mother. 'I take it that we're in my room. We—'

'Oh dear... Darling, I'm sorry but that's something your father wants a word with you about. It's not that we mind, of course...but it's your grandfather. You know how old-fashioned he is and how important public opinion is to him. Your father feels that he just wouldn't be at all happy about you and Caspar...well, especially with the Chester family coming over for the party, your father felt—'

'Are you trying to say that you expect me and Caspar to sleep in separate rooms?' Olivia interrupted her mother incredulously. 'But that's...' She started to shake her head, anger darkening her eyes, her voice crisping authoritatively as she remonstrated with her mother. 'There's no way—'

Caspar touched her lightly on her arm. 'It's okay, I understand. Separate rooms will be fine,' he told Tiggy easily.

Olivia shook her head and pulled a rueful face at him. The sheer intensity of her love for him frightened her at times. Love was a word that was expressed freely and mercilessly in her home, but as an emotion, she wasn't sure she fully understood it—and it left her feeling vulnerable and wary.

She had practically swooned at his feet with lust the moment she set eyes on him. Who wouldn't have done? Six foot two with broad, well-muscled shoulders and physique to match, he had inherited from somewhere or other the facial bone structure of a Native American warrior chief along with the Celtic colouring that was the most compelling of all—black hair and dark blue eyes.

As she walked into his lecture, Olivia simply hadn't been able to take her eyes off him—and she wasn't the only one. She had almost fainted on the spot when he had asked her out, but she had retained enough sanity and enough sense of healthy self-preservation to insist that their first date be somewhere busy and public and to arrange her own transport home just so that she wouldn't give in to the temptation—if it was offered—of going straight to bed with him.

She didn't and it wasn't, but not, as both of them confessed to one another later, because it wasn't what they wanted.

Oh yes, she had wanted him all right—and still did—but now she loved him, as well, loved him intellectually and emotionally as well as physically. He was her lover, her mentor, her best friend...her everything, and she couldn't envisage how on earth her life had ever seemed complete without him, how she had not, for all those years when he had not been there, somehow been conscious of a huge, aching, empty gap where he would one day be.

He was her whole world; he made her complete and yet she found it hard to tell him how much he meant to her emotionally. That was far, far harder than to tell him just what kind of effect he had on her physically, but then Olivia was very leery of emotions, of feeling them and exhibiting them. Her mother was emotional, everyone said so; they also said with varying degrees of sympathy that that was why her mother needed and deserved special handling, special allowances.

Even as a very small child, Olivia was aware that those special allowances made for her mother's emotional nature always seemed to be given at the expense of other people, that in some way or other those closest to her mother had to be less emotional as though to compensate for her mother's excesses.

'You really are the most amazing person,' Caspar had told her one day after she had spent weeks tracking down a particular book she knew he had wanted, presenting it to him with casual indifference. 'You'll do something like this, but just try to get you to tell me that you love me.'

'You know I do,' Olivia returned warily.

'Yes,' he agreed, adding lightly, 'but it would still be nice to hear you say it, though.'

'I know,' Olivia admitted, but she couldn't bring herself to say the small phrase then...and she still couldn't, not even during the most intense moments of their shared heights of passion.

'I just don't believe this,' she told him fifteen minutes later after her parents had left and Jack had gone out to a friend's. She had gone from her childhood bedroom to the small attic guest-room where

Caspar was unpacking his case. 'They might at least have put you up in the room next to mine.'

'It's only for a couple of days,' Caspar reminded her, adding teasingly, 'and I don't mind. In fact, I'm rather looking forward to the rest. Have you any idea how much you move around in your sleep?' he asked her mock-aggrievedly. 'It's been months since I got a decent night's sleep.'

'Two months six days and...eight hours,' Olivia told him lovingly, counting the actual hours on her fingers whilst Caspar grinned at her. 'It's ridiculous of Mum and Dad to expect us to sleep in separate rooms,' she continued, perching on the end of his small single bed.

After studying it, Caspar had already decided rue-fully that there was no way it was going to be long enough for him, and despite what he had said to her, he knew already that he was going to miss having Olivia next to him, and not simply because of the sex, in fact, not really at all because of the sex.

He was thirty-two years old and had had good sex before, and if he was honest, great sex before, but the difference now was that he had never been in love be-fore, never *loved* before, never really believed that love, the kind of love he felt for Olivia, could actually exist. He had watched his parents go through various sets of mix-and-match relationships, taking on part-ners, then abandoning them to take on new ones. He had managed to avoid the trap of an early marriage fa-tally programmed for failure, had realistically ac-cepted that he would marry perhaps some time in his thirties and that maybe it would last long enough for him and his partner to see their children through their teens or maybe it wouldn't and that was all any sensible, mature right-thinking adult could expect.

'It's the fact that it's all so damned hypocritical that really infuriates me,' Olivia complained, nibbling at her lower lip in the same way that she worried over the issue of their not being able to sleep together. 'It's always the same. We've always got to fall in line behind what Gramps decides we should do.'

'Morally speaking...' Caspar started to say, but Olivia shook her head, refusing to let him continue.

'Morally speaking nothing. Gramps just likes controlling other people. He isn't in the least bit concerned about my moral welfare or about any aspect of my welfare,' she declared fiercely. 'He never has been. Now if I'd been a boy...a grandson...' She broke off and shook her head a second time, a rueful smile curling her mouth. 'Look at me. I haven't been back for twenty-four hours and already it's starting. I promised myself when I left home that I'd leave my chip behind me.'

'You've said yourself that you wouldn't really have wanted to go into the family practice,' he reminded her.

'Yes, I know,' she agreed, 'but I should have had the opportunity to choose. Gramps and Dad did everything they could to dissuade me from studying law. Only Aunt Jen supported me and encouraged me. Oh, and Aunt Ruth, as well. You'll like them and Uncle Jon.'

'Your father's twin?'

'Mmm...although they aren't at all alike, well, physically they are, of course, because they're identical, but Uncle Jon...' She stopped in mid-sentence.

'Uncle Jon...?' Caspar pressed but Olivia shook her head.

'I can't really explain. You'll see for yourself when you meet him. It's as though somehow he's always standing in the shadows—in Dad's shadow—and yet...'

She stopped, her brow furrowed in thought. 'It's as though he deliberately makes less of himself and more of Dad. Everyone, but most especially Gramps, focuses on Dad and on Tiggy because she's his wife, and yet to me it sometimes seems as though both of them are somehow unreal, that they're just cut-out cardboard figures with no substance to them....' She gave a small shiver.

'It used to frighten me a bit when I was younger, seeing them like that and wondering why no one else seemed to see them in the same way.' She pulled a wry face. 'Sort of like the old fairy story about the emperor's new clothes in a way, I suppose. You heard Tiggy going on earlier about the flowers, about them making a house a home. Everyone always says what a marvellous flair for décor my mother has, and granted, the house is always perfect but it's not a home. Aunt Jen's house is a home. This place is just like...like a set out of a film or a play...the right furniture, the right colours, the right flowers.' She grimaced again.

'Dad was originally supposed to qualify as a barrister, you know, but something went wrong. I'm not sure what exactly. Oh, Tiggy makes references to how they met, the fact that my father was playing in a pop group, the fact that she was modelling and he fell in love with her on sight. They were married at Caxton

Hall—it was the fashion then. Tiggy was already pregnant with me and that was why they decided to move back to Haslewich. Dad wanted his children to be brought up here, so he abandoned his plans to work as a barrister for our sake...at least that's what I've always been told and, of course, Gramps has never really forgiven me for it. He so desperately wants to have a QC in the family.'

'But I thought there already was, your great-uncle Hugh.'

'Hugh was a QC, yes,' Olivia agreed. 'He was actually appointed a judge last year, but Hugh isn't true family, at least not as Gramps defines it. Hugh is merely Gramps's half-brother. Gramps's father, Josiah, remarried after Gramps's mother died and Hugh is his second wife, Ellen's, son.

'Although Gramps would never admit it, secretly I think he's always been a little bit jealous of Hugh. Ellen's family had money and Gramps's father was, according to Aunt Ruth at least, always that little bit more indulgent towards Hugh than he was towards them.

'It was Ellen's family's money that paid for Hugh to train as a barrister. Gramps, of course, had to go into the family business—there wasn't anyone else who could. I suspect that really he's still disappointed that Dad wasn't called to the Bar, which is why he's so determined that Max will be.'

'Ah, Max.'

'You don't like him, do you?' Olivia questioned.

'Do you?' Caspar returned dryly.

'We've never really got on, even when we were younger. Oh, I know everyone thinks I'm jealous because Max is Dad's favourite, but it isn't that. I just don't think Max is a very likeable person. No one else agrees with me, of course. Tiggy thinks he's wonderful. He flirts outrageously with her and she can't see that underneath it all he's really laughing at her. She'll probably try to flirt with you as she would him. She doesn't mean anything by it...it's just her way...she can't help it, she needs...'

Olivia paused, groping for the right words to explain her mother's vulnerability and then abandoned the attempt, saying quietly instead, 'Sometimes when I see Aunt Jenny watching Max I sort of get the impression that she doesn't like him much herself but, of course, that can't be true. She's his mother after all and mothers always love their children.'

'Do they?' Caspar asked her wryly. 'I'm not sure that's true. What certainly isn't true is that children always love their parents. There's virtually a whole industry growing up now around analysing why so many adult and sometimes not-yet-adult children murder their parents.'

'Mmm... I was reading about that case involving...'

They were off, both of them quickly becoming engrossed in the intricacies of the legal case Olivia had referred to.

She was more beautiful than ever when she was animated like this, Caspar acknowledged, watching her, but never, nowhere ever near so beautiful as she was when she lay in his arms and opened her eyes, her body, her soul to him.

'Caspar,' she complained when she realised that she didn't have his full attention, 'what are you doing?'

'Just testing this mattress,' he explained.

'Why?' she demanded curiously.

'Why do you think?' he responded softly, turning round to kiss her before asking, 'How long do you suppose we have before your parents come back?'

'My bed's bigger,' Olivia whispered between returning his kisses.

'Mmm...' he murmured distractedly, nuzzling the soft, tender flesh of her throat. 'You can show me later. Right now, right now...'

He exhaled in masculine, sensual pleasure as he peeled down her top and exposed the taut curves of her breasts, teasing first one and then the other erect nipple with the tip of his tongue, feeling her whole body quiver in response to his touch.

He could still remember the first time he had gone down on her, the intensity of the quicksilver shudders of pleasure she hadn't been able to conceal from him. Thinking about it now made his own body harden.

'We haven't had any supper,' Olivia reminded him, gasping the words between tiny shivers of responsive pleasure.

'Mmm...who wants supper? I'm going to eat you instead,' Caspar told her lovingly.

Olivia closed her eyes; she loved the way Caspar was so wonderfully vocal in his lovemaking. He wasn't poetic as one would-be admirer had been when she was at college, nor did he talk dirty as some men—and women—enjoyed doing, but he had a way that was somehow totally unique, totally Caspar, a way that was both deliciously erotic and entrancingly funny, and sometimes whilst she was laughing, her own arousal caught her unawares. But not Caspar. He seemed to sense that moment, that second, that heartbeat of time when between one breath and the next, laughter turned to desire and her need for him overwhelmed everything else. Just as it was doing now.

'Caspar,' she demanded, tugging urgently at his hair, feeling the hot sweetness of his breath feeding the soft, fluttering pulse he had so lovingly conjured up with his tongue.

'Mmm...?' he murmured teasingly, knowing full well what that urgent little tug on his hair actually meant.

'I thought you said that Olivia was coming back tonight,' Joss protested when his third attempt to telephone his cousin had met with no response.

'I thought she was,' Jenny agreed, deliberately keeping her back to him and to Jon.

'Well, she can't be there, otherwise she'd have answered the phone, so you must have got it wrong, and now there won't be time to show her the badger cubs,' Joss announced, patently aggrieved.

'Livvy won't want to see the badgers. She's bringing her boyfriend back with her,' Louise told her brother with elder-sister superiority.

'Louise,' Jenny warned, frowning her disapproval.

'So...why should that stop her wanting to see the cubs?' Joss demanded.

Behind her back, Jenny could hear the twins' stifled, knowing giggles.

'Girls!' Joss pronounced with exasperated contempt, then added, 'Aren't you going to eat that pie, Lou, because if you're not...?' He stared hopefully at his sister's plate.

'You're looking tired,' Jenny commented quietly to her husband when they were finally on their own.

'Not really. It's just...well, I suppose this party brings home the fact that we're not getting any younger.'

Jenny didn't say anything; she knew quite well who carried the heaviest part of the burden at work in the practice. She knew equally well that any attempt by her to protest would meet with that same polite, distancing withdrawal that Jon used whenever he considered that anyone was attempting to attack his twin brother.

In the early years of their marriage she had found it unbearably hurtful, knowing that someone else would always come first; that his loyalty, his love for his twin, would always be the most important, would always come before his feelings for her. But then she made herself recognise that it was that same loyalty to David that made him the man he was, the *husband* he was...the *father* he was...and she had said to herself that she must not fall into the same trap as others and try to make her husband what she wanted him to be rather than appreciate what he was. In their marriage at least, he would have the opportunity to be himself—to be an individual. She owed him that much. That much, and *much, much* more. So very much more...

3

'Thank you, Mr Thompson, everything looks lovely, and you'll be here in the morning to finish off?' Jenny asked the man in charge of the team that had erected the marquee.

They had arrived earlier in the day, a dozen or more of them, all neatly dressed in an eye-catching uniform of jeans and T-shirts bearing the marquee company's logo. Most of this group of energetic young men and women, Jenny had discovered, were students working through their summer vacations.

They had erected the marquee with commendable expertise and speed under the watchful eye of the forty-odd-year-old foreman, breaking only for an hour's respite and a picnic meal before going on to hang the interior awnings, put up the lights and erect the connecting 'tunnels' that led from the house to the marquee, one for the guests and another for the caterers.

'We'll be here sharp on the dot at eight,' the foreman assured Jenny.

'And the tables will be set up and the chairs in place by twelve?' she checked.

'By twelve,' he agreed.

'It looks absolutely wonderful,' Olivia approved as the foreman turned to gather his team together.

She and Caspar had called round just as Jenny was on the point of leaving home to check on how things were going and had elected to go with her. Max, who had arrived home late the previous evening, had also announced that he would join them. Jenny wasn't sure why. He was standing on his own, scowling and looking thoroughly bored and irritated.

'I hope having plain cream isn't going to be too dull,' Jenny worried as she turned back to study the interior of the marquee again.

'No, it's perfect,' Olivia assured her. 'So elegant— anything else would have been too fussy...too weddingy.'

The marquee team were piling into the vehicles that had brought them and that Jenny was relieved to see were all neatly parked well away from Ben's precious lawn.

Apart from being present when they arrived to check that everything was in order, Jenny had left the marquee people to get on with their work on their own, having given them her telephone number in case there were any problems, but she had gathered from the comments Ben had made since they arrived that he had spent most of the day keeping a stern eye on their activities.

She wasn't sure whether he was relieved or disappointed that they had worked so efficiently without causing any damage, but she rather suspected it might be the latter.

'Damn fuss,' he muttered now. 'In my day a fiftieth birthday was nothing to make any fuss about. They're forecasting rain, you know.'

'Not until Monday at the very earliest,' Jenny returned serenely.

'I was wondering if I ought to offer Aunt Ruth some assistance with the flowers,' Olivia told her, 'but I don't know whether I'd be more of a hindrance than a help.'

'I'm sure she'd be only too grateful to have another pair of hands, even if it's only to help fetch and carry,' Jenny assured her.

'Make that two pairs of hands,' Caspar joined in.

Jenny smiled at him.

Apart from being introduced to him by Olivia when she had brought him round, neither she nor Jon had had much opportunity to talk to Caspar at any length as yet, but Jenny had liked him immediately.

When one looked beyond the remarkable sexuality of his stunning good looks, there was a steadfastness about him that reassured her maternal heart as well as a certain strength of purpose that told her he was not a man to be deflected from any path he had chosen— any person he had chosen—and it was plain that the person he had chosen, the person he wanted was Olivia.

Jenny watched her niece affectionately. There was no doubt at all that Olivia wanted him, too.

Deep in her heart of hearts Jenny knew with that kind of knowing like a well-spring in the human psyche that cannot be ignored or dammed and was impossible to deny that out of all their children, her own as well as David and Tiggy's, that Olivia was her favourite and extraordinarily special to her. It couldn't be because she was David's child... Her heart had started to beat a little too fast. Fiercely she started to mentally run through the list of things she still had to check up on.

'So, young man, you're a teacher, I gather.'

Caspar inclined his head towards Ben as he spoke. Ben was a tall man himself and it irritated him to acknowledge that this American Olivia had got herself involved with had the advantage over him in that department. Since his accident Ben had started to stoop slightly and he frowned in exasperation as he discovered that he was obliged to take a small step back and actually look up at Caspar.

Americans! Ben didn't like them, *never* had. American servicemen had been stationed locally during the war, loud-mouthed, gum-chewing individuals with more money than sense, bragging and strutting about, turning the local girls' heads and causing all manner of havoc.

'I'm a lecturer,' Caspar affirmed dryly.

'And only over here temporarily, so I understand,' Ben persisted.

'That's right,' Caspar agreed.

'Hmm... Well, over here in this country we have a saying,' Ben told him disagreeably, 'that those who can, do, and those who can't, teach.'

'Gramps,' Olivia protested, but Caspar shook his head gently at her and smiled. If he chose to take it, there was a partnership waiting for him with one of Philadelphia's most prestigious law firms. It would certainly make him far richer than his present occupation, but he enjoyed what he was doing and as far as he was concerned that was more important than making money.

But then, as he would have been the first to admit if

challenged, it was easy for him to make that decision when he was the beneficiary of a considerable family trust set up by his maternal grandfather.

'That depends on the teacher,' he said simply, both his face and his voice calmly neutral, but Jenny, who had overheard the conversation and who happened to be looking at Ben as Caspar made his response, knew that Caspar's refusal to be dominated by him had reinforced Ben's antagonism towards him.

It was just as well that Olivia lived and worked in London and not here, she decided, even though she knew how hurt Olivia had originally been when her tentative hopes of being allowed to join the family business had been contemptuously dismissed by her grandfather.

'The law isn't a business for women,' he was fond of saying. 'They're too emotional, get too involved.'

Her own daughters were going to make him eat those words, Jenny suspected, especially Katie, but then Katie was far tougher emotionally than Olivia. She would never allow her grandfather's views, or anyone else's, Jenny surmised, to deflect her from her goals, a trait she had inherited from Ben himself, and one reinforced by her own family's sturdy ability to withstand whatever shocks life chose to throw at them. As farming stock they had needed that characteristic; *she* had needed it at times.

'No, the only way anyone can really come to know the law is to practice it,' Ben was telling Caspar doggedly. 'I know—I've done it and I don't mean the namby-pamby diluted kind of work you get in some company's legal department like Olivia here does,' he added.

'Olivia is a very highly qualified and professional young woman,' Caspar retaliated.

'Oh, she's passed the exams right enough,' Ben agreed, 'but it takes more than a piece of paper to make a good solicitor. The law isn't sitting at some desk shifting pieces of paper. It's getting out there in it, doing the kind of work young Max is doing. That's the law.'

Jenny could see Caspar stiffening slightly and her heart sank. She knew why, of course. Olivia for all her modesty and her grandfather's deliberate hypocrisy was far more highly qualified than Max and, Jenny was convinced, of far more value to any prospective employer. For starters, Olivia's experience was wider and for another... Well, Jenny knew which of the two of them she would want to handle her most personal affairs and it wouldn't be her own son.

'I'm sorry,' she heard Caspar saying slowly and frowning slightly at the same time. 'Forgive me...I'm still not completely *au fait* with the intricacies of the British legal system but so far as I understood matters Max is still merely a squatter in his present chambers and, as such, unable to take on any potential clients. Olivia, on the other hand, is in charge of her own highly specialised department and I know for a fact—'

'Caspar,' Olivia protested in a stifled voice, 'Gramps doesn't—'

But it was too late. Ben was swinging round to frown at her, sensing a much softer target than the unexpectedly obdurate barrier Caspar had thrown up against him. Ben wasn't used to being challenged and he didn't like it.

'What's this...? Her own department...? What's this...?'

'It's just a small promotion, Gramps. Nothing really at all,' Olivia was already hurriedly protesting. 'Just an interdepartmental thing, but of course—'

'But of course it no doubt carries a whacking great salary increase,' Max interrupted, going over to join in. 'You certainly fell on your feet there, old thing. I—'

'Olivia did not fall on her feet,' Caspar corrected him coolly. 'She happens to be an extremely highly qualified and hard-working lawyer.'

'You would say that,' Max responded. 'After all, she was one of your pupils—out of bed as well as in it.'

Jenny could feel her face burning with embarrassment on behalf of her son, but typically Max was oblivious both to his rudeness and his lack of generosity.

'I hear that there's shortly to be a vacancy coming up in your chambers. Do you intend to apply for it?' Caspar asked Max.

Max frowned. How the hell had Caspar learned about that?

'He doesn't need to apply for it,' Ben interjected, answering the question for him. 'He's already been told that the vacancy will be his and so it should be. He's already had to stand aside once in favour of someone else.'

Max fought to conceal the irritation his grandfather's comment was causing him. Normally he was only too glad to have the old man champion him, but on this occasion just how much did Olivia's damned American know about what was going on?

He had to have some kind of inside information just

to know that the vacancy was coming up. In any other circumstances Max would immediately have started pumping him to discover just how much he knew and if that information included the name of his female rival, but of course he could hardly do that now without admitting to his grandfather that his appointment wasn't as cut and dried as he'd let him think.

Max could feel himself starting to sweat slightly. His grandfather was indulgent towards him—to a point—and Max knew how important it was to Ben that Max fulfilled his ambitions for him. He had already been disappointed once and ultimately David had been forgiven for that disappointment, but Max shuddered at the thought of having to live his uncle's life.

It had been bad enough living under his grandfather's restrictive eye when he was younger; to do so now... His grandfather still held the family purse strings and Max had seen the way he controlled his sons and their lives through them. Max had no illusions about the price attached to being his grandfather's favourite.

But his success meant just as much to him as it did to his grandfather, probably more so. Max liked money and he liked the things it could buy. He wanted to be successful and, if possible, famous, and no mere woman was going to stand in his way.

'Did your mother's shoes arrive safely?' Jenny asked Olivia as they walked back to the car.

'No. She's gone into Chester this morning to see if she can find another pair.'

Olivia hesitated for a moment, remembering the

scene she had interrupted in her parents' bedroom earlier. She still felt disturbed about it.

'Aunt Jenny,' she began, 'I know that you and Mum aren't particularly close, but have you, has she...?'

She stopped abruptly, recalling how on the way here after he had met her aunt and uncle, Caspar had mentioned how much everyone seemed to depend on Jenny. Seeing how not only Jenny's own younger offspring but Olivia's brother Jack, as well, had produced sets of grubby sports kits to be washed, Caspar had remarked wryly that the older members of the family dumped their problems on her in much the same way as the younger ones seemed to dump their dirty washing.

They all *did* have a tendency to turn to Jenny when things went wrong in their lives, Olivia acknowledged but she was an adult now and...

'Is something wrong with your mother, Livvy?' Jenny was asking her but Olivia shook her head, ignoring the temptation to confide in her aunt.

'No,' she replied lightly, 'but you know Mum. She'd be worrying herself silly about those shoes....'

Olivia winced inwardly as she heard her own voice. What would Jenny have said if she had told her what was really bothering her?

She and Caspar had just been on the point of leaving the house that morning when Olivia realised that she had forgotten her jacket. As she dashed back upstairs to get it, she saw that her parents' bedroom door was open and she could hear her mother inside the room apparently talking to herself.

Automatically Olivia had walked into the bedroom. The scene that met her eyes was one she doubted she would ever be able to forget. And neither was the mingled look of shame, guilt, defiance and fear she had seen in her mother's eyes.

'You won't say anything, will you?' she had pleaded with Olivia as she sat surrounded by dozens of glossy carrier bags, their contents plainly never unpacked, the result, Livvy felt sure, of many shopping trips. 'Don't tell your father. He wouldn't... He wouldn't understand....'

Olivia had left without making any response. Beneath her mother's familiar perfume had been another smell, rank and unpleasantly pervasive, a smell Olivia had recognised as actually familiar to her. Her gorge had started to rise in response to it and she had had to leave the bedroom without responding to her mother's plea of secrecy.

'What's wrong?' she heard Caspar asking her quietly as they drove away from her grandfather's. 'You're not brooding over what he said, are you?'

'Who?' Olivia questioned, her face set.

'Your grandfather,' Caspar reminded her. 'I know he must have upset you, dismissing everything you've achieved professionally by...'

Olivia's expression cleared then. Caspar thought she was upset because her grandfather had compared her adversely with Max. Once she might have been but not now, not when...

'No. My grandfather's too old-fashioned and chauvinistic to change now and Max has always been his favourite.'

'Mmm... Well, things will be different in America,' Caspar promised her. When Olivia made no immediate response, he gave her a thoughtful look. 'You're not having second thoughts about our plans, are you?' he prodded, then added, 'You still haven't told your family?'

'How could I have second thoughts?' Olivia challenged him lovingly. 'You know how much you mean to me...how much our future together means to me,' she amended.

She laughed as he warned her softly, 'Just watch it. I don't know what your laws are over here about stopping on the freeway to—'

'This isn't a freeway,' Olivia interjected mockseverely. 'It's a quiet country road and if you want to stop...' She glanced at him provocatively, laughing again when Caspar shook his head at her.

The months they'd spent together had been the happiest of her life and when Caspar had told her that he was due to return to the States at the end of the summer, she had thought at first that he was trying to tell her that their relationship was not one he viewed as potentially permanent.

She had tried not to show her feelings, to reveal to him how devastated she felt, but something must have betrayed her because he had immediately taken her in his arms and held her tight, rocking her protectively.

'No. No,' he told her huskily, 'I don't mean to end our relationship. How could you think it? I love you, Olivia... I want you with me. I want you to come with me...it's just...well, you've worked so damned hard for your promotion and...'

'It's just a job,' Olivia had replied tremulously, and in the emotion of the moment she had meant it. 'You are far, far more important.' She had meant that, too.

Still meant it, even if sometimes she found somewhat daunting the fact that she would virtually have to retrain in the States if she wanted to achieve the same professional status there that she had been well on her way to achieving here at home.

Caspar would never ask or expect her to give up her career for him. She knew that. But he had made it equally plain that there was no way that he envisaged his professional future as lying anywhere other than in the United States.

'We could always commute,' he had whispered to her one night as they lay entwined in one another's arms.

Commute. As Olivia contemplated the emptiness, the loneliness, the bleakness of all the nights they would have to spend apart if they did so, she had known that the option wasn't one she could happily contemplate.

And so the decision had been made. Her notice was already handed in and worked through and she had intended to break the news about her plans for her future to her family at some stage during the weekend. She had not foreseen any problems. Why should there be?

She loved her parents, her family, of course, but they had their lives and she had hers. The old childhood and teenage envy she had felt for Max had long since faded away.

But what about the scene in her parents' bedroom this morning? She bit down hard on her bottom lip. How long had the problem been going on? Did anyone else know? Her father? Surely he must have some inkling. And what about her? She simply couldn't pretend or ignore what she had witnessed despite the pleading look she had seen in her mother's eyes.

Caspar realised that something still troubled Olivia. It was just as well they were only here for the weekend, he acknowledged as he drove back towards Olivia's parents' home. Family gatherings of any kind tended to make him feel claustrophobic, to bring back memories and fears of which, to say the least, he wasn't particularly proud. He could still vividly remember how he had disgraced himself at his father's second wedding.

He'd been taken there by his mother, who had spent the entire previous day patiently explaining to him that her divorce from his father and their consequent relationships with new partners had absolutely no bearing on their shared love for him. He was still their very much loved child.

As a paediatrician, his mother had, of course, been well versed in the kind of trauma experienced by children when their parents' relationship broke down, and not only had Caspar been carefully prepared for the break-up of his parents' marriage and their subsequent divorce, he had also been equally carefully and slowly introduced to their new partners.

In his mother's case, it was an old colleague and friend whom she had known before she married his father. Divorced now himself, he had two teenage children—a son and a daughter—both of whom had been politely distant with Caspar and his mother. His father's inamorata was a younger ex-student who had been tireless in her determination to show Caspar and his father how much she acknowledged the importance of their relationship. Caspar had disgraced both himself and his parents by throwing up all over the bride.

Given his parents' affiliations and careers, the result was perhaps not unexpected. His mother's reaction was to have him and herself undergo months of 'analysis' during which Caspar came close to disliking his mother almost as much as he disliked his analyst. His father chose to proceed with an expensive lawsuit to have his mother proved unfit to have sole charge of him and guilty of poisoning their son against him.

Neither of them had believed him when he told them that his sickness was the result of too much ice cream and a bad case of nerves, and when eventually his father's new wife produced the first of Caspar's half siblings, Caspar was forbidden to go anywhere near the baby, a little girl, just in case his nervous stomach got the better of him.

Caspar was not deceived. His stepmother didn't like him and he didn't think he liked her very much, either.

It was not that Caspar was against families and family life; it was just that as yet he had not seen an example of it that made him feel it was a way of life he wanted for himself. Why, after all, make a liar out of yourself by publicly making promises that were more likely to be broken than kept?

He didn't particularly want to share Olivia with her family; he wanted her all to himself and he freely admitted it. He hadn't had a particularly high opinion of Olivia's father or grandfather before he had met them and now that he had...

How could they value someone as obviously second-rate and unworthy as Max above Olivia? How nature must be laughing at them, mocking them, for their hypocrisy and chauvinism by gifting Olivia above Max.

The two of them hadn't made any firm plans to marry as yet, but ultimately Caspar knew that they would. He had never expected to fall in love so deeply, to want to make the kind of commitment he wanted to make to Olivia, but now that he had...

He didn't want to lose her, he admitted, and part of the reason he had been wary of meeting her family was because he had been concerned that they might oppose her decision to make her home and her life with him in the US.

As Caspar well knew from his own childhood, loving someone made you overly vulnerable, which was why he had initially been so reluctant to acknowledge his feelings for Olivia. He would be glad when this weekend was over and they were free to embark on the next stage of their own lives.

As he turned into the drive to her parents' home, he studied Olivia's profile. Something was clearly bothering her despite her refusal to admit it. He wondered what it was and, more importantly, why she hadn't told him.

'All women are liars and devious,' his father had once said to him. He had been in between marriages at the time and complaining about the amount of alimony his second wife was claiming from him. 'Don't trust any of them, Caspar. Don't make the same mistakes that I've made. They'll tell you they love you with one breath and then with the next...'

Olivia could feel her body starting to tense as Caspar stopped the car. Was her mother at home?

Olivia couldn't see her car. She hated herself for the sense of relief that brought.

Why had she been the one to find out? she asked herself, feeling a defensive, angry resentment that made her ache with shame as her initial shock began to wane. Why hadn't someone else...her father for instance...?

'Olivia?'

She realised that Caspar had said something to her and was waiting for her to reply. Giving him an apologetic smile, she tried to concentrate on what he was saying.

By rights she ought to be confiding in Caspar, telling him what she had seen, but how could she betray her mother when she herself wasn't totally sure... when no one else seemed to know...?

Not sure. Of course you're sure, an inner voice scorned her. You just don't want to accept it, that's all. You just don't want to face up to the truth.

What truth? She only had to close her eyes to be back in her parents' bedroom, to see the disarray, clothes everywhere, that smell... Her stomach started to heave.

'What is it?' Caspar demanded anxiously as she quickly turned to get out of the car.

'Nothing,' she denied.

When David heard his brother's footsteps outside his office door, he reached for the file he had been studying and quickly pushed it out of sight beneath the leather blotter on his desk.

As Jonathon walked in, out of the corner of his eye David could see his bank statement next to the telephone. Trying to be unobtrusive, he angled his arm across it. He could feel the heavy, uneven thud of his heartbeat.

'I was looking for the Siddington Trust file,' Jonathon said, smiling. 'There's a query from the accountants and—'

'Oh, I must have left it at home. I was doing some work on it the other night. I'll bring it in on Monday.'

'You took it home, but—'

'It looks like young Max is going to get his tenancy,' David broke in, overriding his brother.

'Yes...yes...it does,' Jonathon agreed. 'Although, of course, it isn't always wise to take these things for granted.'

'I'll bet Dad can't wait to start bragging to Hugh about it,' David declared, ignoring Jonathon's concern. 'There's always been a bit of rivalry between them on that score, at least in Dad's eyes.'

'I'm sure Uncle Hugh doesn't see it that way,' Jonathon objected. His uncle had been particularly kind to him when they were growing up and Jonathon suspected that any rivalry between the two half-brothers existed more for his father than it did for his uncle.

'Well, Hugh wouldn't, would he?' David countered. 'He's—'

'It will be good to have the family together,' Jonathon commented, unwilling to pursue the matter.

David waited until he was quite sure that Jonathon had gone before retrieving the file he had hidden beneath his blotter and placing it in his briefcase. His fingers trembled slightly as he locked the case. He felt faintly sick and dizzy. It was this damned heat.

He picked up his bank statement and studied it in fresh disbelief. How could they have spent so much? He had warned Tiggy only last month that they simply could not afford to continue spending as they had been doing. He had even threatened to take away credit cards, but of course she had wept and pleaded and in the end he had given in.

It was all very well for Jonathon, he decided bitterly. His brother had never had expensive tastes and had always been careful with his money. Added to that, Jenny must be earning a very useful amount from that business of hers.

Not that he had ever envisaged Jenny as becoming a successful businesswoman all those years ago when they had first known one another. She had been such a shy, diffident girl, so different in every way from his wife.

He had first seen Tiggy perched on the counter of an exclusive and fashionable London wine bar, surrounded by a crowd of admirers whom she was inciting to vie with one another for the chance to take her out.

David had still been playing with the group then and they had just been featured in one of the countless trendy magazines that had mushroomed into existence during that era. Someone recognised him—one of the other models who had been in the wine bar with Tiggy—and she had attached herself to him.

He could still remember the sharp frisson of excitement and challenge he had felt when he glanced across the narrow room and saw Tiggy looking back at him, knowing that she was deliberately ignoring all the other men who were clamouring for her attention.

Impossible then and now, of course, to ever imagine Jenny posing negligently on a bar top wearing one of the shortest skirts ever made, revealing acres of long, coltish leg, her pouting mouth painted in the palest of frosted pink lipsticks, her face deadpan pale, her eyes enormous in their thick rim of black lashes and even blacker kohl.

Jenny never pouted, and had she worn kohl eye make-up her father would have made her wash it off. Her legs were sturdily and sensibly constructed to carry her over the fields of her father's farm, not delicately thin and fawn-like. Where Jenny was healthily robust, Tiggy had been fragile, delicate and vulnerable. Where Jenny had stoically contained and controlled her emotions, Tiggy had gone from tears to laughter and back again in the space of a heartbeat. Where Jenny had been familiar, safe and dull, Tiggy had been deliciously different and dangerous.

And nothing had changed, he reassured himself. He had seen the expression, the envy, in other men's eyes when they looked at Tiggy and compared her with their own dully comfortable middle-aged wives.

Tiggy was the kind of woman who flirted by instinct, who appealed to everything that was male in a man. She certainly had done to him. He had been completely bewitched by her. Bemused. Besotted.

They had gone on from the wine bar to a nightclub, a whole crowd of them, Tiggy giggling as she openly bought a small handful of 'uppers' and insisted that he take one of them.

It hadn't been any particularly big deal—everyone took drugs in the sixties; it was part of the London scene—only unfortunately the senior members of the chambers where he was in pupillage hadn't seen it that way.

There had been his late arrivals and early departures and the days when he had never made it into chambers at all, waking up late in the afternoon in Tiggy's small flat and her even smaller bed to while away what was left of the day in her arms. This behaviour had ultimately cost him his career.

He had to make a choice, the head of chambers had told him sternly when David had been summoned to his room to account for himself. The Bar or Tiggy and the life he was leading with her.

There had been no choice to make, really. He already knew what was expected of him, what his grandfather would expect of him.

He had been given twenty-four hours to think it over and he had gone back to Tiggy's flat to tell her what had happened and to collect his things. Only when he had arrived there he had found Tiggy in a flood of tears—and pregnant with his child.

The sight of her vulnerable face and childlike body, her copious tears, had swept aside all his carefully prepared speeches. He loved her. He couldn't live without her. She was having his baby. His grandfather would understand. He would have to understand.

They were married three days later at Caxton Hall.

As he kissed his new bride, David had told her sternly that henceforward there were to be no more drugs, no more partying all night and sleeping all day. They had their baby to think about.

Docilely Tiggy had agreed, wrapping her arms around him and kissing him passionately whilst she told him how much she loved him.

It was a pity that he wasn't still going to be a barrister, she told him. He would have looked so deliciously stern and forbidding in his court robes, but she would be just as happy married to a famous pop star and she had no doubts he was going to be famous.

David hadn't had the heart to tell her that his career as a pop star had ended almost as soon as it began.

Three weeks later when the bank announced that he had overspent his allowance and that they couldn't allow him to withdraw any more money from his account, he had told Tiggy that they were going to visit his family in Cheshire.

'Cheshire?' she had repeated. 'But we will come back to London?' David hadn't told her before the trip up North that a return to their London lifestyle would not be possible.

In the end, though, she had seen that there wasn't any alternative.

The wild crowd she had run with had dropped her as quickly and carelessly as it had picked her up. She was yesterday's news now, yesterday's girl; the sixties were like that. And neither of them had been willing to consider terminating her pregnancy although for different reasons.

A part of David was proud of the fact that he had fathered Tiggy's child while Tiggy had heard all the terrifying stories the models passed around and frightened themselves with—tales of unimaginable horror about girls who had been left to die in their own blood, or worse.

Tiggy's own family, a respectable middle-class shopkeeper and his wife would have disowned her had she tried to go home to them. David loved her, she knew that, and she desperately needed to be loved. David would keep her safe, protect her from the demons that stalked her and surely they wouldn't have to live in Cheshire for ever.

To David's relief, his father had taken to Tiggy straight away and even semi-growled his reluctant approval when David had explained to him just why they had had to marry so quickly.

The dismissal from his training for the Bar had been less easy for Ben to accept but David had known how to win him round. He always had.

Oddly enough, it had been his mother, Sarah, the quiet, self-effacing one, always willing to fall in with whatever her husband wished, who seemed almost to dislike Tiggy. But then, as David himself had observed, Tiggy was not the kind of woman that other members of her sex took to easily. Jenny, thankfully, had been the exception, welcoming Tiggy into the family with genuine warmth.

She and Jon had been married for several years by then. David suspected that Jenny had been so kind to Tiggy because she herself had been pregnant when she married Jon, but since he was not given to introspection he had not dwelt too deeply on the subject. He was thankful that he had managed to appease his father enough for him to agree to settle all his debts and that he and Tiggy could make a fresh start in the secure environment of his birthplace.

David grimaced as he refocused on his bank statement. He would have to talk to Tiggy again, make her understand.... He had started to sweat heavily and there was a pain in his jaw. He touched it experimentally. He would have to make an appointment to see Paul Knighton, their dentist.

Unlike Jon, he was not looking forward to the weekend. Fifty! Where the hell had all the years gone? Fifty...and look at him. He pushed the bank statement into a desk drawer and then locked it. His head ached and he felt slightly sick.

Probably that damned high blood pressure young Travers had warned him about the last time he had had a check-up.

It wasn't going to be easy talking to Tiggy...making her listen. She had been very upset the previous evening, complaining to him that Olivia thought more of Jenny than she did her and then in the same breath begging him to reassure her that she still looked as attractive as ever, fretfully comparing herself with Olivia.

'Olivia's in her twenties,' he had pointed out unwisely, cursing himself under his breath as he recognised his folly. Only it had been too late to recall his words then; the damage had been done and the consequences so predictable that he could reel off each stage of them. He knew exactly what he would find when he went home this evening and exactly how Tiggy would react if he tried to talk to her about what she was doing to herself, to him, to their life together.

If anyone had told him on the day they married what lay ahead of them, he would have laughed at them in disbelief.

Wearily he passed a hand over his eyes as though unwittingly trying to obliterate the painful memories from his consciousness.

4

━━━━◄━━━━

'Tiggy.'

Olivia paused hesitantly on the threshold of the small sunny sitting room. Her mother was seated at the pretty antique desk Olivia could remember her father buying her one Christmas. As she turned round to smile at her daughter there was no hint of the morning's anxiety and trauma in her expression. In fact, she looked almost serene, Olivia recognised as she watched her tuck the cheque she had been writing into an envelope and seal it.

'I'm just paying a few bills,' she informed Olivia. 'Your father isn't back yet. I thought we'd have dinner in Knutsford at Est Est Est tonight. It's always been one of your favourite places and… Where's Caspar, by the—'

'I'm here,' Caspar responded, following Olivia into the sitting room.

'He really is the most deliciously gorgeous-looking man,' Tiggy told Olivia, dimpling Caspar a teasing, flirtatious smile.

This was her mother at her best, at her most irresistible, Olivia acknowledged as she watched her. It was impossible to feel irritable or envious of her ability to charm or even to question her need to have to do so.

'And so tall,' Tiggy was trilling as she stood provocatively close to Caspar, looking doe-eyed up at him as she asked him, 'Just how tall exactly are you?'

'Six-two or thereabouts,' Caspar obliged her good-humouredly.

'And you've got the muscles to match,' Tiggy breathed poutingly as she ran one polished fingertip down Caspar's bare forearm. 'Oh my...'

Over her mother's averted head, Olivia sent Caspar a pleading look as she witnessed his withdrawal from her mother's touch. She knew how volatile her mother's mood swings were, how quickly she reacted to other people's opinion of her, how vitally important it was to her that others liked and approved of her.

As a child Olivia had simply accepted her mother's needs as an intrinsic part of her character, but now that she was an adult... Her forehead started to pleat in an anxious frown of concern.

'I'd better set my alarm when I go to bed tonight,' Olivia told her mother. 'I promised I'd be at Queensmead early tomorrow morning to help Aunt Ruth with the flowers. Oh, and Aunt Jenny said to remind you that the Chester crowd would be arriving about lunch-time. She said to let her know if you needed any extra bedding or anything. Apparently she's been through the old linen cupboard at Queensmead making sure that Gramps would have enough of everything to cope with Hugh's family. Nicholas, Saul and Hillary and the children are staying there and she says she found enough bedding to equip a small hotel.

'What's wrong?' she asked uncertainly as she saw

the way her mother's expression had changed, her fingers plucking tensely at the cuff of her silk shirt.

'I don't know *why* we have to have Laurence and Henry and their families staying here,' she fretted. 'After all, it isn't as if... That's far more than anyone else is having to put up and Mrs Phillips can't give me any extra time because Jenny has already booked all her spare hours.'

Laurence and Henry were brothers and her father's second or third cousins. Olivia was never quite sure which. They were a little older than her father. Laurence had three grown children and Henry four plus three grandchildren; they belonged to the original Chester family from which her own family had sprung.

'Is the competitiveness with the Chester side of the family shared by you?' Caspar had asked her curiously.

Olivia had shaken her head. 'No, it's all past history so far as I'm concerned and although technically they are family, we've never been that close—weddings, christenings and funerals are about the only times we get to meet these days.'

'Why on earth couldn't they have stayed with Jenny and Jon?' her mother was still protesting.

'Probably because they don't have enough room,' Olivia pointed out gently.

'There's plenty of room at Queensmead,' her mother retorted.

'Yes,' Olivia agreed, 'but Uncle Hugh and his family are staying there.'

Although she didn't say so, she suspected that

Jenny would have been reluctant to place so much of a burden on Ben's shoulders by filling the house.

'Come on, Tiggy,' Olivia coaxed her. 'You know you've always enjoyed entertaining.'

'Yes, but that was before... You know I like to do things properly but your father keeps complaining that we can't afford...' She stopped, chewing on her cheek, her eyes suddenly filling with tears whilst Olivia felt a small, cold finger of unease run warningly down her spine. So far as Olivia knew, her parents were reasonably well off.

Certainly as a child she had never been aware of any lack of money or any necessity to economise. She had always assumed that the practice, although only small, brought in a comfortable and secure income for her father and his brother, given that it was the only firm of solicitors serving the town and its outlying rural district.

Her mother, she realised, was given to exaggeration and Olivia reassured herself that her petulant outburst was probably caused by her father's complaining about her mother's well-known propensity to indulge in designer clothes and expensive make-up.

Olivia was aware that her mother had very little idea of what it meant to watch her spending or live within a given budget. It was not unknown for her to send all the way into Chester for a specific item she required for one of her dinner parties, or to order her current favourite fresh flowers from some expensive Knightsbridge flower shop in London because they were unavailable closer to home.

'I expect Gramps wanted to have the Chester contingent staying with you because he wanted them to be impressed.' Olivia did her best to soothe her mother, biting betrayingly on her bottom lip when she saw the sardonic look Caspar was giving her as he witnessed her overt attempt at flattery. He would, no doubt, take her to task for it later. If Caspar had a fault it was that he did not believe in any gilding of lilies or any sugar-coating of pills.

'Well, yes, I suppose you're right,' her mother conceded, brightening a little. 'Jenny is a dear, of course, and a wonderful cook but...well...she doesn't have much idea of interior design, does she, and the house always seems to be full of children and animals.'

Olivia privately thought her aunt and uncle's home with its lovingly polished antiques, its bowls of homemade pot-pourri and freshly cut garden flowers came as near to her ideal of what a home should be as anything possibly could. She much preferred her aunt's use of the wonderful old fabrics she found on her buying trips—rich brocades, velvets as soft and supple as silk and finely woven cottons and linens—to the modern, and to Jenny's eye, often too pretty, flounced and frilly fabrics that her mother chose to decorate her own home with. But she said nothing.

She knew that her mother took pride in keeping her home as up to the minute and fashionable as she did her wardrobe. Growing up she had become used to the mood of dissatisfaction that would descend on her mother every year when the glossy style bibles she liked to buy pronounced their views on what was currently either in or out of fashion. And whole rooms were refurbished to fit in with their dictates, her mother worrying almost obsessively over every tiny detail, not satisfied until she had found just the right lampshade or the favoured *objet d'art*.

'Has she always been so dependent on other people's good opinion?' Caspar asked her later on that night when they were in bed. Olivia had sneaked upstairs to his attic room, feeling very much like a naughty schoolgirl—it was ridiculous that her mother should feel she had to comply with Gramps's outdated and old-fashioned ideas when he wasn't even there to see them.

'Yes,' she confirmed, 'although...'

'Although what?' Caspar prodded when she paused.

'I...I'm not sure. I can't remember her ever being quite so... I suppose it's very difficult for her. She's always relied so much on her looks as a means of bolstering her self-confidence and she still looks stunning, of course, but...'

'But she's getting older...and more desperate,' Caspar supplied for her.

In the darkness Olivia nodded her head.

Because a part of her had always secretly wished that Tiggy could be more like Jenny...more of a traditional mother and not the almost fey, childlike creature she actually was, the whole issue of her mother and her mother's vulnerability and her own feelings of guilt was one that even now Olivia didn't feel entirely comfortable with.

It was bad enough feeling the way she did without adding to that sense of betrayal by discussing her mother's shortcomings even with someone as close to her as Caspar. She had seen earlier how much he had disliked her mother's overcoy, flirtatious behaviour and had felt torn between protecting Tiggy and agreeing with him.

Slipping out of the narrow bed, she told him, 'I'm thirsty. I think I'll go down and make myself some tea. Would you like some?'

'Please. Want me to come with you?'

Olivia shook her head. 'I shan't be long,' she promised, bending down to kiss him lightly on the mouth before pulling on her robe and padding barefoot to the door.

She knew the house well enough not to need to switch on any light, and besides, the moon was almost full, casting a sharp, clean light in through the windows.

Only the odd creaking board betrayed her presence as she went downstairs. In the hallway she could smell the scent of the white lilies that were her mother's favourite flower.

The kitchen door was ajar and she paused outside it, tensing as she heard the sound of a packet of food being torn open. Biscuits by the sound of it, she guessed as she heard the crunch of someone eating them far too quickly for the health of their digestive system.

It must be Jack. He had obviously sneaked downstairs to get something to eat, Olivia decided as she heard the fridge door being opened. Growing boys were notorious for their appetite, and according to her father's complaints at dinner tonight, Jack was no exception.

Hesitating no longer, Olivia walked into the kitchen and reached for the light switch as she did so. Light flooded the kitchen, revealing the figure crouched almost coweringly in front of the half-open fridge door.

All around her the floor was littered with empty food cartons and packages and even cans, Olivia noticed in shocked bewilderment and disbelief as she stared from the rubbish-strewn floor and work surfaces to her mother's ashen face.

'Tiggy...' she whispered, 'what is it...what's...?'

But even as she asked the question, Olivia knew the answer, just as she had known earlier that morning when she'd walked into her mother's bedroom and seen those glossy, expensive bags of brand-new, unworn clothes scattered all over the room and had smelled that sickening, nauseous smell of fresh vomit overlaid by the heavy, cloying, non-disguising scent of her mother's perfume. Had known and had tried desperately all day to ignore what she had seen just as she had tried to ignore her own shaming feelings of anger and resentment at having been confronted by the evidence of her mother's abject misery and despair. For whatever else could be responsible for what her mother was so plainly doing and what, Olivia had guessed with a burst of unwanted, sickening self-awareness, she must have been doing for many, many years?

Anorexia, bulimia—these were the words one associated with vulnerable, almost self-destructive young adolescents and surely not adult women in their forties, but there was no escaping the evidence of her own eyes.

'Oh, Mum,' she whispered chokily, still half-hoping that it was all a mistake, that her mother would stand up and smile at her and that somehow the chaos, the carnage all around them would disappear; yet it was all too clear from the remains of the food her mother had obviously just forced down for whatever reasons of self-hatred and hunger and need that she had been motivated into the kind of behaviour that left the kitchen looking as though it had been ravaged by a dozen or more starving people.

Torn food wrappers, empty cans, opened cartons of ready-made meals, scattered remnants of a loaf of bread and more, were tossed on the floor as though someone had just emptied a dustbin on it.

Sickly Olivia stared at the mess. How *could* any one person possibly eat so much? She looked at her mother, her face waxy and sallow, her eyes dull and heavy. She was struggling to breathe properly, her hand surreptitiously massaging her stomach beneath her robe.

'Why?' Olivia whispered achingly. 'Why...?'

'I don't know...I don't know...'

Tiggy had started to shiver and cry, wrapping her thin arms around her bent knees and rocking herself to and fro as she pleaded with Olivia.

'Don't tell anyone...don't tell your father...I didn't mean to spend so much...I couldn't help it.... You understand, don't you?' she appealed to her daughter.

But Olivia, remembering how the sight of all the bags of unwrapped and unworn clothes strewn across her floor had shocked her, could not find the words to give her mother the reassurance she so desperately needed.

'Don't tell your father,' her mother was repeating. 'I promised him I wouldn't do it again. He doesn't love me when I'm sick,' Olivia heard her mother saying, her eyes filling with fresh tears as she looked pathetically at her daughter. 'He tries to pretend, but I can tell...he won't come near me....'

She was sobbing noisily now like a small, hurt child. She even looked like a child with her thin arms and her hunched-up body. Olivia wanted to go over to her and put her arms round her, hold her, but the stench of the food she had consumed, the memory of how her bedroom had smelt after she had voided whatever she had stuffed herself with previously, made her gorge rise and she simply couldn't do it...couldn't bear to be near her.

As she swallowed against her own nausea, Olivia wondered why it had taken her so long to realise what was happening, *why* she had not guessed...questioned—

'Olivia?'

She tensed as she heard Caspar coming into the kitchen. She had forgotten all about the tea she had promised him, and now as her eyes met his across the width of the room she saw that he had recognised what was going on as immediately as she had done herself.

'I didn't know,' she heard herself whispering to him as though there was some need for her to justify her own ignorance.

Behind her, her mother was struggling to stand up.

'I want to go to bed...I'm tired,' Olivia heard her saying. She was speaking and moving like someone heavily sedated or drugged, which Olivia recognised dully she possibly was with so much food crammed into her body.

'Let her go,' Caspar told her as Olivia started to protest.

Could this really be her mother? Olivia wondered wretchedly as she watched her shambling out of the kitchen, heading, not for the stairs, but for the down-stairs cloakroom.

'Oh God,' Olivia whimpered. 'Oh God, Caspar. I don't...'

Automatically she started to pick up the debris her mother had left behind. Then abruptly she paused and turned round, her eyes filling with tears. Wordlessly he held out his arms to her.

Still too shocked to articulate her feelings, she half ran, half stumbled into Caspar's open arms, closing her eyes against the too-vivid images of her mother that refused to stop tormenting her as she buried her head against his chest.

In a world that had suddenly become frighteningly unreal, the warmth of Caspar's embrace as he held her felt as blessedly familiar as the hardness of his body. She could feel the steady beat of his heart, so much calmer and slower than the frantic, raised pace of her own, smell his scent, hear his breathing, all of them things she knew well and could recognise, giving her a sense of safety and security that she badly needed.

Emotionally she felt much the same sense of shock and disbelief that people must have experienced when they discovered the unsinkable *Titanic* was ac-tually sinking, the decks no longer stable beneath their feet but tilting; Caspar was her only place of refuge, her only piece of stable ground. How could her mother, her pretty, slim, delicate and dainty mother be that same gross, unrecognisable person she had just seen cramming food into her mouth like, like...?

She started to tremble violently, as distressed by her

own thoughts as she was by what she had just witnessed.

'Caspar...' As she whispered his name she opened her eyes and looked anxiously up into his face, wrapping her arms tightly around him as she started to kiss him with a frantic, fierce passion.

For a second he seemed to hesitate, but then as though he sensed her need, he started to return her kiss, responding to its hunger and need, and inevitably, because he was a man, despite the fact that he knew it was an emotional need that was driving her rather than physical desire, becoming aroused by it, his hands coming up to cup her breasts.

'Oh God, Livvy,' he told her hungrily, 'you feel so good I could eat you....'

Eat her!

Olivia stiffened, wrenching her mouth away from his, nausea churning her stomach.

The sound of the very word 'eat' brought back all the dreadful images she had been trying to suppress—the sight, the sound of her mother as she indulged in her orgiastic binge, a parody of sexual pleasure, which Olivia had instinctively recognised as bringing her physical release, a release from any form of self-control, of emotional restraint.

'Livvy, what is it?' Caspar demanded.

He was still holding her, still touching her, his hands caressing her breasts, his thumbs gently stroking over her nipples. Olivia gave a violent shudder of disgust and pushed him away. It was his love she wanted, his support, the reassurance of his arms around her, not sex.

'Let's go back to bed,' Caspar whispered.

'Go back to bed!' Olivia's eyes widened as she stared at him, the feeling of relief and gratitude she had experienced when he had first held out his arms to her replaced by a sense of alienation and resentment. 'Caspar, how can you say that?' she demanded. 'Sex is the last thing I feel like right now...the very last thing. You saw my mother, you...' She turned away from him, pacing the kitchen whilst Caspar frowned.

He should have guessed, of course, been prepared, but somehow he had allowed himself to believe that she would be different, that she was different, but here she was making it plain that for all she had said about them, when it came down to it, her family, her parents, other people, were far more important to her than he was himself.

Olivia was completely unaware of what he was thinking or of the effect her action in pushing him away from her had had on him. Neither did she have any inkling of the old childhood feelings of not being good enough, of not being wanted, it had awakened in him. Instead, completely absorbed by her own tangled feelings of shock, disgust, fear and guilt, she told him, 'This morning when I walked into her bedroom, she was there surrounded by carrier bags, all of them full of clothes, still wrapped in their original tissue paper, never even worn. Not just one or two of them, there were dozens, everywhere, and the smell...' She gave a small shudder, remembering the rank, muscle-clenching, gut-heaving odour that had filled her parents' bedroom. 'I should have said something *then*...done something...'

'Like what?' Caspar challenged her. 'Your mother obviously has an addictive personality, Olivia.

Binging, whether on food, shopping or love, is all part and parcel of the same thing. It's a driving need, a compulsion, to fill an emptiness that can never be filled in the way that such an addict attempts to fill it.'

'But I should have guessed...known...done something...' Olivia protested, her voice thickening with tears of pity and compassion for her mother's plight. Like an adult who has suddenly realised that they have failed a small child, she felt guilty, helpless, unbearably saddened and filled with an aching pity and the need to put things right, to make things better.

'How could you have?' Caspar asked her tardily, his own emotions under control now or so he told himself.

Unlike her, he seemed completely unmoved by her mother's behaviour, Olivia reflected, but then Tiggy was not *his* mother, and Caspar, as she had already sensed, had a certain hardiness if not hardness about him, a certain tough outer shell he could draw around himself when he chose to do so.

'Natural self-protection,' he had called it when she had once questioned it. 'Everyone needs some,' he had added.

'But you must have been moved by what we saw. Felt something,' Olivia had pressed. They had been watching a current affairs programme at the time and she had been reduced to tears by the plight of the villagers in the far-off, achingly poor, barren environment in which they lived.

'Of course,' Caspar had agreed, 'but my emotions are of no use or help to them.'

'No, but through them you could be moved to do something that would help,' Olivia had protested.

'You mean I could allow my emotions to be manipulated to the point where I automatically put my hand in my pocket?' Caspar had demanded cynically.

'A multibillion-pound aid industry has been built on that very premise,' he expounded, 'and yet there are, as you have just seen, still thousands upon thousands of starving human beings. Yes, I feel that it's wrong for any human being to have to live in pain and poverty. Yes, I know it's wrong that we waste so much so thoughtlessly, that we're so materialistic, but even though we have so much whilst others have so little, you cannot make all people equal, Livvy.

'The best you can do, all you can do, is to help them to help themselves and that does not always necessarily mean giving financially. You wouldn't applaud an adult who gave a child craving their attention a hundred dollars to play with instead, would you?'

'It's not the money, it's what it can buy...what it can provide,' Olivia had insisted, but she had known that it was an argument that Caspar would not allow her to win. He was much tougher than her, much harder, much more inclined to stick to his chosen convictions, not a man who could ever be influenced by the actions of those around him, not a man who would ever go with the crowd unless it suited him to do so.

She remembered all this now as she looked at him.

'There must be something I could have done... something I still *can* do...to help,' she faltered as she saw the cynical way that Caspar was watching her.

'Such as?' he derided. 'From the looks of her I would suspect that your mother is in the grip of an addiction that she's had for a long, long time. She *does* need help, yes—professional help,' he added pointedly. 'What you're doing now,' he added with curt emphasis as he indicated the rubbish-strewn floor that Olivia was cleaning, 'only makes it easier for her to continue with what she's already doing. In effect, what you're doing is actually encouraging her to continue doing it.'

'No. That's not true,' Olivia protested emotionally. 'I'm just trying to tidy up in case—'

'In case what?' Caspar challenged her. 'In case someone else realises what's going on? Don't you think your father already knows? He might have closed his eyes to the situation, but scenes like this must have happened before.'

When Olivia bit her lip, he reiterated harshly, indicating the littered floor, 'The best way you can help your mother is not by doing this, by covering up for her and protecting her, but by compelling her to face reality and to seek professional help.'

'But, Caspar, you saw her, she was...she's—'

'An addict,' Caspar repeated relentlessly, adding, 'Just ask yourself this, Olivia. If you'd come down here and found your father surrounded by empty bottles of alcohol, would you have been so keen to clear up after him and help him conceal what he was doing? I don't think so. Can't you see?' he asked her. 'The nature of the addiction is the same. It's just that the substance, the pattern of behaviour your mother is addicted to to find release from reality, to escape from life, is different, less socially disruptive—'

'I don't want to talk about it any more tonight,' Olivia told him. 'I can't. It's the party tomorrow,' she added unnecessarily, 'and I can't...' She closed her eyes, fighting back the relentless surge of panic she could sense threatening her.

It was pointless feeling that she couldn't cope with what she had discovered; that she didn't *want* to cope with it. Someone had to. How long had her mother been behaving like this? Why had no one else seen, recognised...heard what was obviously a cry for help, the soundless, agonized wail of a soul in torment. And Caspar wasn't helping. Why couldn't he be more compassionate, more understanding? Why couldn't he understand how guilty she felt, how afraid, how compelled almost to do something, anything, to help her mother to ease her own guilt for having gone on so carelessly and unknowingly with her own life without realising what was happening at home?

When they got to the top of the first flight of stairs, it was almost a relief to be able to turn away from Caspar and announce, 'I'd better sleep in my own room, just...just in case—'

'Just in case what?' Caspar challenged her acidly. 'Just in case your mother needs you?' He shook his head. 'You're heading down a no-exit street, Olivia,' he warned her. But Olivia shook her head mutinously, inclining only her cheek for him to kiss and maintaining a stiff distance between their bodies.

Couldn't he see how upset she was, how shocked, how much she needed him to be on her side, to show her that he understood, that he cared? Couldn't he for once forsake the higher ground of his own beliefs and come down to where she stood for her sake, instead of expecting her to make the too painful journey up to him?

'It's all very well for you to sit in judgement of my

mother and say what should be done,' she told him
tiredly, 'but it's *my* mother we're talking about...oh,
what's the point?' She shook her head, too emotionally drained to continue arguing with him but still
half-hoping as she heard him walk towards the
second flight of stairs that she would hear him pause
and turn round, come back to her, but of course he
wouldn't...didn't...

Oh no...his principles were much too important to
him to do that. So important in fact that they obviously mattered far more than her...than her feelings...her needs...her.

5

———————◆◆———————

Ruth opened her eyes cautiously and then expelled her breath in a quiet sigh of relief. The weather forecasters had been right; it was going to be a fine day.

She had purposely left her curtains open the previous night and now, through the uncovered window, she could see the clear, pure light blue of the dawn sky already being warmed by the strength of the rising summer sun.

Swinging her bare legs out of bed, she started to hum one of her favourite hymns—not because she was particularly religious but, living so close to a church that was home to one of the county's best choirs, one naturally became accustomed to hearing them sing and this particularly rousing hymn had always appealed to her and somehow seemed suitable for the bright promise of the day.

Not that the weather was of any special concern to her other than as to how it might affect her floral displays, but it was important to Jenny and Jenny was important to Ruth, far more important than even she, Jenny, realised, Ruth acknowledged. In fact, in her heart, Ruth cherished the same intensity of emotion and love for Jenny that she would have given to the daughter she had never actually had.

A small shadow crossed her face as she padded

barefoot across her bedroom floor, the boards waxed and polished, their rich darkness broken here and there by soft rugs.

Ruth knew that her brother, Ben, would not have approved of her bare feet and even less of her bare body, which was perhaps not the prettiest sight in the world, she admitted wryly to herself. She was, after all, a woman in her late sixties, but these days mercifully she no longer needed to be constricted or constrained by the disapproval and wishes of the male members of her family, and if she chose to sleep in her skin instead of bundling herself up in something society deemed appropriate for a woman of her age, then so be it.

She had not always enjoyed this kind of freedom— far from it—which was perhaps why she valued and appreciated it so much now, she reflected.

As a girl her behaviour had been very rigidly controlled by her parents, especially her father; he had had very old-fashioned ideas about the way a girl should be brought up and allowed to behave. She paused on her way to the bathroom, sadness momentarily clouding the still-bright cornflower blue of her eyes. When she was young many men had been smitten by the intensity and vivaciousness of her eyes. More than one young man had actually proposed to her on the strength of them, but then those had been dramatic times with the young men on the verge of adult life, poised also and much more precariously on the edge of death, as well, about to go to war with no knowledge of whether or not they might survive, and because of that...

She had far better things to think about this morning than the past, Ruth reminded herself briskly as she prepared to step into her shower. It was going to take her the best part of the morning to do the flowers for the boys' party and that was if everything went according to plan.

Pieter was due to arrive with the order in less than an hour's time. She had arranged to meet him at Queensmead, which would save her the trouble of having to transport the flowers there and risk any damage to them. And no doubt when they did arrive, Ben would be on hand to carp and complain. She and her elder brother had never entirely seen eye to eye. He reminded Ruth far too much of their father. Hugh she liked more.

Ben's sons were her nephews but she loved Jenny, Jon's wife, above them. And as for the coming generation, she had never made any secret of the fact that she simply could not take to Max despite the fact that he was Ben's favourite—despite it or because of it. She hesitated a moment before stepping into the shower, a new and necessary addition to her bathroom the previous winter. She had finally been forced to admit that the rheumatism that had plagued her for several years was making it not just difficult but also downright dangerous for her to climb in and out of the huge, antiquated Edwardian bath the house possessed.

Not even the fact that Jenny was his mother could endear Max to her, but Olivia she quite liked as well as Jenny's twins, and as for Joss, he might have been named after her own father but that was the only similar thing they shared in common. A mother might not be allowed to have favourites but there were no such embargoes placed on great-aunts.

She looked forward immensely to Joss's unheralded visits, his unexpected arrivals at her front door, almost always bearing some small odd gift, odd to other people, that was. She herself had found nothing odd in the smooth, water-washed pebbles he had brought her from the river or the fossils he had found on one of his forays into the countryside; the hedgehog he had rescued and the litter of kittens he had found abandoned and half-drowned in a sack in a muddy pond. The hedgehog had recovered, to be released back into her long back garden; the kittens had thrived and been found safe homes—none of them her own—and the pebbles and fossils had pride of place on one of the shelves of her antique marquetry china cupboard. She had drawn the line at the fox cub and announced firmly that he would be better cared for in a local animal sanctuary, but she had visited the place with Joss and been with him when the cub was eventually set free.

Ruth had accompanied him on long country rambles and imparted to him all her own not inconsiderable knowledge of the area and its history. He was her special link with the future just as she was his with the past.

Somehow, out of their family gene pool, the two of them shared a bond that made them close in ways she had not experienced with any other member of her family.

Ben didn't approve, of course, and she knew quite well that had Joss been an elder child, an elder son, there was no way he would have been allowed to follow his own inclinations and desires. She didn't know whether to be amused or saddened by the knowledge that out of all of them Joss would probably be the one to most easily fulfil his grandfather's most cherished hopes and ambitions.

The law for him wasn't so much a chosen career path as an instinctive calling. On their rambling walks around the town and its environs, he had lectured her on the importance of the Romans to their own civilisation, focusing not as another child might have done on their fighting skills, their feats of technical engineering, but their laws.

Oh yes, Joss was a Crighton and potentially the best of the lot of them.

Olivia was a Crighton, too, of course, but in Ben's world, female Crightons simply did not count.

Poor Olivia. Ruth had watched her growing up, had seen the hurt in her eyes when her father and her grandfather rejected her in favour of Max, when they praised him for achievements far, far below her own, whilst ignoring every single one of her triumphs.

Ruth sympathised with her. She, too, had once dreamed of a career in law. Certainly it had been much more difficult in those days, but she had been a clever girl and had determined to win a place at university. But the war had inevitably changed all that. She had had to help her father when Ben joined the RAF. She had provided an extra pair of hands in the office and had worked in the home, as well. No one would have dreamt of being so self-indulgent as to have domestic help when every available spare pair of hands there was was needed to provide for 'our boys'.

Ah yes, her father had needed her help during those turbulent years. But once the war ended, things were different, very different in her case, because she...

She gave a tiny shake of her head. What was the matter with her? It didn't do to dwell on the past; it couldn't, after all, be changed. There was no going back, but seeing Jenny in the churchyard kneeling at the grave of her first-born son had...

She remembered the look she had seen on Jenny's face the other day after she had left her small son's graveside. Ruth and Joss had planted some tiny white scilla bulbs in the grass around it the previous autumn.

'White is good for babies,' Joss had commented sturdily as he drilled the holes for the bulbs.

They had planted bulbs, too, around the family crypt and beneath the monument to the town's war heroes. Ruth's fiancé had been one of those who had never returned from the war. She had originally met him through Ben. They had trained together as young fighter pilots. Charles had been shot down over France and reported first missing and then dead. He had been his parents' only child and they had never really recovered from his loss. Initially opposed to their engagement because of the short length of time Ruth and Charles had known one another, they had longed desperately after his death for Ruth to tell them that the couple had broken society's rules and that by some miracle she was carrying Charles's child, but unfortunately she hadn't been able to give either them or herself that hope.

Charles...she could barely even remember what he looked like these days and yet at the time...

The church bells rang out the hour, reminding her of the time. Quickly she finished showering. It wouldn't do to leave Pieter to face Ben in one of his increasingly irascible moods.

Jenny was awake early, too, and like Ruth she breathed a sigh of relief and mentally thanked the powers on high for the clear sky and the bright golden rays of the early morning sun.

Beside her Jonathon was still asleep, but not totally peacefully. He had woken her twice in the night talking in his sleep, a habit he had whenever something was troubling him. She hadn't been able to make any sense of what he was actually saying, only catching his brother's name here and there in his muttered, anxious words. Typical, though, that it should be concern for David that was disturbing his sleep.

As she studied Jonathon's sleeping face, she was overwhelmed by a feeling of tenderness and love. Very gently she leaned across and kissed him, not sure whether to be relieved or disappointed when he continued to sleep.

It had, at various times during their marriage, infuriated, angered and moved her to helpless indignation to see the way her husband always put David first, even though she was well aware of the fact that this was an involuntary reaction, a habit, an instinct indoctrinated into him by his father virtually from the moment he was born. She had, after all, witnessed at firsthand the way David and Jonathon related to one another, not just as Jon's wife but originally as David's girlfriend.

David's girlfriend. How thrilled she had been, how almost speechless her sixteen-year-old self had been when David had first asked her out. A year her senior he had embarked on his A level course while she had still to take her O's.

She found out later that he had only asked her out by accident and that he had originally intended to date one of her classmates. But hearing on the school grapevine that she intended to turn him down, he switched his attention to her, Jenny, instead, simply because she sat next to the girl in class. They had laughed about it together when he told her, even though her own laughter had been slightly tinged with hurt.

She had known, of course, that so far as looks went she was not in David's league and she had known, too, that by the time he had eventually admitted the truth to her, he did genuinely believe that he loved her. She had believed it, as well, for a little while at least and certainly long enough for her to...

She and David had started officially going steady just after her seventeenth birthday, and although they had outwardly accepted her, she had known that in the eyes of David's father, if not his mother, she was not really good enough for him.

She could still remember the long, wet, winter afternoons when she had watched David playing rugby, his father standing at her side, ostensibly supporting his son but at the same time making good use of the opportunity it gave him to talk to Jenny about the plans and hopes he had for him. During these talks Jenny had learned all about the great future that lay waiting for David and how very far away from her it was going to take him.

There was no point to her, a hard-working Cheshire farmer's daughter, hoping that she could follow

David to university; her parents had her future mapped out for her as clearly as David's did his.

Once she had left school after taking her A levels, she was going to train as a receptionist at one of the big hotels in Chester. Her godparents had connections there and through them Jenny was virtually assured of a job. In between times she would continue to help out on the farm, where there could never be too many pairs of hands and where there was certainly no time for any shirkers.

Oh yes, she had always known what was ultimately to come, Jenny reflected, had even perhaps hastened it on herself by calmly refusing to let him buy her an engagement ring to celebrate his passing the coveted Oxford entrance exams. Jenny was relieved. She realised quite well whom his parents—his father—would have blamed if he had not done so and it wouldn't have been David.

The night she had told him—the night she had done what she knew his father expected of her, what he had been priming her to do for months—would remain for ever in her memory. David hadn't believed her at first when she told him it was over, that it was time for them to part, and then, then he had been both angry and, she also sensed, slightly relieved.

David had never liked being cast in a bad light or being seen as anything other than totally perfect. Amongst their peers, their local circle of friends, he made sure it was known that she had been the one to end their romance and only Jonathon seemed to suspect the truth and guess that she had done it for David's own sake, knowing that he needed his freedom and that once he was at university she would only become an encumbrance and perhaps even an embarrassment to him.

Unlike David, Jonathon was not going on to Oxford even though his A level grades were good enough to justify him doing so—better in fact than David's. Not for Jonathon the higher echelons of the legal profession; Jonathon would be studying law, it was true, but at a far humbler level than David.

No one had seemed too surprised when Jonathon and Jenny had announced they were getting married and she suspected that Harry's birth, less than seven months after their marriage, would have caused a lot more gossip than it had if it hadn't been for his subsequent death.

She had offered Jonathon a divorce then. After all, the reason they had originally married no longer existed, but Jonathon had shaken his head and told her firmly that so far as he was concerned, marriage was for life and she had been too emotionally drained by Harry's death to want to argue with him.

And their marriage had been a good one, she told herself firmly now, even if...

Shaking her head, she reminded herself silently that she had far too much to do to lie in bed thinking about the past. She wanted to get to Queensmead as early as she could just in case there were any unforeseen problems.

She knew, of course, that Ruth was more than capable of taking charge but she also knew that Ruth and Ben did not always see eye to eye.

'If he'd just admit that he's getting older, that he's suffering from rheumatism, I'd feel a lot more sympathetic towards him,' Ruth had commented tartly to

Jenny the previous winter when Ben was being particularly difficult. 'But oh no, it's our fault that he's in a bad mood. But then that's Ben for you. Nothing is ever his fault. He is never the one to blame.'

'I expect he feels it would be admitting to a weakness to complain that he's in pain,' Jenny had soothed her aunt-in-law.

'*In* pain, he *is* a pain,' Ruth had countered forcefully.

Jonathon waited until he was sure that Jenny was safely in the shower and unlikely to come back to bed before opening his eyes. He had been aware of her leaning over and kissing him and of her hesitation as she wondered about waking him up and he had held his breath, dreading having to respond to her uncertain overtures.

He hadn't slept well, his rest fragmented by uncomfortable dreams. In one of them he had been hunting frantically for a missing school book, a child once again, knowing that if he couldn't find it, he would be morally obliged to take responsibility for its disappearance, even though in reality the book was David's.

Like a child, he squeezed his eyes tightly closed against the memory. But he wasn't a child any more, shouldn't think like a child, just as he knew he couldn't go on ignoring certain facts that had to be confronted and that knowledge weighed heavily on his heart as he faced the prospect of the newly dawning day. Their birthday. Not *his* birthday, never just *his* birthday, but always *theirs*, David's and his. David's...

When the shower stopped running, he kept his eyes closed, even though he knew that Jenny would be going downstairs and not returning to their bedroom.

She had worked so hard for today but instead of looking forward to it he was dreading it, conscious of an uncomfortable sense of foreboding, a heaviness of spirit, a dark presence almost that seemed to be pressing against his body.

From the past he could hear the angry echo of his father's voice on another birthday morning—their seventh—as he stood in front of the imposing man, tears of disappointment and, yes, anger, too, filling his eyes as he answered his father's question.

'But I didn't want a new bike...I wanted something else...something different...something that David hasn't got,' he had told his father passionately. He could still remember how angry his father had been, how disgusted.

'You're jealous of your brother, that's what it is,' he had accused Jonathon. 'My God, I don't believe it. Don't you realise how lucky you are to have a brother.'

To Jonathon, it sometimes didn't seem so lucky and at seven he had still been young enough and stupid enough to say so, even if only indirectly through his disgruntlement with his birthday present—a new bicycle had been David's choice. He would have much preferred a train set.

In the end he hadn't had either, at least not immediately. The bike had been confiscated until he had repented of his ingratitude, and as for the train set...

David had never been interested in trains and since their father strongly believed in giving them both the same, the train set had never been forthcoming.

He could still remember the look on Jenny's face the Christmas they had bought one for Max. Like David, he hadn't been particularly interested in trains and they knew this even before they had bought the set but, for some reason, Jenny had been insistent that they get it.

She had tried to stop him when, after the New Year, he had quietly packed it all up again, telling him, 'Maybe if you played with the trains together…?'

But Jonathon had shaken his head, pointing out to her, 'He much prefers the pedal cart that David gave him.'

He had planned to give the trains away but for some reason Jenny had kept them, and when Joss was born… A few years later, Joss had humoured him by showing an interest in the set but Jonathon didn't want his young son to have to bear the burdens of adult expectations and prejudices that he had had to carry.

Fifty… Where had all those years gone? What had he actually done with them? What had he actually achieved? Increasingly lately, he had been asking himself those questions, knowing that he could not supply any satisfactory or comforting answers.

Oh yes, he had been a dutiful son, a good brother, husband and father, but what about *him*? What about himself? More and more these days he had felt as though he barely knew what or who he was, as though frighteningly he had no real self, no real identity, as though he was forever doomed to be merely David's brother…David's twin, a mere shadow figure. And yet why should that disturb him now when for so many years he had been content to remain in his twin's shadow? Why should he be feeling this stronger and stronger pull to be something else, to do something else, just for himself? Was this a mere male mid-life crisis or something more?

Today was not the day to start asking himself these kinds of questions, Jonathon warned himself wearily, not when other far more portentous and troublesome questions still remained unanswered. Questions that weren't purely self-indulgent. Questions that involved others and their futures, their lives. Questions that he knew would have to be asked and answered.

But not today...

In Pembrokeshire, Hugh Crighton was awake early, too. His inability to sleep past the early-morning fingers of sunshine stroking in through the windows of his solidly built stone farmhouse was caused not by any excitement at the prospect of the day ahead of him but by the persistent crying of his youngest grandchild, little Meg.

Saul, his elder son, his wife, Hillary, and their three children had arrived late the previous evening—several hours after they had originally been expected, with both adults in what was plainly not the best of moods and three children very obviously fractious.

Hillary, Saul's American wife, and his own wife, Ann, had put the children to bed whilst he and Saul and his younger son, Nicholas, had broken open a bottle of wine.

As Nicholas had remarked to his parents after supper, Saul and Hillary were apparently going through a rather difficult patch in their marriage.

'All married couples encounter problems from time to time,' Ann had responded protectively.

'Mmm...but there are problems and there are problems,' Nicholas had countered and then refused to be drawn on exactly what he had meant.

Hugh knew that Saul and Hillary's marriage had been stormy, but this was the first time he had seen the children so obviously affected by their parents' differences.

Saul had a tendency to retreat to a position of lofty solitude and disdain when he was angry, an aggravating habit that Hillary, who was far more emotional and volatile, insisted was sulking. Saul could be exasperating, Hugh admitted, but Hillary seemed to take delight in fuelling the fires that lit that particularly unproductive side of his personality rather than taking the trouble to use her inherently feminine skills of diplomacy and tact to coax him round.

'You'd better not let Hillary hear you saying that,' Ann had warned him mildly when he voiced the comment to her. 'She's a very modern young woman and modern young women do not believe in coaxing men round.'

'No,' Hugh had agreed regretfully. During the course of his career, he had seen at firsthand considerable evidence of this refusal on the part of what had once been deemed the gentler sex to make good and full use of the assets nature had given them and could only inwardly regret it.

Perhaps he was old-fashioned, but it seemed to him that male and female relationships had lost something with the onset of modern feminism.

Ann, thank goodness, just like his own mother, was one of those quiet, gentle, loving women who liked nothing better than mothering and spoiling everyone who came within their ambit.

Their marriage had been a good and happy one and if occasionally his hormones had been given a potentially dangerous tug by the sight of a slender female leg or the curve of a pretty pair of breasts, he had always had the good sense to remind himself of what he stood to lose by following his natural male instincts.

As a barrister and now as a judge, he had seen all too clearly for himself the havoc that could be wreaked when men and, regrettably all too commonly these days, women gave in to their basic urges. Take away the human lust for sex and money and there would be no need for men like him, no need for courts or prisons or even for laws.

Little Meg had finally stopped crying but it was too late for him to go back to sleep now.

They were due at Ben's at lunch-time and they were staying with him overnight after the birthday festivities. He would much rather have come straight home to avoid too much socialising with the family. Saul and David did not really get on. Saul was always at his sarcastic worst with David, a fact that had led Hillary the last time they had all got together to accuse Saul of being jealous of his elder cousin.

Her accusation had had just enough truth to make Hugh wince and the silence between them on the drive back home afterwards had been more difficult to bear than an outright argument.

Just enough truth and yet, at the same time, no way near enough understanding either of him as her husband, her lover and father of her children, or of him simply as another human being and, as such, flawed and vulnerable and in need of a gentle touch on any tender places.

Saul, too, had heard Meg's cries and gone to her. His thoughts were also on the day ahead. He generally enjoyed any family gathering, but he'd keep clear of David if at all possible. To Saul there was something exceedingly irritating about a man who went through life so carelessly, so openly filled with self-satisfaction and approval of himself, who expected others to automatically accord him the same high esteem and respect that he was accustomed to receiving from his father and his twin brother when it was patently obvious that he was simply not deserving of them.

Oh yes, David had the charisma, the self-confidence to initially blind a new acquaintance with the fool's gold of a magnetic personality, but in Saul's view this persona had no depth and no real foundation. Moreover, he was dismayed by David's selfishness and lack of regard for others. It galled him that people should be so easily deceived by David's shallow charm and it galled him even more that he himself should feel not only resentful of his possession of it but sometimes almost actually envious.

Even now, adult though he was, he still felt uncomfortable with the way his reaction to David focused his attention on the dual aspects of his own personality that he would prefer to ignore. In the main he was the dedicated, serious professional that other people assumed him to be, but he was also aware that there was a far less, to him at least, acceptable side to his personality, a tendency to seek the limelight, to crave the attention and, yes, admiration of others, a weakness that he both disliked and mistrusted.

It wasn't, he knew, the differences between himself and David that made him dislike David so much—

and to some extent Max, who was very much the same type of man—but the similarities. He feared that the weaknesses he could see so clearly in them might somehow be a family trait that he, too, had inherited and that, although now he had well under control, could one day push its way to the surface....

And what hurt him was that Hillary couldn't recognise this, couldn't, didn't love him enough to try to find out and understand what really lay at the root of his dislike for David.

David overslept primarily because he had been woken up in the night by the sound of Tiggy in the bathroom. He had known what that meant, of course, and had turned over, pulling the duvet up high around his ears, trying to blot out the sound of her nausea.

In the early days of their marriage when he had naïvely assumed that her constant bouts of sickness were caused initially by her pregnancy and then afterwards by her delicate stomach, he had been overwhelmed by a mixture of helplessness and protective concern towards her, anxiously hovering, wanting to do something to help ease her discomfort, even though the sound and smell of her sickness made his own stomach heave. He had loved her then, blinded by her fragile beauty and the feelings of triumph and relief that had followed their marriage. Triumph because he had won such a prize away from the other men who had surrounded her in London and relief because her pregnancy and their marriage had taken everyone's attention away from the real reason he had been asked to leave chambers and give up his plan to qualify as a barrister.

By silent collusion and an unacknowledged mental sleight of hand, it became an accepted part of the folk-lore of their family history; the reason he had returned home had been because of his marriage, because of his desire to do the right thing and stand by Tiggy. Publicly at least, his decision not to continue with his training for the Bar had been seen not as a failure, but as a tribute to his sense of honour and fair play.

Only his closest family had known the real truth and even they....

To their clients it had been delicately hinted that Jon was having trouble coping with the amount of work in the practice, and when anyone asked, he had simply shrugged gracefully and assured them that no, he was not too disappointed to have had to give up his plans to qualify as a barrister, and those who heard him make this statement had decided that such a man, a man who put his duty and his responsibility towards his family and more specifically his brother first, was exactly the kind of upright, honest and morally sound man they wanted dealing with their most intimate legal affairs.

Business had boomed, and if Jon had ever resented being cast as the less able of the pair of them, he had certainly never said so. But then, Jon had never been one for voicing what he thought or felt. Look at the way he had married Jenny so quickly after his own romance with her had ended without ever having said a word to him about wanting her for himself.

He tensed as he felt Tiggy stirring beside him. He wanted to ignore her but she was already reaching out to touch him, running her fingertips hungrily over his chest. His heart sank even though he knew that her surge of sexual energy meant that today was going to be one of her good days.

He had come to know her moods so well. They followed a recognisable pattern and he'd learned them almost by heart. All week she had been edgy, highly emotional, clingy, demanding, in tears one moment and so filled with anger and bitterness the next that it seemed her fragile body could scarcely contain such intense feelings.

He knew exactly what to expect—the frantic bouts of shopping, the purchase of clothes, shoes, make-up, anything to fill yet more glossy carrier bags that would never be emptied but merely hidden away in an agony of guilt and self-disgust as she abased herself in an orgy of remorse, begging for his forgiveness, promising that she would never, ever do it again, theatrically pleading with him to destroy her cheque-book, her credit cards. But what was the use?

Once he had played her games with her, believing her, hoping that this time she meant it; that in time she would realise what she was doing to herself, to him, to their lives, but why bother destroying a cheque-book when he knew she had others secreted away just as she had other credit cards? But the game had to be played according to her rules and these were simply things he was not permitted to say. She had to be allowed to play out her role of guilt-ridden supplicant to the full, unable to cease berating herself verbally until he had granted her the 'forgiveness' she required.

After that would come the lull...sometimes for a

few days, sometimes only a few hours, and then it would start...the furtive disappearance from their bed in the middle of the night, the inexplicable appearance of mounds of food in the kitchen followed by...

The first time he realised that her bouts of sickness were not caused by any weakness or by the fact that, as he had always thought, she barely ate enough to keep herself alive, but by her huge consumption of food in eating binges that could last for hours before she finally fed herself into a state of emotional and physical stupor, he had been shocked rigid.

Afterwards, of course, would come the purging, going on and on until she was satisfied that her stomach was finally empty, her body restored from its temporarily bloated, obscene distension to its normal svelte, almost too thin, delicacy, and then and only then and oh, the blessed relief of it, finally those few wonderful hours when she was relaxed and at peace, sated by her orgy of self-punishment almost like a drug addict after a mammoth fix. Contented, calm, until the whole cycle started again with the frantic need for reassurance that she was loved. The refusal to let him touch her because her body was loathsome was almost immediately followed by what amounted to an almost frenzied need for sex.

Lately, as she was doing now, she had become increasingly sexually aroused during what he normally thought of as his own period of respite from the stress of what she was.

Sex... God, what a joke, and to think that when he had met her, when he had married her, he had wanted her so much....

Now the mere thought of having to touch her, of being touched by her, brought him out, as it was doing now, in a cold, drenching sweat of impotency and a physical rejection not just of her but of everything and anything to do with sex.

Even though he knew that in refusing her he was doing the worst possible thing he could do and that this refusal only served to hasten the speed of the whole appalling cycle of her unbalanced behaviour, he just couldn't force himself to behave any differently.

It wasn't simply that he didn't want her any more, he recognised, he... He what? Loathed her, hated her, resented her.

In the early days before he realised there was no point, that the whole situation...that *she* was beyond any kind of help, he had tried to persuade her to seek professional advice. Her response had been to threaten to kill herself. She had rung him at work to tell him that he would soon be free of her and he had rushed home to find her sprawled naked and drunk across their bed, an empty bottle of painkillers at her side. He had no way of knowing how many she had managed to take. Fortunately their doctor had been very understanding, but that had been over fifteen years ago and David knew that such a situation would never be handled with such discretion now.

Duncan Flitt had been a contemporary of his father. They had played golf together and been old friends. Between them they were the unofficial keepers of much of the area's secrets. Today things were different. The local medical practice was serviced by four doctors, all of them several years his junior. It also boasted an acupuncturist, a reflexologist and several counsellors.

Tiggy's caressing hand had reached his belly. He froze, tensely aware of the resistant slackness of his penis and the fact that it was going to remain in that limp state.

Beneath the bedclothes, Tiggy moved towards him, rubbing her naked breasts against his arm as she did so. David cringed. The odour of her vomit still clung to her skin or perhaps it was being exuded from it, he decided as he swallowed down his own reciprocal nausea. As she leaned across to kiss him, her breath smelled initially of mint but beneath the mouthwash's sharpness he could still smell the sour taste of her night-time activities. The bathroom would stink of it, as well, and because Olivia was home he couldn't use the spare bathroom, not without the risk of arousing her suspicions.

Olivia... No doubt it was her arrival that had precipitated Tiggy's latest attack. Not that she needed much of an excuse any more; anything and everything could set her off. Increasingly, though, she had recently begun to fret over the fact that she was growing older, flirting increasingly openly with younger men, behaving in a way that was totally inappropriate for the wife of a man in his position. As yet he did not think that she had actually gone so far as to have a real affair but he suspected that given the right opportunity...

An affair. Dear God, if only she would. If only she would find someone else to take over from him the unwanted burden of her emotional and physical demands, her constant need for reassurance, her scream-

ing outbursts that he did not love her, her accusations
that there was someone else, that he no longer wanted
or loved her.

'Happy birthday, darling....'

Mutely he endured the unwanted intimacy of her
kiss, not daring to provoke her by withdrawing from
her and yet, at the same time, aching to be able to do
so. Her hand had reached his penis now. He cringed.

'What a poor, sad little boy,' she was cooing in his
ear. 'Doesn't he want to come out and play, then...?'

David gritted his teeth.

'Is he all hurt and sulky, then?' Tiggy teased. 'Does
he want Mummy to stroke him and kiss him better...?'

David shuddered violently in a reaction of rejection
and disgust. 'We've got to get up,' he reminded her
hoarsely. 'The birthday...'

'I thought that was what I was trying to do,' Tiggy
countered, pouting, but David was already moving
away from her, throwing back the duvet.

'You said last night that you'd got to help Jenny,' he
reminded her as he pulled on his robe.

David was beginning to look dispiritedly middle-
aged, Tiggy decided. He had recently put on weight
and that, coupled with the flaccid smallness of his penis, was decidedly unerotic. Unlike her, he seemed to
have no interest in looking after himself, in keeping
his body fit and his weight down. Surreptitiously she
touched her own stomach. It felt reassuringly taut and
flat. She breathed out in relief and examined her polished nails. One of them was scratched. She frowned.
She must have done that last night when... Hurriedly
she pushed the thought to one side.

What had happened last night? What happened on

all those dark, frightening nights like last night wasn't something she wanted or needed to think about during the day. It was over now and best forgotten...a silly habit she had fallen into but which she could break...end...any time she liked. David knew that and she knew it, too. She realised she had been a bit naughty of late, overspending, but David didn't understand how lonely she felt sometimes. He had his own busy life at work and she was at home here all day on her own.

Of course, she had her girlfriends...but...she wasn't like Jenny, the kind of woman who could busy herself with good works, children and cooking. She needed more than that. She was not a country person. David should take her out more...make more fuss of her, *show* her that he loved her. She might be in her mid-forties but she was still a beautiful and desirable woman. All right, Olivia might be younger than her but she would never be as attractive. Why, when she had been Livvy's age she could have had her pick of a couple of dozen men even though she had been married to David at the time, and a mother.

Her dress was hanging up over the bedroom door, a body-hugging shimmer of silver-shot silk that looked like mother-of-pearl when she moved in it. It was a size eight, a perfect fit; she touched her stomach again. She could hear the shower running. David was still in the bathroom. Perhaps she ought to try it on again, just to make sure...

6

'Anything else I can do?'

'No. I think we've just about finished now,' Ruth assured Olivia as she stepped back to eye the arrangement for the top table, tweaking a couple of stems judiciously.

'The flowers look wonderful.'

Ruth gave her great-niece a wryly amused smile, hearing the genuine admiration in her voice and guessing what lay behind it. 'What were you expecting,' she mocked her gently, 'or can I guess? Something twee and stilted, overwired flowers that would have looked more artificial than real, poor things?' She shook her head reprovingly.

Olivia laughed. 'Something like that,' she admitted ruefully. 'Certainly nothing like this.'

She gestured towards the vibrant tumble of softly natural flowers set in some sort of wire concoction filled with moss—a theme that Ruth had repeated throughout the huge marquee in varying forms. Moss, fruit and even vegetables as well as flowers had all been utilised to create the wonderfully rich falls of cascading colour that Olivia was now admiring.

'No wonder Aunt Jenny was so insistent on plain cream hangings for the marquee,' she commented to Ruth.

'Jenny and I were both in agreement that we wanted to get away completely from the prettiness of bridal tulle and dainty pastels.'

'Well, you've certainly done that,' Olivia assured her, gently touching the silky petal of one of the vividly coloured geums and poppies Ruth had used to create the harmonising masses of reds, oranges and yellows that were her colour theme for the event.

On the far side of the marquee, Jenny herself was going round each of the tables checking that everything was in place. The caterers had already arrived and were busy getting themselves organised.

Ben, who had been generally getting in everyone's way and grumbling all afternoon, had finally allowed Hugh's wife, Ann, to coax him back to the house, leaving Jenny free to make her final inspections in peace.

'Caspar seems to be getting on well with Hillary,' Ruth commented, glancing across the marquee to where the two of them were deep in conversation.

'Well, they are both American,' Olivia responded neutrally. She had never particularly taken to Hillary without really being able to say why.

It was Saul, she had noticed this afternoon, who had to take charge of their children, including little Meg, but then, in fairness, Olivia had to admit that she had no idea how much time Saul normally spent with his children, perhaps not very much, and hence Hillary's determination that on this occasion she deserved a small break from them.

Saul had taken them back to the house now in order to start getting them bathed and changed in readiness for the evening ahead.

Her own brother, Jack, like his cousin, Joss, had

been dragooned into helping out with the carrying to and fro of Ruth's flowers and other materials. Was he aware of their mother's problem...?

All day long Olivia had been trying to push the events of the previous night to the back of her mind but they couldn't be ignored for ever, of course. Sooner or later she would...

She would... She tensed as she heard Caspar laughing. Hillary was standing beside him, her hand on his arm, and as Olivia watched she leaned across him to tuck a discarded cream rose into the buttonhole of his jacket. It was an intimate gesture and one that Olivia instinctively resented, her body stiffening as she watched the way Caspar responded to Hillary, apparently oblivious to her own presence.

'Why don't you take Caspar home?' she heard Ruth suggesting gently at her side. 'There's nothing else to do here now apart from a bit of clearing up and the boys can help me with that.'

'Aunt Ruth...' Olivia paused. She desperately wanted someone to confide in, someone to talk to about her concern for her mother and her own shock at what she had discovered, but as strong as that need was, her sense of loyalty to her mother prevented her from giving in to it. Ruth had never really approved of Tiggy and if Olivia told her what was going on...

'What is it, dear?'

'Nothing...' Olivia backtracked. 'I'll go and get Caspar.'

'Flowers all done?' Caspar enquired as Olivia went across to join him.

'Yes,' she confirmed as she slipped her arm through his and gave Hillary a cool smile.

Ostensibly Saul's wife had come down to the marquee to join the other helpers but so far as Olivia was aware she appeared to have spent most of her time chatting to Caspar.

'We really ought to leave,' she warned Caspar now as she looked pointedly at her watch. 'The Chester crowd will be arriving soon and I promised Mum that we'd be on hand to help out.'

'Poor you,' Hillary butted in sympathetically looking, Olivia was perfectly aware, not at her but instead at Caspar as she turned her body slightly towards him and with an air of complicity that Olivia knew only too well was designed to exclude herself. 'You must be finding it a little intimidating being engulfed by such a large family. I know I did the first time I met them all. I felt quite alienated and alone—the only American and very much an outsider.'

'That would have been your and Saul's wedding day, wouldn't it, Hillary?' Olivia interrupted her coolly, reminding her, 'I don't think you'd met the whole family before then, had you?

'Caspar, we really ought to be going,' she repeated without waiting for Hillary's response.

'That was a little bit harsh, wasn't it?' Caspar commented critically once they were in the car and out of Hillary's hearing.

He felt slightly on edge and irritable and was still smarting from Olivia's sexual rejection the previous evening even though he was loath to admit it even to himself.

'What was a little harsh?' Olivia queried even

though she knew exactly what he meant. The day would have been stressful enough with only the tension of working so hard to get everything just right for tonight without the added burden of worry and anxiety she was having to carry of the discovery she had made about her mother. The last thing she needed now was any kind of disharmony between her and Caspar. But it irked her that he didn't seem able to see what kind of woman Hillary was, and if she was honest, it had annoyed and hurt, yes, hurt her, too, that he had seemed content to spend so much of the afternoon with Hillary. It still rankled that he hadn't been more understanding last night.

'You know what,' Caspar countered as she started the car. 'That comment you made just before we left.'

'Really?' Olivia challenged him, changing gear too quickly, the raw, grating sound of the clashing gears further exacerbating the already irritated and edgy state of her nervous system. 'I don't think so, Caspar. In fact, if you want my honest opinion, I find it rather odd that Hillary should have made such a statement at all, but then she's the type of woman who never misses an opportunity to grab any male interest and sympathy she thinks might be available.'

'Aha!' Caspar responded, his face suddenly relaxing into a teasing smile. '*I* understand. You're jealous and—'

'*No*, I am *not* jealous,' Olivia denied angrily. 'I just don't happen to like Hillary very much, that's all. She's a very predatory woman, very cold and calculating and far too—'

'American,' Caspar finished for her, his voice suddenly hardening as his smile disappeared. 'No wonder she feels so isolated and alienated if that's the way your family treats her,' he continued, his voice grim with contempt.

'Is *that* what she told you...that she feels isolated?' Olivia demanded, suddenly beginning to lose her temper. She knew she was handling the situation badly, allowing it to balloon into something far more important and potentially dangerous than it should have ever been allowed to be, but she still felt afraid and hurt from last night's discoveries and from Caspar's refusal to share her feelings over them.

'We *did* discuss how difficult she was finding it to adjust to life in this country,' Caspar agreed evenly in a tone of voice that warned Olivia that she wasn't the only one fast losing patience with their conversation. But she was too wrought up, too on edge—too much in need of the very large helping of TLC he seemed to have been unable to give her the previous night but that he appeared to have had no trouble at all in handing out generously to Hillary this afternoon—to apply logic and restraint to her thoughts and emotions—or her reactions.

'Oh, did you?' Olivia demanded angrily. 'Well, she certainly seemed to be getting a *very* sympathetic hearing from you, judging by the way she was all over you,' she fumed, 'and she was certainly getting far more understanding from you than I got last night. But then I suppose the two of you are on a compatible wavelength, being fellow countrymen,' she finished sarcastically.

'It certainly helps to create a bond,' Caspar agreed calmly, 'and I have to say, Livvy, that she seems to be dealing far more responsibly with the threatened breakdown of her marriage than you are with—'

'The threatened breakdown of her marriage,' Olivia interrupted him, shocked. 'What are you talking about? There's nothing wrong with her marriage to Saul. In fact—'

'No?' Caspar countered grittily. 'And how would you know that? According to Hillary, none of you has made the least attempt to welcome her into the family or to find out why she's so unhappy or to help her to adjust to a different way of life.'

Olivia discovered she was shaking slightly as she turned into her parents' drive and stopped the car. 'I don't believe I'm hearing any of this. If Hillary feels that we've neglected her—in any way—then I would suggest that the fault, if there is one, lies more with her than with us. What else did she tell you?' she demanded.

'Not an awful lot other than the fact that there's a history of antagonism and dislike towards Americans in the family.'

'What?' Olivia stared at him in disbelief. 'Now I *know* she's been lying to you. What on earth made her say a thing like that? It's completely untrue. She's the first American to marry into the family and—'

'To *marry* into it, maybe. But not the first to be involved with a member of it,' Caspar interrupted her grimly. 'There was Ruth's affair with an American major during the war and—'

'Ruth's what?' Olivia couldn't keep the shock out of her voice and she saw Caspar frown as he recognised it.

'We'd better go inside,' he muttered, turning to open the car door.

Olivia stopped him, grabbing hold of his sleeve, her eyes passionately alive with anger and hurt as she told him, 'Oh no, you can't leave it there, not after saying something like that. I know *nothing* about Ruth's having an affair with *anyone*. She was engaged during the war to a British airman who was killed in action.'

'Well, according to Hillary, who I gathered heard the story from Hugh, she was involved with an American major who was stationed locally, but when your grandfather and her father found out about the relationship they reported the major to his superiors and insisted that the relationship had to end. Apparently an American, in those days at least, wasn't good enough to marry into their family! And Hillary says that kind of prejudice does tend to be passed on from one generation to the next.'

Appalled and confused, Olivia could think of nothing constructive to say. It was bad enough having to be forced to admit that she knew nothing of any relationship her great-aunt may or may not have had with an American but what was even worse was feeling that a barrier of doubt and mistrust had somehow sprung up between them. Caspar now seemed to believe that her family had some deep-seated dislike of Americans. Troubling, too, was her own inability to be able to do anything to convincingly refute it and thereby undo the damage that Hillary had so carelessly inflicted.

'But you know how I feel about you, Caspar,' she offered weakly. It was all she could think of to say as she touched him appealingly on his arm.

'Do I?' he responded unforgivingly. 'I wonder why you're going out with me, exactly. Is it because I'm American perhaps, because I'm a way of getting back at your grandfather?'

Without giving her a chance to reply, he got out of the car and loped towards the house, leaving Olivia with no option other than to follow him. She knew that once they were inside they would have no opportunity for any private conversation, not with the house soon to be full of visitors and the party only a matter of a few hours away. Yet she desperately wanted them to resolve their argument and make their peace with one another. She must convince him to retract his unjustified accusation about the basis of her feelings for him.

It was both unfair and illogical of him to throw that kind of accusation at her and then walk away without allowing her to defend herself from it. It left her feeling almost as though he had *wanted* to pick a fight with her; as though... As though what? But *if* so, then why? It was so unlike him, so alien to the maturity and the deeply grounded sense of himself she so admired and enjoyed in him.

Dispiritedly Olivia followed Caspar into the house. Behind her on the drive she could hear the sound of cars arriving—the Chester 'lot' no doubt! Squaring her shoulders she firmly put her own thoughts and fears to one side.

7

A little nervously Jenny smoothed down the skirt of her dress. Jon hadn't seen it as yet. In fact, no one had seen it apart from Guy Cooke.

She had been initially amused and then very touched when he had announced several months earlier that he was taking her to Manchester in order for her to buy an outfit for the birthday ball.

'Manchester?' she had queried, half-inclined to refuse to go, not sure whether he was serious or simply subjecting her to his sometimes wickedly dry sense of humour.

'What on earth for? Chester is much closer and—'

'Chester may be much closer but it doesn't possess an Emporio Armani,' he had countered, enlightening her obvious confusion by explaining, as though trying to instil comprehension of some arcane adult concept to a very small child, 'Armani, my dear Jenny, just in case you are the only person on this globe who is unaware of the fact, is a designer—*the* designer so far as the vast majority of elegant, successful women are concerned. He designs clothes for *women*—not girls, you will note, not models, not fashion victims, but *women* with a capital W and there is a branch of his vast network of retail outlets in Manchester selling clothes from his diffusion range.'

'Thank you, Guy,' Jenny had retorted wryly, 'but yes, I have heard of him and as for buying one of his designs or even looking...' She had shaken her head and laughed. 'My budget doesn't run to that kind of extravagance.'

'An Armani is never an extravagance,' Guy had corrected her and then added smugly before she could argue further, 'and besides, this is a diffusion range we are discussing with suitably modest prices. If you won't come with me, then I shall just have to go by myself,' he had added determinedly, 'and choose something for you by guesswork.

'I mean it, Jen,' he had informed her sternly, 'you are not going to this do wearing some dowdy, dull "bargain" bought at the last minute because you haven't had the time to get anything else and because we both know that if you had you would not spend either it or Jon's money on something—anything—for yourself. For once in your life *you* are going to be dressed in something that does you justice and for once in your life, even if *you* won't put yourself first, then I'm damn well going to see that someone does!'

Jenny had had to sit down.

'But why?' she had asked him, honestly bewildered by the obvious strength of his resolution.

'Why? If I said because you deserve it, you'd find some way of arguing me out of it,' he had told her frankly, 'so instead I'll say because even if you yourself don't recognise it, you owe it not just to yourself and to Jon but to me, as well, and to this business and before you come up with any more arguments, the business is going to pay for it. No, I mean what I say,

Jenny,' he had repeated. 'Either you come with me or I'll go by myself and—'

'And you'll what?' she had teased him gently. 'Make me wear whatever you choose or send me to bed in punishment instead with a glass of water and some dry bread?'

She had only meant it as a joke but she saw the look in his eyes as he told her oh so gently and oh so quietly, 'If I ever got the opportunity to send you to bed, Jenny, it most certainly wouldn't be in punishment and as for *making* you wear it... Well, let's just say I don't imagine it would be beyond my powers to work on Jon to ensure that *he* persuaded you to wear it.'

Bravely Jenny had met the look in his eyes.

There had been odd occasions before when her woman's instincts had told her that Guy wanted more from her than just friendship, instincts that she had dismissed as the over-active imagination of a middle-aged woman. Now she knew she had been wrong, or rather that she had been right.

But they had still gone to Manchester, mainly because Guy had already preempted her by going behind her back to inform Jon of his plans and to get his assistance.

Jon, Jenny suspected, had little idea who or what an Armani might be but Guy's comments had struck an unfamiliar raw chord within her, reminding her of how she had felt at the annual family get-together at Christmas dressed in the familiar security of her 'good suit' and humiliatingly conscious of how different she looked, not so much from Tiggy but from the other women present there, as well, women who were probably no more physically attractive than she was herself and certainly no younger but who seemed to have a confidence, a pride in themselves, that she had always lacked. Even Ruth had been more trendily dressed than she was herself, a fact that Joss had pointed out to her at the time.

She had been unnerved at first on stepping into the solidly built King Street building that housed the Armani store. The female assistants, every one of them impeccably dressed and groomed, all seemed to possess the same Italianate good looks. They exuded a certain air that initially she had found slightly intimidating but that, on closer inspection, melted away to reveal a genuine helpfulness that soon had her forgetting her doubts and allowing herself to be coaxed into trying on clothes that ten minutes beforehand she would have totally refused to even consider wearing.

In the end she had bought the dress she was wearing tonight—a handful of cream crêpe in the simplest of styles that fell from a sort of Empire-style bodice to her ankles in a swathe of material that owed nothing to the vagaries of fashion and everything to the eye of the master who had designed it.

It was, as the enthusiastic saleswoman pointed out to her, a dress designed to complement and flatter a woman's figure. Without a single frill or flounce and without coming anywhere near fitting tightly to her body, it somehow still seemed to subtly emphasise all her good points, Jenny had realised as she stared at her own reflection in silent astonishment.

It was a dress that made her look and feel very much a woman; a dress that brought back all her teenage yearnings and longings to be seen as desirable...yearnings and longings that she thought she had packed sensibly away with all her other memories of those years. Yearnings and longings that she had told herself sternly were most certainly not appropriate to a woman of her age. And yet, she had still bought the dress and a trouser suit, as well, which she was saving for the family lunch they were having the next day.

The dress went beautifully with the pearls that Jon had given her for their twenty-fifth wedding anniversary, reflecting their creamy colour and satiny texture. She held her breath a little as she fastened them.

The phone was ringing as Olivia walked across the hall on her way to join the others in a predeparture drink in the drawing room. She answered it automatically, asking the caller to wait as she went to find her father.

'There's a call for you,' she told him. 'The Cedars Nursing Home.'

David could feel himself starting to sweat and he knew that his heart was beating far too fast. He could feel the tension invading his chest, tensing his muscles, his whole body, and with it the accompanying nausea of fear.

His palm was so damp he had to wipe it as he picked up the receiver and cleared his throat. 'Yes, David Crighton here.' His jaw was aching again. He massaged it with his free hand, turning his back towards the half-open drawing-room door as he listened to what his caller had to say.

Upstairs in his attic bedroom, Caspar grimaced as he finally managed to knot his bow tie and reached for his jacket. He wasn't looking forward to the evening ahead and not just because of his quarrel with Olivia who, in his opinion, had been wrong to blame Hillary for it even if it had been her revelations that provoked it.

He had noticed a change in Olivia over the past few days; suddenly the family that, at a distance, she almost disdained had become all-fired important to her. Suddenly he and his views were no longer apparently of any value to her. Look at the way she had dismissed his advice over her mother's obvious need for professional help and counselling.

'It doesn't matter how much they quarrel with one another, in the end they always stick together,' Hillary had warned him this afternoon. 'They stick together and they shut you out,' she had added emphatically with a bitter look in the direction of her husband.

'I suppose I should have seen the writing on the wall when Hugh told me about Ruth,' she had added, 'but at the time I didn't realise exactly what he was telling me, any more than I realised exactly what it meant when I discovered that it was part of Ben's grand plan for the family that ultimately Saul should marry Olivia.'

Saul should marry Olivia! Caspar frowned his lack of comprehension. Olivia had never said anything to him about there being any family hopes that she might marry her father's cousin. But then she had never mentioned the fact that her great-aunt had apparently had an extremely passionate relationship with an American major who, according to Hillary, had virtually been co-erced into giving her up.

How much more was there about her family, about herself, that Olivia hadn't told him?

* * *

'You look just as I've always known you could look, should look. You look wonderful, perfect. You look...you.'

Strange how such words, such emotions, when expressed by one man, the wrong man, could mean so little and could cause more embarrassment and self-consciousness than pleasure and yet the same words when said by the right man...

Logically, of course, Jenny should have expected, anticipated, that Guy would be the one to praise and admire her appearance, take a long look at her as she welcomed him and then seek her out at the first opportunity to take hold of her hand and draw her close to him as he told her what he felt. But for some reason she was still idiotically hoping that...

The meal was over and the band had started to play. Several couples were already dancing.

'Jenny! Goodness! You do look—'

Jenny tensed as she saw the look Tiggy was giving her and heard the critical edge in her voice, but before she could say anything more, Ruth interrupted firmly, 'You look wonderful, Jenny. I love your outfit.'

There was no mistaking the sincerity in Ruth's voice, or the warm approval in her eyes as she, too, studied her, Jenny recognised, and even David, who was standing slightly behind Tiggy, was looking at her now, his eyes widening slightly and then lingering on her.

'It's Armani, isn't it?' she heard Tiggy demanding as she self-consciously forced herself to break the eye contact David was maintaining with her. Ridiculous of her to start blushing like that. David was her brother-in-law, that was all, even if once...

'Yes, yes, it is,' she answered Tiggy hastily.

'What on earth made you buy it?' Tiggy persisted. Her eyes had narrowed, her voice was slightly shrill and she looked almost unhealthily pale, Jenny noticed. 'It isn't you at all.'

'Mother...' Olivia upbraided her mother warningly, giving Jenny an apologetic look as she started to draw Tiggy away.

Jenny frowned as she watched them. It wasn't like Tiggy to be bitchy or unkind and her comments were making Jenny have second thoughts about the advisability of wearing her new outfit. Perhaps Jon hadn't said anything about it not because he simply hadn't noticed that she looked any different but because he had not wanted to upset her by criticising her appearance.

'Tiggy's wrong, you know....' Her head came up as she heard David's voice. He smiled warmly at her. 'It does suit you.'

As tongue-tied as a small child, Jenny could only stand there and shake her head mutely.

'Tiggy's just jealous of you, that's all.'

'Jealous of me?' Jenny stared at him. 'She can't possibly be,' she protested. 'Not when she's...'

'Not when she's what?' David prompted, taking hold of her arm and starting to draw her towards the dance floor.

Jenny shook her head again. 'I can't dance with you now, David,' she told him huskily. 'The caterers—'

'Of course you can,' he told her. 'The caterers can wait, but I can't. Mmm...you feel good,' he murmured as he turned her into his arms and began to dance.

Helplessly Jenny realised that David wasn't going

to let her go and that it would cause less fuss to give in and dance with him than to go on protesting.

Unlike Jon, David had always been a good dancer, a natural dancer, and her face grew hot in the darkness of the subtly lit dance floor as she remembered what was said about men who were naturally good dancers. Too good, she decided shakily as he ignored her efforts to keep a respectable distance between them and pulled her closer to him.

'What's wrong?' he whispered against her hair. 'You used to enjoy dancing with me like this once.'

Jon was standing on the opposite side of the dance floor talking to Ruth. He didn't appear to have seen them.

'You look wonderful tonight,' David told her softly, his hands sliding up to caress her back. 'You look wonderful, you feel wonderful...you are wonderful, Jenny, and I wish to hell I'd never been stupid enough to let you go.'

'David...' Jenny protested, finding her voice at last.

'David what?' he demanded roughly.

His breath smelt faintly of drink, which must surely be why he was talking to her like this, Jenny decided.

'How many years is it since we last danced together like this, since we last held each other like this?' he asked her.

Jon had seen them now, and out of the corner of her eye Jenny could see him frowning slightly as he watched them. Max had seen them, as well, and there was no mistaking the expression in his eyes as he glowered at David's dinner-suited back.

'Do you know what I'd like to do right now?' David was murmuring to her. 'I'd like to—'

'David, we really ought to get back to the table.' Jenny almost gabbled the words in her haste to bring the situation back to normality. 'There are still the speeches and the toasts.'

'And the congratulations and the kisses,' David agreed, turning his head to look right into her eyes. 'You haven't kissed me yet, Jenny.'

'Yes, I have,' she corrected him. 'I kissed you earlier when you arrived.'

'No, you didn't,' David denied. 'You gave me a dutiful, sisterly peck on the cheek, yes, but you didn't kiss me. I can still remember the first time you kissed me, Jenny. You tasted of blackberries and fresh air....'

'David...' Jenny protested. 'Stop it.'

'You tasted of blackberries and fresh air,' he repeated, ignoring her, 'and it was the most delicious kiss I've ever had. You were the most delicious...'

To Jenny's relief the band stopped playing.

'We must go back to the table,' she told David firmly. Her heart was beating far too fast and her face was far, far too flushed. She felt...she felt...

The last thing, the very last thing she needed tonight was to be reminded of how she had once felt about David or how... When he finally let her go with obvious reluctance, Jenny made her way quickly back to their table, but she knew that the damage had already been done.

'I can still remember the first time you kissed me,' David had told her. Well, so could she, although her memories of it were, she suspected, different from his.

It was true that she had been picking blackberries and no doubt her hands and her mouth had been stained with their juice, but it had been David and not she who had instigated the kiss, David who had teased and challenged her by guessing that she had still not been properly kissed, demanding, when she denied it, that she prove it to him by showing him just how expert and experienced she actually was.

She had put down her basket of blackberries and walked slowly towards him, her head held high, her pride refusing to allow her to back down and inwardly feeling more terrified than she had ever felt in her whole life.

From before the previous Christmas the other girls in her class had been boasting about their new-found skills in the art of snogging and whilst she had smiled and pretended not to care that she was excluded from this new game, in private she had secretly studied every kiss she'd seen in films, endlessly wondering and worrying how she would fare when a boy finally kissed her. And now that that day had come it wasn't just any boy; it was him...David Crighton.

Screwing up her courage as tightly as she had already screwed up her eyes, she pursed her lips and made a despairing dart in David's direction and then stopped, her face burning with humiliation as her lips made contact only with thin air.

Opening her eyes she saw that David had moved to one side and was watching her in amusement, his mouth curled into a wide smile.

'You really haven't a clue, have you?' he had told her, shaking his head.

'Yes, I have,' Jenny had fibbed.

'Liar,' he had chided her softly, adding with a smile,

'It doesn't matter, though. In fact, I rather like the idea of being the one to teach you.'

'I don't need anyone to teach me anything,' Jenny had stormed at him.

'No?'

She had turned round, intending to retrieve her basket and walk away, only David moved faster, planting himself between her and the blackberries, walking towards her slowly as she backed away from him until she could back away no longer. He had, she discovered, trapped her very neatly between his body and the stone wall behind her.

What happened then was, of course, inevitable. He had kissed her tightly closed lips once briefly and then a second time less briefly and then...and then he had bent down and picked up a handful of blackberries from the basket, popping one into his own mouth before offering one to her.

Naïvely she had opened her mouth for it—and for him. The fate of the rest of the blackberries he had removed from the basket was something that left her trembling and weak-kneed for weeks afterwards every time she thought about it, although the sensual intimacy of it was spoiled for ever for her when illuminatingly she later overheard another girl describing David's favourite trick of passing sweets from his own mouth to a girl's.

She had ended up with her mouth ripely stained by blackberries, a fact that gained her a scolding from her mother for eating the fruit she had wanted for a pie but that thankfully, at the same time, helped to disguise her tell-tale swollen lips.

Odd, but she never ate blackberries these days, blaming her aversion on the seeds.

Out of the corner of her eye, she could see Jon shifting uncomfortably in his seat; the toasts were about to begin. Apart from that one small hiccup when David had insisted on dancing with her, everything had gone perfectly and according to plan. Even Ben had praised the food and Jenny had lost count of the number of guests who had come up to her and praised the décor of the marquee and in particular the richness of Ruth's floral arrangements as well as doing a very gratifying double take as they noted her own appearance.

The quartet engaged to play through the meal had been an excellent if expensive idea and the cream backdrop had provided exactly the right touch of quiet elegance for the women's gowns and the men's dinner jackets. Even the younger members of the family had behaved impeccably. So why did she have this dull, heavy feeling, of emptiness almost, of... disappointment...?

David was getting to his feet whilst the eagle eye of the catering manager checked that everyone had a full glass of champagne; Jenny could see the look of pride and love in Ben's eyes as he watched his heir, his most loved son; and she knew without having to check that the same look would be mirrored in Jon's eyes. The feeling of heaviness intensified.

David cleared his throat. He knew his speech off by heart and had no need really of the notes he had placed on the table in front of him; that had always been one of his gifts, the ability to memorise whole tracts of written material.

He glanced round the marquee. His shirt collar felt tight and he was hot, too hot, his stomach muscles tense, the meal he had eaten lying like a millstone in his stomach. That damned phone call. A spasm of pain ripped through him, paralysing him with its intensity. It seemed to spring out of nowhere, forking through him like lightning and with the deadly speed of a poised snake. First came the sharp sting of its poisoned bite and then the burning flood of its deadly aftershock; it was a pain like no other he had ever experienced or dreamed of experiencing. All around him he could hear noise but it no longer seemed to touch him; only the pain could touch him.

Someone was screaming. It was Tiggy, Jenny recognised sickly as she and Jon struggled to get David into a recovery position, his body a leaden weight in her arms. She must not use the word 'dead'. Not yet...please God, not yet.

'What is it...what's happened...?'

That was Ben, his voice querulous and shaky, the frightened voice of an old man, as he stood helplessly watching the chaos erupt around him.

Someone—one of Hugh's sons, she couldn't see which one—was trying to calm everyone down, to stem the panic that had flooded the marquee when David slumped across the table just as he was starting to give his speech.

'The ambulance is on its way.'

Jenny turned gratefully towards Neil Travers. 'Thank God you were here,' she told their doctor simply. 'If you hadn't been...' Unable to stop herself, she asked anxiously, 'How is he? Will he...?'

'I don't know,' he replied, shaking his head. 'It's too soon to say. Right now he's alive. We won't know any more until we get him into hospital. He's obviously had a pretty major heart attack, how major we won't know until—' He broke off as they both heard the wail of an ambulance siren. 'You stay here with him,' he instructed Jenny unnecessarily. 'I'll go and tell them what's happened.'

As they waited for the ambulance crew, Jenny turned to look at her husband. If anything, his face was even greyer than David's, his skin putty-coloured. He had been the first to react to David's collapse, reaching out to him as he yelled at her, 'For God's sake, do something. He's had a heart attack.'

Almost single-handedly he had tenderly lifted his brother off the table and placed him carefully on the ground. He had not said a single word since and that was because he was, Jenny knew, expending every single ounce of energy he had in willing his twin to stay alive, his hand clasped tightly around David's as though he could physically pour his own strength, his own life's blood, into his brother's inert body. It was as though no one else, nothing else, existed for him.

'David...David...' Tiggy started to scream, trying to throw herself over her husband's motionless body as the ambulance crew placed him on a stretcher, and she had to be physically restrained by Olivia and Caspar.

Jenny winced as Olivia used the flat of her hand to give her mother a short, swift blow against her cheek, not out of pain for Tiggy but more out of sympathy for Olivia.

All round her she could see the shock and disbelief mirrored in people's faces as they found themselves unable to fully take in what had just occurred.

'What's happened to Uncle David?' she heard one of the younger children asking in panic. 'Is he dead...?'

It was one of Saul's children who asked the question and Hillary immediately tried to silence her.

Poor child. She hadn't, after all, done anything wrong. Jenny sympathised even if Ben was looking at the girl as though he would like to murder her.

'David...David...where is he? I want to be with him. Where is he...?' Tiggy was crying noisily.

'They're taking him to hospital, Tiggy,' Jenny said, trying to soothe her. 'He's in the best of hands now and—'

'They can't take him without me. He could die without me. I should be with him....'

'Uncle Jon's with him, Mum,' Olivia was telling her mother quietly whilst she looked appealingly at Jenny, silently asking her for help, just as all of them were looking to her for help, Jenny realised as she looked round at the shocked faces that surrounded her.

She took a deep breath and then said as calmly as she could, 'Caspar, if you could take Olivia and her mother and Ben to the hospital. You can use my car and—'

'I'll drive them,' Saul interrupted her tersely. 'It will be quicker,' he added as Caspar looked as though he was about to argue. 'I know the way. Come on,' he instructed, taking hold of Tiggy's arm and relieving

Olivia of her weight so that she was able to go over to Ben and gently guide him towards the exit.

'I can hold the fort here,' Ann, Hugh's wife, told Jenny. 'You'll want to get to the hospital yourself.' She patted Jenny on the arm. 'Don't worry, David and Jon might be twins, but that doesn't mean that Jon...'

Quickly Jenny shook her head. 'No. No, I know it doesn't,' she agreed, anticipating what Ann was going to say. How many other people were wondering the same thing. David had had a heart attack...would Jon be stricken down in the same way?

'They're two separate people, Jenny,' Ann was reiterating firmly.

'I know that,' Jenny agreed, 'but I sometimes wonder...'

Shakily she took a deep breath. Now wasn't the time to start losing her temper or her self-control and especially not with Ann.

'Are you sure you don't mind taking charge here? I *would* like to be there....'

'Of course I don't mind,' Ann assured her. 'You'll ring us—'

'Just as soon as I hear anything,' Jenny promised. She could see Ruth standing a little apart from everyone else, Joss close to her side, her arm pressed around him. 'I'm going to the hospital,' she told Ruth. 'Ann's offered to take charge here, if you want to come with me.

'Max,' she called out, summoning her elder son who virtually hadn't moved from the moment David had collapsed and whose face was still blank with disbelief. 'Max,' she repeated more sharply when he looked uncomprehendingly at her, waiting until she was sure she had got his attention before telling him, 'Laurence and Henry will want to know what's going on. We can't all go to the hospital. I want you to stay at the house with them. As soon as we know what's happening, we'll give you a ring.

'Luke will drive his parents and his Uncle Laurence back and James will take the others. Apparently Luke is the only one his father will trust to drive his Rolls, and fortunately, since he was late arriving, he hasn't had anything to drink,' Jenny explained to her son.

The mention of Luke's name seemed to have caught his attention.

'God bless Saint Luke,' Max sneered nastily under his breath, causing Jenny to draw a sharp breath and then bite down hard on her bottom lip. Quarrelling with Max was the last thing she had the energy for right now.

Behind his back, Ann gave a brief understanding shake of her head. 'Don't worry,' she mouthed reassuringly, 'I'll sort everything out here. You go.'

As she drove her car into the parking area for the hospital's new cardiac unit, Jenny acknowledged the irony of the fact that she herself had been extremely active in helping with the fund-raising for the unit and was more grateful than ever for all those people who had contributed their time and their money to making its existence possible. Whether or not the unit and the skills of its specially trained staff would be enough to save David's life was another matter.

Shakily she released her seat-belt and turned to smile as reassuringly as she could at Ruth.

The receptionist's greeting was a comforting blend

of professionalism and sympathy. 'The specialist is still with your brother-in-law,' she told Jenny, once she had given her name. 'If you'd like to join the others in the waiting area.'

'Joss, why don't you and Jack go and get your mother and me a drink?' she heard Ruth instructing her younger son. 'It's given them a bad shock,' Ruth told Jenny when they had gone.

As they walked into the waiting room, Jenny automatically looked for Jon. He was at the other side of the room with Olivia and Tiggy and hadn't seen her walk in. Tiggy was crying and Jon had his arm around her. Gravely Jenny watched them.

'It's Livvy I feel the most sorry for,' Ruth announced unexpectedly. 'If she's not careful, she's going to find herself turning into a leaning post for Tiggy.'

'You stay here with Ruth while I go and have a word with your father,' Jenny instructed Joss when he came back in, carefully carrying their coffee.

Jon still looked as though he was in shock, Jenny noted as she reached him and saw the way he was barely able to focus on her, even recognise her, his face almost a total blank.

'Is there any news yet?' she asked him anxiously. It was Olivia who answered her.

'No, nothing concrete. They've confirmed that Dad's had a heart attack but as yet they don't know...'

She put her hand over her mouth as her eyes started to fill with tears.

'Come on now, take it easy. At least he's still alive and he's in the best place...safe hands...'

Olivia gave Saul a grateful look as he had obviously

overheard Jenny's question and come across to join them.

He had been marvellous on the way to the hospital, taking charge calmly and easily, even managing to stop her mother's hysterics without betraying any of the disdain or disapproval she suspected that Caspar might have shown, and once they had got to the hospital he had dealt equally efficiently with everything there, even managing, Olivia noticed, to have a discreet word with one of the nurses to make sure that a professional eye was kept on Ben who, shockingly, seemed to have aged a decade in as many minutes, turning from a domineering, irascible patriarch into an almost frighteningly frail and vulnerable old man.

Just like the rest of the family, she had always known, of course, how much David meant to him and it made her heart ache with pity for him now to see the debilitating effect David's heart attack had had on him.

Uncle Jon, too, looked equally devastated although in a different way. He had remained with her father right up until the specialist had arrived to examine him, and the moment he had walked into the waiting room, Tiggy had run over to him, flinging herself into his arms, demanding, 'He's not dead, is he? Tell me he's not dead. I can't live without him. I can't...'

'No. He's not dead, Tiggy,' Jon had reassured her.

No, David wasn't dead, thank God. Thank God. No doubt it was the shock of seeing his brother collapse in front of him—his fear for him, his love—that was responsible for the feelings he was experiencing now. He had the oddest sense of somehow not really being a part of what was going on around him, of somehow having stepped outside himself, seeing himself as though his mind, his spirit, had somehow become detached from his body.

His movements, his behaviour, his words, were all automatic, instinctive. He was acting as he always had, as the dutiful, responsible brother.

He tried to put himself in his twin's shoes, to imagine what it would be like if he were the one lying in the hospital bed. Would Jenny be weeping over him, distraught, inconsolable at the thought of losing him?

Or would she be looking at David and thinking...wishing...

He had watched them dancing together earlier, their bodies so close, Jenny's head resting against David as he whispered in her ear. What had he been saying to her?

Jon had never been under any illusions about Jenny's reason for marrying him. If it hadn't been for the baby... And he, after all, had been the one to insist that they did get married. He couldn't blame Jenny for that. He had known all along, too, how she had felt about David. Had known how almost relieved his father had been when he announced that he and Jenny were getting married and he had discovered why. Once married to him, Jenny could not pose any threat to the future Ben had planned for David. There had been the expected stern parental lecture, of course, about the fact that Jenny was pregnant and he had sat stoically through it, speaking only once to defend Jenny and to remind his father that creating a new life took two people and not just one.

He had seen the relief in Jenny's eyes when David had written to say that he couldn't make it home to attend the wedding and then naïvely he had taken that to mean that Jenny hadn't wanted David there; that she no longer wanted him in her life.

He knew that Jenny had tried very hard to make their marriage work just as he had done himself; that she had been a good wife and was an even better mother—that could never be called into question—but he had seen the look in her eyes earlier in the evening, watching her as she stood in front of the bedroom mirror studying her reflection, not realising that he was there.

Her face had looked unfamiliarly flushed, her lips half-parted, her eyes shining with…with what? Expectation…excitement…because she had known even then that David…?

It had shocked and disturbed him to see her looking so different…so…so…desirable and…feminine. She had not looked like the Jenny he was familiar with and an odd sensation had gripped his chest as he realised the trouble she had taken with her appearance; revealing herself as a serenely sensual and feminine woman had not been done for his sake. Never once in all the years they had been married could he ever remember Jenny taking the trouble to dress like that for him.

And there had been no doubt that David had been impressed, and not just David. Jon wasn't blind. He had seen the way the male guests had looked at Jenny, a quick, startled frown of semi-recognition followed by a much longer and far more sexually appraising study of her feminine attributes.

What had David been saying to Jenny whilst they danced? Had he been telling her how attractive she was, reminding her that the two of them once…? And what had Jenny felt, or did he really need to ask himself? As a teenager Jenny had loved David even if she had sturdily dismissed her feelings as a mere teenage crush when she had accepted his proposal of marriage.

David was his brother, his twin brother, and he had been raised from childhood in the belief that that relationship created a closeness between them, a bond formed on his part by unquestioning love and loyalty and on David's by a careless affection that must come before everything else and everyone else in his life.

David might now be dying, but all he could see in his mind's eye was not his brother's stricken face as he collapsed, but his brother as he danced with Jenny.

Of course he wanted David to live. Of course he did. So why did he feel this hollowness inside, this emptiness, this almost complete and total lack of emotion?

Tiggy was still crying and trembling. Automatically his arm tightened protectively around her. Here at least was someone whose feelings were not tainted, whose sole concern was for David. He couldn't bring himself to look at Jenny, to see what she was feeling, to read what was in her eyes, just in case...

Jack still had his arm around his mother whilst she clung weepily to him, Olivia noticed. *She* would have liked the support and comfort of Caspar's arms around her right now, she reflected, but he'd stayed behind, probably seeking out Hillary for company and support.

'Try not to worry. I'm sure they're doing everything they can.' Saul gave Olivia's hand a comforting squeeze as he picked up on her tense anxiety.

The waiting-room door swung open and the specialist walked in. He looked tired and grave-eyed as he began to speak in an even graver voice.

'David is out of immediate danger—for the moment. But...' He paused and looked round the room, choosing his words carefully as he took in Tiggy's tear-drenched, pale face and Jon's equally tense, too rigid one. Ben was holding on to Hugh's supporting arm whilst Ruth stood slightly behind him, Joss's hand tucked comfortingly within her own.

Without knowing she had done so, Olivia took a step closer to Saul, glad of the male comfort of his arm and the heat of his body as he drew her closer.

Only Jenny stood alone, somehow positioned so that the specialist was closest to her, and perhaps for that reason he addressed himself more directly to her than anyone else. To an unaware onlooker it might have seemed as though Jenny were the sick man's wife and Jon and Tiggy the married couple.

'He's had a very serious heart attack,' he continued, pausing briefly as Tiggy sobbed audibly and clung harder to Jon, 'and in fact he's very lucky to be alive. But he *is* alive and...' He paused again and it was Jenny who stepped into the silence.

'What exactly is it you're trying to tell us?' she asked quietly.

'David is a very seriously ill man. The next twenty-four hours will be critical. Until then, we won't know—'

'You mean there's a danger that he could have a second attack? Is that what you're trying to tell us?' Jenny demanded.

'It does happen,' the specialist warned them gravely, 'but hopefully...'

'Can…can we see him?' Jon asked huskily.

The specialist shook his head. 'No. I'm afraid that won't be possible. Not at this stage. It's imperative that he's kept calm and sedated. In fact, the best, the only thing you can all do for him right now is to go home and try to get some sleep, because…' As he saw the quick, frowning look Jenny gave in Ben's direction, he beckoned to a hovering nurse, then took Jenny aside and said reassuringly, 'I'll prescribe something for your father-in-law. I know his own heart's not as strong as it might be.'

'Tiggy's very upset, Jenny,' Jon announced ten minutes later as Saul started to usher everyone back into the corridor. 'She can't be left on her own. I think I'd better go back with her tonight, just in case she needs me.'

'Yes, of course,' Jenny agreed, quietly refraining from reminding him that Tiggy had a house full of Chester relatives to turn to should she decide she needed a shoulder to cry on during the night in addition to her daughter and her daughter's boyfriend.

What would be the point after all? Jon simply wouldn't understand. He would expect her to accept, just as he had always accepted, that David's needs and wishes and therefore the needs and wishes of David's closest relatives must automatically take preference over everything and everyone else.

As she got back into the car, she remembered that he had never commented on her dress. Silly to cry over something as senseless as that when she had so many more important things to cry over. Appallingly selfish of her, too, to even be thinking of her own hurt at Jon's lack of response to her tonight, to have that at the forefront of her mind rather than, if only momentarily, David's heart attack.

It wasn't that she wasn't concerned for David; of course she was. He was, after all, Jon's brother and as such... She and Jon hadn't even managed to have a dance together; she couldn't, in fact, recall the last time they had danced together. This was so wrong. She shouldn't be thinking about her own selfish needs when David was so desperately ill. Why hadn't Jon said anything about her dress? Hadn't he liked it? Didn't he...? *Stop* it, she warned herself. You're not a teenager any more; you're an adult.

8

Well, at least the specialist seems pretty optimistic that David's over the worst.'

Olivia turned towards Saul.

'He's over the worst,' she agreed, 'but Mr Hayes has warned us that it's going to be some considerable time before he's completely out of danger—they're keeping him in intensive care until the end of the week but he won't be allowed home immediately. Mr Hayes says there's no question of his being able to go back to work for at least three months, and even then...'

'No,' Saul returned gravely. 'It's going to be hard. What will Jon do, do you think, hire a locum?'

'I don't know. No one's really discussed what's going to happen with the practice as yet,' Olivia admitted. 'We've all been too concerned about Dad, but something will have to be done.'

'Mmm...I wish I could offer to help out myself, but...' He spread his hands expressively. 'It just isn't possible. The company's heavily involved in negotiating some new contracts with Japan. I can't go into details, but from the legal point of view it's proving pretty complex. Hillary's always complaining that she hardly sees me any more, or rather she used to. I get the impression these days that the less she sees of me the better.'

The bitterness in his voice made Olivia wince. It had become increasingly obvious over the past three days, when Saul had elected to remain in Haslewich with his family until the immediacy of the crisis with David was over, that he and Hillary were no longer happy together. Olivia felt very sorry for him. It was plain that he adored his three children and she suspected that he struggled to make his marriage work more for their sake than his own.

They were in the drawing room of Queensmead along with the rest of the immediate family who had gathered there to hear the latest bulletin from the hospital on David's progress.

It had been Olivia's turn to see him today. She and Jon had been taking turns in accompanying her mother to the hospital on her daily visits to see her husband who was now conscious and able to communicate, although still quite heavily sedated and in intensive care. It had been tacitly acknowledged by the family that Tiggy was far too shocked and distressed by her husband's heart attack to endure the trauma of seeing him without some family support.

Hugh and Ann had remained at Queensmead until the immediate danger was over but had had to return home as Hugh was due to sit on the Bench. Saul, though, had opted to stay on in his father's stead, telling Olivia wryly that he might as well use up what little holiday allocation he had left.

'I had hoped we might get away, take the kids on holiday somewhere, but Hillary says the last thing she wants to do is spend any length of time cooped up with them and me. She was talking about flying home to see her family on her own.'

His face had been bleak as he delivered this last piece of information and tactfully Olivia had made no comment. Besides, she had enough problems of her own to worry about.

Caspar had moved into her room following her father's heart attack and last night... She closed her eyes, not wanting to have to think about the problems that were surfacing in her relationship with Caspar or the mixed-up feelings of panic, resentment and anguish they were causing her.

How was it possible for their relationship to have changed so much? Yes, of course she had been aware of Caspar's leftover feelings of rejection from his childhood. He had talked quite openly about them, as she had done about her own. She had thought that she understood Caspar and that he understood her and that even whilst he occasionally drew attention to her inability to verbally admit to her feelings for him, he knew that her fear of actually saying the words 'I love you' in no way lessened her commitment to him just as she had thought that his own wry awareness of his need to rewrite the emotional history of his childhood by placing himself first in her emotions meant that he had come to terms with it.

Now she was not so sure. It had shocked her to discover that far from being the mature adult she had believed him to be and someone she could lean on and respect and even look up to as she had never been able to do with her father, Caspar was just as capable of behaving emotionally and irresponsibly albeit in a different way. Just as able to be selfish and demanding, just as able to ignore her needs and focus on his own. Just as masculinely capable of putting pressure on her to get what he wanted from their relationship without giving a second thought to what she might want or need. Just as he had done last night...

Tensing, she wrapped her arms around herself. It had been at her suggestion that Caspar had moved into her room. She missed the comfort of his body in bed, his warmth...just knowing that he was there. Dismaying, too, was the knowledge that she had been more disturbed and upset by the discovery that her mother was suffering from an eating disorder than she had been in some ways by her father's heart attack and shamingly she knew why. A heart attack was something that could be explained, discussed, understood. Her mother's bulimia...

She had wanted desperately to talk over her feelings with Caspar, to know that he not only understood but sympathised, empathised, with what she was feeling; to see if he realised how torn she now felt. How much on the one hand she longed to be able to simply walk away and escape, to turn her back on the situation here at home and start a completely new life with him in Philadelphia. A life where she would be judged only on her own merits and by people who knew nothing and never would know anything of her family background. And yet on the other how guilty she felt, how compelled to do something to protect and help the vulnerable person she now saw her mother to be.

She felt so confused...so helpless. More than anything she needed Caspar's understanding...she needed time. But Caspar quite obviously wasn't prepared to give her either.

Last night, when she had turned to him, wanting to

talk... She closed her eyes again and was instantly back in her own bedroom, the faint light of the moon shining through the curtains.

'Caspar,' she whispered softly, 'are you awake?'

'What do you think?' she heard him grunt, the bed-clothes rustling as he raised an arm, pushed them aside and slipping it around her, his mouth nuzzling the soft, warm skin of her throat. 'Mmm...I've missed you.'

He was apparently too engrossed in enjoying the taste of her flesh to register her tension.

'Caspar,' she started to protest, but he ignored her, throwing one leg across her body as he slid his hand along her jaw and turned her to face him, his mouth opening hungrily over hers.

Olivia hesitated a second before she started to respond. It wasn't that she didn't want to make love. It was just that right now it was more important to her that they talked. She needed to vocalise what she was feeling and Caspar was the only person she felt she could talk to.

It felt so disloyal, hurt too much, to have to admit that the love she knew she ought to feel for her mother simply wasn't there and that she felt guilty—guilty because all she could feel was pity and compassion. But Caspar's hand was already moving towards her breast. His body was already aroused.

His thumb stroked her nipple and in the darkness she tried to recapture her normal feeling of sensual delight at his touch. The first time they had made love she had wanted him so much, ached for him so much, that she had actually had a small orgasm whilst he had been kissing her breast, teasing first one and then the other erect nipple with the tip of his tongue. The gentle roughness of his teeth, the mind-blowing eruption inside her when he started to suck slowly on her nipple had been incredible sensations.

She had been mortified with embarrassment, but Caspar had simply laughed, teasing her that if that was her reaction to his sensual stimulation of her breast, he couldn't wait to find out how she reacted when it was a far more intimate part of her body he was orally stimulating.

As it happened he had been right; he couldn't wait and neither could she, but they had made up for their impetuosity later, and for the first time in her life Olivia discovered that it wasn't only the man who derived pleasure from the warm caress of a woman's mouth on his sex.

She had been a little hesitant at first to pleasure him in such a way, especially when her own body felt so languid, so deliriously satisfied, and so her touch had been a little cautious and uncertain.

Caspar hadn't hurried her, though, or tried to force the pace of an intimacy she wasn't ready for. Yet, if she was honest, she had rather enjoyed the sense of power their intimacy gave her, especially when she had felt him start to swell and harden as he responded to the gentle pressure of her mouth and the stroke of her tongue.

Totally absorbed in his reaction of what she was doing, it had been several minutes before she recognised not only the fact that she was squirming rather obviously on the bed but the reason why she was doing so, the reason why her breasts suddenly started to ache again, her nipples re-engorged, her chest was flushing with sensual heat.

When she did realise that the desire recharging her sexual batteries had nothing to do with anything that Caspar had done to arouse her and owed its being quite simply and rather shockingly to the fact that she was becoming sexually aroused by so intimately caressing him, she was so surprised that she released him and sat up abruptly.

'What's wrong?' Caspar had asked her, sitting up himself and reaching out to take her in his arms. 'If you don't like it...'

Olivia had shaken her head. 'No. No, it's not that,' she had told him.

'Then what?' Caspar had pressed her when she didn't go on.

'I...I want you,' she had confessed huskily as she looked from his aroused body to his face and then betrayingly touched her fingertips to her own mouth, her face warming as she added, 'Doing that...being so...I didn't think...I never knew...'

Later Caspar had shown her that he was equally vulnerable to the sensual effect of that kind of intimacy when he laid her gently on the bed and even more gently moved apart her legs and then knelt between them, touching her, stroking her slowly, watching her eyes, holding her gaze so that he could see her reaction as he slowly lowered his head towards the soft, damp tangle of her pubic hair.

Olivia had closed her eyes, trying to suppress the moan of pleasure she could feel building in her throat as he slid his hands beneath her thighs, lifting her, tilting her, setting her legs over his shoulders as he started to explore the tender, sweet intimacy of her, unerringly finding the place where she was most sensitive, most responsive, and caressing it until she could no longer hold back her response.

But that had been then; this was now. Beneath the stimulation of his tongue, her nipple had started to stiffen, her body responding to him even if her mind was not.

Beneath her fingertips she could feel the crispness of his hair, but where normally she would have buried her hands in it to keep him, to hold him even closer to her body, tonight what she really wanted to do was to push him away. How could he not know...not sense that she simply wasn't in the mood? Was he really so blind, so oblivious to her feelings, or did he simply not care? Was it more important for him to satisfy his own needs than hers?

The pressure of his mouth on her breast was increasing. He had moved their bodies closer together. She could feel his hardness pressing against her and for the first time in their relationship Olivia experienced a need to simply get their lovemaking over and done with as quickly as she possibly could.

Tonight the foreplay she normally loved and enjoyed so much was merely an unwanted and resented duty. Since his need for sex was quite obviously so all-consuming, all-important, far more important to him than what she might want or need and since he was so obviously ready, why didn't he just go ahead and get it over with?

She moved impatiently against him and then ground her teeth as he misinterpreted her invitation and started to caress her with his hands, sliding them down over her hips, massaging her belly and then her buttocks in the way she normally enjoyed before sliding one hand between her thighs.

Olivia tensed and finally so did Caspar.

'What is it?' he asked her. 'What's wrong?'

So he'd finally noticed there was something wrong.

'Nothing,' she told him curtly, then added, 'Look, Caspar, can we please get this over with? I'm tired and if you want sex as you obviously do...'

Olivia knew even as she was saying it how awful her words must sound but she just couldn't help herself. Was it her fault that Caspar was so blind, so selfish that he couldn't tell for himself that she just wasn't in the mood, that what she wanted was to be held and comforted, to be listened to and not simply treated as a means by which he could relieve his sexual tension?

She could feel him watching her in the darkness and wasn't surprised when he started to move away from her. Caspar had never been the kind of man to force unwanted sexual overtures. He had once told her that for him to enjoy sex, the pleasure had to be mutual, both partners giving and taking, both sharing the desire, the wanting, the arousal. But then just as she was about to turn over, he suddenly reached out and took hold of her, pinning her beneath him with a speed and strength that took her off guard, and when she looked up at him in stunned shock he told her angrily, 'Very well, if that's what you want...'

'Caspar,' Olivia started to protest but it was already too late. With the weight of his body keeping her pressed to the bed, he was already starting to enter her.

Her body, she recognised, must have been more

aroused, more responsive than she had thought because it was certainly accepting him easily enough
now, despite her efforts to tense her muscles against
him.

'I thought you wanted me to get it over with,'
Caspar reminded her grimly as he felt her efforts to resist him.

He had started moving faster, harder, and to her
shock Olivia realised that a part of her was almost enjoying the knowledge that she had made him angry. It
seemed as though in pushing him into anger she could
allow herself to acknowledge her own sensual and
sexual needs.

She stiffened as she found that her body was quite
definitely starting to respond to the fiercely rhythmic
thrust of Caspar's within it. She wanted to push him
away, to stop him doing what he was doing, to reach
out and scratch him with her nails, bite him with her
teeth, fight against his sexual possession of her and at
the same time...at the same time...

She gave a sharp gasp as the first fluttering contrac-
tion of her orgasm caught her off guard and then it
was too late, much too late for her to do anything but
wrap herself around him and call out his name as the
intensity of her own need swamped and engulfed her.

They had never used sex as a means of hurting one
another before, not physically and certainly not emotionally, but they had done last night. After it was over
she had turned her back on Caspar, feigning sleep
when he had tentatively touched her and whispered
her name.

After a while she had felt him move away and turn
his back to her whilst she had stayed stiffly where she

was, aching to be able to turn to him and be taken in his arms and yet too angry...too hurt to allow herself to tell him so.

When she had woken up this morning, Caspar was already in the bathroom. They had been treating one another with guarded politeness all day. Stubbornly Olivia told herself that Caspar was the one in the wrong and not her. He should have known how she was feeling; he should have seen...understood. She was disturbingly conscious of a growing feeling of alienation between them, a reluctance on her part to feel able to confide fully in him, to tell him about the hours she lay awake at night, worrying not just about her father but also about her mother, listening for the betraying sound of her mother creeping downstairs to repeat the self-destructive binging and vomiting cycle of behaviour that she had witnessed before the party.

Now she smiled tiredly as Jon came over to join her and Saul. Of all of them Jon was the one who was taking her father's illness the hardest, Olivia suspected. After all, not only was he her father's twin brother and bound to be psychologically affected by his heart attack, he was also the one who had to bear the brunt of the family's panic and fear, especially her mother's and his own father's. In her mother's case, that fear had been displayed in bouts of hysterical tears and a need to cling to him both physically and emotionally, which must be hard enough for him to bear, but when it came to her grandfather... Judgementally Olivia glanced across the room to where her grandfather was sitting.

Perhaps he didn't mean to give the impression that he wished it had been Jon who had been stricken with a heart attack and not David…that if he had to lose one of his sons he would prefer it to be Jon and not David. But, nevertheless, that was the impression he had given and Jon must have inevitably been hurt by such accusations—despite his enviable stoicism and quiet acceptance of his father's angry claims that it was due to his own failure to shoulder his fair share of the burden of running the practice that David had been overworked to the extent that his heart had damaged by the strain.

'Livvy and I were just wondering how you are going to manage with the practice,' Saul commented. 'I imagine your best option would be to get a locum in and—'

'No.' The swiftness with which Jon rejected Saul's suggestion surprised Olivia. His voice, normally gentle and controlled, had been almost harsh. 'I…I haven't had time to come to any decision about the practice as yet,' Jon told them stiffly as Olivia and Saul instinctively exchanged surprised glances. Such vehemence and intensity were so foreign to Jon's nature that it had caught them both off guard a little.

'But you will have to make a decision soon,' Jenny interposed quietly from her seat near by. 'You can't possibly run the practice on your own. There's far too much work and besides—'

'Besides what?' Jon challenged her, ignoring Olivia and Saul's presence as he turned round to face his wife, his voice and eyes suddenly sharply bitter. 'Besides what?' he demanded again. 'Besides I'm not David and therefore not capable of running the practice by myself?'

'Jon. You know I didn't mean anything of the kind,'

Jenny reproached him. He had changed so much over these past few days that sometimes she hardly recognised him. She knew how much pressure he was under, how anxious and concerned he was for David...how caught up with supporting not just Tiggy but his father, as well; and she sensed how hurt he must have been by Ben's obvious belief that he was not capable of stepping into David's shoes. But it was impossible for him to do two men's work indefinitely and that was all that she had been going to say.

'I could help out for a while....'

As soon as she had said the words, Olivia wondered what on earth had possessed her. She was already committed to going to America with Caspar. All their plans had been made.

'Oh, Livvy, could you? But what about your own job?' Jenny exclaimed in obvious relief.

Olivia was conscious of Caspar listening to her and watching her from the other side of the room. Hillary was at his side, a place she was frequently to be found of late, she reflected a little bitterly. As Hillary reached up and whispered something to him, Olivia's chin tilted stubbornly.

It was too late for her to retract what she had said now and besides... 'I'm...I'm between jobs at the moment,' she told her aunt quite truthfully. 'I...I haven't got round to telling the family yet, but I actually handed in my notice at work some time ago, so there's no reason why I shouldn't step into Dad's shoes and help out at the practice for a little while at least.'

'Could you, Livvy. That would be marvellous, wouldn't it, Jon?' Jenny exclaimed as she turned to her husband. 'It would—'

'What's this, what's this?' Ben was demanding, having obviously been told by Max what was going on.

'Livvy's just offered to help out at the practice until David's well enough to go back to work,' Jenny explained to her father-in-law.

'To do what? She can't! She's only a girl and she's not—'

'I might be a girl, Gramps, but I'm also a fully qualified practising solicitor,' Olivia heard herself reminding her grandfather in a coolly firm voice. But despite her outward control, inwardly her heart had started to beat too fast and she could feel the familiar turmoil beginning to churn her stomach. 'I know it's what Dad would want me to do,' she added, looking her grandfather squarely in the eye. 'Unless, of course, Max wants—'

'That's impossible,' Ben told her testily. 'You know that perfectly well. Max is trying for the Bar.'

'Are you sure you know what you're taking on?' Saul murmured in her ear. 'It's not going to be easy for you, you know. I dare say that Jon isn't as much of a dyed-in-the-wool traditionalist as Ben, but you're still talking about a very old-fashioned country practice with very old-fashioned country clients.'

'What are you trying to say to me, Saul?' she challenged him sharply. 'That I'm not up to the work?'

'No, of course not,' he denied. But despite his denial, as she looked round at the expressions on people's faces, Olivia suspected that none of them really believed that she was capable of stepping into her father's shoes.

'Livvy,' she heard Jon beginning hesitantly and her resolve hardened and along with it her voice.

'I've made up my mind, Uncle Jon,' she told him grittily, 'and I'm not going to change it. I'll be at the office first thing tomorrow morning.'

She held her breath, waiting for one of them to call her bluff, then released it slowly when none of them did. They needed her, she recognised bleakly, even if none of them, apart from Jenny, was prepared to admit it. Well, she would show them. She would show them that she was just as professional as any male Crighton they'd care to name, and a good deal more so than some of them, she decided as she glowered darkly at Max, who was watching her with his usual smug contempt.

She wondered if he'd told Ben that his elevation to full junior membership in his chambers wasn't by any means as cut and dried as he'd implied and then decided that if he hadn't, it was his own business. She wouldn't want to be in his shoes, though, if the final selection went against him as Caspar was pretty sure that it easily could.

'Why?' she had asked Caspar when they had been discussing it. 'On what grounds?'

'Plenty,' Caspar had returned. 'He's the wrong sex for starters and in addition to that I doubt that he's strictly fully competent enough to win the selection.'

'He passed his exams.'

'Just,' Caspar pointed out pithily, 'and he's not popular. Oh, I know what you're going to say,' he continued, holding up his hand to stop her before she could begin to speak. 'And, yes, I agree that to have the reputation of being held a little in awe by your peers is no bad thing for a barrister, but in this case I wouldn't say his peers hold him so much in awe as in contempt.'

Olivia gave him a wry look. He wasn't telling her anything she hadn't already heard. The legal world was, after all, a relatively small and close-knit one through which gossip and rumour tended to spread pretty quickly.

Now, as she looked at Caspar across the width of her grandfather's drawing room, her heart missed a beat. How was he going to feel about her impetuous decision to step into her father's shoes at the practice and the temporary hold it would put on their own plans? He would understand just why she had felt compelled to offer her assistance, wouldn't he?

'Fine. You felt you had to do it for your father's sake. Very daughterly. But what about *us*, Livvy? What about *me*? Surely *I* had a right at least to be consulted about what you were contemplating.'

Olivia winced as Caspar stopped pacing the floor of her bedroom and swung round angrily to confront her. 'I didn't stop to think,' she confessed. 'I just...I thought you'd understand....'

'Oh, I *understand* all right,' Caspar told her grimly. 'I *understand* very well that you just couldn't resist the opportunity to win your grandfather over, to get his approval, to have him say how much he values you...how much he appreciates you...how he loves you. But it isn't going to happen, Livvy, because your grandfather will never admit that he could possibly make an error of judgement or that a woman could possibly be as good a lawyer as a man. He *can't*. It would mean going against everything he believes in and he's too old and too set in his ways to do that.

'You can think about that when you're trying to fill your father's shoes and abandoning a perfectly good pair of your own in the process and you can think about something else, as well,' he told her bitterly.

'*I* value you. *I* appreciate you…*I* love you, but *my* feelings no longer seem to matter to you. Just like the plans we've made. Still, at least I found out before it's too late. There's no way I intend to build my life around a woman who is always going to be running home to her family whenever she thinks they need her, who is always going to put them first, who's as addicted to the way they withhold their love and approval from her in just the same way that her mother's addicted to—'

'That's not true,' Olivia interrupted him furiously. 'I'm *not* abandoning you for my family, Caspar. And as for our plans, I'm simply putting them on hold for a few weeks until my father's well enough to go back to work. You *know* what your trouble is, don't you?' she challenged him, as angry now as he was himself, refusing to listen to the small inner voice that warned her to exercise restraint and caution.

'You're very good at accusing *me* of clinging to a childhood pattern of behaviour; of misinterpreting my motivation for offering to help as some childish need to gain my grandfather's approval. But what about *you*? What about the fact that you're still acting like the little boy who couldn't bear not to come first? It's not *my* fault your parents divorced, Caspar. It's not *my* fault that your father had other children. Oh, this isn't getting us anywhere,' she finished tiredly as she saw the look in his eyes. The last thing she wanted was to quarrel with him, not now when she needed his support and his understanding so badly. As she pushed the heavy weight of her hair off her face, she looked pleadingly at him, her stomach tensing nervously as she saw his stony expression.

'No, it isn't,' he agreed coldly. 'But then perhaps that's because there's nowhere left for us to go. You've made your decision, Olivia...your choice, and you made it without feeling any need to discuss its implications with me. I think that says all that needs to be said about how much you value our relationship, don't you?'

'Caspar, what are you doing?' Olivia demanded anxiously as he started to walk towards the door.

As he opened it he paused and looked coldly at her before saying, 'I think you already know the answer to that. It's too late for me to leave for London this evening, but first thing in the morning I'll make arrangements to do so. After all, there's very little point in my staying on now, is there?'

'Caspar,' Olivia protested, but it was too late; he had already gone and yet, alongside her despair, Olivia was acutely conscious of a sharp sense of resentment she couldn't completely smother.

Yes, she had acted impetuously, and yes, she should, with hindsight, have talked things over with Caspar before making that offer to Jon. But to make those accusations about her motives, to have reacted the way he had without making any attempt to understand her feelings or her situation...to virtually demand that she focus her life on him and only him...?

After all, he hadn't wanted to listen to her last night, had he?

Olivia couldn't forget how alienated from him she had felt when he had refused to understand how upset she had been about her mother. At least now she would be on hand if her mother should need her, something she was sure that Saul with his far more compassionate nature would understand.

Wearily she looked out of her bedroom window. She could see Caspar standing in the garden. He had his back to her, his hands in his pockets, his hair ruffled by the late afternoon breeze. She would have to go down and talk to him, make him understand, make him see her point of view...apologise to him for not having consulted him...show him that she did love him, and that once she had discharged her duty to her parents, her family, they could be together as they had originally planned.

He would have to understand that she couldn't go back on her word to Jon. Not now... If she did, it would simply confirm everything that her grandfather was so scathing about concerning the ability of her sex to commit itself to a career, to put logic first and emotion second. But would Caspar understand? Perhaps Saul had been right this afternoon when he had claimed wryly that Americans have a different way of looking at life...a different set of priorities.

At the time, whilst she had been sympathetic, Olivia had put his disenchantment down to the fact that he and Hillary were having marital problems. Now she wasn't so sure...

'Well, at least Livvy's offer to help out at the partnership will take one problem off your shoulders,'

Jenny commented to Jon later that evening after their return from Queensmead.

'Yes,' he agreed tersely. They were both in the kitchen. Jenny was starting preparations for supper.

Jenny looked thoughtfully at him. His terseness only confirmed what she had already guessed—that for some reason he was reluctant to accept Olivia's offer of help. She was sure about one thing; it wasn't because of Olivia's sex. Jon, after all, had been the one who suggested, albeit rather tentatively, to both David and Ben when Olivia had first expressed an interest in training as a solicitor, that they take her on themselves as an articled clerk. It had been David and, of course, Ben who had vetoed the idea.

'You don't sound very keen,' she pressed when he made no further attempt to answer her. 'You can't run the practice on your own,' she told him. 'You need—'

'Yes. I do realise that, Jenny,' Jon snapped, interrupting her. 'But it would make my life much easier if certain members of this family would stop trying to decide what's best for me and allow me to make my own decisions.'

Jenny stared at him. She knew, of course, that by 'certain members of this family' he meant her, but his criticism was so grossly unfair and out of character that she could hardly believe he had uttered it.

'Jon,' she protested.

'I have to go and see Tiggy,' he told her curtly. 'She's getting herself into a terrible state over some problem or other with the bank and I promised her I'd go round.'

'Olivia's at home,' Jenny reminded him, trying to

keep her voice deliberately neutral. 'I'm sure if she knew that Tiggy was worrying about something like that, she would sort it out for her.'

'Yes, I'm sure she would,' Jon agreed, 'but perhaps Tiggy feels more at ease asking for *my* help rather than Olivia's. She feels that Olivia disapproves of her... considers her too irresponsible. They do have rather conflicting personalities. You've said so yourself,' he reminded her when Jenny remained silent.

'I doubt I ever said that they have conflicting personalities,' Jenny corrected him gently. '*Different*, yes. But I'm sure you're wrong in accusing Olivia of disapproving of her mother.'

'I'm not accusing Olivia of anything. Just repeating what Tiggy told me...a confidence she's given me,' he underlined. 'You might try to be a little bit more compassionate and understanding yourself, Jen. I know you and Tiggy aren't exactly close and that in the past she has tended to be rather dizzy, but that doesn't mean that she doesn't feel...'

He paused, looking uncomfortable and self-conscious as though aware that he had said too much, betrayed too much. But since when had he felt it necessary to defend Tiggy from her? Jenny wondered grimly, and more importantly, why should he feel it necessary to do so?

'Olivia has always been much closer to you than she has to her mother,' he pointed out, but he couldn't quite meet her eyes, Jenny noticed, and the way he was playing with the cutlery she'd been laying on the table for supper gave away his inner tension.

'Olivia and I *have* always been close, yes,' she agreed, 'but that doesn't mean... Tiggy can sometimes tend to overreact to situations,' she began to explain carefully. 'She needs—'

'She needs help,' Jon interrupted her, 'and that's not something she should be made to feel ashamed of needing.'

'No, it isn't,' Jenny agreed. Her hands, she noticed distractedly, were trembling slightly as she reached up for a serving dish. Why? Not because Jon was defending Tiggy, surely. Uneasily she reflected on his implied criticism of her. All she had been going to say was that in her opinion Tiggy needed careful handling, but she could see that Jon was in no mood to listen to her, never mind welcome her interpretation of his sister-in-law's volatile personality. In fact, in his present uncharacteristic mood, he would probably take any attempt on her part to put forward her own viewpoint as an unwanted disparagement of his own judgement of the situation.

Once they would have sat down together and discussed the whole thing amicably, but recently he seemed to be so touchy and on edge, taking umbrage at the slightest thing. Only the previous evening he had lost his temper with Joss just because their son had quite innocently and unintentionally knocked over some papers Jon had been working on.

Jon had apologised to Joss later, but normally such an apology would not have been necessary in the first place because her husband would never have lost his temper over such a trivial incident.

Of course, Jenny appreciated the difficulties he was facing. David *was* his twin after all, but knowing he was carrying a double burden of anxiety both as David's twin and his business partner, surely it made more sense for him to welcome Olivia's offer of assistance instead of acting as though in making it she had given him yet another set of problems to deal with.

'Things could be worse,' she told him mildly, trying to inject some measure of light-heartedness into the situation. 'It could have been Max who offered to stand in for David.'

'Max!' Jenny was unprepared for the look of loathing that suddenly darkened his eyes. 'No, never! Max is far too selfish, too self-obsessed, too concerned with his own needs and not anyone else's to even think of—'

'Jon, he's your son,' Jenny felt bound to remind him, disturbed by such an explosion of antagonistic emotion from a man who was normally so placid and prone to give others the benefit of the doubt. She didn't want to have to point out to him that Max's selfishness had been increased a hundredfold by his grandfather's, and to some extent David's, thorough spoiling and indulgence of him.

She herself wasn't happy with her son's behaviour any more than Jon, but like any mother she was sorely tempted to defend her child. She wanted Jon to see that the faults he so deplored in his elder son were the same faults to be found in his twin brother who had—or so it sometimes seemed to Jenny—been elevated in the combined consciousness of Jon and his father to a state approaching sainthood.

However, this was quite obviously not the time to remind Jon that much of what was now happening could be directly attributed to David's own refusal to moderate his lifestyle.

'Max may be my son,' Jon repeated in angry disgust, 'but as we both know he'd much rather have had David as his father—even as a child he used to revel in the fact that people often mistook him for David's son and perhaps...' He stopped and shook his head, then without giving Jenny the opportunity to object he got up and walked over to the door, stopping only to tell her brusquely, 'Don't bother with any supper for me. I'll eat with Tiggy.'

'Mum...where's Dad?'

Hastily Jenny tried to regain control of her chaotic thoughts as Louise came into the kitchen.

'He's gone to see your Aunt Tiggy. She needs his help with something. Finish setting the table, will you please, Louise? It's almost time for supper.'

'Again,' Louise grumbled as she picked up the plates. 'He's always over there. In fact, he might as well move in with her, then at least she wouldn't be ringing him up all the time.'

'This is a very difficult time for her, Louise,' Jenny responded quietly.

'It's a very difficult time for all of us,' Louise countered feelingly, 'especially Dad.'

'Yes, well, Olivia's offered to come home and help your father out at the practice.'

'Has she? I bet Caspar won't like that. Still...I expect Hillary will do her best to comfort him. Are she and Saul going to get a divorce?'

'Louise!' Jenny warned. It was quite frightening at times to realise how much modern teenagers absorbed and how aware they were of adult concerns and personal problems, far more surely than when she had been a girl.

'I like Saul. I think he's very, very sexy,' Louise pronounced, ignoring her. 'I don't suppose it will take him long to find someone else. It's a pity that...'

'That what?' Jenny asked with maternal suspicion, but typically Louise refused to be drawn, simply shaking her head.

Really, in far too many ways, Louise was more adult, more knowing, than she sometimes was herself, Jenny reflected wryly. But for once her mind wasn't fully on the potential problems Louise, far too swift and determined to emerge into womanhood, was likely to cause. Other more immediate concerns about the recent scene with Jon had left her shaken and dismayed.

She squeezed her eyes tightly closed against the threatening onslaught of tears. She dared not let Louise or anyone else see her crying. But, she wondered in silent anguish, whose shoulder was she supposed to cry on? Whose arms were supposed to hold her? Who was supposed to listen and sympathise with her pain and fears whilst her husband did all those things for someone else?

It had shocked her to hear Jon speaking so bitterly about Max. She had always felt guilty about the fact that Max and Jon weren't closer; that Max had always instinctively turned to David. Nature perhaps wasn't always wise in the way she passed on family traits and characteristics. She herself had always been wary of making too much of Max's startling psychological resemblance to David rather than to Jon; she had assumed that, like her, Jon believed it was a subject best left alone.

It had disturbed her to hear the resentment in Jon's

voice and to see the accusation in his eyes. And more than that, it hurt her deeply, knowing that he had deliberately walked away without allowing her to defend herself or tell him that, given the choice, she would rather her son had inherited his virtues and his strengths rather than David's weaknesses.

9

Jon paused uneasily as he got out of his car. There were lights shining from the upstairs window, which he knew belonged to David and Tiggy's large bedroom—only Tiggy's bedroom now and for some time to come if, as the specialist warned, David was going to have to remain in hospital for the present.

'I thought the idea these days was to get the patient back on his or her feet and home as quickly as possible after a heart attack,' Jon had commented when the specialist had taken him through his proposals for David's treatment.

'There are heart attacks and heart attacks,' Mr Hayes had responded enigmatically, 'and there are patients and patients.'

Olivia's car was parked outside and Jon's heart sank slightly as she opened the door to his knock.

'Tiggy's upstairs,' she told him and took him through into the small sitting room that he always associated with David's wife.

Like her, it was delicate and feminine and somehow always seemed to smell of her perfume. David had his own study on the other side of the hall, which reminded him...

'I'd like to have a word with you before Tiggy

comes down,' Olivia told him as she handed him the glass of dry sherry she had poured him.

Jon's heart sank a little further. He had no need to ask her what she wanted to talk to him about.

'I know that nothing will ever persuade Gramps, and to some extent Dad, too, since he always tends to fall in line with Gramps's views that a woman, any woman, but most especially a Crighton woman, is capable of being a competent lawyer, but I thought that you were different, Uncle Jon. I *am* qualified, you know, and... But from the look on your face when I offered to stand in for Dad until he's fit enough to return to work—'

'Olivia, I know how well qualified you are,' Jon interrupted her dryly, 'and as for your competence...' He gave her a wry look. 'We both know that you are far, far more than merely competent, but—'

'But you still don't want me working here in the practice.'

'It isn't a matter of what I may or may not want,' Jon hedged. 'You know—'

'What? That Gramps doesn't approve? You can't run the practice on your own. It's obvious from what Mr Hayes has told me that at least part of the cause of Dad's heart attack was the stress he was under at work. You don't have time to advertise and interview and—'

'There are agencies that supply temporary cover,' Jon started to point out, but Olivia overruled him, shaking her head, her chin firmly, stubbornly, set.

'Yes, I know, but...' She stopped speaking and walked impatiently over to the fireplace before turning round and demanding, 'If I were male...if I were

Max, for instance, you wouldn't think twice about accepting my offer, and—'

'Olivia, I promise you, any reluctance you might imagine there is on my part to take you on has nothing to do with your sex.'

'Hasn't it? Then prove it,' Olivia challenged him.

Jon closed his eyes tiredly; there was no point in continuing to oppose her. He couldn't carry the workload of the practice without help. He hadn't had a chance to go through David's desk or files yet, but if the backlog of work there was as large as he suspected... How could he explain to Olivia that the reason for his reluctance to accept her offer was because he... If only he had had more time. If *only* he had had some warning, he might have been able to...

'It isn't that I don't appreciate your offer, Olivia,' he told her quietly.

'Good,' she returned firmly. 'Then that's settled. I'll start tomorrow morning.'

'What's settled?' Tiggy demanded as she walked into the room. She was wearing some kind of housecoat-type garment, Jon noticed, a floaty, chiffony affair in soft pastels that reflected the delicate purity of her skin.

She had never been exactly robust-looking, but since David's heart attack, she seemed even more vulnerable and fragile.

'It's settled that I'm going to be filling in for Dad until he's fit enough to go back to work,' Olivia answered her mother. She frowned slightly as she commented, 'I thought you said you were going upstairs to get dressed.'

'Yes, I did...I was,' Tiggy agreed. Jon noticed she

hung her head almost as though *she* were the child and Olivia the parent. 'But...' She turned to Jon, her eyes wide and appealing as she told him huskily, 'I started thinking about David and...' Her mouth started to tremble, her eyes filling with tears. 'You won't be cross with me for not getting dressed properly, will you, Jon? After all, you are family. I'm so glad you're here,' she added without waiting for his response. 'The bank keeps ringing up and—'

'I would have spoken to the bank, Tiggy,' Olivia interrupted her. Her mother gave her a tearful look.

'I know you would, but it's better if Jon talks to them. He's a man and...'

She bit her lip as Olivia replaced her empty sherry glass on the silver tray with unnecessary force.

'Oh, Saul rang,' Tiggy told her. 'He wants you to ring him back.' She waited until Olivia had left the room before turning to Jon and saying apologetically, 'Olivia isn't in a very good mood, I'm afraid. I think she and Caspar have had a row. Oh, Jon.' She stopped talking, her voice suspended by her tears. 'Perhaps I shouldn't be burdening you with my problems, but I know David—'

'Shh...it's all right,' Jon started to reassure her, 'and you're not burdening me. I *want* to help.'

'Oh, Jon.' The misty-eyed look she gave him was full of gratitude and trust. 'I don't know what I'd have done if it hadn't been for you. I'm not like Jenny or Olivia. It doesn't matter what happens, they always seem able to cope, but I'm not like them.'

No, she wasn't, Jon acknowledged. He couldn't remember the last time that Jenny had needed him, turned to him, wanted him.... His heart missed a beat.

He hadn't let himself think about their quarrel as he drove over here.

'Am I a nuisance, Jon? I'm sure Jenny...'

'No, of course you aren't.'

Later he wasn't sure how it had happened. One moment he was reaching out automatically and a little awkwardly to pat her reassuringly on the arm; the next Tiggy was in his arms, fragile, fragrant and fatally feminine, clinging to him and crying out her anxiety and fear.

His awareness that she wasn't wearing anything underneath the chiffon affair and that her breasts felt pert and firm came too late for him to do anything about his body's unexpected reaction to her. He could feel the soft warmth of her breasts against his body, the scent of her filling his nostrils. He had an overwhelming urge to...

When Tiggy nervously whispered, 'We mustn't. Olivia might come back,' he suddenly returned to his senses—to reality—his face flooding with hot, guilty colour as he released her and stepped awkwardly back from her, unable to look directly at her as he started to apologise.

'No, it's not your fault,' Tiggy stopped him shakily before bursting out in an anguished voice, 'Oh, Jon, you don't know how much I've needed someone like you. David hasn't... Our marriage...' She stopped and shook her head. 'I shouldn't be talking to you like this. You're his brother...his twin.' She gave him a sad smile. 'But who else can I talk to...confide in...trust?' She lifted her hand to her head.

'My head aches so much I can't think. There are so

many things I ought to do...things that I know that Jenny would be able to do, but I just can't...'

It hurt him that she so constantly felt the need to compare herself unfavourably with Jenny. How well he himself knew that feeling of envy, the sense of shame and self-dislike it brought, the guilt and self-contempt.

'You and Jenny are different people,' he told her gently.

'Yes, I know,' she agreed, giving him a slightly wobbly smile. 'But I can't help thinking that if Jenny had been David's wife, she would have seen what was happening, she would have known...done something... I just know that everyone blames me for his heart attack,' she confessed brokenly.

'No, you mustn't think that,' Jon denied. 'Of course it wasn't your fault. How could it be? Look...I have to go, but don't worry. I'll speak to the bank in the morning.'

There was something else he had to ask...something he had to do. He paused and then took a deep breath.

'Tiggy, I was wondering...the keys to David's desk here, do you...?'

'They're upstairs,' she told him instantly. 'Do you want them? I'll go and get them for you.'

She was so trusting, so guileless, he could taste the sour bile of his guilt.

'If...if you don't mind, there are some papers...some files.'

'I shan't be a moment.'

He closed his eyes as he watched her leave, his forehead beaded with sweat, his heart thumping. He silently prayed to God not to be right, not to let the suspicions that had been gathering round him like dark clouds be confirmed.

Tiggy returned, smiling her innocent triumph, as she gave him David's keys. 'I'm not sure which ones are for his study desk,' she confided, her forehead puckering.

'Don't worry, I'll find them,' Jon reassured her. The telephone had started ringing and he held his breath in relief as she went to answer it.

Feeling like a thief, he hurried into David's study, flicking through the keys Tiggy had handed him until he found the ones for the desk. The drawers were a jumble of unanswered mail and unfiled correspondence all thrown haphazardly on top of one another. He could see the familiar buff edge of the file poking out from underneath a thick, untidy wad of bank statements. His heart started to beat very fast.

He had just removed the file when the study door opened. He froze as he heard Olivia exclaiming, 'Tiggy... Oh, Uncle Jon, it's you.'

'Yes. I was just getting some papers...your mother...'

Olivia frowned as she watched the awkward way he tried to conceal the buff file he had removed from her father's desk amongst some of the papers he had picked up.

'I, er, promised your mother I'll ring the bank in the morning.'

'Won't you need to take Dad's bank statements, then?' Olivia suggested quietly.

'What? Oh yes...' He reached for them almost reluctantly as though he didn't want to touch them, Olivia noticed.

Her instincts warned her that something was wrong. Jon looked pale, ill almost, but then none of them was exactly behaving normally at the moment. Take Saul for instance. She had telephoned him at Queensmead to discover that he wanted her advice.

'Hillary and I have decided to separate,' he had told her tautly. 'She wants to go back to the States. As yet we haven't made any plans to divorce, but I suspect it will only be a matter of time before we do so. I'm going to need a good divorce lawyer, Livvy. I want full custody of the kids. There's no way they're going to be passed between us like parcels and no way do I intend to be an absentee father. You're more up to date with these things than me. Is there someone you can recommend?'

'I'm like you. I work in industry,' Olivia reminded him. 'Wouldn't Max have more idea?'

'Max!' Saul had snorted with derisive contempt. 'The only ideas he's got are how to extract more money out of Ben. Come over if you can, Livvy, please. I need someone to talk to...or are you and Caspar...?'

'Caspar's gone out,' Olivia told him shortly, not wanting to tell him that she and Caspar had quarrelled.

'So you can come over, then?'

'Yes,' she agreed after a small pause, 'I can.'

She had gone into the study thinking her mother was there and intending to tell her that she was going out. She hadn't expected to find Jon there and expected even less to see the almost guilty way he seemed to be furtively going through her father's papers.

Tiggy appeared at the door. 'Did you find what you were looking for?' she asked Jon.

'Yes, yes, I have,' he told her, adding, 'Look, Tiggy, I must go.'

'Yes, I know you must,' she agreed wanly. 'Jenny will be cross with me for keeping you so long, but you will come with me when I go to see David tomorrow, won't you?'

'Yes, of course I will,' Jon assured her gently.

'I'm going to Queensmead to see Saul,' Olivia told her mother, then turned to Jon and asked him quietly, 'What time shall I be at the office in the morning?'

A shadow crossed his face before he reluctantly answered, 'I normally like to be there around eight-thirty.'

'Fine, eight-thirty it is,' Olivia agreed.

'Are you sure you're doing the right thing?' Olivia asked Saul, concern etching her features. He had met her at the door as she arrived and had plainly been waiting for her, shaking his head as she turned towards the house.

'Do you mind if we talk outside? It's easier for me somehow. We could walk down to the river. Remember how much you used to love it as a kid?'

'I can remember how exasperated you got when I disturbed your fishing expeditions.' Olivia laughed. 'Remember the time I fell in...?'

'Can I ever forget it? You terrified the life out of me, and I'm sure your mother thought I'd pushed you in deliberately.'

'I'll bet there were plenty of times when you wanted to,' Olivia teased him.

'The temptation was certainly there,' he agreed wryly, 'and I don't just mean the temptation to give you a ducking....'

'Oh?' Olivia frowned as she looked questioningly at him.

'No,' he returned softly. 'Dunking you wasn't what I had in mind at all the night I caught you skinny-dipping.'

This time, Olivia's 'oh' was low and vibrant with remembered teenage embarrassment. 'It was midsummer night's eve, and I—'

'You were standing there perched on a rock in the middle of the river stark naked, curtsying to the moon,' Saul interrupted her huskily, 'and you looked—'

'A complete idiot,' Olivia supplied ruefully for him. 'No...a complete naked idiot,' she amended, tongue-in-cheek.

'You looked like a young acolyte, a moon maiden, offering herself up in sacrifice, virginal and pure; as innocent as a child and yet as knowledgeable as Eve. I wanted to reach out to you, take hold of you. You had been in the river and I could see the water still running off your skin, your breasts, your belly, your... The moonlight turned your body the colour of moonstones, pale and almost translucent. I wanted to bury my face between your legs and lick the drops of water from your skin. I wanted to join you in your pagan nakedness, your sensual abandonment to the night and the moon, and then you turned your head and saw me and—'

'Fell off my perch and into the river,' Olivia finished for him shakily. She was glad of the concealing darkness around them, not because Saul had evoked the embarrassment her adolescent self had experienced at being so shamingly discovered by her so much older and more sophisticated male relative cavorting around naked in the river, but because of the sensations, the emotions, his words had aroused in her now.

'I never knew you could be so poetic,' she finally managed to say as she struggled to dismiss the surge of heat she could feel invading her body. It would serve no good purpose and only add fuel to embers, which, she suspected, given half a chance, could start to burn very dangerously out of control if she admitted to Saul that if he had done all those years ago any one of the things he had just described, he would have made the magic of the night complete.

Hadn't she, after all, gone down to the river to fulfil an old local tradition that said a girl should offer a prayer to the midsummer night's moon to be granted the love of the man of her choice? And in those days, Saul...well, she had certainly had a mammoth crush on him.

Right now, Saul was feeling very vulnerable, she reminded herself. His marriage had broken down and he had turned to her for support and advice as a close family member...her father's cousin, she reminded herself firmly.

'It was just as well it was you who caught me and not Gramps,' she commented lightly, 'even if I didn't think so at the time, considering the ticking off you gave me.

'Is there no way you and Hillary can give your marriage a second chance?' she asked him, changing the subject as they walked down the path that led through Queensmead's more formal gardens and through the water meadow bordering the river.

'A second chance?' Saul derided cynically. 'Our marriage has had more second chances than I've had hot dinners. No, Meg was the result of our last attempt at a second chance,' he admitted frankly, 'and I wish to God she hadn't been. No child should be conceived as a Band-Aid to fix an ailing marriage.'

'Oh, Saul,' Olivia protested, automatically reaching out to touch his arm sympathetically.

The years that separated them no longer seemed the vast gulf they had appeared to her at fifteen when she had been at the height or rather the depths of her mammoth crush on him. Nor did Saul himself really appear to resemble the Godlike remote creature she had built him up in her mind to be in those days. She rather preferred him as the fallible human being he actually was, she admitted ruefully, and whilst the awe in which she had once held him might have gone, her awareness of his sexuality certainly hadn't.

Quickly she released his arm, causing him to stop and look searchingly at her in the dusky half-light before very firmly taking hold of her hand and gently tucking her arm back through his own.

'Caspar can't object,' he told her, 'if that's what you're worrying about. We are cousins.'

'It wasn't and we're not...cousins,' she clarified. 'Well, not first ones, second maybe...heavens, I'm beginning to sound like Gramps. He always makes such a big thing of the fact that he and your father are half-brothers.'

'Mmm... Well, it's always amazed me to see the different ways he treats your father and Jon. If I were Jon...' He stopped and shook his head.

'What will you do now?' Olivia asked him, changing the subject again. 'What will happen to the children if Hillary does go back to America?'

'If she does? Believe me, there's no "if" about it. This afternoon she was on the phone organising her flight. I've got to go back to work, of course. The parents, or rather Mum, has offered to help out with the kids for the time being but that's only a temporary solution and it means uprooting them, which I don't really want to do. I suppose my best option is to take on a nanny to look after them.'

'Where's Hillary now?' Olivia asked him. They had almost reached the river and she could see it gleaming darkly under the shadows of the clouds that raced across the moon.

'She's got a dinner date, would you believe it? I don't know who with.' He laughed bitterly. 'Trust Hillary. You know it wasn't very far from here that I saw you on that night,' he reminded her.

'I can't remember, was it...?' Olivia replied untruthfully, adding as she turned her back on the river, 'We'd better go back, I—'

'Livvy...'

'Yes.'

She knew what was going to happen, of course. She wasn't fifteen any more and she knew perfectly well what that particular note in a man's voice meant. She could have ignored it. Ignored Saul, but instead...

Instead, she turned back to him and he stepped towards her, lifting his hands to touch and then cup her face, stroking her skin with those long, lean fingers, learning its contours with delicate and very deliberate sensuality.

'Saul!' She reached to catch at his hands and remove them from her face but it was too late to avoid the downward movement of his head, the warm male pressure of his mouth, his kiss.

She ended it as quickly as she could, willing her own lips not to give in to the temptation to respond; stepping back from him quickly and determinedly and starting to walk back down the path they had just come without waiting for him.

'Livvy, I'm sorry,' he apologised as he caught up with her. 'I shouldn't have done that.'

'No, you shouldn't,' she agreed lightly.

'Still friends?' he asked her.

'Still *friends*,' she repeated, emphasising the second word meaningfully.

Saul laughed as he caught hold of her hand, dropping it again as she tugged it away from him.

'All right, all right, I get the message,' he assured her, adding ruefully, 'Caspar's a lucky man, although I get the impression that he wasn't too pleased when you offered to stay on here to help Jon.'

'Did *he* tell you that?' Olivia asked sharply.

'Not in so many words.'

'It won't be for very long. Just a few weeks until Dad gets back on his feet.' Not even to Saul could she admit that it wasn't just because of her father that she felt compelled to stay. There was her mother, as well. So far there had been no repeat of the ugly scene Olivia had walked in on. But her mother was so frighteningly vulnerable; look at the way she was clinging to Uncle Jon. She needed someone to be there for her.

But Olivia knew that there was no point in trying to tell Caspar how she felt. He had made his views on her mother's condition quite plain enough.

'You wanted to see me, Grandfather?' Max paused edgily just inside Ben's study door.

He had just been on the point of leaving for Chester, ostensibly on a self-imposed mission to update the Chester side of the family with the latest news on David's progress, but in reality, he had planned, after discharging this duty, to spend the rest of the evening indulging in a little R and R away from the claustrophobic atmosphere of Haslewich. He knew of a club where the membership rules were pretty elastic, provided you could afford to break them, and the girls... Then when his mother had informed him that his grandfather wanted to see him, he had been tempted to put off answering Ben's summons until the morning, but he knew quite well that his mother would refuse to lie for him.

Just what the hell did the old man want? Had that interfering American boyfriend of Olivia's been dropping hints to him about the chambers vacancy? Max could feel himself starting to sweat slightly. By rights he ought to be back in London finding out who his female competitor was and doing all he could to sabotage her chances of getting what was rightfully his, but until they had had some concrete news about David's condition, he hadn't dared to leave. He knew exactly how Ben would view his departure if he did.

He had never seen the old man so off balance. Mentally Max rehearsed his defence. His grandfather was bound to share his view that it was unfair that his right to the tenancy was being challenged—*threatened* by a woman. Ben's views on women entering the legal profession were, after all, no secret. It had amused Max to watch Olivia trying to worm herself into Ben's good graces earlier. Much good it had done her. It was obvious that neither Ben nor Jon wanted her around.

Luckily the fact that *he* had trained as a barrister and not a solicitor meant that there was no point in his offering to make a similar sacrifice, which was just as well because he had no intention of doing so. The thought of ending up like David, trapped in Haslewich, brought him out in a cold sweat.

Ben had some papers in front of him on his desk and Max's heart started to thump heavily as Ben beckoned him closer and he realised what they were.

'I've been going through my will,' Ben told him heavily. 'At my age it's a necessary precaution, although...'

He paused and looked from Max to the fire whilst Max tried not to betray his impatience. What the hell did the old man want? Had Caspar spilled the beans or not?

'As things stand, David, as my eldest son, will inherit Queensmead and the bulk of my personal assets,' Ben began solemnly. 'I have, of course, left certain personal bequests—your allowance is one of them. At least until...'

Max gritted his teeth. He knew all this, they all did, so what was the point in the old boy's going over it again now? Was he going senile or something? Had David's heart attack affected his brain?

'However, your uncle's heart attack changes everything.' Ben spoke slowly, reluctantly, almost as though the words were physically painful to him. 'I can't ignore the fact that David might not...'

He stopped and Max watched dispassionately as Ben tried to control the way his hand shook as he picked up his will. The old man was getting frail. How old exactly was he?

Max was beginning to relax now that he knew Ben hadn't sent for him because he had found out about the potential problems with his tenancy in chambers. His stance eased, becoming indolently nonchalant as he leaned against the wall, his hands in his pockets.

'I can't ignore the fact that David could die before me. In the normal course of events, Queensmead would pass to Jack, but the boy is only ten and his mother...well, in my opinion, women and property don't mix. They never have. It would only take some smooth-talking scoundrel to come along and Queensmead could pass out of the family for ever. I can't take the risk of that happening.'

'David isn't dead yet, Grandfather,' Max pointed out.

'No,' Ben agreed. His eyes suddenly filled with tears as he cried out in a muffled voice, 'My God, what *is* it about this family? Why must we lose those...have the best taken from us...? When my father died, I made him a promise that one of my sons would be called to the Bar and fulfil the ambition that was denied to him.'

Max impatiently shifted his weight from one foot to the other. He knew all about Ben's promise to his father; he had heard the story more times than he cared to remember. The old man really must be going senile to start repeating it all over again.

'David should have made good that promise for me. His circumstances changed and he couldn't, but you can. I intend to change my will,' he told Max abruptly, 'and leave Queensmead and the bulk of my estate to you, on condition that you are a fully practising barrister at the time of my death.'

Max had difficulty in controlling his shock—and his elation. My God, and to think when he had come in here he had expected... Hastily he pulled himself together. Ben might be suffering from the shock of David's heart attack at this point, but he was still an extremely shrewd old man; it wouldn't do for him to guess what was going through his own mind right now, especially his plans for Queensmead once it actually became his.

His grandfather might view the house and its land as some kind of sacred cow, but he most certainly did not. Haslewich was growing and one day Queensmead's farmland could be a prime development site.

My God. Max could feel the elation singing through his veins. It would make him millions. Forget any paltry potential barrister's fees. Abruptly he checked himself. Queensmead could be his but first he had to fulfil that one vital condition. He knew his grandfather well enough to know that it would be there, written into the will in an unbreakable clause that could not be got round or overset. He was starting to sweat again.

If securing the tenancy had been important to him before, it was nothing to what it meant to him now. That girl...that female, whoever she was, would have to be removed from the picture and he didn't care

what means he used to make sure she was. He had to
have that tenancy; he couldn't afford to waste any
more time. David could have a second fatal heart attack tomorrow. His grandfather could die just as easily.

Swiftly he lowered his head, not wanting Ben to see
his expression just in case it betrayed him. 'That's very
generous of you, Grandfather,' he said quietly, forcing
a solemn expression into his eyes as he lifted his head
and looked squarely at him, 'and I promise you that
I'll do my best to live up to the...trust you're placing in
me.'

'You're a good lad, Max,' Ben told him emotionally.
'Another David.'

Oh no, he would never be another David, Max determined, exulting as he listened to his grandfather
outlining exactly what he planned to do. He would
never let himself get trapped the way David had done,
his whole future destroyed.

'Right now I'd give anything to be able to trade
places with Olivia and stay on here...be on hand...' he
told Ben untruthfully, 'but I don't have that choice,
that freedom.' Cleverly he managed to imply that in
having it, Olivia was somehow less dedicated to her
career than he was himself, that she was somehow
slightly feckless and irresponsible in not having the
commitment of a job to return to.

It was a skill of his and one he had honed to perfec-
tion over the years, using it ruthlessly whenever he
felt the need—and sometimes, if he was honest, just
because of the pleasure it gave him to do so—as he did
now. He had never really liked Olivia. Miss Goody-

goody. Well, if she thought that she was going to impress the old man with what she was doing...

'I have to go back to London.' Too right he did and the sooner the better. The sooner he found out just who this woman competing with him for the tenancy was, the better. 'Queensmead will be safe with me, Grandfather,' he lied as he clasped the older man's hand. 'I can promise you that.'

10

Olivia didn't drive straight home after she left Saul; instead she drove into Haslewich and parked her car on one of the empty, narrow side-streets just off the main square, unwilling to admit, even to herself, just why she felt so reluctant to return home.

She wanted to see Caspar, wanted to talk to him...*needed* to talk to him but not just yet, not whilst she was still feeling so...so what? she asked herself as she locked her car and started to walk towards the town square, tucking her hands firmly into the pockets of her coat as she did so.

It seemed strange to be walking through her home town at this time of the evening without any real purpose, rather like a tourist instead of an inhabitant, but had she been a tourist she would have surely had Caspar with her, her arm tucked through his, his dry, witty sense of humour making her laugh as it had done so many, many times in the past.

In the past? But she and Caspar *weren't* in the past...were they? Her heart started to beat a little bit too fast, her walking pace increasing. It would be easy to put her own sombre, reflective mood down to Saul's revelations about his marriage but she knew that wouldn't be entirely honest.

Her doubts, her feeling that she and Caspar were

not, after all, as harmoniously in step with one another as she had so naïvely believed, had not been brought on by the realisation that Saul's marriage was in difficulty.

She paused, her attention caught by the floodlit façade of the church, its Norman tower standing stoutly square. As she absent-mindedly studied the familiar sight, Olivia couldn't help contrasting the staunchness of the faith of those long-ago builders not only in their God, but also in themselves and humanity, with the present-day malaise of world-weariness and cynical disaffection.

It was indeed a truly awe-inspiring thought that in an age where merely to reach adulthood was an achievement, and to live much beyond one's thirtieth year almost a miracle, that men, *people*, should have committed themselves to the construction of a building that would take not only their own lifetime to complete but the lifetime of their sons and grandsons after them, as well.

Instinctively she shifted her gaze away from the church towards the row of Georgian houses where Ruth lived. As a young girl she had been puzzled by the fact that Aunt Ruth lived alone, that there was no uncle, no children; and later as a teenager she had been initially surprised and then had a vague sense of amusement and a slightly patronising superiority at the dullness of the life Aunt Ruth had chosen for herself compared with the wide horizons that were going to be hers.

Oddly she had never felt curious about Ruth's life, or her past, simply taking it for granted that she should accept worthy spinsterhood following the death of her fiancé.

Her forehead puckered as she studied the windows of Aunt Ruth's house. Where did this American, whom Caspar claimed her great-aunt had been involved with, fit into the picture and why had she never heard about him? Head down, deep in thought, she continued walking into the square when a group of noisy teenagers, laughing and tormenting one another, erupted into the square several yards away from her. A couple of them, she suspected from their coal-black hair and familiar features, were members of the semi-notorious Cooke family. One of them saw her watching them and paused to return her scrutiny with a bold-eyed, challenging sexual stare. Olivia grimaced as she looked away. He must be all of fourteen.

She walked on until she reached the building that housed the practice's offices. They were a world away from the modern hi-tech building where she had worked in London and from the life she would have shared in America with Caspar.

Would have shared. Would still share, she corrected herself quickly. Caspar meant so much to her. She couldn't bear to lose him and there was, in truth, no real reason for her to lose him, she reassured herself, quickening her pace as she hurried back to her car, suddenly, desperately, anxious to see Caspar, to be with him.

Yes, maybe they did hold opposing views of what was happening here in Haslewich. They were, after all, both strong-minded, intelligent people who couldn't always be expected to see completely eye to eye on everything. Indeed, sometimes they were bound to think and feel very differently, and the more important the issue, the more intense those differences were likely to be, but that didn't mean that they couldn't be resolved, that a compromise couldn't be reached. She could quite simply follow Caspar to Philadelphia rather than arrive there with him, and in that time she could stay here and help Uncle Jon whilst Caspar picked up the threads of his life in America. It would only be for a few weeks. They could keep in touch via the telephone, even if they couldn't...

Her hands were trembling slightly as she unlocked her car door.

There was a light on in her bedroom as Olivia drove up in front of the house and parked her car. Unlocking the front door, she took the stairs two at a time, aching, anxious to be with Caspar; to tell him what she had been thinking. She pushed open the bedroom door and then came to a full stop.

Caspar obviously hadn't realised she was already in the house. He was standing with his back to her, peering out of the window; his skin still had a damp sheen to it from his recent shower, minute droplets of moisture still edging their way down his spine and gathering in the small hollow at its base.

Olivia's mouth had gone very dry, her legs felt wobbly and her heart was thudding with so much excitement that it might have been the very first time she had seen him naked, she thought, and fighting down her urge to go up to him and wrap her arms tightly around him, she said his name instead, knowing even before he turned around that the moment he saw her face he would know exactly how she was feeling.

She had never been any good at concealing from him just how much she wanted him, she acknowledged ruefully, as he responded to the soft sound of her voice saying his name.

'Oh, Caspar,' she whispered shakily, ignoring his stiff-armed attempt to hold her away from his wet body as she gave in to the temptation to be close to him and wrapped her arms tightly around him. 'What are we doing to one another? Why are we arguing...quarrelling when...'

'When what?' Caspar demanded gruffly.

She could feel the pressure of his hands gripping her upper arms but she was past worrying about what effect his wet skin might have on her clothes now, her only regret being the fact that they had become an unwanted barrier between them.

'When we could be doing this,' she told him huskily, lifting her face towards his and sliding one hand behind his head to guide his mouth down towards hers.

For a moment he seemed to hesitate, looking deeply and searchingly into her eyes whilst she looked back at him, her pupils already dilated, her eyes cloudy with longing. Her whole body, her whole being was awash with a soft flood of aching tenderness from the full force of her new-found knowledge that what they felt for one another, what they had together, was far too important, too strong...too vital, to be threatened by any quarrel.

Together they would find a way to reach a happy compromise.

His mouth felt unfamiliarly immobile, cool and slightly dry, almost unresponsive, but even as she started to frown and draw back from him, Caspar reached for her, taking control of the kiss, taking control of her, she realised as his mouth moved firmly on hers, his hands cupping her face, his body...

Eagerly Olivia moved closer to him.

'You're wearing too many clothes,' Caspar told her rawly between kisses.

'Mmm...I know,' Olivia agreed, but her need to feel his mouth moving against hers, to hold on to their closeness and intimacy made her reluctant to stop kissing him, even for long enough to get undressed, and in the end, what had in recent times become a mundane chore relegated to the end of the day when both of them prepared for bed became instead a deliciously agonizing, passion-building and wickedly sensual extravagance of snatched kisses and caresses interspersed with fumbling fingers and hasty tugs as they both struggled to remove the damp clothes that obstinately clung to her body and cast them aside to lie unregarded on the floor before they finally collapsed onto her bed in a tangle of trembling but blissfully naked limbs.

'Mmm...you feel so good, taste so good,' Olivia marvelled in an ecstatic sigh as she licked her way as delicately as a small cat across Caspar's torso.

'Feeling good isn't how I'd describe it,' Caspar groaned as her tongue stroked tantalisingly below his ribcage and then drew a sinfully erotic circle around his navel. 'In fact, right now, what you're doing to me feels like...it feels like...oooh,' he groaned through gritted teeth as her tongue dipped lower.

Olivia tried to tease him mockingly by demanding huskily, 'Go on, what does it feel like?' although in reality she was just as aroused by their love play as he was.

Turning the tables on her, he caught her off guard, picking her up and rolling her easily beneath him as he countered trenchantly, 'Why don't I just give you a demonstration, see how you like that kind of torture?'

Only torture wasn't the word she would ever use to describe the sensual movement of Caspar's mouth against her body as he lovingly caressed every feminine responsive centimetre of her skin.

'Caspar, no more,' she whispered. 'I can't wait any longer. I want you. I want you inside me…deep, deep inside me…now.'

Olivia could feel her whole body shudder as Caspar complied with her sensual demand.

Right from the very first time, the sex between them had been so good, so right…. She had felt incredibly good about being so intimate with him, about being so open with him. It wasn't only the love but, in many ways just as importantly, the trust she had in him that gave her a sense of security, a sense of being protected and safe that made it possible for her to be completely at ease with him sexually and emotionally, to be open with him about her needs as a woman and to be equally responsive to his needs as a man and it was this openness between them, this honesty, that for Olivia made their relationship so special and why she hated the way things had been between them over the past few days.

The sense of closeness, of wholeness, of oneness she felt now in the aftermath of their passionately intense physical lovemaking had brought gentle, vulnerable tears to her eyes, and as she lay in his arms, a feeling of such love and happiness welled up inside her that she wanted desperately to somehow convey to Caspar just how much their love, their relationship meant to her. There was always, she knew, a sentence, a verbal commitment to him that whilst meaningless to others, would show Caspar just how much he did mean to her.

She reached out to trace the shape of his jaw, his mouth, with her fingertips and told him softly, 'Caspar...I do love you....'

For a moment he looked startled...shocked almost, and then he was hugging her, holding her so tightly that she had to protest laughingly that she could hardly breathe.

'At last...at last,' she heard him saying exultantly. 'Say it again Livvy. Tell me again....'

'Say what?' she teased and then happily complied with his demand, whispering the words first against his ear and then against his mouth. When she felt his lips moving against hers as he said the words back to her, the desire she had thought completely satiated started to burn again as they kissed and touched and then kissed and touched some more.

'Mmm...that was wonderful,' Olivia sighed blissfully as she snuggled up against Caspar.

'That!' complained Caspar mock-indignantly.

'Very well, then *you* were wonderful,' Olivia confided sleepily. 'I'm so glad we're not fighting any more,' she added sombrely. 'I saw Saul earlier. He seems to think that his and Hillary's marriage is virtually over.'

'Yes, I know,' Caspar said, stifling a yawn.

'You know?' Olivia demanded, suddenly alert as she leaned up on her elbow and frowned down at him. 'How do you know?'

Something about the way he hesitated before replying and then looked away from her made her clench her stomach muscles and watch him warily.

'I, er, Hillary told me when we had dinner together this evening....'

'You had dinner with Hillary! You invited another woman out to dinner without telling me?' Olivia demanded, spacing the words out carefully, all her earlier pleasure draining away as she stared at Caspar in shock. 'Why didn't you tell me? Why?'

'It was a spur-of-the-moment thing,' Caspar answered angrily. 'For God's sake, Livvy,' he expostulated, pushing his fingers irritably into his hair, 'it's past two in the morning, and right now the last thing I feel like doing is being cross-examined as if I'm guilty of a major crime. You just said yourself how much you hate it when we fight and yet here you are—'

'I'm not fighting,' Olivia interrupted him tersely.

'No? Then you're sure as hell giving a fair imitation of it,' Caspar retorted grumpily.

'Caspar, we're lovers, we've planned a future together. I wouldn't go out and have dinner with another man and then not tell you about it.'

'No, but you're quite happy to change all our plans and have me looking a fool while you announce that you're staying here and playing the dutiful daughter and niece, that it's far, far more important to you than being with me, even though it's been made plain to you that your sacrifice isn't either necessary or wanted,' Caspar came back with angry ferocity.

Olivia sat upright in bed and stared at him through the darkness.

'Caspar, I explained about that,' she protested. 'It will only be for a few weeks...I thought you understood...and tonight...' She paused and bit her lip before continuing. 'Tonight, when I told you I love you...I thought—'

'You thought what?' he interrupted her savagely. 'You thought because you'd made the big sacrifice of finally committing yourself verbally to me that that made everything okay. That I'm dumb enough, besotted enough, to go away and wait patiently until you're ready. Was that what tonight was all about, Livvy?' he demanded bitterly. 'Was that what all the passion...all the hunger, all the sex was for, to keep me quiet? Well, I've got news for you...it didn't work.'

'Caspar,' Olivia protested, but he had already turned his back on her, hunching his body as close to the edge of the bed as he could.

Well, let him sulk if he wants to, Olivia decided wrathfully. She wasn't the one who had spoiled things between them. Not this time. No, Caspar had done that all by himself. Why hadn't he told her that he'd had dinner with Hillary? And even worse, would he ever have told her if she hadn't just happened to stumble on the truth?

Had tonight's seemingly passionate and intense lovemaking simply been a ploy on his part to make her come to heel...to make her commit herself to him verbally, to give him the words of love he wanted just so that he could use them against her in the kind of emotional power struggle she had so foolishly believed their love meant too much to either of them for them to enter into? And if she had been wrong about that, how much else had she been wrong about, as well? Did Caspar really love her at all? Quietly she, too, lay down, her own back firmly turned to him.

'Olivia, have you got a minute?'

Uncertainly Olivia looked across the kitchen at Caspar. She had woken early in anticipation of going into the office but Caspar wasn't there beside her. Even as early as it was, he must have dressed and gone downstairs ahead of her, thus depriving her of any opportunity of talking privately with him in the comforting intimacy of her bedroom.

'I've decided to go ahead and call the airline this morning,' he told her tersely.

An ominous sense of foreboding gripped Olivia. 'Call the airline if you like, but I'd hoped we weren't going to do that until we went back to London.'

'We weren't,' Caspar agreed, emphasising the 'we' before adding grimly, 'But then we weren't planning to spend more than a few days here saying goodbye to your folks.'

Olivia stared at him in dismay. 'But, Caspar, that was before my father had his heart attack. Can't...?' She dug her teeth into her bottom lip, willing herself to stay calm whilst she begged, 'Caspar, please don't do this to me...to us... Caspar...' Her voice shook so much she had to stop speaking.

'Livvy...look, it isn't too late,' Caspar told her urgently, crossing the space between them and grasping her hands. 'Tell your uncle you've changed your mind...that you can't stay. I'll get us seats on the first available flight and we—'

'No...no, you know I can't do that,' Olivia protested, drawing her hands free of Caspar's grasp. 'Caspar, why won't you understand?' she pleaded, pressing her hands to her aching head. 'I have to stay.'

'No, you don't,' Caspar countered brutally. 'You want to stay. You, Olivia, and no one else. Your uncle doesn't want you here and neither does your grandfather. You want to stay because—'

'Because it's the right thing for me to do. My father—'

'The right thing?' Caspar laughed bitterly. 'You already know my views on that subject,' he told her angrily.

'I've never seen you like this before,' Olivia protested, her teeth starting to chatter, even though she wasn't particularly cold. As a child she had never liked 'scenes' or 'quarrels'. One of the things she had liked most about Caspar had been his calmness, his logical approach to things, his ability to bypass the kind of emotional response and overreaction to life's hazards that had been such a familiar part of her childhood.

'What you are trying to say,' Caspar challenged her, 'is that you've made a mistake...committed yourself to the wrong guy. Well, I guess that feeling goes both ways. Maybe I'm not too thrilled to discover that you aren't exactly the woman I thought you were, either,' he told her hurtfully.

Olivia stared at him, unable to fully take in what he was saying. 'Caspar,' she protested, but as she took a step towards him, he stepped back from her, leaving her standing frozen in disbelief in mid-step as she read the rejection in his body language.

'Perhaps it's for the best that we both found out the truth before we got in any deeper.'

The truth. What truth? She *loved* him...*he* loved her...wasn't that all that really mattered? *Was* it? If she turned round now and told him that she had changed her mind, that she would break her promise to her uncle and return to America with him, was that really the kind of basis she wanted to build her future, *their* future on? Wouldn't she in effect be setting a precedent that meant that every time she had to make a decision he didn't share, that ultimately he would expect her to give in and back down? No matter how small the issue or how large. As a lawyer she knew very well and better than most the danger of setting any kind of precedent. She swallowed painfully.

She had never imagined that Caspar, *her* Caspar, could be capable of such small-mindedness, such self-ishness...that he could quite willingly sacrifice their love. The knowledge physically hurt her and all at once she knew what people meant when they said something felt like a blow to the heart, a heavy weight...a sickening burden. She felt all of those things and more, but at least she had her pride to sustain her, the same pride that had carried her through all the rigours of her legal training without the support and encouragement of her family. She had survived that and she would survive this. Somehow...

'If that's what you think,' she agreed quietly, keeping her voice as low as she could so that it wouldn't betray her by breaking.

Without waiting for him to make any further response, she walked past him and hurried upstairs. Even though she fumbled for several seconds with the door, he made no effort to catch up with her; to take her in his arms and tell her that he had been wrong; that he couldn't bear for them to be apart; that he still loved and wanted her.

Perhaps it *had* all been a mistake, she admitted. Perhaps she had mistaken something far more shallow and ephemeral for love. After all, love—real love, enduring love, the kind of love she believed *they* shared—surely couldn't be destroyed so easily.

Caspar watched her walk away from him, her back ramrod straight. He ached to call her back but his pride wouldn't let him. Listening to Hillary last night as she detailed all her complaints against not just Saul but also his family had underlined for Caspar all the doubts he had felt about the viability of his relationship with Olivia ever since their arrival here in her home town—and if he was honest with himself, reawakened the destructive ghosts of his own childhood.

Here was Olivia telling him he wasn't important enough to merit her concern, that there was no way she was going to put him first.

To Caspar the obvious emotional closeness that bonded the various members of Olivia's family together in an acceptance of one another's flaws and faults in a way that was totally alien to the way his own family network worked was something he instinctively rejected, even found threatening, not just to his relationship with Olivia, but to his deeply held belief that such closeness was at best a self-deluding fiction and at worst a means of control leading to the potential destruction of the individual.

As a child he had seen at close hand how apparently easily the adults around him discarded one relationship to enter into another. From that he had come to believe that human emotions could only be stretched so far, that an individual could only encompass one really meaningful emotional tie at a time. He had seen his father, and his mother, too, form intensely close bonds with their current partners, giving all their emotional support to that partner and the children of that union. Growing up, he had been on the outside of that closeness, excluded from it; as an adult he had no intention of suffering the same fate.

It wasn't that he was jealous of Olivia's involvement with her family; it was simply that he could not see the point in wasting his emotions on a relationship with someone who apparently wasn't prepared to commit herself as fully as he was to it.

Although in returning to America he was returning to his home town and family, the life Caspar had envisaged there for Olivia and himself had involved just the two of them and any children they should have. They would socialise with his family, no doubt, but they would have separate lives and they would not have been allowed to trespass emotionally into Caspar and Olivia's private life. Just as he had never been allowed to trespass into his parents?

Yesterday when discussing her husband and his family, Hillary had complained that she had never truly felt a part of their lives; that she had always been made to feel different—an outsider. That no allowance had ever been made for the fact that she might have different needs, different desires, different goals from theirs.

'Saul should have married an English girl, preferably one from Cheshire and even more preferably, one from his own family,' she had told Caspar bitterly, adding sardonically, 'Olivia would have been perfect for him, of course.'

Of course. And Caspar had not been oblivious to the look of sensual appreciation and sexual awareness in Saul's eyes as he watched Olivia.

He went up the stairs and walked past Olivia's room without stopping.

Inside her room, Olivia released her breath. Let Caspar behave like a spoiled child if that was what he wanted. *He* hadn't made *any* effort to understand her feelings, so why on earth should she kowtow to his?

Jenny tensed as Jon turned over in his sleep and muttered something. She had always been a light sleeper and his restlessness had woken her up. She glanced at her alarm; it would soon be time to get up anyway.

Why had he thrown those bitter comments about Max at her before he went out yesterday evening? Neither of them had ever discussed the deep vein of selfishness and self-interest that ran through Max's character, setting him so much apart from both of them, but most especially from Jon. Perhaps that was one of the biggest flaws in their relationship—the fact that they did not discuss such things but tended to ignore them. They were both placid, natural peacekeepers preferring harmony to discord, although Jon, she knew, would never shrink from standing up for some moral code he felt was being broken—no matter what the cost of doing so might be to himself.

Jenny not only realised how much stress David's heart attack had placed Jon under, but she'd also seen how much stress he'd been under before it happened. Did he really think she wasn't aware of the increased amount of time he was having to spend at work—and couldn't guess the reason for it? If she had said nothing, it was merely because she knew the futility of embarking on a discussion that might lead to any criticism of David, however slight. And now it seemed that Jon had taken on the role of providing Tiggy with emotional support as well as everything else.

Tiggy. Jenny could still remember quite vividly how wretchedly insignificant and unattractive she had felt beside her the first time they had met. Tiggy had been so glowingly beautiful, the soul of life and enthusiasm, clinging adoringly to David's arm.

In comparison she had felt lumpish and plain, boringly unsophisticated, a woman who knew nothing of the heady excitement of the life Tiggy and David had lived in London and that Tiggy so obviously still missed.

Even pregnant, Tiggy had possessed that air of fragility and delicacy. She had been dreadfully sick almost throughout her pregnancy and it had been touch-and-go at one stage whether or not she would have to be hospitalised. All of them had been surprised when Olivia had proved to be such a strong, healthy baby. The hospital staff had fussed more over Tiggy than Olivia, Jenny remembered, just as Jon was fussing over her now.

Oh really. She threw back the bedclothes and

swung her feet out of bed. Surely she wasn't silly enough to be jealous. Poor Jon had enough to cope with as it was. It would soon be dawn and she was too wide awake to sleep now, and besides, it wasn't just Jon who was on her mind.

Max had left for London shortly after his return from his visit to his grandfather yesterday in a mood that Jenny could only describe as unusually euphoric. There had been an air of hostility and excitement about him, a look of secrecy and triumph that had left her feeling edgily suspicious.

It had been so out of character, so unlike him. Max liked to portray himself as someone who was rather hard-done-by, someone to whom life had been slightly unfair. He enjoyed putting others at a disadvantage by making them feel they had misjudged him. He enjoyed manipulating people, Jenny recognised honestly as she padded downstairs to the kitchen.

It was a Crighton family trait, of course, laughably and roguishly charming in Joss, but in Max it had somehow manifested itself as something sour and spiteful, even destructive.

As expected, he hadn't told her why Ben had wanted to see him and she hadn't asked him. They didn't have that kind of relationship. Probably her fault for clouding his birth with her sadness over the earlier birth of the son who had not survived. Who could tell what thoughts, what emotions, the child in the womb absorbed from its mother? And yet he had been a dearly wanted child.

Lost in her thoughts, she started to fill the kettle.

In London Max, too, was awake early, his mind buzzing with plans. He had one hell of a lot to do and time might not be on his side.

As he showered in the bathroom of his fashionable flat, he was quickly sorting through various plans he had made the previous evening on his drive back to London for discovering the identity of his rival and discarding those that were either too time-consuming or too impractical. He had taken the flat on ready-furnished—it had originally belonged to a city whiz-kid who had fallen flat on his face in a currency-market débâcle. Fortunately the bank had discovered the misdemeanour in time, the whiz-kid was fired and his assets disposed of quickly and unceremoniously by his ex-employers.

Max had been lucky enough to hear about the flat on the grapevine and bought out the remaining lease for next to nothing, promising to keep his mouth closed about whatever he knew concerning the potential disaster.

As he shaved, he studied his reflection dispassion-ately. He had his grandfather's patrician nose and his father's and uncle's height and breadth of shoulder. His hair was dark—not quite black but almost, his eyes an unusual, clear pale grey. He was, in short, damned good-looking. He grinned at himself, reveal-ing even, strong white teeth, then frowned as he re-turned to contemplating the problem of discovering his competitor's identity.

It was pointless even thinking about pumping the chambers clerk who loathed him. Most of the other members didn't like him much more. Max had never seen the point in wasting his time being pleasant to someone unless he felt they could be of use to him, and besides, it was always easier, in Max's view, to get a woman on his side than a man, which, of course, had potential side benefits, many of which he had investigated over the years.

The only women who worked in chambers were secretaries, two of whom were old enough to be his grandmother and possessed the kind of battleaxe temperament that rendered them totally unsusceptible to Max's particular brand of charm. He mentally ran through what he knew about the other three.

No point in even trying to worm anything out of Laura, the clerk's secretary-cum-assistant. She had a mammoth crush on a senior partner and would doubtless go running to him to tell him the moment Max tried to pump her for information. That left the other two: Wendy, the placid, anaemic-looking little blonde with buck teeth and bad breath, and Charlotte, the sultry-looking brunette who had already made it clear to him that he could be a serious contender for her affections, or rather for her determined ambition to become the wife of a barrister, and Max did not intend to make the mistake of misjudging either her determination or her ability to achieve her ambition. She was certainly socially ambitious enough to make a good wife for a barrister, but when *he* eventually married, Max had his own plans *and* his own ambitions.

There were barristers and barristers and he knew which camp he wished to be in and a helping hand in the right direction from an influential in-law would certainly not go amiss and neither would a wife with the kind of family money to enable them to mix in the right sort of social circles. But he was not ready for marriage yet, not by a long shot.

These plans had, of course, been laid before he learned that his grandfather had decided to change his will, but there was no harm in doubly securing the future. And there were still plenty of wealthy families with daughters who found considerable appeal in the prospect of a son-in-law who, if he made it to the higher echelons of the legal profession and became a High Court judge, could ultimately be granted a title.

Max, who knew the story of his family history in what to him was excruciatingly boring detail, had often reflected that, in the original Josiah's shoes, he would have given in to family pressure and allowed them to dictate his choice of wife.

Finished in the bathroom, Max didn't waste time going into the kitchen. He never bothered eating breakfast. His cupboards rarely contained any food. He either ate out or bought himself something microwaveable. So far, his lifestyle and eating habits had had no discernible effect on his physique.

As he pulled on his suit jacket, he glanced at his watch. He had never seen the point of arriving virtuously early for work when there was no one there to log such virtue, but this morning he had his own reasons for wanting to get there ahead of time.

Had he felt he could get away with it, he would have had no compunction whatsoever about going through the clerk's confidential files himself, but in order to do so he would have had to 'borrow' his keys, a task that taxed even his skills.

No. It would have to be Charlotte.

He grimaced slightly as he caught the smell of the new cologne he had used with deliberate generosity.

It had been a gift from his last girlfriend. Charlotte, he suspected, would like it.

It must be something to do with the fact that she was having to stand in the street outside the office waiting for Uncle Jon to arrive that reduced her to the state of a nervous schoolgirl, Olivia decided as she glanced at her watch and then up at the church clock just to check that she had the right time.

She had seen Caspar briefly again before leaving this morning. His manner towards her had been withdrawn and wintry. He had simply told her the time of his flight to London, from where he would eventually return to the States, dashing her hopes that he might have had a change of heart. She wished they could reach a compromise that would allow their relationship to continue. One look at Caspar's face, though, had warned her of the futility of such an exercise. Caspar didn't *want* to compromise.

And so she had left the house without saying any of the things she had so desperately wanted to say and half an hour earlier than she had planned, which was why she had been pacing the pavement outside the offices for so long. She expelled a small sigh of relief as she suddenly saw Jon emerge from one of the myriad side-streets off the square. It was just gone twenty-five past eight.

'Olivia.'

He didn't smile as he greeted her. He looked as though he hadn't slept, Olivia noticed. Her father's illness had aged him slightly, giving his features a gauntness that made him appear rather intimidatingly austere.

As Olivia waited for Jon to unlock the door, she wondered how Saul was feeling this morning. Was it some kind of omen, some secret twist of fate, that both of them should be experiencing relationship difficulties at the same time?

The shop over which Josiah Crighton had first started his practice had long since disappeared; the family now owned the whole building. But at Ben's insistence the offices were still on the first floor as they had been in Josiah's day, the downstairs rooms now having been converted into a reception and waiting area.

As she followed Jon up the narrow, creaky stairs, Olivia remembered nostalgically how exciting she had found it as a child to come here and how fascinated she had been by the rows of old-fashioned, heavily bound law books that filled the shelves of the small gallery at the top of the stairs.

Of the two rooms, her father's office had always been the larger and Olivia paused a little uncomfortably outside its door, then turned to Jon. 'If you would prefer Dad's office...?' she suggested.

Jon shook his head. 'No, it's all right. As a matter of fact I prefer my own,' he told her as she continued to hesitate. 'It's quiet and it gets more light.'

A little uncertainly Olivia opened the door to her father's office. She frowned as she surveyed the interior; it looked much larger than she remembered. Then she realised that the heavy bank of metal filing cabinets that ran along one wall had gone.

'Where...?' she began, staring at the empty space.

'We moved them into my room,' Jon explained calmly to her but Olivia could sense that for some reason her question had discomforted him. 'We're in the process of putting everything onto computer and since I was the one who attended the induction course, David thought I might as well deal with that side of things.'

A simple enough explanation but Olivia felt oddly uneasy. Something, she didn't quite know what, didn't ring fully true about it.

'It will take me a few days to get into the routine,' she told Jon. 'I'll have to familiarise myself with Dad's cases and clients, of course, read up the files. I know you deal with most of the conveyancing side of things while Dad handled all the family trusts and wills.'

'Broadly speaking, yes,' Jon agreed, but he wasn't looking at her, Olivia noticed, and once again she was aware of an odd tension in his voice that she suspected wasn't purely because he hadn't wanted to accept her offer of help.

She must not be too sensitive, Olivia warned herself. She was here to help not cause more problems.

'Well, I'm here to do whatever I can,' she said, smiling. 'I'll need a list of Dad's clients and—'

'Er, I'm afraid we didn't do things quite so formally,' Jon interrupted her. 'It wasn't really necessary and then we often found we were overlapping interests.'

Olivia frowned. That wasn't how she had understood the practice was run. She had always been under the impression that the two brothers clearly divided their workload and their fields of operation.

'Well, if you would give me some keys to Dad's desk, I'll go through his diary,' Olivia suggested.

It was several seconds before Jon produced her father's keys and Olivia had the distinct feeling that he didn't really want to give them to her. Heavy-hearted she went into the office and firmly closed the door behind her.

Tiny motes of dust danced in the sunshine streaming in through the room's windows. Olivia went to open one of them to let in some fresh air. The room smelled of lavender polish and old wood.

Her uncle had mentioned switching from their traditional filing system to computers, but to judge from the way the screen and keyboard had been pushed to one corner of her father's desk virtually out of reach, she doubted that he had ever made much use of it.

Beneath the window the town was stirring sleepily into life, shops starting to open, one or two people walking through the square.

Determinedly Olivia turned her back on the window and walked over to her father's desk. It was over a hundred years old, a heavy mahogany partner's desk with a faded leather top. Her grandfather had used it, and before that, his father; very gently she touched the antique leather. The whole room breathed tradition; it hung heavily in the air so that her shoulders bowed automatically beneath the weight of it. Perhaps if Caspar had come here, seen this, he might have understood.

Caspar... She looked at the telephone. He wasn't leaving until around noon. There was still time for her to telephone him...go home.

Resolutely she turned her back on the temptation of the telephone as she unlocked her father's desk. She found his diary easily enough, the drawers surprisingly almost too neat and tidy, as though someone had already been through them...as though...

She sat down and opened the diary. No appointments for today, thank goodness. That would give her time to start doing some reading up. None for tomorrow, either, or the day after. Olivia started to frown as she flicked through the diary and found it empty of any appointments other than the odd half days pencilled in for golf.

Uneasily she started to look back through the diary, her muscles tensing as she studied the empty pages. Perhaps her father had another diary and this was simply one he used to record his golf matches. Yes, that must be it, she decided eagerly as she put it down and started to search through the drawers a second time.

And found nothing. Nothing!

Blankly she reopened the diary and restudied it once again. Earlier in the year there had been a clutch of appointments, but these had gradually tapered off until there were barely more than two or three a week and then even less, which meant...

'Olivia.' She stiffened as the door opened and Jon came in. 'The post has arrived,' he told her. 'If you'd like to come into my office we can go through it together...oh, you've found your father's diary,' he commented unnecessarily.

'Yes,' Olivia agreed. She took a deep breath and then forced a smile, remarking, 'Luckily he doesn't appear to have any appointments this week, other than a game of golf.'

'Oh yes, that is lucky,' Jon agreed, smiling back, but his smile seemed forced, even if he did seem to relax a little bit as she got up to accompany him to his office. Because he was becoming more accustomed to the idea of having her working in the practice, or because she hadn't made an issue of her father's virtually empty diary?

In contrast to her father's office, Jon's seemed smaller than she remembered, and of course there were the familiar filing cabinets, plus some modern additions to house the computer system. But unlike her father's desk, his was almost covered in files and papers, and his diary, which lay open next to his keyboard, looked pretty full, as well.

'So the practice hasn't become a complete *Marie Celeste* of the legal world,' Olivia couldn't resist saying.

'Er, excuse me...?'

'We do still have *some* clients, Uncle Jon,' Olivia explained dryly. 'I had begun to think from the state of my father's office and his diary that the practice might be completely devoid of them.'

'Oh...yes. Oh yes...I see. Well, you know how it is. Sometimes one side of things can be busy and sometimes it's the other....'

'Mmm. I suppose so. You mean that people don't die in Haslewich in the summer?'

She was being unfair, Olivia recognised remorsefully as she saw the almost hunted look in her uncle's eyes.

'I'm sorry,' she apologised. 'It was just that I had the impression from Tiggy that Dad was very busy.'

'Oh yes, he was...it's just... Well, to tell the truth, Olivia, I came down the other day and—'

'Cleared out Dad's desk,' Olivia supplied gently

and yet she knew she had made it sound more like an accusation than an acceptance of kind intent.

'I just wanted to check that there was nothing that was urgent, that was all,' Jon told her stiffly.

Had he, after all the years of playing second fiddle to her father, both in the family and in the practice, suddenly rebelled and seen...seized the opportunity to assert himself and take over his brother's role? Guiltily Olivia tried to dismiss such a disquieting thought. Jon, so far as she knew, had never been anything other than fully supportive of her father. But there must surely have been times when he had felt *some* resentment, *some* jealousy, *some* sense of anger at being pushed into second place?

She stole a look at her uncle as he started to go through the post with her, handing her each letter to read and meticulously explaining its origins.

An hour later she decided that there was nothing she need feel too apprehensive about. Most of the letters had seemed pretty straightforward; the practice did not deal with complex litigation cases or even the more complex European and international intercompany legal wranglings that were her particular field.

'I'm going to have to leave soon. I've got an appointment with Lord Burrows at eleven,' Jon told her. 'He wants to go through some of the tenancy agreements for his farms.' Yes, it was a world away from the kind of work *she* was familiar with, Olivia acknowledged as Jon added, 'and then I promised I'd go with your mother when she visits your father.'

So far as she could see, *her* day's work was going to consist of drafting a new will, chasing authority for some details they needed on a conveyance, clarifying

a property boundary and reading through the half-
dozen or so files that Jon had entrusted to her.
Nowhere near enough to keep her thoughts too busy
to stray to Caspar—unfortunately.

11

Max's first set-back of the day came when he walked into the poky little room that housed the chambers' two secretaries and their equipment to discover that Charlotte wasn't there.

'She's at the dentist,' Wendy told him in her nervous little-girl whisper that always aroused in him the desire to torment her by pretending he couldn't hear her. He knew that she felt intimidated by him and that she disliked and resented him, just as he knew that she was too nervous and fearful to dare to complain when he arrived in the office at ten to five in the afternoon with more than half an hour's 'urgent' typing for her to do.

Charlotte would never have stood for such bullying tactics and it amused Max to witness the skilful way she always managed to pass on the main burden of the work to Wendy and yet at the same time give the impression that she was the one who was the more efficient and hard-working of the pair.

Charlotte and he were in many ways, he suspected, two of a kind, which was why they tended to treat one another with a certain amount of healthy respect. Like him, he imagined that Charlotte had chosen to work at Gray's Inn because, of the four Inns of Court, Gray's was the one with the reputation of providing the best social life, and he already knew that there was no way that Charlotte would provide him with the information he wanted without requiring some form of payment in kind.

'Well, when she comes back, tell her I want to see her, will you?' he asked Wendy.

She had flushed a painful shade of unflattering pink when he walked into the room and now her whole face and throat were dyed an unpleasant shade of puce. She was more than likely still a virgin, he reflected—and very likely to stay that way.

In his own office, his desk was piled high with work, none of which was likely to earn him anything more than a meagre few hundred pounds. Once he had his tenancy all that, of course, would soon change. *Once* he had it. He glanced at his watch. How long did it take to visit the dentist, for God's sake, if indeed that was where Charlotte was?

He sat down and reached for the first file, studying the note pinned to it impatiently. Another no-hoper. My God, why the hell did these people bother? He glanced contemptuously at the letter of instruction from the acting solicitor, formally requesting counsel's opinion as to the feasibility of their client's claim. A five-year-old could see that there *was* no claim. No claim, which meant no case, which meant no fees.

He reached for the next file.

In the end it was almost lunch-time before Charlotte came sauntering into his office, her hair and make-up glamorously immaculate as always, the skirt of her suit just that little bit too short, the jacket just that little bit too fitted for a woman who took her career seriously.

'You wanted to see me?'

The glossy red lips pouted provocatively as she stood in front of him, making sure he got the full benefit of the long length of her legs and the full curve of her breasts, Max observed, leaning back in his chair, hands crossed behind his head as he looked her lazily up and down.

'I always enjoy seeing you, Charlotte,' he assured her mockingly.

The look she gave him suggested that he stop wasting her time.

'You know it's the annual dinner dance the month after next,' he commented, watching as Charlotte eyed him warily.

The annual dinner dance was an external prestigious event with tickets strictly limited, supposedly on a first-come first-served basis, but in reality available only to preselected applicants.

For the first time this year, Max had managed to obtain two tickets, illegitimately, of course, through the good offices of the wife of a certain junior judge who just happened to be on the selection committee and with whom Max had had a judiciously planned flirtation, which had resulted in the then bedazzled lady in question getting his name onto the requisite list.

Charlotte, unless she was invited to the affair by a ticket holder, would have no chance of attending, a fact that they both knew, just as they both knew how beneficial it would be to her in her quest for the right husband if she *could* be present. There was no limit to the kind of contacts and opportunities an enterprising girl like Charlotte could find at such an event.

'Is it?' Charlotte now countered with deliberate vagueness.

Max allowed himself an indulgent smile. 'I've got two tickets for it and as yet no partner.' He paused. If anything, Charlotte looked even more wary.

'I need some help...some information...' Max told her quietly. This was the risky bit. The unprotected leap from one position of strength and safety to another. There was no guarantee—as yet—that Charlotte would take the bait he was offering. She could choose to expose him instead, and if she did...

'What information?' she asked him carefully.

Max allowed himself to start to relax.

'Nothing too unreasonable,' he assured her easily. 'Just a name...'

'A name...what name?' Charlotte demanded, her eyebrows lifting.

'Not what, whose,' Max corrected her loftily.

This was the second hazard; even if she had access to the information he wanted, she might decide not to give it to him, and again he was risking potential exposure.

He paused for a second and then, reminding himself of how much was at risk, told her bluntly, 'There's another applicant for the upcoming vacant tenancy— a woman. I need to know her name.'

'Only the tenants on the tenants' committee have access to that kind of information,' she reminded Max.

'The tenants and the chambers clerk,' Max agreed smoothly, 'but at some stage an appointment has to be made...letters have to be written.'

'Laura deals with all that kind of correspondence,' Charlotte informed him.

Max raised his eyebrows.

'All right, I'll do what I can,' Charlotte agreed, 'but I'm not promising anything.'

'Neither am I,' Max warned her smoothly.

They exchanged looks.

'I'll have to wait until Laura leaves this evening.'

'Excellent. You'll be able to do some extra typing for me then, won't you?' Max remarked.

Charlotte gave him a warning look and asked mock-sweetly, 'These tickets, do they include the dinner or are they just for the dance afterwards?'

'They include everything,' Max assured her, 'the dance, the dinner and the pre-dinner cocktail party. I hope you've got a suitable dress.'

Charlotte smiled at him.

It was a pity in a way, Max mused after Charlotte had gone. He had worked hard for those tickets, damned hard, far too hard to have wasted a ticket on someone like Charlotte under normal circumstances, but then these were not normal circumstances, and in view of what he ultimately stood to gain, some sacrifices had to be made.

The practice's cases might not involve the huge sums of money she was used to dealing with but they were certainly far more interesting, Olivia decided after she had finished reading through the tangled history of one of them. A land dispute had sprung up between two brothers, both of whom claimed to have rights over a piece of land left by their uncle. Both men were already relatively wealthy local farmers but this piece of fiercely disputed land also contained a stream, and it was access to the stream that was the real cause of the dispute. The problem was exacerbated by the fact that at some stage the course of the stream had been altered, diverted, as one brother claimed, so that it now ran through the other brother's land instead of running in its original course on his land.

Olivia had spent most of the morning poring over old maps and deeds, which in itself was an unfamiliar enough task to her to be intensely absorbing, but trying to read the fine old-fashioned writing was beginning to make her eyes ache. Then she remembered seeing a small magnifying glass on her uncle's desk.

He had already left for his first appointment, but his office door was open and she could see the magnifying glass beside some papers. She went inside and walked over to get it. As she reached out to pick the glass up, her attention was caught by the open wallet of bank statements on the desk. They were her father's, she realised, and her uncle had presumably been going through them because they were folded back to show the month of February. One item on the statement was ringed in red, and without intending to do so, Olivia found she was studying it, her heartbeat registering her shock when she discovered that the circled item related to a credit to her father's account of almost a quarter of a million pounds.

Her father was not the kind of man who had ever managed to accumulate large sums of money. As a family they lived well, very well in fact, but both her parents in different ways tended to be financially extravagant; they were not savers or investors, which meant that her father either must have been given the money or...

Her heart thumping heavily, Olivia sat down in her uncle's chair and pulled the statements towards her. The money had been deposited by credit transfer. From her grandfather perhaps? Olivia knew that there had been occasions in the past when her father had had to apply to Ben for a 'loan' but she, perhaps naïvely, had always assumed that the sums her father had borrowed had been for much smaller amounts.

She flicked forward through the statements and then stopped abruptly as she came to another credit entry—easy enough to find since the bulk of the statement entries were for withdrawals, withdrawals that ran to sums far in excess of her father's drawings from the practice.

This time the credit was smaller, one hundred thousand pounds, and it was dated very recently, only days before her father's heart attack, in fact. More slowly this time, Olivia turned back to the first statement and started to go carefully through them all.

By the time she had finished, she felt ice-cold and her hands were shaking so much she could hardly turn the statements. By her rough calculations, in the past five years her father's account had been credited with close on two million pounds. Where had he got such a vast sum of money? What had he spent it on? So far as she could see, it had been absorbed by her parents' day-to-day living expenses, by extravagance and overspending to a catastrophic degree. Yes, she could see where the money had *gone*, but where had it come from?

She had a nauseous feeling that she already knew, if not the exact source of the money, then at least the type of source it was most likely to have come from.

She closed her eyes and took a deep breath, trying to steady herself.

'Oh, Dad, how could you...?' she whispered shakily.

Her glance fell on a file that had been tucked underneath the statements. It looked very like the one Olivia had seen her uncle holding in her father's study the previous evening. Reluctantly she picked it up and glanced at the name. JEMIMA HARDING—TRUST FUND.

Her fingers were trembling so much she could hardly open it. She knew the Harding family, who lived in Haslewich. They had originally been local landowners; some of their land had been sequestered for use as an American army base during the war, and more recently the same land had been sold off along with the land the Hardings still owned close to a huge multinational chemical and drug conglomerate, which had its British headquarters several miles outside town.

That sale had made Jemima Harding a millionairess. It had also enabled her only son to buy the fast sports car in which he had met his death and, so local rumour said, brought about the split between her and her husband that had ultimately led to their very acrimonious divorce and her reverting to her maiden name of Harding.

She was an old woman now, in her late eighties, Olivia reckoned, living in a residential home.

She was also one of her father's clients; he was her sole executor and held power of attorney over her financial affairs. Was that where the money had come from? Olivia wondered bleakly. Had her father used those powers to transfer money from Jemima's account into his own? It would have been easy enough for him to do and easy enough to keep hidden—just so long as Jemima remained alive and no one questioned what was happening to her estate.

The cold, icy calm of deep shock had fallen over her. She was distantly aware of neatly placing the file where she had found it along with the statements, of getting up and even remembering to collect the magnifying glass she had originally come for before walking back to her father's office. But once there she felt her legs starting to buckle beneath her and her whole body starting to shake so much that she was forced to cling to the back of a chair, unable to move, unable to do anything other than stand there shivering violently and trying to force her emotions to accept what her brain insisted they had to know.

Her father had stolen money from someone else. Her father had defrauded someone who trusted him. Her father was no different from the thief who broke in during the night, the con man who deceived vulnerable old folk out of their savings and pensions. Her father...

She swallowed uneasily. Uncle Jon...had he *known*...? Had he guessed? Was *that* why...? Her head started to pound. The temptation to run back to Jon's office and go through the statements again, to convince herself that she was wrong, that she had misread the evidence, misunderstood what she had seen, was so strong she had to forcibly prevent herself from moving.

Her father...

'Has he been under any unusual stress?' the specialist had asked them and she had wondered guiltily

then if she ought to mention her mother's 'problem'
but had decided not to do so since she was not sure
whether her father was aware of it. The stress caused
by that knowledge would have been bad enough, but
this...

How on earth had he managed to live with himself,
knowing what he had done not once, but regularly,
consistently, over a period of five years? How *could* he
have done it?

Abruptly, achingly, Olivia longed for Caspar. And
not just for him, but the means of escape he could have
provided from the appalling dilemma she now faced.
If only she had never seen those statements, opened
that file. If *only* she was now safely on her way to
London with Caspar.

It shocked her that she, who had always privately
thought of herself as strong and independent, should,
the moment she was tested, become so mortally afraid
and vulnerable, and even worse than that, a moral
coward who, instead of facing up to what she had discovered, simply wanted to run and hide herself away
from it, preferably in the safe sanctuary of Caspar's
arms.

Caspar. She looked at her watch. It still wasn't too
late for her to catch him before he left, she decided fe-
verishly. If she drove straight to the airport, there was
still time before his flight took off for London.

She couldn't tell him about her father, of course.
Caspar would never, never understand that kind of
deceit and dishonesty—a violation rather than a
straightforward theft—so much worse somehow coming from a person who was, after all, in such a great
position of trust. But still, she needed him. Needed the

loving warmth of his arms, the security he provided, and the escape...

She had already pulled on her jacket and picked up her handbag without being aware of doing so. As she hurried through the downstairs foyer, she told the receptionist quickly, 'I'm...I'm just going to the airport to see a friend.'

Oh dear God, *why* had she looked at those statements? *Why* hadn't she simply turned the other way? What was happening to her and to her life? *Why* did she have to discover these things about her parents that she would much rather have not had to know? Not even the silent threat of the police video cameras was enough to prevent her from speeding as she drove towards the airport, overtaking other vehicles with an uncharacteristic recklessness, terrified that she would somehow miss seeing Caspar. She had to see him...she had to...

The airport had changed since her last visit, expanded into a vast complex that had her gritting her teeth as she hunted frantically for a parking space and then abandoned her car half in and half out of it. She locked the door and started to run towards the departures lounge, praying that Caspar would not already have been called through for his flight.

The escalator taking her down into the departures lounge was packed and she fidgeted nervously as it progressed slowly, tortuously, into the hall itself. Suddenly she caught sight of Caspar's familiar back and froze.

The urge to call out to him, even though she knew he wouldn't hear, was so strong that she had to bite the inside of her mouth to stop from doing it. He was, she realised, talking to someone. He moved and she was able to see who it was.

Hillary.

The shock rocketed all the way through her body— the sudden sickening sensation of the blood draining from her head inducing a feeling of faintness, the nauseous lurch of her stomach, the weak shakiness of her legs.

Hillary. What was *she* doing with Caspar?

As Olivia watched them, Hillary reached up and whispered something in Caspar's ear. He turned to smile at her and Olivia's heart turned over inside her chest. Hillary moved her head and started to kiss Caspar, her body moving subtly closer to his. Caspar had his hand on her shoulder.

Olivia thought for a moment that she was actually going to faint. Disbelief, anguish and hot, furious anger all combined to produce a pain like nothing she had ever previously experienced.

Was *this* why he had ended their relationship? Not, as he had accused her, because he doubted the strength of her feelings but because his own for her had changed. Because *he* no longer loved her, wanted her. Because of Hillary. Hillary who, like him, was an American. Hillary who, like him, thought nothing of the ties and responsibilities of being part of a family, the duties... Hillary who could walk away from her children and her husband just as he could walk away from her. But if he thought that in Hillary he had found someone who would put him first, he was very, very wrong, Olivia decided savagely. Hillary was the kind of woman who would never put anyone other than herself first.

She was down in the departures lounge now but she didn't waste any time in going over to Caspar. Instead she headed straight for the exit.

Caspar. Her lover. Her refuge...her sanctuary... She started to laugh bitterly.

'...and you needn't worry about work, David, because Olivia is going to stay on and help out at the office and—'

'No!'

Tiggy looked nervously at Jon, appealing silently to him for help as David interrupted her. Jon had offered to wait outside whilst she went in to see her husband alone, but Tiggy had begged him to go with her.

She was uncomfortable and ill at ease when she was with David, Jon had noticed, but then he suspected that very few people would have not found the battery of technical equipment that had originally surrounded his brother when he was in the intensive care unit intimidating and they had been warned that David must not become upset or overexcited, which he quite plainly was now.

'It's all right, David,' he soothed his brother as he discreetly rang for the nurse, mentally cursing himself for not having warned Tiggy not to mention the fact that Olivia was helping out at the practice.

Ten minutes later after the nurse had shown them out of David's room, having first firmly reassured a tearful Tiggy that David was not about to suffer a second heart attack but that he did need to 'rest', Tiggy flung herself into Jon's arms.

'Oh, Jon, I'm so frightened,' she wept. 'They keep

saying that David will soon be able to come home, but I'm afraid that if he does...'

'Don't upset yourself,' Jon comforted her. 'I'm sure the doctors won't allow David to leave here until they're sure he's well enough to do so.'

'He just doesn't seem the same any more,' Tiggy persisted weepily. 'Why was he so angry about Olivia?'

'He's probably upset at the thought of her disrupting her own career plans,' Jon fibbed. 'Don't let it upset you. That won't do either you or David any good.'

'Oh, Jon, you're so understanding. Jenny is *so* lucky to have you,' Tiggy sighed as she nestled close to him. 'I used to tell David that he should watch his weight. You're much much fitter....' She lifted her head from his shoulder and reached up to touch his hair, telling him coyly, 'Why don't you try a different haircut, something more modern. It would suit you.'

'I don't think so,' Jon replied, laughing, recalling the hairstyles favoured by his younger son and his friends. Even so, it was flattering to receive Tiggy's compliments and her interest. Jenny would certainly never have said anything like that to him, but then Jenny had never been the type to think of flattering a man.

'Oh, Jon—' Tiggy's mouth trembled pitifully as she tried to smile '—will you think me very dreadful if I say that recently I've been feeling that I married the wrong brother?'

Jon had to swallow hard as he hugged her. She aroused in him the same kind of emotions he had felt on first holding each of his newborn children. Only with Tiggy there was an extra ingredient, a sensuality, a sexuality—a charge that left him feeling both elated and ashamed.

Jenny was his wife and Tiggy was David's and what worse kind of betrayal could there be than for him to covet his twin's wife?

'I don't want to go home yet,' Tiggy was whispering to him. 'Can't we go somewhere...?'

'I really ought to get back to the office...' Jon began, but Tiggy clung tightly to his arm.

'We could have lunch. Everyone has to have a lunch-hour. Please, Jon,' she pleaded, 'I don't want to be on my own.'

As his plane started to climb into the surprisingly blue Manchester sky, Caspar stared bleakly through the window. Only now could he acknowledge that, il-logical though it was, a part of him had gone on ex-pecting, hoping, right until the last call for his flight to London, that Olivia would appear.

And yet so strong was the hold of the angry, jealous child within him that even knowing that, he had not been able to allow himself to walk over to a telephone and call her.

If she had loved him enough, then she would auto-matically have put him, his needs, his desires, his wishes, first; so rang the stubborn child's voice within him.

Only she had not...did not. Think how you would feel in her shoes, how you would behave; how you would react, given that kind of ultimatum, the analyti-cal adult voice of his grown-up self demanded. Would *you* give in to that kind of emotional blackmail?

Would you want a relationship with the kind of person who wielded it?

Tiredly he pushed his hand into his hair. It would probably never have worked anyway; Olivia would have needed to retrain to be able to work back home. Lawyers there did not command the same kind of respect from the community that they did in Britain. The whole system was different, more political, more hard-nosed, and Olivia, despite her academic intelligence and ability, had a certain feminine softness about her that he—and, he suspected, other men, too—found subconsciously alluring. Because men liked women to be vulnerable?

He moved irritably in his seat. She might be soft-hearted but she sure as hell could be stubborn, as well. Yet in her shoes wouldn't *he* want to prove the doubting Thomases amongst her own family wrong, to prove that she could do the job as well and indeed better than any of them? Wouldn't that have been a challenge he'd have found impossible to resist? So why expect Olivia to resist it?

She had caught him off guard last night. He had never had any intention of having dinner with Hillary. It had been obvious virtually from the first moment they had met that she was looking for a way to justify leaving her marriage and someone to support her in that decision. As a fellow American and someone like her who was outside the family, it was only natural that she should turn to him, but in listening to her, there was no doubt that he had placed himself in a highly invidious position. Olivia had already made it plain that she supported Saul, but by the time he had run into Hillary last night, he had been almost glad of an opportunity to widen the rift between Olivia and himself. Well, he had certainly found it and meeting Hillary by chance at the airport this morning had not been particularly welcome.

It was just as well that her family lived out on the West Coast, making any future contact between them highly unlikely. He still had a few days before he actually left the country, he comforted himself as his plane started to circle Heathrow. Time enough yet for Olivia to contact him...or for him to contact her.

There was no going back now, Olivia acknowledged, no, not even if she wanted to. What she had seen at the airport had convinced her of that. Their quarrel, the reasons for it, the events leading up to it, she could understand if she divorced herself from her own emotions and studied the situation dispassionately. This didn't mean to say that she felt she was in any way in the wrong, simply that there were realistically strong arguments for both Caspar and herself to feel aggrieved and angry, but the speed with which Caspar had quite obviously replaced her in his life—and in his bed, too, judging from the way Hillary had been draping herself all over him—no, that could not be forgiven or understood. That was treachery, betrayal on a grand scale. As a family, they seemed destined to suffer badly from it, both as the betrayed and the betrayer, she reflected soberly as she drove back to the office.

Well, she knew what she had to do. There was no avoiding the issue now, no escape, no cowardly walking away.... And the first person she'd have to tackle had to be her uncle Jon, and after that... Her hands were shaking as she locked the door of her car.

Haslewich was a small town and her grandfather a very upright and proud man. She dared not think what it would do to him when word got round about what her father had done. The whole family would be affected by it, each and every one of them tainted by it. The bile rose in her throat, sour tasting and heavy.

Jon was in his office when Olivia walked in. 'I need to talk to you,' she said without preamble.

'What is it?' he asked her after he had waved her into a chair. 'Have you changed your mind, decided to go to America with Caspar after all? If you have, don't worry—'

'No, I haven't changed my mind,' Olivia interrupted him quietly. 'I wanted to, but I discovered that I'd left it too late.'

When she didn't elaborate Jon shifted his weight uncomfortably from one foot to the other.

'It's all right, Uncle Jon,' Olivia told him gently, 'I know now why you didn't want me working here.'

She could see Jon physically stiffening as she spoke and she could see, as well, the way his glance strayed betrayingly to the place on his desk where he had left those incriminating bank statements. He had put them away now as well as the file.

'I know what Dad's been doing,' Olivia pressed on firmly. 'About the money he's taken, stolen from Jemima Harding's trust fund. When did you find out what was going on?'

For a moment she thought that he was going to attempt to deny the whole thing. He took a deep breath, paused and then walked over to the window before saying tiredly, 'I've been suspicious for a while, but stupidly, I suppose, with hindsight...I didn't want to...I thought that perhaps... You mustn't judge your father too harshly, Olivia,' he told her. 'God knows what kind of pressure he must have been under. I only wish...' He stopped and shook his head.

'Oh, Uncle Jon, how could he?' Olivia demanded, suddenly giving way to her emotions, too wound up to keep still she started to pace the floor. 'How could he do something like that...?'

'I don't think he ever meant things to go so far,' Jon tried to comfort her. 'I imagine that he just meant to borrow the money at first, that he fully intended to pay it back, but as things stood—'

'He couldn't do it and so instead he just borrowed more,' Olivia interrupted bitterly. 'Only he wasn't borrowing it at all, was he, Uncle Jon? He was stealing it,' she retorted sharply. 'I still can't believe it.'

Jon winced as he listened to her. He felt so guilty— as much to blame as David himself. He should never have allowed David to have so much control over such a vulnerable client, especially not when he knew... But that was all in the past and he had sworn as David's brother, his twin, sworn on the Bible to his father that the one unfortunate mistake of David's— that small silly bit of foolishness when David was in London—was something that would never again be mentioned between them. David had escaped a formal charge then because no one, least of all the important client he had been involved with, wanted it to become public knowledge that a junior, as yet unqualified barrister, had almost got away with swindling him out of a considerable sum of money.

Instead the whole affair had been hushed up. David hadn't actually spent any of the money; that had been repaid. He had been dismissed from chambers and David himself had sworn tearfully to both his father and to Jon himself that he would never be tempted to do such an idiotic thing again. It had simply been the pressure of the way he was living, the crowd he was running with, the fact that Tiggy was pregnant, that had led him into such temptation in the first place. He had never really intended to steal the money, simply to use it, borrow it, until his allowance came through, that was all.

Ben, of course, had to believe him, accept his excuses and his remorse, because to do otherwise would have meant that he had to accept that David was not what he had always so proudly believed him to be. And Jon had accepted the vow of silence imposed on him by Ben because, well, because David was his brother and he had grown used to always shielding and protecting him, helping to maintain the fiction that he was the character their father had established for his favourite son. Who was really to blame if David found maintaining the burden of that character too difficult? David or Ben? And who, after all, was he to sit in judgement on the brother he had been brought up to revere?

Over the years he had done his best to be careful about exposing David to any kind of temptation, but then he had perhaps started to become overconfident, to relax a little too much. He had avoided seeing what was happening because he hadn't *wanted* to see it, and because of that laxness…

The burden of the way he had turned his back on his responsibility, the way he had let not just David but Ben, as well, and yes, Olivia and all the others down, too, weighed unbearably heavily on his shoulders.

David had, of course, escaped from his burden of responsibility just as he always escaped or downright avoided it; after all, Jon wasn't going to take the risk of accusing him now with fraud when to do so could bring on a second and potentially fatal heart attack. But Jon did not like admitting to such thoughts and so he quickly pushed them to the back of his mind. They were not the kind of thoughts he had been brought up to harbour about his brother.

'Uncle Jon, what are we going to do?' Olivia asked him huskily. 'There's no way that the money can be repaid and even if it could…' She spread her hands helplessly. 'He's guilty of theft…and fraud…and of professional misconduct of the worst possible kind.'

As he listened to his niece and heard the anguish in her voice, Jon forbore to remind her that her father had never qualified either as a barrister or a solicitor and therefore the question of professional misconduct at least did not arise, or at least not in the sense that she meant.

'It will kill Gramps,' she whispered, 'and this…' She lifted her hand to indicate their surroundings. 'No one will… It could destroy all of us…the whole family.'

Jon couldn't deny it. Who would want to hire a firm of solicitors in which one of the partners had been convicted of fraud? The Crighton name, of which his father was so chauvinistically proud, would be ruined. There was nowhere so comfortable and safe as a small town, and nowhere so cruel once you had broken its moral laws, transgressed its ethical boundaries. And the legal world was in many ways very similar to a small town; gossip spread fast and lethally through it. Only the fact that the only other person apart from the client to know about David's earlier transgression had been felled by a stroke within days of having confronted David had prevented the news of *that* transgression from spreading. Jon was sure of it.

But this time the truth couldn't be hidden. Jemima Harding was eighty-nine and in poor health; she couldn't live for ever and sooner or later—probably sooner—someone was going to start questioning the disappearance of that two million pounds from her accounts.

'There isn't anything we can do,' Jon told her heavily, and for the first time as she looked into his eyes Olivia saw just how great a burden her father had placed on his twin brother.

'Someone will have to tell Jemima Harding...and the bank...and—'

'Yes,' Jon agreed. 'I've already made an appointment to see her accountants,' he said quietly. 'I know the senior partner reasonably well.'

They looked at one another in heavy silence. Jon had no other option open to him, Olivia realised. If he withheld the fact that he knew of David's fraud and did not act upon it, technically he would be as guilty as her father, just as she would be herself.

'Would you like me to come with you...when you see the accountant?' she offered.

Jon gave her a ruefully tender smile. 'No,' he replied gently. 'It would be best if no one other than ourselves knew that *we've* had this conversation. In fact, it would be best if we had not had it,' he added firmly.

'Oh, Uncle Jon.' Olivia shook her head as she went over and hugged him swiftly. 'You always put other people first. You always want to protect them.'

As he returned her embrace, Jon reflected guiltily that she was wrong. He hadn't thought about protecting Jenny last night when he'd been holding Tiggy in his arms. Why had he done it? He didn't know what was happening to him. Increasingly over the past few months he had discovered aspects of his character that bewildered and sometimes shocked him. It was like looking in a mirror and seeing an unfamiliar reflection, turning a corner of a well-known street and seeing a totally unknown view, an experience that was both unsettling and alarming.

Lying in bed at night next to Jenny, unable to sleep, he sometimes found himself worrying, questioning where they were going, and even more disturbing, why they should bother going on at all.

Their children would soon no longer really need them. Their marriage. Their lives together had become predictable and routine. But where once he had actually found its steadiness and sameness a comforting security, just recently it had felt more like a prison. He was fifty years old and it was as though he had suddenly woken up to the reality of life itself and seen for the first time how much he had missed out on. Realised how many times he had not done things. The chaotic turmoil of his own thoughts left him feeling confused and agitated; the intensity of his emotions—new emotions many of them—shocked him.

It was almost six months since he had first begun to suspect what David was doing, from a chance remark by their bank manager that David and Tiggy were very fortunate to inherit such a substantial fund of money from her parents. Since he knew that Tiggy's parents were both still alive and lived in comfortable but very modest circumstances on the South coast, his suspicions had immediately been alerted.

He had tried to discuss the subject with David, but typically his brother had fobbed him off, initially avoiding the issue and then claiming that their bank manager must have misunderstood.

But Jon had not believed him. He closed his eyes briefly. The knowledge that he doubted his brother's word, his probity, his honesty, had caused him many sleepless nights as he swung from feeling guilty at his own suspicions to fearing that they might be true, his pain, misery, anger and hopelessness accompanying the sense of loss and loneliness.

For the first time in his life, he was forced to confront the truth. David, his brother, his twin, was a liar and a thief. The anger that had filled him, the sense of betrayal and resentment, had been like a flood-tide sweeping through his emotions and his beliefs, destroying whole segments of the person he had always thought himself as being, leaving him stranded in a no man's land of confusion and doubt, knowing only that now he had a desperate need to sever himself from the role of his brother's most loyal supporter.

In place of the loyalty and love he had been taught to feel for David, he now felt a huge weight of unexpressed and inexpressible anger, not just against David and his father, he acknowledged tiredly, but against virtually everyone, including himself.

Only Tiggy with her vulnerability, her helplessness, her neediness, seemed able to reach the old tender emotions and ready compassion that had once been the benchmark of his whole personality. A part of him longed, yearned, to be able to tell Jenny how he felt, to be able to share his confusion, his anger, his sense of self-loss and pain with her, but he was afraid to do so, fearing not just her judgement of him but also his being forced to judge himself.

In the final analysis, no matter what his criminal actions, David *was* still his brother and he was betraying him by revealing what he had done and, more importantly in his own heart, by being unable any longer to go on loving him.

He glanced at his watch and told Olivia quietly, 'It's gone six. You go. Your mother doesn't like being left on her own.'

'She's probably gone shopping,' Olivia said, trying to smile, but then, as she realised where the money had come from for her mother's compulsive shopping trips, her face crumpled.

Why…why…why hadn't she gone with Caspar as they had planned? If she had…if she had, nothing would have changed, except that Jon would have been left to carry the burden of her father's dishonesty by himself, she reminded herself sternly. The least she could do as her father's daughter, her parents' daughter, was to be here to share that burden with him.

As he watched Olivia leave, Jon acknowledged sombrely that whilst he had no clear idea yet what exactly it was he wanted to do with the rest of his life, he knew that it could no longer continue as it had. More than anything else, he needed time and space to think. Time away from Jenny's sad, reproachful eyes and from the knowledge that lay between them. Perhaps with hindsight, it would have been better for them not to have married in the first place. Which was the more cowardly act? To stay in a marriage simply because it was there or to admit the truth and face up to reality, as he had been forced to admit the truth about David.

There was an estate agent's on the opposite side of the square. He had noticed absently when passing it that one window was devoted to properties to let....

12

'Hello...I didn't expect to see you here today.' Guy smiled warmly at Jenny as she walked into the shop.

'No, I'm just on my way back from the hospital,' she told him.

He studied her covertly. She had lost weight over the past few days and it suited her, emphasising the elegant bone structure of her face and narrowing her waist. She had always had neatly defined wrists and ankles; Guy, to whom such things were important, had noticed them the first time they met.

To him there was a natural elegance about Jenny's body, about the way she held herself and moved, which far surpassed the more common theatrical mannerisms and poses that Tiggy affected.

In his mind's eye, Guy could transform her into the woman he knew she could be, the woman she should have been—with her dark hair worn slightly longer and styled differently, its natural curl allowed to emphasise the shape of her face and worn in a soft bob, Italian style, the warm tones of her skin accentuated by clothes in mouth-wateringly delicious shades of honey and cream deepened through to cinnamon.

Guy, unusually perhaps for such a strongly heterosexual male, had an eye for colour and line, a sensitivity for style that caused him to flinch in almost physical pain when he was forced to witness other people's apparent blindness to the necessity of creating visual harmony.

It amazed him that Jenny, who could pick just the right piece of furniture, just the right fabric and accessories to decorate their window, could fail appallingly to apply that talent to her own wardrobe and person. He had hoped their triumphant excursion to Armani might have changed things, but so far he hadn't once seen her wearing the trouser suit they had bought.

'How is David?' he asked politely as he watched her pushing her hair off her face with fingers on which her wedding ring had become loose.

He had never taken to Jenny's brother-in-law, whom he privately considered to be both a weak and a rather vain man.

'He had a bit of a set-back, although he's stable again now,' Jenny replied. She frowned a little, remembering that the nurse had told her that David had become upset during Jon and Tiggy's visit.

'His wife had been talking to him and he became very agitated, so we had to ask her to leave,' she'd repeated.

What exactly had Tiggy been saying to him? Jenny wondered, her heart giving a funny little nervous beat.

'What's wrong?' Guy asked her softly.

She gave him a wary look, then shook her head, denying, 'Nothing.'

To put into words her fears and confusion about the change in Jon's behaviour would give them a weight and power she couldn't bear them to have. There had been many times during their marriage when she had felt isolated, and alone and very vulnerable, but never one when she had felt quite like this, when she had known instinctively that her marriage was being threatened by another woman.

Not deliberately, of course. Tiggy could never be so cold-blooded. But... Was it really any wonder that Jon should be so attracted to her? She was all the things she herself was not and she had always known that he had not married her out of love, or at least not out of love for *her*, she amended mentally; there had never been that wild, passionate flaring of sexual excitement between them. In its place, though, they *had* shared a harmony she kept hoping would compensate for all that they did not have.

'I must get back,' she told Guy. 'Jon will be home soon and—'

'I saw him earlier. He was in the Italian restaurant with David's wife.'

'Yes,' Jenny agreed distantly. 'He would have been.'

Guy looked searchingly at her, wondering if she was aware just how much she had revealed in those sad, almost bitter, words. He had seen for himself the intimacy Jon and Tiggy were sharing, Tiggy putting down her fork to reach across the table and touch him, not perhaps as a lover but in a way that betrayed almost as clearly how she felt about him, and if Jon had not been equally intimate in return, he certainly hadn't made any attempt to withdraw from her.

Gravely he watched Jenny leaving the shop. It was too soon yet for him to do or say anything. He had waited all these years, he could wait a little longer.

Wearily Jenny made her way home, her heart turning over uncomfortably as she saw Jon's car parked

outside the house. It was unusual for him to be home
so early these days and again all her instincts warned
her that his presence now was not a good omen.

He was waiting for her as she walked into the
kitchen.

'There's something I have to tell you,' he said
sombrely.

'Is it very important or can it wait until after dinner?' Jenny asked with forced brightness.

'I...I won't be in for dinner. I've got a meeting in
Chester.'

It wasn't true, but Jon knew that there was no way
he could sit down and go through the same stifling
routine without breaking the promise he had made
himself and either saying or doing something that
would hurt her.

'The children,' she began, but Jon shook his head.

'The girls are upstairs doing their homework and
Joss has gone round to see Ruth.'

'Oh, well, I'll just put the kettle on and—'

'Jenny...'

The stifled impatience in his voice stopped her.

'I...I can't stay here any longer...I need to be on my
own.... This house, our life...'

You, he might just as well have said, Jenny acknowledged as she listened to him in anguished silence.

'They...I...' He stopped and shook his head.

'What is it you're trying to tell me, Jon?' Jenny asked
as calmly as she could. 'That our marriage is over, that
you want a divorce?' Despite all her good intentions,
her voice cracked painfully over the last few words
and Jon winced as he heard her pain.

'No...not that. Not a divorce—a separation.'

'What about the children?' Jenny protested.

'They'll manage. They won't need us much longer,' Jon told her, guilt driving him into anger. 'And anyway, they've always related more to you than they have to me.'

Jenny bit her lip. 'What are you trying to say...that I've been too possessive with them, that...?'

'No,' Jon denied wearily. 'Jenny, I don't want us to argue. If we're being honest with one another, we both know...' He paused. 'I know we married for the best motives but—'

'But?' Jenny pressed him determinedly.

Let *him* say it. Let *him* say what she had always privately known...feared, but he obviously couldn't. His glance slid away from hers. He edged closer to the door...to his exit...his escape.

'Where will you go?' she asked him and then regretted her question. Now it was her turn to be afraid of what her eyes might reveal, to look directly at him. She knew, of course. He would go to Tiggy, but when he answered, it seemed she was wrong.

'I...I don't know. I'm going to look for somewhere to rent. It's for the best, Jenny,' he said almost plaintively. She could hear the pleading note in his voice and her heart ached not just for herself but, ridiculously, for him, as well. She wanted to hold him, much as she might have done one of the children, to comfort him and reassure him that she understood, that he was forgiven, but how could she when that wasn't what she felt at all?

'When—' she moistened her dry lips '—when will you go?' she asked him quietly.

'I don't know. Just as soon as I can arrange something. There's no point in drawing things out.... I'll move my things into the spare room in the meantime.' He saw the look she gave him and winced a second time.

'The children,' she whispered. 'What are we going to tell them?'

Jon shook his head. 'I don't know....'

'I could tell them that...that it's just a temporary thing,' she suggested huskily. 'They might find that easier to accept.'

'Tell them whatever you think best,' Jon replied. He was looking at her almost pityingly, Jenny recognised as she felt the first stirring of something other than pain and shock, the first awareness of the mortality of the blow struck not just at her heart but also at her pride.

You're the one who's doing the leaving, she was tempted to say. You explain it to them. But instinct and habit urged her to stay silent. She felt oddly weak and light-headed without either the energy or the will-power to fight or argue with him. 'I'd better get on with supper,' she heard herself saying mundanely. 'Did Joss say what time he would be back?'

She was behaving like someone out of a bad play, she decided as she fought down a near hysterical desire to break into laughter. The stupid, dull, boring, soon-to-be-cast-off wife, too unaware, too caught up in the events of her monotonous daily routine to realise what was happening.

'No, no, he didn't,' Jon was answering her.

She didn't watch him as he opened the door and walked into the hallway. She couldn't.

* * *

Max drummed his fingers impatiently of the top of his desk. It was almost seven o'clock, well past the time when he would normally have left chambers, but when five-thirty had come and gone with no sign of Laura getting ready to leave, he had gritted his teeth, cursed his grandfather under his breath and sent Charlotte a warning look when she had started to pout.

'Still here, Charlotte?' Laura had commented with a wintry look. 'That's not like you.'

'Charlotte has agreed to work late to finish some typing for me,' Max had cut in.

'Really?' Laura had responded in an even frostier tone. 'You *do* surprise me.'

Only by reminding himself of what was at stake had Max been able to prevent himself from retaliating. In the end it had been nearly half past six before she had finally and, he suspected, reluctantly gone.

'Wait,' Max had cautioned, shaking his head warningly and taking hold of Charlotte's arm to restrain her when she would have rushed over to the other woman's desk virtually the moment she left.

'Give her another ten minutes,' he instructed Charlotte, 'just in case she decides to come back.'

She hadn't returned, but even so Max had retreated to his own office whilst Charlotte produced her unauthorised set of keys and proceeded to unlock Laura's desk.

Now it was nearly seven o'clock and she still... Max stiffened as his office door opened.

'I think I've found what you want,' Charlotte told him. 'The senior partner has had lunch with a certain Ms Madeleine Browne, that's Browne with an *e*, of course. Three times in the past two months and he's also written her initials in his diary next to the time of the committee meeting.'

Madeleine Browne... Swiftly Max scanned his memory to see if it held any trace of the name and found it didn't.

'Oh, and by the way,' Charlotte informed him with obvious relish, 'there's something else you should know. This Madeleine Browne—' she paused importantly '—she only just happens to be the head's goddaughter. Now,' she added briskly, 'about the ball...'

The head of chambers' goddaughter, he might have known. Max fumed as he made his way back to his flat. Well, at least he now knew who his adversary was. The thing he had to do next was to find a way of eliminating her from the contest, and the easiest way to do that would be to discredit her in the eyes of the committee. As yet he wasn't sure just how this was going to be accomplished, but there was bound to be a way. There always was—and he would make damn sure that he found it.

It would be essential to find out as much as he could about her. What her strengths were, and her weaknesses, and he did not necessarily have in mind her professional strengths and weaknesses.

Head of chambers' goddaughter or not, sexual equality laws notwithstanding, he was determined that *he* would be the one who got the vacant tenancy and not Ms Madeleine Browne, with or without an *e*.

'Aunt Ruth.'

Ruth looked down at her great-nephew. She and Joss were walking through the water meadows where, as a girl, she had picked watercress. There were no cress beds here any longer, even though she and Joss had mounted a vigorous and secret campaign to re-introduce the cress to its natural habitat.

'Why is it, do you suppose, that a person who seems okay...you know, okay, suddenly seems, well...different?'

Ruth frowned as she heard the note of anxious constraint in his voice. 'Which person in particular are we talking about here, Joss?' she asked gently. 'You?'

'No, not me,' he replied, shaking his head and causing her to exhale a small sigh of relief. She kept herself reasonably up to date, read papers and magazines, watched news programmes and the like, but she didn't really think she was up to dealing with any youthful questions about sex or drugs.

'No, then who?' she asked.

'It's Dad,' Joss admitted, scuffing the toe of his shoe on the ground.

'Your father?' Ruth frowned. 'Well, I expect he's very anxious about David.'

'He spends a lot of time over at Uncle David's house,' Joss informed her, studiously casual. 'With Aunt Tiggy.'

Ruth's heart sank. 'Does he? Well, I expect there are a lot of things that Tiggy needs his help with.'

'Yes, that's what Mum says,' Joss agreed.

Ruth hesitated, not sure just what to say. How far to probe. In the end she decided that since he'd brought up the subject, she owed it to him to deal with it responsibly and give him the opportunity to air his obvious concern rather than pretend it did not exist. And so instead of drawing his attention to the fact that several of their plants had at last appeared to have taken root, she prompted, 'But you don't agree?'

'Dad's different,' he confessed in a muffled voice. 'He's been different for...well, before Uncle David had his heart attack.'

'Different how, Joss?' Ruth prodded gently.

'I don't know, just different. Not like Dad somehow. Sort of as if...I think he might be having, you know, problems with Mum,' he stated judiciously. 'Lots of people at school have parents who are divorced,' he informed her casually.

Ruth felt her concern turn to alarmed disquiet. 'Your parents aren't getting a divorce, Joss,' she told him. 'What on earth put that idea into your head?'

He gave a small shrug, his eyes suddenly sombre and very wise. 'I don't know...it just came.'

'Have you talked to them about...about this?' she asked.

'No...you see,' he said earnestly, 'I don't think that Mum would want to be divorced and...Aunt Tiggy is very pretty, isn't she?'

Ruth didn't try to lie to him. 'Yes, she is,' she agreed quietly. 'But your mother... People don't always fall in love because of the way the other person looks, Joss,' she reminded him.

'No, I know, but Aunt Tiggy needs someone to look after her and now that Uncle David isn't there... Dad likes it when people need him,' he added with an almost adult perceptiveness that half shocked Ruth, even though she knew already how intelligent and astute he was.

'Your Aunt Tiggy is married to David and your fa-

ther is married to your mother,' she finally managed
to say as she tried to assimilate his words.

Was his fear just the product of some childish imagination, or did it have a deeper and more dangerous
cause? Was Jenny and Jon's marriage in difficulty?
Jenny had said nothing to her and to think of Jon considering a divorce as Joss had suggested seemed im-
possibly far-fetched. If it had been David now...

'I'm sure there's nothing for you to worry about,
Joss,' she tried to reassure him gently as they turned
round and started to head back.

'Oh, it's not me I'm worried for,' he declared firmly.
'It's them, Mum and Dad. He needs Mum. I know he
might not think so, but he does. And she needs him.
Aunt Ruth, could I stay with you tonight instead of
going home? We could go and watch the badgers,' he
coaxed her winsomely.

'Joss, I don't think that would be a good idea,' she
began and then as she looked at his face, she changed
her mind and added, 'We'll see what your mother
thinks, shall we?'

'I know that Mum won't mind. I'll go and ring her
when I get back, shall I?'

Thoughtfully Ruth watched him. She did so hope
that he was wrong and that his suspicions were ill-
founded.

She had planned to visit Ben tomorrow. Saul and
his mother were leaving in the morning and she knew
that Ben, despite his claims to the contrary, would
miss their company. She dared not think, however,
how he would react to the possibility of a relationship,
an affair, between Jon and Tiggy. Jon must know himself how fiercely and furiously Ben would oppose any

attempt on his part to replace David in Tiggy's life, and the mere fact that he could, if indeed he actually was even considering doing so, betrayed how very deeply involved Jon was.

Tiggy's feelings did not worry her nearly so much. Tiggy she likened to a pretty clinging plant that needed constant support, *any* support, and that would just as happily attach itself and cling to one plant as another, her emotions like roots, safely shallow and easily transferred.

But Jon... Jon was a different matter entirely and that he who had always put David's needs first should even begin to consider taking his wife from him seemed grossly out of character.

Always supposing, of course, that Joss had not completely misread the situation. He *was*, after all, only a boy still. He could be wrong. She hoped he *was* wrong. Ruth admitted her brother could be a very determined man. She hadn't forgotten the pressure he had put on her when... But that was all in the past now and in the end he and her father had probably been right. She could never have lived with herself, knowing that she was responsible for the break-up of someone else's marriage no matter how much she had loved the man concerned, and then there was the fact that he had lied to her, deceived her, letting her believe that he was free to love her when all the time he had a wife and child back home in America.

She bit her lip. Why on earth was she thinking about all that now? It was over fifty years ago.

Olivia heard the phone ringing as she was stripping off the clothes she had worn for work. Somehow they felt tainted by what she had discovered, the cloth soiled and grimy, although she suspected in reality it was merely the dust from the office she could feel.

When her mother called up that the phone was for her, her heart started to thud heavily. Caspar. It had to be! As she raced downstairs in her underwear, she was already repeating what she was going to say to him. Only it wasn't Caspar; it was Saul.

'Saul,' she repeated mechanically, her voice dry and empty of enthusiasm.

'You sound down,' Saul sympathised. 'Bad day at the office?' he teased. 'Fancy telling me all about it over dinner?'

'Oh, Saul...it's very kind of you, but I don't think...'

'Look, if what happened the other night is putting you off, don't let it,' he told her softly. 'I meant what I said. I won't...'

What he had said the other night? What was he talking about? Olivia wondered in confusion.

'You needn't worry that I'm going to come on to you, pressure you,' Saul went on, 'and besides, I've already fixed up a babysitter. Louise has offered to sit with the kids and Mum's still here, as well.'

Saul thought her hesitation was because she was afraid he might try to flirt with her. Olivia didn't know whether to laugh or cry. She couldn't hurt his feelings by telling him that she had all but forgotten that small brief incident by the river and she certainly could not tell him why.

'Please...'

Olivia wavered. What was the point in staying at home in case Caspar rang? What was she going to do if he did? What was she going to say? Nothing could alter what she had seen.

'I...yes...all right,' she agreed.

'You might at least try to sound more enthusiastic,' Saul chided with a mock-aggrieved laugh, adding, 'I'll try to be round to pick you up in half an hour.'

'Mum, where's Dad?'

'He's had to go out,' Jenny told Louise without turning to look at her. The kitchen smelt of baking, betraying, no doubt, that the mix she had just slid into the oven was Jon's favourite upside-down apple cake. How silly of her to have made it. The girls wouldn't eat it—Louise had loftily announced only the previous month that they were far too old now for the childish treat of scraping out the mixing bowl and neither of them had ever been great cake eaters anyway. Perhaps she could give some of it to Ben. Baking soothed her. She could well remember how busily she had baked in those months when her mother was dying and again when... She winced as she accidently burned her wrist on the hot door of the Aga.

'I don't suppose you could give me a lift round to Grandad, could you?' Louise was wheedling. 'Only I promised Saul I'd babysit and—'

'You suppose quite rightly,' Jenny retorted. 'What's wrong with using your bike?' Tiredly she turned to her daughter, her eyes widening as she saw what Louise was wearing.

Surprisingly the Armani trouser suit was only just a little too large for her. She was already taller than Jenny anyway. Even more disconcerting, it looked good on her, which was more than could be said for the make-up she was wearing.

'You aren't planning to babysit wearing my suit, are you, Louise?' Jenny asked with what she felt herself was commendable calm. But then, what was the potential loss of a designer trouser suit when you were faced with the more drastic loss of a husband?

Louise looked at her, opened her mouth to argue, then changed her mind. 'I was just trying it on, seeing how it would look. After all, it's wasted hanging there in your wardrobe, and you'll never wear it, we both know that,' she finished disparagingly.

'Louise...' Jenny began warningly.

'Oh, all right, then,' she conceded, sulking. 'I'll go and take it off.'

'I think that would be a very good idea,' Jenny agreed firmly. 'Jeans and a T-shirt would be a much more sensible alternative.'

What on earth had motivated Louise to try to get away with going out wearing her trouser suit and not just any trouser suit, but the Armani, which Guy had told her—after she bought it—made her look incredibly sexy. That was nothing to the way it had looked on her daughter, who Jenny was nearly sure had been wearing the jacket with absolutely nothing underneath; there had certainly been more than just a suggestion of provocative thrust of taut, uplifted teenage nipple showing through the supple fabric.

For whose benefit? Surely not Saul's. He was easily twice her age, and besides, improbable though the idea of Louise falling for Saul was, Jenny decided it would do no harm to discuss her suspicions with Jon—just as a precaution. Then chillingly she remembered that there would be no more long, cosy chats with her husband as she snuggled up in bed beside him and they talked over the joint and separate events of their day. That there would be no more *anything* with Jon.

Hastily she wiped her eyes. The last thing she wanted was for Louise to come back in the kitchen and find her crying.

'Young Saul took Olivia out to dinner last night,' Ben announced abruptly.

Ruth looked at her brother. Only Ben could refer to Saul as 'young' as though he were no more than a teenager and Olivia much the same.

Ann had already informed Ruth about the break-up of Saul's marriage, and Ruth, guessing what was going through her brother's mind, felt bound to point out to him, 'Olivia considers herself fully committed to Caspar, Ben.'

'Pooh, she'll soon come to her senses. Americans, none of them can be trusted. You know that....'

Ruth could feel herself tensing. No matter how often she promised herself that this time she wouldn't end up quarrelling with him, Ben almost always managed to provoke her into forgetting her vow and this occasion was no exception.

'You really are the most ridiculously biased man,' she told him forthrightly. 'People are *individuals*, Ben, no matter *where* they come from. A hundred or so years ago you'd have been the sort of man who objected to his daughter marrying someone from outside the Cheshire border. Olivia loves Caspar and her relationship with him is a far different affair from mine... I...I made a mistake,' she countered tautly, 'but that doesn't mean that all Americans are—'

'Lying cheats,' Ben supplied angrily for her. 'What about Saul's wife, then, going off like that and leaving three children? What kind of woman does a thing like that, deserting her own children?'

Ruth winced. 'Sometimes a woman doesn't have any option,' she answered quietly. 'And the fact that Hillary is American has no bearing whatsoever on her decision to leave Saul. He *wanted* to keep the children, as you well know. They were all born here, this is their home, and no doubt in leaving them here with Saul, Hillary is trying to put their own interests first.'

'Rubbish,' Ben snorted. 'They're all the same, the whole lot of them. Young Olivia will soon find out the truth...just like you did.'

'I hope not,' Ruth returned. She wouldn't wish what had happened to her on anyone else, least of all someone like Olivia. 'The fact that Grant lied to me when he pretended that he wasn't married, that he was free to...' She stopped and swallowed fiercely before forcing herself to continue. 'The fact that he deceived me had nothing at all to do with his nationality. Any man, whether English, Welsh, Scots, French, Polish, Dutch, any man could have done the same. Grant just happened to be American.'

'They were all the same,' Ben argued angrily. 'Coming over here, lying and cheating, seducing innocent young girls, turning their heads... Don't think I don't know.'

'But you *don't* know, Ben,' Ruth contradicted him gently. 'You see, originally *I* was the one who chased Grant, not the other way round.' She smiled sadly as she saw his face. 'Oh yes, it's true. I know how much it offends that steely Crighton pride of yours to hear it, but *I wanted* Grant and I wanted him very badly. He was like a breath of fresh air, an irresistible magnetic force...he was just so different from anyone else I'd ever met....'

'You don't know what you're saying,' Ben remonstrated gruffly. 'You were still grieving for Charles.'

'No,' Ruth told him firmly, shaking her head. 'I did grieve for Charles, yes, but as a friend, not as a woman. Oh, I know we were engaged but that was just because it was the done thing. I was young and, I suppose, rather silly. I got caught up in the urgency of the whole war thing. Charles was going away into danger. He wanted the security of having someone to come back to, of reassuring himself that he would come back. I gave him the security, but that was all I gave him. I was sad when he was killed, of course, but I never mourned him as a lover. I never mourned him in the way I did Grant,' she added under her breath.

'He seduced you,' Ben insisted fiercely.

'No,' Ruth corrected him with gentle determination. 'If you must know the truth, Ben, *I* was the one who seduced *him*.' Her mouth curved in a tender, reminiscent smile. '*He* was the one who was reluctant, responsible....'

And he was also the one who was committed to someone else, who was married and not just married but had a child, as well. He'd never told Ruth that, not then, when she had pushed him back into the sweet-smelling long grass of the water meadow and teased him with the soft shape of her breasts, breasts, which they both knew were bare beneath the flimsy covering of her frock, nor later when she had lain beneath him, crying out her joy at the feel of him inside her, surrendering herself to it and to him. No, he had not told her then, nor had he mentioned them at any other time.

It had been left to her father and brother to tell her the truth. For a long time she had thought that the pain of losing him would never leave her, but eventually it had, the sharp agony of her original grief softening to a dully monotonous ache, and that ache, over the years, fading to an occasional twinge of pain whenever she allowed herself the dangerous pleasure of thinking about him. And anyway, by then she had other pains to bear, other hurts to hide. Grant. She had no idea if he was even still alive, and she did not want to know, either, she told herself firmly.

She could see Ben massaging his bad leg. She knew how much David's heart attack had upset and frightened him and she was filled with remorse for having argued with him. It was not his fault that he was the way he was. He reminded her sometimes of a great, lumbering, clumsy and anachronistic primeval beast on the edge of extinction, bewildered by the fact that he no longer had the power or strength he had taken for granted for so long. To Ben the Crighton name was sacrosanct, the upholding of it a sacred trust. Ruth smiled sadly to herself. He was so badly out of step with the times, it was almost laughable, but somehow she didn't feel like laughing.

On her way home she intended to call round and see Jenny to find out if there was any real substance to Joss's fears. Distasteful though the idea of prying into someone else's private life was to her, she felt she owed it to her great-nephew to at least take his fears seriously enough to make some attempt to alleviate them. If they *could* be alleviated.

13

Madeleine Browne. A triumphant smile curled Max's mouth in cynical satisfaction as he looked down at the name he had doodled. In the three relatively short weeks since he had first discovered her name, Max had found out rather a lot about her.

First and foremost, and the most serious hurdle, in his eyes at least, to his ousting her from the race to gain the chambers vacancy was the fact her grandfather on her mother's side was one of the country's most prominent Law Lords and her father was a senior High Court judge; moreover, she was not merely Madeleine Browne, but Madeleine Francomb-Browne, although apparently during her time at university she had decided to drop the first half of her double-barrelled surname.

She lived, very appropriately, in a small house in Chelsea down by the river, which belonged to her father and which she shared with a friend—a 'girl' friend, her circle of friends predictably in the main 'girls' she had been at school with. She was, in short, a typical product of an upper-middle-class background, the type of girl who thirty or even twenty-five years ago would never even have dreamt of having any kind of career other than the pursuit of a suitable husband and Max heartily wished that she had chosen that option now.

However, in the midst of all the unhelpful and predictable information he had gathered about her from various sources, there was one fact that glittered as brilliantly as a cut and polished diamond. And that was quite simply, God alone knew for what reason, that she had, during one summer's vacation while she was studying, taken a part-time job, no doubt as some kind of general dogsbody, at the chambers headed by Luke Crighton in Chester. Max had no idea why on earth she had chosen to work there when, thanks to her family's influence, she could have worked anywhere—if indeed she had needed to work, which seemed highly unlikely—but what he did know was that it was a golden nugget of good fortune, which he fully intended to turn into the maximum advantage for himself.

He had done all his homework, checked and double-checked all his information, plotted his strategy carefully and meticulously, and now it was time to put his plan into action.

He left work at his normal time, went home, showered and changed, and then set out for Chelsea. It didn't take her long to answer the door to his knock. She might have all the social advantages, Max decided chivalrously as he studied her, but she was certainly nothing very remarkable to look at.

Plain brown hair cut into a neat bob, brown eyes, a small round face to go with her equally small and gently rounded body. As she saw him studying her, she flushed deep pink and looked shyly self-conscious.

'I'm sorry,' he apologised, giving her his most charming and winning smile, the one that revealed the delicious dimple in his chin and made him look even more raffishly attractive than he had any right to be, as an adoring ex-girlfriend had once told him. 'Luke told me that you were only a tiny little thing, but I hadn't thought...'

'Luke?' she questioned, looking both flustered and curious, and reacting to his opening gambit just as he had planned and intended that she should.

'Yes, Luke Crighton, my cousin,' he explained, conveniently leap-frogging the interfamily complexities that in reality made Luke something like a fourth or fifth cousin rather than the much closer connection that referring to him as his cousin implied.

'Luke Crighton?' She was frowning slightly now and looking both embarrassed and confused.

Max took a couple of steps towards her, causing her to retreat into the house and allowing him to follow her inside. It was a simple enough manoeuvre to master and one he had used to good effect many times in the past.

'There,' he explained mock-ruefully, 'I told Luke that you probably wouldn't remember him. You worked in chambers with him in Chester some time ago. His father, my uncle was...'

'Oh yes...' Her face cleared. 'Of course, Luke...'

Her colour deepened and she looked both flattered and self-conscious and Max knew perfectly well why. He resisted the temptation to laugh. Did this plain, dull-looking little thing really believe that Luke was likely to have remembered her?

'So you're Luke's cousin...er...please come in.'

A little awkwardly she ushered him into a very Colefax and Fowler furnished sitting room, which Max guessed, as he cast a brief eye over it, probably cost more to decorate than he was likely to earn in a full year, and as for the value of the antiques he could see scattered around the room... Its whole ambience shrieked family wealth and family status and his resentment against her grew. Why the hell couldn't she have been satisfied with what her type did best? Living in the country and breeding, *that* was what she was designed for. You only had to look at those softly rounded hips....

'Er, can I get you a drink?'

'Thanks,' Max accepted easily. 'Dry sherry if you've got any.'

She had, of course, and it pleased him to notice that her hand trembled noticeably as she handed him a glass.

'So, how is Luke?'

'He's fine, still based in Chester, of course. I saw him when I went home for a family celebration a few weeks ago. We were both reminiscing about our misspent youth and he happened to mention you and suggested that I call and pass on his regards.'

'Oh...I see...how kind. I'm surprised he even remembered me, really,' she told him guilelessly. 'I was only there the one summer and we didn't keep in touch. I hadn't realised... And what do you do?' she asked him politely.

'I'm in pupillage at the moment,' he told her. 'Or rather, I'm waiting for a vacancy.' He pulled a wry face. 'I could move straight into chambers in Chester, of course, but I prefer to be independent, to make it on

my own rather than rely on family patronage.' He
gave her a crocodile smile and waited.

'Oh yes,' she agreed, stammering slightly, 'I...I
couldn't agree more.'

'Mmm...good sherry,' he commented, pointedly
studying her legs as she quickly responded to his hint
and took his glass away to refill it.

She had the kind of neat, delicate ankles that
plumpish girls often had and they looked as though
they were rather nicely tanned beneath her sheer
stockings.

'What about you?' he asked her, accepting his
newly filled glass and the comfortable easy chair she
indicated. As he slid nonchalantly into his seat, he noticed the way she perched uncomfortably on the edge
of hers. 'Luke mentioned that you were planning to
study for the Bar yourself after university.'

'Did he? I didn't realise he knew...I didn't think...'

Max held his breath as he heard the note of uncer-
tainty enter her voice. He was really going to have the
ground cut from under him if she came out with some
comment about not having made up her mind what
she was going to do when she worked in Chester. Max
had always preferred the bold manoeuvre over the
cautious, preferring to gamble for high stakes rather
than low and he guessed that with her family background, her choice of career would be automatic and
unquestioning, just like her acceptance of his lies
about Luke's remembering her.

'Well, yes...I've taken my Bar exams and have been
in pupillage,' she acknowledged, allowing him to start
to relax, 'but I'm not sure...that is, as yet I haven't
quite... Mummy and Daddy thought I might like to

take a year off before...' She bit her lip and looked acutely self-conscious.

'Mummy's on the committee of a charity that helps homeless children all over the world and she wants me to go with her on her next tour. I'd like to but... Well...I'm the only one, you see, and I feel I owe it to Daddy to...to preserve the family tradition. He and my grandfather would never say anything, of course. They'd never push me, but one does feel that one has some kind of obligation.'

'Sounds rather like my people, especially my grandfather,' Max responded with another crocodile smile. 'It must be something to do with the way they were trained.'

'Oh...what does he do?'

'He's retired now,' Max told her smoothly. No need to mention at this stage that the elderly man had only made it as a country solicitor. 'But I do understand what you mean about upholding a family tradition. As a Crighton, it's expected that one will become involved with law one way or another. As you say, one feels a sense of responsibility and duty.' He gave her a complacent look, which was rewarded by a shy smile.

'It's nice to talk to someone who knows...who understands...' she started to confide. She broke off and said instead, 'It isn't always easy, is it? One seems to be sort of caught in the middle of things, caught between one's family and—'

'And those who think that because of your family, your history and connections, that everything is so much easier for you,' Max suggested sympathetically.

She gave him another smile. 'Yes, yes, exactly that, and yet in many ways it can be harder because one

feels that...' She spread her hands and admitted, 'I feel
guilty myself sometimes, especially when I see how
hard other people have to work. I even feel guilty
about...well, it isn't easy to find a place in chambers,
and there are people with outstanding qualifications
who just don't...'

She stopped again and looked at him. She had a
habit of leaving her sentences unfinished and waiting
for someone else to finish them for her—an indication
of the fact that there had always been someone around
to complete life's more mundane chores for her, Max
decided resentfully. But he kept that resentment hidden, the expression on his face benignly and decep-
tively understanding.

'My...my friend, Claudine, who shares here with
me, she has the most wonderful qualifications but because she doesn't have any family background in the
law she has been finding it most awfully difficult to
get a place in chambers and yet I know she would
make the most wonderful barrister.'

'Perhaps your father could help her,' Max suggested carelessly. He didn't have the remotest interest
in her friend, whoever she was, and even less in her
problems in getting a toe-hold on their very slippery
and steep career ladder. Why the hell should he? *He*
had enough problems of his own.

'Well, yes...' she agreed, looking awkwardly uncomfortable. 'Daddy could do something but...'

But he probably felt disinclined to use his un-
doubted power for the advancement of someone who
was not 'family'. That was, after all, how the system
worked, how *life* worked, Max acknowledged cynically, but he kept those thoughts to himself, glancing

with apparent regret at his now-empty glass and getting to his feet, telling his unsuspecting hostess, 'I really must go. I've taken up more than enough of your time. I hope I haven't held you up, delayed you on your way out?'

'No...not at all... I wasn't going out and...and I really enjoyed talking to you,' Madeleine told him shyly. 'Please...please remember me to Luke when you next see him.'

'Oh no,' Max told her softly, moving in for the kill. 'I don't think I can do that.'

She gave him a startled look.

'I've enjoyed...talking, as well,' he continued in that same soft, meaningful voice, not giving her the opportunity to speak or question. 'In fact, I've enjoyed it so much that...will you have dinner with me one evening?'

'Oh...oh yes, I'd like... Yes, that would be very nice,' she amended quickly.

Got her, Max crowed in silent triumph. Not that he had had any doubts. She wasn't his type, of course. Too plain, too dull, too 'nice'. If he could make her blush and tremble simply by looking at her and talking to her, it didn't say much for her sexual experience, and naïvely awkward, properly brought-up virgins held no sexual appeal for Max. But then, it wasn't her virginity he was interested in taking from her, was it?

'Yes...it will be,' he agreed softly. 'Very, very nice.'

Whilst she was still blushing and looking confused, he told her, 'I'm free on Thursday if you are.'

It was only two days away but he didn't want to give her any time to start having doubts and asking

questions and he certainly didn't want her thinking
that he was free at the weekend.

'Thursday? Yes...yes...that would be lovely.'

Max smiled. 'Thursday it is, then.' He frowned as he
heard someone opening the door.

'Maddy... Oh...I'm sorry, I didn't realise you had a
visitor.'

The girl who came in was everything that
Madeleine was not. Slender, elegantly narrow-boned
and just exactly the right kind of height. Her hair was
shoulder length, thick and naturally wavy and a deep
rich brown with honey gold highlights around her
face, which was smooth-skinned and perfectly
shaped, her eyes a deep sea green and her mouth the
kind of mouth that automatically made Max think of
sex.

'Oh, Claudine...this is Max...Max Crighton...
Max...this is Claudine...my friend.'

'Max Crighton.' There was a certain quick, sharp as-
sessment in her eyes as they studied him, a very definite sense of cool withdrawal and hesitation, which
Max countered by looking pleasantly through her
rather than at her.

She was the kind of woman who took for granted
that her looks would make her the focus of any male
attention, he decided, and that air of cool withdrawal
was no doubt a trick she employed to increase her de-
sirability. Well, in this instance, she was wasting her
time, and ignoring her, he turned back to Madeleine.

'I'll see you on Thursday,' he told her warmly. 'If I
pick you up here around seven-thirty...?'

'Yes, yes, that will be fine,' she agreed huskily.

* * *

Claudine waited until he had gone before tackling her friend. 'Max Crighton...you know who he is, don't you?' she warned Maddy forthrightly.

'Yes... Yes. I know,' Madeleine agreed quietly. 'But Claudine...'

'What was he doing here?'

'He... I know his cousin...'

'You never said anything.'

'No...I didn't think...'

'You're sure you want to see him again, then?'

'Yes...yes, I'm sure...'

'Be careful, Maddy,' Claudine warned her. 'You know he—'

'I like him, Claudine,' Madeleine interrupted huskily, turning her back so that Claudine couldn't see her betraying expression. It was all right for Claudine; men fell for her on sight, and she never felt shy or awkward in their presence. She never had to sit in a corner and feel excluded, unwanted, unattractive. She didn't have to bear the burden of knowing that her parents were disappointed by her lack of good looks. But Max had made her feel special, different...and he hadn't even looked properly at Claudine. She knew— she had been watching him, holding her breath, waiting for the familiar male reaction to her friend's loveliness, only it simply never came. Max just hadn't seemed to notice how stunningly lovely Claudine was. Instead he had focused on her and it was her he had invited out.

Frowning, Claudine studied her friend's tense back, torn between wanting to voice her suspicions and warn her friend and knowing that if she did so, she would risk hurting her by implying that Max Crighton could have some ulterior motive in seeking her out.

Madeleine had been a good friend to her and Claudine felt intensely protective towards her; despite all her material and social advantages, she was essentially a rather lonely and shy girl who had allowed others to bully and dominate her.

'He was nice to me, Claudine, kind...' Madeleine continued in a muffled voice without turning round.

Claudine stifled her doubts and said bracingly instead, 'I should think he jolly well ought to be,' then couldn't resist double-checking, 'Who exactly is this cousin of his, by the way? Why haven't I heard you mention him?'

It was quite depressing how easily and quickly one slipped back into the familiar routine, Guy decided gloomily as he set out for the shop the morning after his return from holiday.

Three weeks sailing in the Greek islands had given his skin an even deeper colour and toned up those muscles that didn't get daily use in his job.

Well, he might have been away for three weeks but he doubted anything would have changed in Haslewich; it simply wasn't that kind of town. He was glad, though, that today was one of Jenny's days in the shop. He had thought about her a lot whilst he was away, but then, what was unusual about that?

He knew there were a lot of people who would have been astonished at the strength of his feelings for her. Sometimes he warned himself about it. After all, she was a woman some years his senior, placidly and happily married, a woman, moreover, who was simply not the type one connected with intense and unrequited feelings of love and lust.

There was a trade fair coming up soon and he wondered, as he had on many similar occasions in the past, what his chances were of persuading her to attend it with him. An overnight stay in some secluded, romantic little hideaway might just... Who the hell was he kidding? he taunted himself as he reached the shop and felt in his pocket for his keys.

He frowned as he started to insert them in the lock and then realised that it was already open. Turning the handle he walked in, his frown deepening as he saw Jenny come through from the back room.

She looked different somehow, thinner, frailer, and she wasn't smiling her usual warm, generous smile. Instead she looked tired, strained and distinctly on edge.

'Jenny,' he exclaimed fondly, 'I wasn't expecting you to be here before me. I thought you'd be glad of the opportunity to have some time off after three weeks of covering for me,' he joked.

'I had to come into town to drop Joss off for the school bus,' she told him tersely. 'So I decided I might just as well come straight here.'

Guy watched her thoughtfully. When Jenny couldn't drive Joss all the way to school, Jon normally dropped Joss off for the bus, not Jenny.

She had turned away from him and proceeded to dust a small, delicate china figurine, her face averted from him.

'Did you have a good holiday, Guy?' he asked himself conversationally, his gaze on her down-bent head. 'Why, yes, Jenny, I did, thank you.'

He had only meant to tease her a little. It was so unlike her not to make the enquiry, not to be genuinely and keenly interested in others, but instead of laughing and apologising as he had expected, her hands fumbled with the figurine, causing it to slip through her fingers and smash down onto the floor, breaking into several small pieces.

Immediately Guy dropped to his knees to pick them up and then stopped as he looked towards Jenny and saw that she was standing motionlessly beside him, an expression of mingled shock and despair in her eyes as they welled with tears.

Guy contritely rose to his feet and put his hand out to comfort her. 'Hey, it's only a piece of china,' he reminded her gently, 'and not even a particularly valuable one at that.' He smiled reassuringly at her. It was so unlike Jenny to be clumsy. He couldn't remember her ever fumbling with anything before, never mind actually dropping something. She was always so careful and deft.

She was crying now, silent tears flooding down her cheeks. As he watched in distress, she lifted her hands to cover her face, her shoulders heaving as the tears slid through her fingers. Such grief couldn't possibly be caused by the simple loss of an ornament, Guy knew.

'Jenny, what is it? What's wrong?' he asked.

For a moment he thought she wasn't going to tell him. The sight of her grief, all the more shocking because of its very silence, as though the pain was so great that she couldn't endure the added agony of giving it voice, made his own stomach muscles clench in angry helplessness. Automatically he moved closer to her, wrapping both arms around her.

He was right. She had lost weight; he could feel her bones through her skin. She seemed tiny and fragile, frighteningly so.

'Jenny,' he urged, wanting to hold her even closer and yet afraid to do so in case he hurt her.

'All right,' she acquiesced, misunderstanding the reason for the pleading, questioning way he said her name. 'If you must know, Jon has left me.'

Guy felt his whole body stiffen in surprise and disbelief. 'Jenny,' he muttered huskily, totally unable to voice his stunned emotions.

'Jenny what?' she demanded tearfully.

'Jenny, it can't be true....'

'Oh, but it is true. You'll hear all about it soon enough.'

He couldn't see her face, but he sensed that she had stopped crying although she was trembling in his arms as though her body was unable to contain the intensity of her pain and outrage.

'The whole town's been talking about it...and who can blame them? If they think they've got something to talk about now, just wait until they find out *why* he's gone.'

She began crying again. Great noisy, gulping sobs this time. Guy held her tightly.

'Why *has* he gone, Jen?' he questioned gently, as gently as though he were speaking to a child, somehow knowing that this was what she needed, that possibly for the first time in her life she needed to be allowed to behave instinctively and emotionally instead of sensibly and logically, to put herself first instead of others.

'He's fallen in love with Tiggy—Tania,' she admitted painfully, pushing herself away from him slightly and looking up into his face, her eyes full of misery and despair. 'And who can blame him? You only have to look at her...'

'She's nowhere near the woman that you are, Jen,' Guy told her roughly. 'My God, if he's left you for her, then he's a fool.'

'No, not a fool. He's just doing what he's always been taught...trained to do. All his life he's been taking responsibility for David and now that David is so ill, what could be more logical than taking responsibility for David's wife, as well?'

She started to laugh a wild, dangerous laugh, one on the edge of hysteria, that made Guy's heart ache unbearably for her.

He wanted to be able to offer her some form of comfort and reassurance but he suspected that there was none that she would accept—or at least not from him. He had always known how much she loved Jon and he assumed that Jon felt the same way about her, yet despite his awareness of her suffering, he could not help wanting to take advantage of the opportunity that fate had given him.

'Look, why don't we close the shop for an hour? We aren't normally that busy on Monday morning. We'll go and have a cup of tea and you can tell me all about it.'

'Oh, Guy.' Fresh tears started to fall. 'I still can't really believe that it's happening, that Jon has actually gone. A temporary separation, to give him time to think, that's what he's calling it. The children, everyone else, thinks...' She bit her lip. 'Everyone else thinks it's because of David...the shock of his heart attack and that Jon is...that he will—'

'That he's having a mid-life crisis accelerated by David's illness,' Guy supplied for her. 'Perhaps he is.'

Jenny shook her head. 'I don't know...I don't know anything any more,' she told him painfully.

'It *could* just be a temporary thing,' Guy felt bound to comfort her. 'You've been married a long time and—'

'Jon married me because he felt he had to, not because he loved me,' she broke in tensely.

Guy stared at her.

It was the first time in all the years he'd known her that she had referred to the fact that she was pregnant when she and Jon had married.

There had been a certain amount of gossip at the time, of course. He, as a schoolboy, had overheard something about it without being particularly interested in what it meant and later he had assumed that the subsequent death of the child shortly after his birth had been so painful that the subject was simply never referred to. It had never occurred to him to question the happiness of the marriage.

'The two of you may originally have married because you were carrying Jon's child,' he agreed, 'but—'

'No.' Jenny shook her head, her eyes darkly sombre as she looked not so much at him as through him, he realised, as though she was looking back into the past. 'No,' she continued, 'I wasn't carrying Jon's child. It was David's....'

Guy willed himself not to betray his shock or to ask her any questions. Instead he simply took one of her hands and, holding it gently between his own, said quietly, 'Come on...let's go and have that cup of tea.'

She went with him as docilely as a small child, watching whilst he locked up the shop and then allowing him to guide her down the street.

He knew exactly where he intended taking her—the only place where they could be guaranteed the degree of privacy he knew they, she, needed—but cautiously he took a circuitous route towards it. Generation upon generation of Cookes had learned to value the habits and instincts of stealth and caution and to stake their lives on them. Now it wasn't so much his life that was at stake as Jenny's reputation. This was still very much a small country town after all and Jenny was now in the highly invidious position of being a 'single' woman.

He felt her tense slightly as he led her along the maze of narrow back streets and then out onto the road that led to his own house, but she didn't say anything as he drew her arm through his own and walked her towards his home.

'I've never been inside your house before,' she commented as he led her through the small front door.

'No,' he agreed.

He wondered how she would react if he told her how often he had pictured her here, and not just here downstairs in his little living room, but upstairs in the huge old oak four-poster that virtually filled the open-plan upper storey of the house. When he had initially bought the bed he found he had to have the small existing bedrooms knocked into one to accommodate it and a small extension built out over the kitchen to house the bathroom.

The bed had at one time come from the local castle, or so local rumour had it, although how on earth it had ever actually been moved from its original place, Guy had no idea. He had bought it from a farmer's wife who had complained that she was sick of the huge, ugly old thing. He had had to employ someone to take it apart and rebuild it again but it had been worth it.

From his neat and compact kitchen he could watch Jenny as she stood in the centre of his living room, slowly taking in her surroundings. Did she realise yet what she had told him? Had she meant to tell him or...?

The kettle boiled, he made the tea, poured two cups, put them on a tray and carried it through to the living room.

'Now,' he instructed, 'sit down and tell me everything.'

'I've already told you,' Jenny said heavily. 'Jon's left me, he's in love with Tiggy....'

'Where is he living? Has he actually moved in with her?' Guy frowned, trying to imagine old Ben's reaction to the news that Jon had usurped his brother David's place in his own marital bed.

'No...no, he's renting somewhere...a house... Oh, he keeps pretending that it isn't because of Tiggy—he keeps saying that—but I know the truth,' she told him fiercely. 'I *know* it's just a matter of time before...'

'What about David? Does he know...is he...?'

Jenny shook her head. 'No...I don't think so, unless Tiggy's told him. He's out of hospital now but he isn't at home. He's staying in a nursing home at the moment. The specialist felt that he needed to rest and avoid any kind of strain, and of course Tiggy agreed. Well, she would, wouldn't she?' she added bitterly.

'So it isn't just Jon who...? Tiggy feels the same way, does she?'

Guy hated himself for asking such a question when he saw the way Jenny winced and bit down hard on her bottom lip.

'Yes,' she agreed hoarsely. 'Yes...she seems to be as much in love with Jon as he is with her.'

'Jen...' Guy paused delicately. 'In the shop you said that...at least you implied—'

'That when Jon married me I was pregnant with David's child,' she finished tiredly. 'Yes, it's true, I was.' She looked up at the ceiling, trying to control the tears she could feel threatening to fall. This morning the last thing she had intended to do was confide in Guy like this; in fact, she had been dreading his return, passionately wishing that he wasn't coming back. She had grown unexpectedly adroit at avoiding people recently, at refusing to allow them to get close enough to her to ask questions and offer sympathy. Even Olivia and Ruth had met with a firm rebuff when they tried to sympathise with her.

She didn't want sympathy. What she wanted was to have her husband back and her life restored to normalcy and no amount of commiseration was going to achieve that for her. She even found, to her shame, far from welcoming people's concern, she almost actively resented them for it. It made her feel like...like a beggar forced to accept the charity of others and be openly grateful for it.

And she had certainly never intended to tell Guy about David's baby. She started to shiver slightly. She still had no clear idea of why she *had* done, apart from the fact that now Jon had gone, there seemed no real point in keeping it a secret any longer. It was as though the guilt and shame she had felt, both then and all through the years of their marriage, not in having conceived David's child, but in having allowed Jon to sacrifice his own life in order to protect all three of them—herself, the baby and, of course, most importantly of all in Jon's eyes at any rate, David himself—had finally been forced to a head, which had burst this morning like a suppurating wound expelling its poison.

'What's wrong?' she demanded fiercely as she saw the way Guy was looking at her. 'Have I shocked you?'

'No, it's not that,' Guy denied quietly. 'It's just that I never imagined…you aren't…'

'I'm not what…not the type?' Jenny smiled bitterly. 'No, I don't suppose I am, but that doesn't make it less a fact.

'David and I had been dating for some time when I found out that what I'd thought was love was in reality nothing more than a silly teenage crush on my part and just a way of passing the time before going to university on David's. We went our separate ways without any animosity, David to university and me back to school.' She gave a small shrug. 'My mother had been unwell for a while and then we discovered that her illness was terminal. I was needed at home to help take care of her. Jon and I were…friends, nothing more...just friends. When I found out I was pregnant...' She paused and bit her lip a second time.

'You told him because he was David's brother...?'

'Something like that,' Jenny agreed. 'Although it was more him who told me. I fainted one day while he was up at the farm. It never occurred to me that I might be pregnant but Jon guessed straight away. When he suggested that we should get married, I was so relieved to have someone take the responsibility off my shoulders, that I agreed.' She looked at Guy. 'I know what you must be thinking, that I was selfish...that I used Jon...that I deserve to lose him now, but—'

'No, I don't think any of those things,' Guy assured her gravely.

How old must she have been? Seventeen, eighteen at the most, a very young and very frightened girl whose mother was dying and who had no one she could turn to.

'I *knew* that Jon didn't love me...how could he? But he convinced me that it was the right thing to do, that the baby, David's baby, had the right to be brought up amongst his own blood relatives. He told his parents that *he* was the father when his father tried to stop our marrying. I think...I always felt that perhaps their mother knew, but if she did, she never said anything. Sarah was very kind to me throughout and she...'

Jenny swallowed and forced back the aching burn of the tears searing the back of her eyes.

'I was so well all through the pregnancy that I couldn't believe it when they told me...' She took a deep breath, her voice choking with tears. 'They said it was his heart, that the...'

Jenny had to stop speaking as she relived the pain of hearing the doctor tell her that her baby had died shortly after his birth.

'It was all for nothing, you see,' she told Guy in anguish now. 'All for *nothing*. Jon need never have married me after all, because in the end there *was* no baby.'

'Jen, please, my darling, don't...' Guy begged her, unable to endure her suffering, the unguarded words of tender endearment spoken before he could recall them, but Jenny seemed not to notice.

'Afterwards...after the funeral, I offered Jon his freedom but he wouldn't take it and I didn't...' She raised her head and looked directly at Guy. 'By then I had fallen in love with him. He was, is...all the things that David could never, ever be and I loved him desperately, but he never really loved me. He never said anything, but I've always guessed, always known.'

Guy could think of nothing to say, could find no words to comfort her.

Jenny had finished her tea. She looked at her empty cup and then said quietly, 'We ought to get back to the shop. It's almost lunch-time.'

She was curiously light-headed, Jenny realised as she walked towards the door without waiting to see if Guy was following her. She felt empty, purged almost, and strangely separate from herself, as though she had somehow gained the ability to step outside of her body and watch herself as an observer, curiously detached from her own pain, temporarily insulated from it.... Her heart temporarily missed a beat. Temporarily... How apt. Everything in life was, after all, temporary, wasn't it? Life itself was fleetingly unstable and not to be relied upon.

14

———➤ ◄———

David reached for the remote control switch of his television and settled himself more comfortably in his chair. He really ought to be taking more exercise. The specialist had reproved him the previous day when he had called at the nursing home to check up on him. These days, heart attack patients were not encouraged to spend too much time in bed, it seemed, even those who'd had attacks as serious as David's.

Mr Hayes had been dubious at first when David had insisted that he wanted to go somewhere else to recuperate instead of going straight home from hospital, but ultimately David had managed to talk him round.

'You've had a very lucky escape,' the specialist had told him.

A lucky escape. If only that was true. He might have earned himself a respite but that was all. Sooner or later he was going to be called to account. By now, Jon would no doubt have discovered what he had been doing. It would probably have been better if he had *not* survived, David decided morosely. Had Jon said anything to anyone else yet? He got out of the chair and walked over to the window. The nursing home was surrounded by neatly manicured lawns and paths wide enough to take a wheelchair.

Tiggy had been to see him this morning; he had pretended to be asleep. She hadn't stayed very long, thank God. The main drawback to his present existence was that it gave one too much time to think. And there was one thing he had definitely decided and that was, no matter what the outcome of the financial mess he had got himself into, he could no longer stay married to Tiggy. Didn't any of them realise the burdens they had placed on him, the way they had controlled his life? His father, his brother, Tiggy, all of them, with their expectations and their demands.

Ben had filled him with such an unbearable mixture of resentment and guilt, weighing him down with the overwhelmingly relentless pressure of his love, his determination that David would be all the things he had not been able to be. God, he shuddered when he thought about the way he had been sacrificed on the family altar, his life mapped out for him virtually from the moment of his birth, no choice allowed, every indulgence given, just so long as he kept his feet immovably placed in the dead men's shoes his father had created for him.

But he wasn't his father's dead twin. He *wasn't* his grandfather. Had he been given a choice, the last career he would have chosen would have been the law. Deep down inside himself, soul deep if there was such a thing, he had a craving, a yearning, a need for challenge and change, limitless horizons, excitement and even danger.

In the drug-filled days following his heart attack, he had dreamt of it, travelling storm-swollen rivers through vast jungle terrain, beset by swirling, foaming rapids, huge thundering cataracts, and being swept along almost to the very brink of death—the ultimate adventure.

He had known then that he couldn't go on with his present life. Oh for the days when a family's black sheep was shipped out to some far-flung shore. Oh indeed.

And Jon, Jon with his quiet, watchful gaze, his loyalty. Jon should have been the chosen one. If he had... Jon who as a boy had covered for him and taken the blame for so many of *his* misdemeanours. Jon whom, if the truth were known, he sometimes almost hated for his very generosity towards him and whom he almost always envied because he was not their father's favoured child. Jon, too, was a burden—a living reminder of all his own fallibilities and weaknesses, of all that he himself could never be.

And last but not least, of course, Tiggy...Tiggy...his wife. She was the greatest burden of them all. There was no way that he could ever live with her again. No way that he could ever go back to his old life. No way at all.

'Is there still no word from Jemima Harding's accountants?' Olivia asked Jon anxiously a few weeks after her discovery of her father's less than honest actions.

He shook his head. 'Not as yet. The original meeting had been cancelled and the partner dealing with Jemima's affairs was apparently on holiday. I called in at the home yesterday to see Jemima. She's not at all well,' Jon reported grimly.

'What will happen if...when she dies?' Olivia asked worriedly. But she already knew the answer to her own question. 'Has...has Dad said anything to you about...?'

Again Jon shook his head.

It was incomprehensible to Olivia that her father could so apparently easily dismiss what he had done. Surely he must realise that his fraudulent activities, his *theft*, were bound to have come to light.

Olivia watched her uncle as he checked through the post. When she had first learned that he and Jenny had decided to separate, she had been stunned. They had always seemed so happy together. She was uneasily aware of how much her mother had started to lean and depend on Jon since her father's heart attack and she just hoped...

So far, as far as she knew, there had been no recurrence of her mother's nightmarish eating binge and Olivia had slowly started to relax a little and to tell herself hopefully that it might just have been a one-off incident and that her fears about her mother were groundless.

She had an appointment later on that morning to draw up the will of an old lady who lived several miles outside town and who, because of her incapacitating rheumatism, Olivia was to visit rather than the other way round.

Jon was due to appear in court in Chester that afternoon with one of his clients and Olivia had been slightly disturbed when her mother had announced the previous evening that she intended to travel to Chester with Jon in order to do some shopping.

Saul had returned home, but he had kept in touch, ringing her almost every day. They were light-hearted, amusing telephone calls, outlining the problems he was having in finding a suitable nanny for the children.

'I don't suppose *you* feel like taking pity on me and stepping into the breach,' he had teased on one occasion.

'Certainly not,' Olivia had refused.

'Ah, so *you've* heard the stories, as well, have you?' he challenged her.

'What stories?' Olivia had asked curiously.

'Oh, you know, the ones where the father always falls for the nanny,' he had told her wickedly.

Be careful, Olivia had warned herself after he had rung off. It would be dangerously easy to resurrect her teenage fantasy for Saul, to assuage her damaged emotions and fill the empty space in her life with him.

She had heard nothing from Caspar and no longer expected to even though, ridiculously, her heart still started to beat much too quickly whenever the phone rang at home; and she still rushed to collect the post. But even if he did get in touch with her, what good would it do at this point? She was hardly likely to be granted a work permit in the US now or even an entry visa, not with a father who was soon to become a convicted criminal.

In a world where so much could be determined by human intervention, it came as even more of a shock to discover that fate, nature, destiny, call it what you would, could *still* have such a devastating and unanticipated effect on human lives.

'So you're Jon's daughter, you say...?'

'No, David's,' Olivia patiently corrected the old lady she had come to see. The niece who looked after her, calling at her cottage every day to check up on her, had been dismissed following Olivia's arrival.

'No doubt she's decided that she wants to leave her bits and pieces to my sister instead of me,' Margaret had told Olivia dryly. 'She's like that. Mind you, if you ask me, they're all inclined to go a bit that way when they get old. I suppose we'll be the same if we live that long. She's ninety-one next time....'

'Ninety-one...' Olivia gazed at the tiny, wizened figure on the chair opposite her own.

'David's...' The old lady's gaze sharpened. 'Oh yes, I remember now...came home with some young American, didn't you? So our Margaret told me. What's happened to him?'

'He's gone back to America,' Olivia replied tersely. 'Now, about your will...'

'Gone back, has he? Oh well, he's not the first to do that by a long chalk. You want to ask your Aunt Ruth about that. A real to-do over *her* Yank there was, her father up in arms about what was going on, and her mother sending her off to her family in Yorkshire.'

Olivia frowned. Caspar had said something about her great-aunt being involved with an American, but she had forgotten all about it in the turmoil of her father's heart attack and the discovery that had followed.

'Not told you about it, has she?' the old woman asked. 'Well, dare say she wouldn't. Never liked the Yanks, her father, and there was a real to-do up at the house when he found out what was going on. My daughter Liza used to work there then and she came home full of it.' She chuckled. 'Not that your grandfather had it all his own way. She had plenty of spirit

about her, did your Aunt Ruth, but my Liza told me
that they'd found out he was married, this American
of Ruth's, and that was that, then. The poor girl was
broken-hearted. Had to be sent to Yorkshire to get
over it. It's a long time ago now. Quick, before our
Margaret comes back...about my will...'

'How do you feel about taking pity on me and
having dinner with me tonight?'

'Saul...how can I?' Olivia protested, laughing after
she picked up the telephone and heard Saul's voice.
'You're in—'

'No, I'm not,' he interrupted softly. 'I'm right here in
Haslewich, well, almost...'

She could hear the warmth in his voice and a huge
wave of desolation and loneliness swept over her.
'What...what are you doing up here?' she asked him
chokily. 'I thought—'

'Business. I've got a meeting in Chester in the morning. I'm staying at the Grosvenor. I could drive over
and collect you and—'

'No...no...I'll drive to Chester,' Olivia countered. It
would do her good to get out. She had spent far too
many nights worrying and brooding over problems
for which she knew there were no solutions.

'Good girl,' Saul said quietly before asking, 'How
soon can you get here?'

The Grosvenor was right in the centre of Chester.
The doorman welcomed her with a well-trained smile
and a brief admiring glance as she walked past him
and to the foyer, where Saul was waiting for her.

He looked dangerously handsome in his elegantly
cut dark suit and Olivia noticed the way his glance fell

appreciatively on her body as he greeted her, her pulse rate picking up betrayingly as her body registered the interest and responded to it.

'Mmm...you look good enough to eat,' Saul told her as he ignored her attempt to hold him at a distance and bent his head to kiss her very firmly and lingeringly on the mouth. 'So good in fact,' he murmured wickedly as he lifted his mouth from hers, 'that I—'

'Saul,' Olivia warned him reprovingly.

'All right,' he said, laughing, 'but you can't blame me for trying. I like the dress, by the way,' he remarked. 'Black suits you. Have you heard anything from Caspar?'

Olivia shook her head. 'What about you? Has Hillary...?'

'She's been in touch via her lawyers,' he replied dryly. 'Looks like she's very eager to get the divorce through. I wonder why. Perhaps she's already lined up her next victim.'

Olivia could feel her heart starting to thump unevenly. Did Saul know about Hillary and Caspar?

'Saul...' she began, but before she could ask him, he was leaning forward and whispering to her.

'Your lipstick's all smudged.'

'And whose fault is that?' Olivia challenged him indignantly. 'Now I'll have to go and repair it.'

'I've got a better idea....' As his thumb pressed gently against her lower lip and his eyes looked deeply into her own, she saw there the unmistakable message of desire; Olivia took a steadying breath and determinedly stepped back from him.

She felt as though she had just drunk a large glass of champagne much, much too quickly and, as a result, had become deliciously light-headed and slightly dizzy. Anticipation delicately threaded with sensual and sexual arousal curled headily through her body and she was tempted to cast aside her cares and behave illogically and, yes, even irresponsibly, to allow herself to imagine what it would be like to feel the warmth of Saul's arms around her, the heat of his mouth on hers, the hard male pressure of his body.

Be careful, she tried to warn herself. Saul is family, a relative...a friend...and not a potential lover. She had come to Chester simply to have dinner with him and to talk. That was all, she reminded herself firmly, that was *all*.

'You've hardly touched your meal. Would you prefer to order something else?'

Jenny shook her head and looked apologetically at their waiter as he came to remove their plates, hers barely touched, and Guy's empty.

'I'm just not very hungry,' she admitted and then added untruthfully, 'I ate with the children before I came out.'

She still wasn't quite sure exactly what she was doing here in Knutsford's premier bistro with Guy when she should have been at home doing the ironing and when, after all, she saw him almost every day at the shop as it was. She just knew that when he had telephoned out of the blue and suggested they go out together for a meal, for some reason without really allowing herself time to think, she had agreed.

For *some* reason... Now she *was* trying to ignore the truth. She knew perfectly well what had prompted her to accept Guy's invitation. It had been Olivia who had

informed her quite innocently that Jon had taken her
mother to Chester with him. Hot tears burned the
back of her eyes. There had been many times during
the years they had been married when she had ached
with the pain, the almost unbearable weight of her
love for Jon, knowing that loyal, caring, compassionate though he was, he couldn't possibly return it, but
there had never been a time when she had felt like
this, when her whole body seemed to be reflecting the
emotional agony of not just her loss, but even more
hurtfully, her searing jealousy of Tiggy.

Knowing Jon the way she did, she knew how painful it must be for him to have fallen in love with his
brother's wife. Jon, predictably, denied that his decision to leave had had anything to do with Tiggy but
Jenny knew better.

Oh yes, she had seen the covert, pitying looks of
other people when they saw her in the street and
somehow, most shaming and hurtful of all, the way
some women, women whom if anyone had asked her
beforehand, she would immediately and confidently
have claimed as friends, now seemed to avoid her, almost as though being deserted by one's husband was
akin to having a contagious disease that she might in-
advertently pass on to them.

'I just need some time to myself...some space to
think,' Jon had told her angrily when she tried to persuade him to stay, but he had not told her the whole
truth, and not even to Ruth had she been able to admit
her sense of failure and hopelessness, her feeling that
somehow she had always known this would happen,
that one day Jon would suddenly realise all that he
had missed out on, all that he had given up for her.

No, not for *her*, she corrected herself tiredly, but for David. It was for *David's* sake that he had married her in the first place, not her own. For *David's* sake and the sake of the baby she had been carrying. *David's* baby...

Jon stared unseeingly out of the large picture window of the house he was renting and into the darkness of the garden beyond it. The house was quiet, too quiet, almost oppressively so, empty of the bustle and clamour he was used to. It was odd how it was the thing he had taken the most for granted; the thing he would, if asked, have said he would miss least of all. He actually found himself yearning for the din of children banging noisily up and down stairs, slamming doors, calling out to one another, playing loud music and having even louder quarrels. And through it all, that never-ending, irritating cacophony, came the gentle, warm, soothing sound of Jenny's voice.

Jenny... He closed his eyes, leaning his forehead against the glass. He could still see the look of shock and bewilderment in Jenny's eyes when he told her that he wanted to leave; could still hear the pain in her voice. She had tried to put up a bold front, even asking him practical questions about his plans. But although he knew he had hurt her terribly, he had been intent only on what he perceived was his own right to satisfy his own needs.

Jenny... He could still see in his mind's eye the way she had looked when he had guessed that she was pregnant with David's child, the fear she had tried so bravely to hide, her determination to take sole responsibility for what had happened, her clear-sighted resolution.

He had seen Louise earlier this evening in Hasle-wich, but when she had seen him she had deliberately crossed the road to avoid him, turning her head away from him. That had been after he had got back from Chester.

Chester. He let out a small groan, inwardly cringing as he relived what had happened there earlier in the day.

It had been his suggestion that he take Tiggy to the Grosvenor's bistro for lunch and he felt ashamed now to admit that he had enjoyed the envious looks of other men as Tiggy clung to his arm and flirted co-quettishly with him. Being with her made him feel like a different person, the person he decided he had al-ways meant to be but whom no one had ever allowed him to be—a different Jon, not good old staid, depend-able, reliable, self-effacing Jon, but the kind of Jon who'd quite naturally be with the kind of woman whom other men would watch with appreciative envy, the kind of Jon who would quite naturally lunch in places like the Grosvenor's bistro instead of snatch-ing a sandwich at his desk.

What a fool he had been creating a fantasy ego for himself, which in the end he simply had not been able to live up to—and worse.

Tiggy hadn't eaten much lunch, claiming that she wasn't very hungry, but she *had* drunk several glasses of wine, which was no doubt why she had whispered to him afterwards that instead of going their separate ways—him to court and her to do her shopping—they should spend the rest of the day together.

At first Jon hadn't suspected what she had really meant, which just made the whole farcical thing more appalling. It was only when Tiggy had laughed about the fact that they need not even sign the register with a fictitious name since they were in actuality a Mr & Mrs Crighton, that the full impact of what she intended them to do had struck him. And what had he done after all these weeks of behaving like a lovesick adolescent, all these weeks of determinedly denying that his decision to leave Jenny had anything whatsoever to do with Tiggy whilst at the same time secretly revelling in the knowledge of his desire for her?

Had he leaped at the chance she was offering him, his mind, his emotions, his body ablaze with the desire to consummate his love for her?

No, he had not. He groaned again. Even now, he still couldn't wholly believe how crassly, how cravenly he had behaved, how humiliatingly, how faint-heartedly and cowardly.

His body, far from being inflamed with passion, had instead been flooded with terrified fear, and even worse, that part of it that should at the very least have started to stir with rampant sexual excitement had chosen to beat a rather hasty retreat. His mind, instead of encouraging him to seize the opportunity Tiggy had given him, had commanded his tongue to start babbling inanities about the impossibility of their doing any such thing; had produced excuse after excuse whilst Tiggy simply stood and listened, watching him in disbelieving silence. And as for his emotions!

Jon opened his eyes and moved away from the window. That had been the worst blow of all, because instead of feeling the surge of pleasure and excitement, of love and delight that he *should* have experienced at Tiggy's suggestion, what he had actually felt was a tidal wave of shocked distaste, acutely aware that the very last thing he wanted to do was to take Tiggy to bed and, equally strongly, that the only body he wanted curled up next to his own in bed was that of his wife.

In the illuminating half-dozen or so seconds it had taken him to absorb all these self-revelations, he had been so stunned and distracted that it hadn't even occurred to him how Tiggy might be feeling.

He couldn't really blame her for the hysterical scene that had followed or for her accusations against him, or indeed for her refusal to travel back to Haslewich with him. He winced, remembering some of the things she had said and winced even more as he tried to understand why on earth he had ever imagined himself even remotely attracted to her.

What on earth had he done, and why? It was all so clear now.

Because for years he had been jealous of David, secretly resenting him and having to play a subordinate role. He had been a fool, Jon decided bleakly, a complete and utter fool, and he would give any-thing...*anything* to be able to simply wipe out the past few weeks, climb in his car and go home.... Home to Jenny and his children, *their* children... Home...to Jenny. He looked at the telephone and then frowned as it suddenly started to ring.

'Uncle Jon?'

'Yes, Jack,' he greeted David and Tiggy's son.

'It's Mum. Can you come round? She's...she's not very well.'

'Jack, what is it, what's wrong with her?' he demanded urgently, his heart sinking with foreboding, but his nephew had already replaced the receiver.

Quickly reaching for his car keys, Jon headed for the door.

Guy was just on the point of asking Jenny if she wanted a liqueur when she stood up, abruptly pushing her chair back, and said, 'Guy, I'm sorry...but...I want to go home.'

At first he thought that she mustn't be feeling well and he immediately called the waiter over and got to his own feet. Once they were outside, Jenny couldn't bring herself to look at him as she hurried to where he had parked the car. She felt so guilty, but nowhere near as guilty as she knew she would have felt if she had stayed.

'Jenny, what's the matter? Are you all right?' he asked her anxiously as he unlocked the car door for her.

'I'm fine, really,' she replied, then added shakily, 'It's...it's...just that this isn't right...not for me. I'm sorry, Guy,' she apologised. 'I know you're trying to be kind, to help, but...'

How could she explain to him how alien all this was to her, how barren and empty it made her feel to be out with him instead of with Jon and how she just *knew* that, no matter *how* lonely the years ahead might be for her on her own, solitude was infinitely preferable to trying to fill the space she had left in her with another man...even a man as kind and caring as Guy?

'I...I guess I'm just a one-man woman,' she told him, trying to force a smile, but she could see from Guy's expression that he wasn't deceived. 'I'm sorry,' she repeated, then turned away from him to look out of the car window.

Guy grimaced to himself...and longed to be able to retort, Not half as sorry as I am, but forced himself to hold back his bitterness and frustration. This wasn't how he had envisaged the evening ending at all.

In Chester, Olivia and Saul had finished eating. The restaurant was nearly empty with only themselves and another couple lingering over their liqueurs, reluctant to let the evening end.

'No, I don't believe you.' Olivia laughed, shaking her head as Saul finished telling her an amusing story about one of his company's overseas clients.

'It's true,' he protested, sharing her laughter. 'Oh, I almost forgot. I've some photographs in my room I promised I'd let Ruth have. Some are of the kids and the others are of her flower arrangements for the party. Perhaps you could deliver them to her for me?'

'Yes, of course,' Olivia agreed willingly, adding warningly, 'I think the waiters are waiting for us to leave, Saul. There's no one else in the dining room now.'

'What...?' Saul looked round and then shook his head in disbelief. 'I hadn't realised it was so late,' he admitted as they both stood up.

Once outside the restaurant he directed her towards the bank of lifts.

'I've never been entirely happy in these things,' Olivia confessed as the doors closed and the lift started to rise.

'Mmm. I know what you mean,' Saul returned, adding teasingly, 'Not that I would object to being trapped in one with you, Livvy.'

They both laughed as the lift rocked gently to a standstill on Saul's floor.

'It's this way,' he told her as they stepped out, removing his key card from his pocket as they reached his room. After he unlocked and opened the door he stood back, allowing Olivia to precede him inside. The room was a good size and pleasantly furnished, but then she wouldn't have expected anything less from the Grosvenor.

The colours and patterns had been carefully chosen to give the room a warm, welcoming look; the queen-size bed, Olivia noticed, had already been enticingly turned down. As she looked at it, Olivia automatically had to stifle a yawn.

'Tired?' Saul asked her sympathetically. 'These past few weeks can't have been easy for you.'

His warmth and sympathy were in such direct contrast to Caspar's attitude. Why on earth couldn't Caspar have been like Saul...sympathetic...understanding...?

'Livvy...?' she heard Saul asking.

She shook her head and told him quickly, 'It's getting late. I'd better go. If you'll give me the photographs...?'

'The photographs? Yes, yes, of course. Now just where did I put them?' Saul muttered under his breath as he went over to a chest of drawers and started to open the top one.

He had shrugged off his jacket as they entered the room, dropping it casually on one of the chairs, and now as she watched him, Olivia was suddenly and very dangerously conscious of just how very masculine a man he was...of just how well muscled his back was beneath its fine covering of soft white cotton.

'Now where the hell did I put them?' Saul was muttering again to himself as he closed the drawer. 'I know,' he announced triumphantly, snapping his fingers and turning round abruptly.

Forgetting that the bed was behind her, Olivia stepped back to avoid him, caught her heel in the fringe of the rug she had been standing on and started to fall.

'Hey, steady,' Saul warned her as he reached out to help her, but as his fingers tightened protectively around her upper arm his expression suddenly changed, the good-humoured amusement dying out of his eyes to be replaced by an expression, a look, that made Olivia start to tremble slightly, unable to draw her gaze away from his and from the desire it held.

'Saul...' she warned shakily.

Olivia could feel her heart beginning to pound. Her knees were on the verge of giving way as she became aware of how Saul was looking at her mouth.

'Saul, don't,' she protested huskily.

'Don't fight it, Livvy,' he told her softly. 'It's what we both want, what we both need.'

'No,' Olivia objected hoarsely. 'You just think that because...because of what's happened, because...because I'm here.'

Saul was still holding on to her, drawing her closer, and weakly she let him.

Very gently he turned her to face him. 'Livvy, you know...' and then he stopped, his eyes suddenly blazing with a fierce hunger as he pulled her even closer and then cupped her face in his hands. 'I should have done this years ago,' he murmured as he fanned his fingers through her hair, the warmth of his breath whispering against her skin, her mouth. 'That night when I saw you in the river, then you wouldn't have said no, would you, Livvy?'

'Please don't,' she protested again, but it was too late. His mouth was already moving urgently against hers and she was responding to it, to him.

She ached so much for this kind of closeness, this kind of physical intimacy, missed it so much.... It felt so good to be held, touched, kissed, *wanted*.

She closed her eyes and wrapped her arms tightly around him, savouring his warmth, his desire. Her impatient hands began tugging at his shirt. His body felt hard and hot, so very hot beneath her questing fingertips. She heard him groan, felt the groan, his chest vibrating to the growled masculine sound of his arousal as she touched him. His body hair felt silky soft and somehow...

She frowned, some random thought trying to surface past the first thrust of the sensual pleasure that speared through her. She could feel his hands on her body, touching her firmly and yet at the same time almost hesitantly, so that her senses easily recognised that it was not his expertise or his desire that was holding him back but rather his need to have her physical confirmation that his touch was welcome.

Olivia gave it. The exhalation of her soft breath, the tiny half turn so that the palm of his hand rested against her breast, the deliberate opening of her mouth to his kiss were, she knew, all that was needed, all that he was asking of her, all that it took for him to slowly start kissing her throat and then her collarbone as he exposed it to his seeking mouth and then went on to expose her breasts to his seeking, tender hands. He was making no demands on her, imposing no rules, giving rather than expecting to be given.

'Mmm, Livvy,' she heard him mouth against her breast, 'you don't know how much I've wanted this...how much I've wanted you.'

She was trembling violently, as much with shocked excitement as with real desire, floating on a protective cloud, buoyed up by the ego-stroking pleasure of knowing she was wanted—desired. Saul's thumb stroked her nipple and she shuddered frantically in response.

'Olivia...'

As she focused on him she saw how desire had turned his eyes almost black, enlarging their pupils, his habitual, faintly cynical expression banished, his skin slightly flushed and hot, so hot that when he buried his face between her breasts and started to kiss the soft hollow between them, she could feel his heat.

And all the time he was kissing her, tasting her, he was still talking to her, praising her, his voice thick and slurred with the desire she could feel so potently pulsing from his body.

It was impossible for her to remain immune to that desire...to him; she could feel her own responsive arousal, see it in the way her nipples hardened and swelled provocatively, inviting the eager caress of his lips, his tongue, his mouth, and eagerly responding to them.

Saul had fully shrugged off his shirt, and with the hand that wasn't holding her, he was struggling with his belt. 'Help me,' he begged her throatily. 'Undress me, Olivia...'

Dizzily Olivia let him take her hand and place it on his belt, her fingers shaking in her response to the sharpness of his indrawn breath and the way his whole body shuddered as her fingertips grazed the bare flesh about his belt buckle.

She tugged at it ineffectually, her hands trembling too much for her to unfasten it properly, welcoming the hard warmth of Saul's hand as it covered hers, helped and guided her.

His belly was firm and flat, the crispness of his body hair activating the sensitive nerve endings beneath her skin as she touched him and felt his arms tighten around her in response. Closing her eyes, she lifted her face towards him. She had been feeling so besieged and beleaguered lately. It felt so good to be held like this, to be wanted, to have hostility and anger replaced with laughter and warmth.

She let her thoughts and her senses drift as he continued to kiss her, willing herself to ignore everything but the pleasure they were sharing, but deep down inside her a small mournful, grieving voice could not quite be silenced.

Something was wrong. Oh, her flesh, her body, her physical senses might be responding to Saul, welcoming the loving sensuality of his touch as it stimulated them. A part of her might enjoy seeing the heat and the need in his eyes as he looked down at her partially naked body, just as part of her enjoyed looking at him, but something was not quite right. Something was just not there, and as she tried to force herself to respond passionately to his kiss, Olivia knew what it was.

'Caspar.'

She didn't realise she had said his name aloud until she felt Saul gently but so firmly holding her away from him, the look in his eyes no longer aroused and passionate but instead rueful and knowledgeable.

'I...I'm sorry,' Olivia faltered. 'I didn't think...I didn't mean...'

'It's all right, Olivia,' Saul reassured her gently. 'I do understand.' He glanced down briefly at her still-naked breasts before releasing her and very tenderly tugging her clothes back in place. When he had finished he looked directly at her and smiled into her eyes. 'It is all right,' he repeated emphatically, 'and I do understand.'

'I didn't mean...it just...'

'I know, I know,' he soothed. 'But that still doesn't stop me from wishing,' he added ruefully.

He touched her face lightly with his fingertips as he started to do up his own clothing.

'I shouldn't have...' Olivia began, feeling guiltier by the minute. Saul was being so nice, so caring. If she had any sense she would make up her mind to forget about Caspar right now and...

It seemed she did not possess that admirable quality because right now the person she wanted more than any other in the world was...Caspar.

'No, *I* shouldn't have,' she heard Saul correcting her firmly. He took hold of her hands. 'Let's both agree that this—' he glanced around the bedroom '—was the result of a little too much good wine and a little too much wishful thinking—on my part at least.'

And then he leaned forward and gave her a determinedly cousinly peck on the cheek before saying briskly, 'Now, just where did I put those photographs?'

'Oh, Max...'

Max grimaced in impatience as he heard the emotion in Madeleine's voice and felt the warmth of her tears on his skin. If there was one thing he particularly loathed, it was women who cried in the aftermath of their orgasm. He might have known that Madeleine would be that type, just as he had known that she would be awkward and inexperienced, fortunately too inexperienced to realise just how manufactured his forced 'desire' for her actually was. Unlike her housemate, Claudine... She would have known and she would most definitely not have cried.

Irritably he suppressed the thought. He had never been attracted to brunettes and certainly not ones like her. She was far too assertive and self-assured, far too—

'Oh, Max! I wish we could always be together....'

Max tensed; this was his cue, the opening he had been angling for, carefully manoeuvring towards. 'So do I,' he lied adroitly, reaching to brush away her tears in a gesture of faked tenderness whilst he smiled his crocodile smile down into her tear-wet eyes. 'But you know the situation. I'm not...I can barely support myself...never mind anyone else....'

He could feel her pulse jump betrayingly beneath his fingers and felt his body start to ease into relaxation and triumph. It had all been so simple. Much, much simpler than even he had anticipated. Madeleine had proved boringly easy to charm and deceive, swallowing every one of the lies he had so cynically told her, gazing at him wide-eyed and adoringly as he relentlessly and ruthlessly manoeuvred his way into her life and her heart.

Prior to meeting her, he had had no clear idea of how best to accomplish his objective, but once he *had* met her... She was almost too persuadable and malleable, and the contempt he felt for her had now spread to include her parents, especially her father. Did he really believe that she had what it took to make a barrister? Oh, she might have the academic qualifications, but the thought of her ever appearing in a courtroom, even defending a case, never mind prosecuting one... And yet, just because of who she was, or rather who her father was, she still had the power to take that vacancy from him, or rather she thought she could.

Cleverly Max had given her no indication that he knew that she was his rival for the tenancy whilst at the same time apparently openly and disarmingly admitting to her how important getting it was to him. Predictably she had flushed bright red and become self-conscious and flustered, and she had even asked him if he couldn't find a vacancy with another set of chambers.

He had been tempted then to tell her crudely and bluntly what he really thought and felt, but he had restrained himself. He would get his opportunity to tell her once she had—as he was quite determined that she would—relinquished her claim on the vacancy in favour of him.

'Oh, there'll always be a vacancy for me in Chester,' he had told her carelessly and untruthfully.

In reality, the old man's pride would never allow him to accept any favours from the Chester branch of the family, even for his favourite grandson. Oh no! It could never be good enough for Max to match the achievements of his Chester cousins. He must supersede them. But Maddy, of course, knew nothing about any of that or about a good many other aspects of his life—and indeed she would never know.

'Chester?' Maddy had demurred anxiously. 'But that would mean you'd have to move there and—'

'And what?' Max had teased her, starting to kiss her and keeping on kissing her until her half-hearted protests had subsided.

Oh yes, he had baited his hook very carefully indeed and now tonight he had caught his prize and was starting to reel it—her—in.

Nothing had been left to chance, from the champagne he had left chilling on ice before he had picked her up for their dinner date, to the new bedding he had left instructions for the maid to put on his bed and the flowers he had told her to arrange.

'Mmm...' Max murmured, gently nibbling her ear. 'I'm not really looking forward to meeting your father. He isn't exactly going to approve of me as prospective son-in-law material, is he? Not when I haven't even got a proper job...'

He could feel her body going stiff in his arms, and as he raised his head to look down into her eyes, the look of mingled hope, disbelief and adoration he could see so clearly there made him smile in cynical satisfaction.

'Oh, Max...' Madeleine whispered. 'I didn't know...I didn't think... Oh, Max, I love you so much.' She flung her arms around him, holding him tightly as she whispered shakily, 'Daddy is going to *love* you...just like I do, and as for your not having a job...'

'Mmm...' Max prodded between kisses. 'As for me not having a job...we can live on love, is that it?'

Madeleine laughed. 'Well...I...I have some money,' she told him shyly, 'and—'

'No,' Max countered fiercely, softening his voice and his grip on her arms when he saw her shock. 'No, my darling, I'm not the kind of man who could ever live off a woman. I know it's chauvinistic and old-fashioned of me, but, well, that's just the way I am.'

'Oh, Max...I do love you,' Madeleine sighed ecstatically. 'Don't worry about the vacancy,' she urged, giving him a happy, secretive smile. 'I just know that everything will work out all right....'

Her eyes shone with happiness as she lifted her face up towards his. 'So please, please stop worrying about it and kiss me instead.'

'Jack, what is it, what's wrong, where's your mother?' Jon demanded anxiously as his nephew opened the door for him. He had driven straight over to the house after Jack's phone call, his stomach churning with anxiety and guilt.

'She's...she's in the kitchen,' Jack replied unhappily, but as Jon headed towards the closed kitchen door he noticed that Jack was hanging back and that he was obviously reluctant to go with him.

As he pushed the kitchen door open, he had no clear idea of what he expected to find, but it certainly wasn't the sight that greeted him.

Tiggy was squatting in the middle of the kitchen floor surrounded by what looked like the contents of a rubbish bin. She was wearing a thin diaphanous robe through which he should have been able to see her body but couldn't because of the way it was smeared with food. At some stage in the evening she had clearly been sick; he could smell the sour, rank stench of it and his own stomach heaved at its foulness.

'Tiggy...'

As he said her name she focused on him but gave no sign of having recognised him. Her eyes were wild like those of an animal. As Jon studied her more closely, he realised in shocked distaste that it wasn't just her gown that was smeared with food but her hair and face, as well. Food and what he suspected must be traces of dried vomit.

His stomach curdled and he had to grit his teeth against his own nausea. As he watched her, almost unable to comprehend what he saw, she started to crawl away from him, scuttling into a corner like a...scared animal, her eyes never leaving his face as she reached a clawlike hand towards him with what looked like a half-eaten wedge of cake. To his shock, she started to ram it into her mouth, the whole time peering at him like some kind of feral creature.

Dear God... What was happening? What was she *doing* to herself? Instinctively, with a feeling of certainty, Jon knew that this was no isolated incident, no single abberation or reaction to outside pressures and the stress of David's heart attack and everything that had happened since. For the second time in his life, he knew what it was to feel pity for his brother.

The first time had been the night of baby Harry's birth when he had experienced the privilege and emotional intensity of witnessing the miracle of birth, of feeling his whole being flooding with love for the small, helpless life he had just seen born, of sharing with Jenny the miracle of that birth.

Yes, then he had felt something for his brother but it had been a very different kind of pity to what he felt now.

'Tiggy!'

'It's no good. She can't hear...she never can when she's like this....'

The sound of his nephew's voice made him turn round. Dear God, no child should have to witness this ugliness, yet Jack seemed so composed, so knowing...so adult. Then he remembered the way the boy had hung back from entering the kitchen.

'Tiggy...' he tried again, but she was eating something else now, refusing to even look at him, never mind show that she was listening to him.

'She'll have eaten everything soon,' Jack said dispassionately, 'and...and then it will be all right... unless...' He paused and looked up at Jon. 'Sometimes it isn't enough and she has to have more and then...'

Jon could see the boy's face starting to crumble as he tried to control his emotions. Automatically he reached for him, held him in his arms and gently rocked him. Dear God, he felt so thin. Far, far thinner surely than Joss.

There were a hundred questions he wanted to ask him, a hundred things he needed to know. He hadn't the foggiest idea of how to handle this situation. Out of the corner of his eye, he could see Tiggy starting to creep along the floor. She held a knife in her hand now. His heart started to thud unevenly.

How much of this was his fault...his responsibility...? How much had he contributed to tipping her over the edge and into this dark abyss she was now inhabiting?

He couldn't deal with this on his own. He needed help...he needed...

His arm around Jack's shoulders, he started to guide him out of the kitchen. In the hallway he picked up the telephone and punched in a number.

'Who are you ringing?' Jack asked anxiously. Jon hugged him reassuringly as he heard the familiar voice on the other end of the line.

'Jenny,' he said huskily before pausing to clear his throat. 'Jenny, it's me, Jon.'

As she heard her husband's voice, Jenny closed her eyes and leaned against the wall, willing herself not to start crying.

'Jon, yes,' she replied. 'What is it?'

'I'm at David and Tiggy's,' Jon told her. He could hear her indrawn breath and added quickly, 'No, Jen, please don't hang up. This isn't... It's not what you think, Jenny. Please listen,' he pleaded.

Tensely Jenny gripped the receiver. Dear God, what was it he wanted to say? Why was he ringing her? What did he want? To tell her that he was moving in with Tiggy...?

'Jen...I...I need your help. Can you come over? Now...please.'

Jon looked down at Jack who was standing stiffly at his side.

'It's Tiggy,' he heard himself saying. 'She's... she's...there's a bit of a problem,' he told her. 'Please come, Jen...now.'

'Yes...yes...I'll be there,' Jenny promised.

Olivia passed the ambulance on the main road as she drove tiredly home. After she left Saul, she had absently got into her car and driven mindlessly though the dark country lanes, the tears pouring down her face as she wept out her pain and despair.

Saul had been so good about everything and so generous, telling her gently that *he* was the one to blame and not her and that he was a fool for thinking what he had.

'Of course you still love him,' he had told her quietly, lifting her chin and looking into her eyes. 'You're that kind of person.'

'Oh, Saul,' she had wept. 'I'm so sorry. How could I...?'

'It's not your fault,' he had repeated.

But he was wrong. It *was*. *She* should have known. She *had* known but had tried to ignore that knowledge, to tell herself that if Caspar could so easily replace her, then she could do exactly the same.

Only she couldn't. She still loved him...still wanted him, still ached for him with her emotions and her body even as her mind acknowledged the impossibility of their ever settling their differences, of his ever being able to accept her as the person she was.

Saul had not wanted her to leave whilst she was so obviously upset, but she had refused to listen to him, and in the end he had been forced to let her go. She had no real idea how far she had actually driven, only that suddenly she realised that she was totally exhausted and needed to get home.

As she turned into the drive, she saw that the house

was ablaze with lights. Four cars were parked haphazardly outside, five including her mother's. Two of
them she recognised. Her stomach started to churn as
she got shakily out of her car and started to run towards the house.

Jenny had seen her arrive and was at the door waiting for her. Olivia knew the moment she saw her face.
'It's Tiggy, isn't it?' she demanded, and although five
minutes earlier she would have sworn that she had no
tears left, all at once she started to cry again.

Jenny wrapped her in her arms and rocked her
soothingly in much the same way that Jon had done
with Jack earlier.

'It's all right, Livvy, everything's all right,' Jenny
crooned calmly. 'Come inside and sit down. Jon,
put the kettle on, would you?' she called out to her
husband as he appeared in the hallway, but Olivia
shook her head.

'I'm fine,' she whispered. 'I think I know what's
happened.'

Behind Jon she could see two other men. One of
whom she guessed, vaguely recognised, was the local
doctor.

'It's Tiggy, isn't it? She's had another...' She swallowed and bit her lip. 'Is she...?'

'Your mother's got an eating problem, Livvy,' Jenny
told her gently, 'and Dr Travers feels—'

'Your mother needs specialised treatment,' the doctor interjected to tell Olivia. 'I've arranged for her to be
hospitalised for tonight. With this kind of disorder
there's always a danger of someone choking to death,
either on the food they've gorged or on their own
vomit.'

'I knew...I knew what she was doing, but I tried to pretend it was just a one-off. I didn't... I should have...' Olivia looked helplessly at Jenny. 'I *wanted* to tell you, but...'

'Livvy, it *isn't* your fault,' Jenny asserted firmly.

'I *saw* her,' Olivia continued despairingly. 'Just after I came home, I found her in the kitchen one night. Caspar told me then that she needed help...treatment...but I...we...we quarrelled about it. I couldn't believe...I didn't want to believe. I should have listened to him...done something then. I should have known....'

'People like your mother are very skilled at concealing their addiction,' the doctor informed her sympathetically.

'Olivia, please believe it isn't your fault,' Jenny repeated.

'What...what will happen to her?' Olivia asked the doctor uncertainly.

He exchanged a look with Jenny and Jon.

'We've agreed with the doctor that your mother should be admitted into a private clinic that deals in eating disorders,' Jenny replied quietly.

'It's too early to say yet how well she will respond to the treatment. Bulimia isn't an easy problem to deal with either for the sufferer or her family,' Dr Travers explained.

'Your father will have to be told, of course,' Jenny added, looking at Jon.

'Yes. I'll have a word with the specialist first, though,' Jon agreed.

After the doctor had left, Olivia started to thank Jenny and Jon for what they'd done, but Jenny stopped her. 'I feel terribly guilty because we didn't realise what was happening earlier,' Jenny admitted.

'There was no way you could have known,' Olivia comforted her.

Jenny shook her head. 'Somehow one tends to associate eating disorders with younger people. There must have been signs, though, indications.... We must have been too busy with our own lives to have noticed them. Livvy, are you sure you're going to be all right here on your own?' she asked Olivia as she prepared to leave.

It had already been arranged that Jack would go home with Jenny, at his own request.

'Yes. I'll be fine,' Olivia reassured her.

15

Jenny only realised that Jon had followed her home as she was pulling in front of the house. She hung back after she had sent Jack inside, wondering what her husband wanted.

These past few weeks had somehow given him a much more noticeable air of authority; he seemed slightly taller, and as she listened to him talking to the doctor, she'd observed how much more positive and even assertive he was. He had, she recognised, for perhaps the first time in his life, stepped out of David's shadow, and as a consequence, was being judged on his own merits instead of being dismissed as merely David's twin. The change suited him, gave him an added air of masculinity and self-assurance.

She looked away from him as he got out of his car and walked towards her.

'Jenny,' he asked her, 'can we talk?'

Her heart sank. 'That depends on what you want to talk about,' she told him eventually, forcing herself to meet his gaze. 'If by talk you mean that you want my shoulder to cry on because of Tiggy...' She paused and looked away from him again before continuing huskily, 'I appreciate the way you feel about her, Jon. I know you...you believe you love her....'

'No...you're wrong. I don't. I don't know which

makes me feel more ashamed,' he told her sombrely as she stared at him. 'The fact that I fell so easily into the trap that nature sets middle-aged men and so whole-heartedly and stupidly embraced my...my belief that life owed me the chance to be infatuated with the idea of falling in love, or the fact that I could so easily and quickly realise that I didn't love her at all.'

'It must have been a shock for you...finding her like that,' Jenny commiserated. She was trying desperately hard to put aside her own feelings and focus on him but it wasn't easy, especially when she still hurt so much.

'If that's a tactful way of saying that you think that was what brought me to my senses, I can, thank God, at least acquit myself of that. No—' he shook his head '—I had already realised the truth before tonight...this afternoon in fact. I was due to appear in court earlier today and I took Tiggy to Chester with me. We had lunch together. Afterwards... Well, let's just say that when the opportunity to put our...our relationship on a different footing occurred, I very quickly discovered that that wasn't what I wanted at all. To be brutal about it, Jen, my body told me in no uncertain terms that it knew exactly who it wanted and it most certainly wasn't Tiggy.

'No, it wasn't Tiggy I wanted to talk to you about.' He looked levelly at her. 'I know I don't deserve it and I wouldn't blame you if you refused, but is there any chance that we can...that I could... I want to come back, Jen. I've missed you and the kids like hell. I...I've been doing a lot of thinking these past few weeks, and although it hasn't been easy, I've come to accept that no matter how much in the past I might have believed otherwise, a part of me has always subconsciously envied David. I see now how jealous I was of him at times, and I resented the fact that *his* needs, that *he* always had to come first.'

'But *you* were the one who always insisted that he come first,' Jenny countered. 'You always made it perfectly clear that your loyalty to him, your love for him, superseded everything and everyone else....'

'On the surface, yes, because I knew that was what was expected of me, but inside... My son, my wife, my father, my friends, everyone loved David more than they did me and so I suppose when someone, and not just any someone but David's own wife, actually seemed to prefer me... I'm not trying to make excuses for myself,' he said. 'There are none. I despise myself for what I did and always will. I guess a part of me must have been thinking, well...Jenny might prefer you to me but Tiggy, *your* wife, prefers me—'

'Oh no, you're not getting off by thinking that,' Jenny interrupted him fiercely. 'I did not...*do* not prefer David.'

'You married me because you were carrying his child,' Jon reminded her quietly.

'I married *you* for almost the same reason *you* married me,' Jenny admonished him. 'I married you for the sake of David's *child* to give him the family, the father, the protection he deserved, just as you married me to give David the protection you believed he deserved. *I* hardly came into it at all. I could have been anybody.'

Jon frowned as he heard the forlorn note in her voice. 'That's not true,' he objected.

'You didn't love me,' Jenny charged.

He looked away from her, his eyes veiled. 'No, perhaps not,' he agreed heavily at last, and then he took a step towards her and reached for her hand. He held it firmly between his own, his action surprising her into looking questioningly up at him. 'Not then, but... Do you remember the night Harry was born?' he asked her huskily.

Jenny nodded her head. Of course she did. How could she forget it? Her first child, the long struggle to give birth, her joy when they handed her her son.

'*That* is when I fell in love with you,' Jon declared softly. 'That was when I fell in love with *both* of you. Yes, up until then, marriage to you had been a responsibility, my duty...for David's sake, the child you were carrying, David's child, but when I saw him born, suddenly he was *my* child. I can't explain properly just how I felt...there aren't the words. I just know I felt this tremendous uprush of love for both of you.'

'You...you never said anything,' Jenny returned weakly, her voice husky with tears and not just because of the memories Jon's words had conjured up.

'I...there wasn't time,' Jon said simply. 'His life was so short, and afterwards... Well, afterwards, when you told me that there was no reason for us to stay married any longer, I felt...thought it inappropriate to tell you how I felt.'

'I...I was just trying to do the right thing, to give you your freedom,' Jenny explained.

'To give me my freedom.' Jon smiled ruefully at her. 'It was much, much too late for that. What I really wanted you to give me was your love.'

'Oh, Jon.'

'It's not your fault,' he assured her. 'No one can love

to order, and the last thing I would ever have wanted you to do was to pretend...fake....'

'But, Jon, I *did*, *do* love you,' Jenny told him. 'Not when we first married. I don't think that I was capable of allowing myself to love anyone then, but later when Harry...you were so...I loved you then,' she admitted simply. 'But it seemed that I'd burdened you with so much already that I couldn't burden you with that, as well.'

'How old are we?' Jon asked wryly. 'And how long have we been married? And it's taken all *this* for us to be able to tell one another how we really feel.'

'I thought you couldn't possibly love me, especially when I compared myself with Tiggy. She's so—'

'*You're* beautiful,' Jon interrupted her gruffly, cupping her face. Then narrowing his eyes he added, 'I've always thought so. I was so damned jealous the night of the party—seeing you look so lovely. That dress...'

'I thought you didn't like it,' she owned. 'You never told me.'

'I couldn't,' Jon admitted. 'I wanted to, but I just couldn't.'

'Oh, Jon...'

'I hated seeing you dancing with David—I would much rather have been dancing with you. Guy didn't look too pleased, either.'

'Guy is only my business partner,' Jenny asserted firmly.

She silently sent up a small prayer of gratitude for the fact that that was exactly all that he was, even if there had been a moment earlier this evening when...

'I feel almost guilty in a way that we should feel like this—have so much,' Jenny whispered huskily to Jon several minutes later after he had finished kissing her. 'Poor David and Tiggy... What do you think will happen?'

'I don't know.... Jen, there's something I haven't yet told you.'

Quietly she waited.

'It's David. He's been taking money from a client's account.' Briefly he explained as Jenny listened in appalled silence.

'Oh, Jon,' she whispered in shock once he had finished. 'How *could* he have done such a thing? What will happen? There's no way we could pay it back even if we sold everything and—'

'I know, I know,' Jon agreed, reaching out for her and wrapping her in his arms. 'There was a message waiting for me when I got back from Chester this afternoon to say that Jemima Harding had died early this morning. The accountants will *have* to be told now, and the bank.'

'Oh, Jon...' Jenny pressed her hand to her mouth. 'Has David said...?'

Jon shook his head. 'We haven't discussed it. I couldn't, not when...'

'And your father?'

Again, Jon shook his head.

'Oh, Jon,' Jenny repeated sadly as she leaned her head against his chest.

It seemed to be a recurring pattern over the years that their moments of the most intimate shared joy were always overshadowed by David. But this time, he wasn't merely casting a shadow over their lives; he was threatening to ruin them. Jon may not have said so, spelled it out in so many words, but she knew all the same. David might have been the one who had stolen the money, broken a trust, but it was Jon who would have to pay. It always was....

Obligingly Olivia broke off another piece of her sandwich for the bird watching her. She hadn't been hungry anyway, she acknowledged glumly as she scattered the crumbs on the grass in front of her. It was a warm, sunny day and she had come into the square to have her lunch but she had no appetite for it.

The doctor had reported back to them this morning that her mother was stable and that she would be transferred to the clinic later in the afternoon. He would advise, he had added firmly, that at least for a few days, her mother not have any visitors.

'She really isn't up to it and sometimes it can be very distressing, both for the patient and the family.'

Jon had told her this morning about Jemima Harding's death. A tear trickled down her face followed by a second. She bent her head protectively over her unwanted lunch as she fumbled in her handbag for a tissue.

'Olivia?'

She tensed as she heard Ruth's voice, but it was too late; her great-aunt had seen her tears.

'Oh, Livvy my dear, I heard about your mother. I'm *so* sorry,' Ruth began saying compassionately as she sat down next to her on the wooden bench and put an arm around her.

'No, that's not it, not why... I'm not crying for Tiggy. I'm crying for myself,' Olivia told her miserably. 'I miss Caspar so much. I hate myself for saying it but part of me wishes that I'd never offered to stay...that I'd just gone with him.'

'Oh, Livvy...it's not too late,' Ruth responded consolingly. 'You could—'

'No, he doesn't want me any more. *He* believes that loving someone means putting *them* first, you see, and he thinks that I don't love him. At least not enough, because according to him I didn't, and even though I do love him, I'm not sure that I can live like that...with that... I would always feel that it was hanging over me. I...'

She started to cry again, her throat aching from the effort of trying to suppress her tears.

'And anyway,' she said, 'I couldn't go now...not with Dad...'

'Your father's over the worst and, by all accounts, well on the way to recovery. He'll be back at work within a month and then... Olivia my dear, what is it?' Ruth asked in dismay as Olivia buried her head in her hands and started to sob in earnest.

'Oh, Aunt Ruth...'

'Olivia, what is it...? What on earth's wrong? What have I said...?'

'I can't tell you,' Olivia replied tearfully. 'I shouldn't have said anything...I...'

'Of *course* you can tell me,' Ruth admonished her robustly. 'You can and you must, and I'm certainly not leaving this bench until you do. Neither one of us is.'

Olivia gave her a watery smile.

'That's better,' Ruth encouraged. 'Now tell me what's wrong.'

Hating herself for being weak enough to give in to the temptation to unburden herself, Olivia did just that. Ruth let her speak without trying to interrupt her and when the younger woman had finished, Ruth looked across the small pretty square in silence.

'I...I shouldn't have told you. You're shocked and—'

'No, I'm not shocked,' Ruth countered lightly. 'I'm not even particularly surprised. Now *I've* shocked *you*. I'm sorry, Olivia, but then, you see, I rather think I know your father slightly better than you do. You find it hard to accept that he could do something so...dishonest. A child needs to be able to trust and respect its parent, so that's no bad thing.'

'Except that I'm not a child.'

'Maybe not, but it isn't always easy to cast off ingrained modes of behaviour and beliefs...ideals. Perhaps that's why it's easier for me to accept than for you.

'You see, to me, your father always has been and always will be the self-willed and rather selfish little boy who always so skilfully shrugged aside his responsibilities and used his charm and his father's unfortunate tendency to spoil him to his own advantage, leaving Jon to be his whipping boy.' She sat quietly for a moment, seemingly deep in thought. 'Has Jon actually seen the accountants yet?'

'No, not yet,' Olivia told her tiredly.

'Good.' Ruth turned round and looked across the square to Jon's office window. 'I'd better go and see him, then,' she said purposefully, a smile warming her face.

'Go and see him...?' Olivia frowned. 'But—'

'Do you know what I think you should do, Livvy?' Ruth interrupted. Without waiting for Olivia to respond, she continued, 'I think you should go and ring that young man of yours. You do love him,' she reminded Olivia when she saw her expression. 'All right, he *may* not be perfect, you *may* have problems to resolve, but tell me this. Which is the worst alternative, living your life with him, problems and all, or living your life without them *and* without him? Don't waste your life in useless regrets, Olivia my dear. Not like... Go and ring him. I insist.'

'Ruth...?' Jon stood up as his secretary ushered Ruth into his office. She might only live across the square but he couldn't remember the last time she had actually come to the office.

'Sit down, Jon,' she told him crisply. 'We need to talk. Olivia has told me all about David,' she announced forthrightly. 'I take it that as yet no one outside the family knows what's happened?'

'As yet, no,' Jon agreed heavily.

'Good. Now tell me, how much exactly did David borrow from Jemima Harding?'

'Borrow...?' Jon gave her a dry look. 'David didn't borrow anything. David *stole*—'

'No, he did not,' Ruth corrected him authoritatively. 'David, rather unprofessionally to be sure, asked Jemima for a loan. Or rather, I should say, a series of loans. The informal arrangement being that he would repay her on demand. Now with her death he naturally feels that the time has come to repay these loans, even though no specific repayment date was originally put on them.'

Jon shook his head. 'If *only*... David *can't* pay back that money. We both know that.'

'*David* can't,' Ruth agreed, pausing before adding calmly, 'but *I* can.'

Jon stared at her. 'Ruth,' he explained patiently, 'it is really generous of you to make such a suggestion, but David took two million pounds from Jemima's trust fund.'

'Yes, I know,' she acknowledged coolly.

Jon stared blankly at her. '*You* haven't got two million pounds.'

'No, I haven't,' she allowed. 'I think at my last count it was closer to five million.'

'Five million! You've got five million pounds!'

'Jon, please don't take offence, but if I were you, I really wouldn't let my jaw sag like that. It really isn't very flattering, not at your age,' Ruth chided her nephew in a kindly voice. 'And no, I haven't gone senile.' She gave him an amused smile. 'I really do have the money, though I must admit I find it rather irksome to have to use it to save David's skin, but then it isn't just David's skin that's at risk here, is it?' she asked Jon gently. 'You and Jenny and most especially Joss are very special to me...most especially Joss. At my age one is allowed to have favourites and there is no way I would want to see his life and future marred by David's weakness and stupidity.

'I was left a quite substantial sum of money by my mother's sister,' she revealed with a smile. 'No, not five million pounds, nowhere near anything like that, but this was many years ago, and I discovered rather to my own surprise that I seemed to have a talent for the stock market. You'll have to see the bank and the accountants, of course. We can't leave *that* to David.

You can explain to them about David's private arrangement with Jemima—'

'They'll never believe that Jemima agreed to lend David the money.'

'Privately, maybe not,' Ruth concurred, 'but I think you probably will find that they'll be as keen to see the whole affair sorted out as discreetly as we are. It won't do anything to improve their professional standing if it gets out that David was raiding Jemima's account right under their noses, will it?' she asked Jon practically.

'Haven't you forgotten something?' Jon asked his aunt quietly after a brief silence.

'What?' Ruth gave him a quizzical look.

'I owe a duty to my family, Ruth, but I also owe a duty to my own profession. I am honour bound to report David for—'

'No,' Ruth interrupted firmly. 'You may be honour bound to report your *suspicions* but that *is* all they are, Jon. *You* do not, after all, have any proof, do you, that David did *not* have some private arrangement with Jemima?'

'Ruth...' Jon protested.

'*Have* you?' she persisted.

'No,' he agreed, 'but we both know—'

'We both know that David borrowed money from Jemima and that is *all* we know. I do understand, Jon,' she went on more gently, 'but while I might applaud the moral strength that makes you sacrifice your own career and life, I can't say the same about what the prospect of your exposing David will do to the new generation. All of them will be tainted by it.

'And besides, we can't *know* what private arrangement David and Jemima may or may not have had,' she repeated. 'Jemima is now beyond answering any questions and as for David... Well, I wouldn't like to say what effect it might have on his health if he were to be subjected to a rigorous questioning.'

'Ruth, don't do this to me,' Jon begged her wearily. 'You know—'

'I know that you're an honest man, Jon, and that's all I need to know. I'm going home now to speak to my brokers and I want you to get in touch with the bank and the accountants and explain the position with regard to David's loans as you feel that your professional code of conduct requires you to do. You will, of course, also tell them that arrangements have been made within the family to repay the loans even though there is no legal recourse or obligation to cover their repayment. I think you will find that both the accountants and the bank will be so relieved at having been spared the necessity of investigating the matter and escaping all the attendant publicity that they will be only too happy to accept your version of events, publicly at least. And as for David... Well, it goes without saying, he can never be allowed to work again either here or anywhere else. I think it would be best if he decided that in view of his heart attack it would be wiser for him to take early retirement.'

Jon looked at her sombrely. 'Ruth, I just don't know what to say....'

'Then don't say anything. I generally find it is the wisest course,' Ruth told him with a smile.

Olivia closed her eyes and gripped the telephone receiver hard. She had rung the number she had for

Caspar and asked for him. What would he say when he heard her voice? What would he do? Would he speak to her or simply hang up? Was she now just a part of his past life, one he only wanted to forget?

She heard a voice at the other end of the line but it wasn't Caspar's.

'I'm sorry,' she was advised, 'but I'm afraid he isn't available.' Olivia's heart sank.

'Is he...? Could I...? When *will* he be available?' she asked desperately.

'I really couldn't say. He's away at the moment on private business and I have no idea when he's going to come back.'

'I...I see.... You don't...you don't have a number where I could reach him, I suppose?' Olivia asked.

'No, I'm afraid I don't.'

Quietly she replaced the receiver.

Well, at least she had tried. Oh, Caspar, where are you? She could feel the hurt building up inside her in a low, slow surge of agony. Whoever had said that time and distance healed all wounds was wrong. They didn't. They just made it worse.

'Oh, Max...I didn't think you'd be here. The clerk said something about your being in court this morning.'

'The case was cancelled,' Max told the senior member of chambers as he stood awkwardly in the doorway of Max's office looking both irritated and self-conscious. Someone was standing behind him, and when he moved slightly out of the way, Max saw who it was. He frowned. What the hell was Madeleine's housemate doing here?

'Well, since you are here,' the senior member began saying fuzzily, 'I suppose I'd better introduce you. Claudine, this is Max Crighton. Max did his pupillage here and he's currently waiting to find a vacant tenancy.'

'Yes...so I've heard.'

She was smiling as she extended her hand towards Max. He took it reluctantly. He hadn't liked her the first time he met her and he still didn't. He also had a suspicion that she had tried to warn Madeleine about him, which made him like her even less.

'Max—' the senior member's voice was just a shade too hearty, his smile just a touch forced '—Claudine Chatterton will shortly be joining us as a junior barrister. She'll be taking over Clive Benson's place when he retires.' He turned to smile at her, but she wasn't looking at him; she was watching Max, her mouth curling into a smile of knowing amusement.

For once in his life, Max knew that he was in a situation over which he had no control and no power. It *hadn't* been Madeleine who was his rival, he recognised in a surge of white-hot fury; it had been *this* woman, *this* woman who was standing there smiling mockingly...tauntingly at him. *Knowing*...

And Madeleine must have known. The stupid little bitch, why the hell hadn't she said something? He stood up, ignoring the nervous look of mingled dislike and distaste the senior member was giving him, then shouldered his way past both him and Claudine, almost pushing them out of his way as he made for the door.

'Oh dear,' he heard Claudine saying smilingly as he

grimly left the office, 'have we done something to upset him?'

Something to upset him? She knew perfectly well, the bitch.... The bitch! Charlotte had been grossly mistaken in her information. Well, someone was going to pay for making a complete fool of him, for lying to him...*cheating* him out of what was rightfully his. And he knew exactly who that someone was going to be.

Madeleine looked startled as she opened the door to him, her surprise turning quickly to dismay as she saw his face. 'Max, what is it, what's wrong...?'

'You know damn well what's wrong!' he shouted, hurling the words at her like blows. 'Why the hell didn't you tell me that Claudine was up for the tenancy?'

'I...I thought you knew....' Madeleine replied nervously, adding pleadingly, 'Oh, Max, please don't be angry. I know how disappointed you must be...how much you wanted to...to prove yourself by your own efforts, but even Daddy admits that to get into the really top sets of chambers, it isn't enough simply...well, you just have to have the right connections and that's why—'

'The right connections! And just where the hell are *her* right connections, or can I guess? Did Daddy put in a good word for her? Why? He's fucking her, is he?'

'Max...' Madeleine's face had gone white with shock. 'Please, I know how you must feel.'

'Do you...do you...?'

Max grabbed hold of her wrists and began shaking her like a rag doll, ignoring her frantic pleas to let her go. God, when he thought of the time he'd wasted to no purpose, when all along...

'I suppose you thought it was funny, did you, the pair of you?' he demanded as he released Madeleine so forcefully that she almost fell against the wall.

As she struggled to keep her balance, she tried surreptitiously to ease the soreness out of her bruised wrists.

'Max, it wasn't *like* that.... I *know* you're upset, but please, please listen to me....'

'Listen to you...listen to *you!*'

'I've spoken to Daddy,' Madeleine desperately tried to tell him, ignoring the searing contempt she could hear in his voice, avoiding looking directly at him and frantically trying to pretend that everything was really all right, that this wasn't really *her* Max.... Maybe once he had calmed down, things would be different and she would forget that he had ever been like this... frightened her like this....

'I...he...he wants us to have dinner with him and Mummy tonight. He...he says there may be a vacancy coming up at another set of chambers.'

She told him the name and Max stared at her in furious disbelief. It was one of the most exclusive sets of chambers in the Inn and he had as much chance of being considered for a vacancy there as he had of flying to the moon.

'Daddy knows the senior member there...he's had a word with him and...well, Daddy said, since he doesn't have a son, it would be rather nice if he could have a son-in-law to follow in his shoes....'

Madeleine swallowed...and then added miserably, 'I'm sorry I didn't tell you about Claudine but, well, she begged me not to. Oh, Max...' Her eyes filled with tears. 'It's been so horrid listening to you talking about it, knowing how much it meant to you and not being able to say anything, but I promised, and...please don't be cross with me...I know you didn't want me to say anything to Daddy...that you wanted to do it on your own but...'

Max's head was spinning. A place in one of London's top chambers...the patronage of one of the country's most senior judges... He looked consideringly at Madeleine, her head bent low, her eyes downcast. It was all there for the taking...with one proviso.

Son-in-law... *That* meant marriage. Marriage to Madeleine. Last night he had been anticipating the moment when he would tell her just exactly what he thought about her, the moment when he would walk away from her, and now...

'Stop crying, Maddy, my sweet, devious, wonderful Maddy,' he crooned as he took her in his arms. 'Of *course* I'm not cross with you. Well, not very much,' he amended lightly. 'It *was* naughty of you to go to your father.'

'I did it for you...for us,' Madeleine whispered, her mouth trembling. 'So that we could be together....'

'Yes, I know,' Max agreed, gentling his tone. 'But *I* wanted to earn the right to tell your father I want to marry you...not to feel—'

'Oh, Max, don't,' Madeleine pleaded. 'I was just trying to help. I just wanted—'

'I know exactly what you wanted,' Max began murmuring silkily, his voice changing, 'and I know exactly what I want, too....'

'Oh, Max, we can't,' Madeleine whispered breathlessly, 'not now. It isn't even lunch-time and... Oh, Max...'

'What time are we having dinner with your parents?' he asked as he slid his hands under her top to caress her breasts.

His mind was working overtime, racing ahead.... He would get his place in chambers *and* his grandfather's money and if the price he had to pay was a few years of marriage to Madeleine, then so what? In three and even four years' time he would still only be in his late twenties. He would have to secure his position financially, of course. Make sure that when they did divorce he didn't lose out and he would have to make sure, as well, that there were no children. There was no way he was going to be forced to support a couple of brats he had never even wanted.

'I'll have to take you home to meet my family,' Max was promising her as he guided Madeleine upstairs. 'They're going to love you.' But as he took her in his arms and started to kiss her, it wasn't Madeleine's small round face he could see, but the amused, mocking expression in Claudine Chatterton's eyes as she stood in the doorway of his office.

It wasn't over...not yet...not by a long shot...

Caspar paused before turning the car into the drive that led to Olivia's parents' house.

He had no idea how Olivia was going to react to his arrival. Initially when he had left her, his mood fuelled by a lethal cocktail of affronted male ego, hurt pride and sense of injustice, he had told himself that in ending their relationship and distancing himself from her, he was simply saving himself the bother of the pointless trauma of trying to pretend that they still loved one another when quite patently they did not.

It had taken him a week of expecting her to contact him coupled with an emotional backlash that began with self-righteous anger and ended with the bitter realisation that she was not going to telephone to make him understand just *what* he had done and—even more painfully—accept why he had done it.

It had never worked as a child, trying to bring his inattentive parents to heel or to command their attention and concern to evoke their parental love, so why the hell had he thought it would work this time and with someone like Olivia, especially with someone like Olivia?

He could now plainly understand how she must have felt—that he had let her down by not sympathising with her need to step into her father's shoes.

The truth was that he had been jealous, jealous of the fact that anyone other than himself could be important. He had visited some old friends whilst he was at home and had sat politely listening to the woman complaining tiredly that her partner was jealous of their two-year-old child.

'It's ridiculous,' she had told Caspar wearily. 'Ricky is his son, and *that's* part of the reason that I love him—because he *is* Gerry's child—as well as for himself, but Gerry can't or rather won't see that. He only sees that Ricky is another male taking my attention away from him. I just can't seem to make him see that the reason Ricky clings more to *me* is because he senses Gerry's rejection of him. Ricky needs Gerry's love.'

Caspar had at first thought she was exaggerating, but it had only been later, turning the conversation over in his mind when he was alone, that he had begun to ask himself if he, too, would turn out to be the kind of father who was afraid of the love his partner had for their children, the kind of man who resented it and actively tried to punish both the child and the mother because of it, the kind of man his own father had been....

Dusk was settling as he drew up outside the house, his arrival activating the security lights. He got out of the car and paused in thought before heading towards the entrance. He had been unnecessarily hard on Olivia, especially with regard to her mother, he acknowledged. As a child he had had no one to protect him from the realities of his parents' chaotic lives. *Was* that in part why he had refused to give Olivia the escape route of believing that her mother's obvious problem was simply a minor abberation?

He still didn't feel that it would serve any useful purpose to try to deny that Tiggy had a problem, which so far as he was concerned needed professional treatment, but he *could* have handled the situation differently, been more cautious, more circumspect, in his appraisal *and* his comments, he conceded as he rang the doorbell and then stood back to wait.

Olivia was upstairs when the doorbell rang. She almost decided against going down to answer it; she didn't really feel up to seeing anyone. Jon had already rung her earlier to tell her about Ruth's visit.

'I didn't mean to tell her,' Olivia had confessed. 'I don't really know why I did. She caught me at a weak moment, I suppose....'

'Well, I must admit that I'm certainly grateful that you did,' Jon had told her. 'Oh, at first I wasn't really convinced by what she said but I have to say I was wrong and she was right. The accountants and the bank did seem loath to ask too many questions about David's "loans" and I got the impression they were just happy that the money was being repaid. There are no heirs, of course. Inland Revenue will get the bulk of Jemima's estate and we must hope that they, too, are content to accept the status quo.'

She knew that it couldn't be either him or Jenny calling. Jon had told her that they were going out for a celebration meal.

'Alone,' Jon had told her wryly, adding, 'Ruth's babysitting and Jack says to tell you that he's going to call round tomorrow for his sports kit.'

Jack. Olivia bit her lip. She felt that she ought to have insisted on taking charge of her brother, but there was no doubt that he was better off with Jon and Jenny. Staying with them, not only would he have the company of his cousins to occupy him and stop him from brooding, but as Jenny had pointed out, since both he and Joss were at the same school, it made things far simpler to have the two of them under one roof than two separate ones. *She* certainly would have found it hard to give him the time and attention she knew he needed. It was gone six o'clock most evenings before she got home and she left at eight in the morning.

She and Jon had found themselves working together as a team as Jon himself had commented, and they were now beginning to get through the backlog of work her father had stacked up. There was a good deal of satisfaction to be found in managing to achieve a clear desk, Olivia had decided, and what surprised her even more was that she didn't really miss the fast pace of her previous job.

She *did* miss Caspar, though.

Tiredly she went downstairs and opened the door.

'Caspar!' She cried out his name in disbelief, staring at him as though she couldn't believe her eyes, which in truth she couldn't.

'Is it too late to admit that I've been a fool and say that I've changed my mind?' Caspar asked simply. 'I thought I was already a man, Livvy, whole and complete, but I've discovered over these past few weeks that I'm not. Nowhere near. I can't be a man if I can still behave like a spoiled child. And as for my being complete, I will *never* be complete again without you.'

'I tried to ring you,' Olivia could only think to say as she stepped back so that he could walk into the house, 'but you weren't there....'

'No, I was probably on my way here,' Caspar agreed, 'praying with every mile that you weren't going to give me the treatment I deserved and tell me to go straight back again. Is it too late, Livvy?' he asked her directly.

Olivia shook her head and then told him rawly, 'Yes, very much too late for me to stop loving you. Oh, Caspar,' she wailed as she flung herself into his arms, 'I've missed you *so* much. I've *wanted* you so much. I thought it was so important to assert my independence and not let you bully me emotionally by demanding to be the most important person in my life, but that's exactly what you are...*who* you are,' she amended.

'Stop talking, woman, and let me kiss you,' Caspar commanded lovingly as he drew her into his arms, tightening them possessively around her. He started to bend his head towards her whilst Olivia reached up eagerly towards him, but then he stopped and glanced up and down the hallway. 'Where are your parents?' he asked her in a whisper. 'The kind of behaviour I'm about to indulge in right now isn't something I feel I want anyone to witness.'

'Dad's in a nursing home,' Olivia explained, 'and Tiggy...'

As Caspar saw the sadness darken her eyes, he held her even more tightly and watched her tenderly.

'You were right about her, Caspar. She was...she did need help. Hopefully she's going to get it now....' Quietly she told him what had happened.

'Uncle Jon and I went to the clinic this afternoon and talked to the specialist who runs it. She was very kind but very honest, as well. She says there aren't any statistics to show how many bulimics recover simply because, as yet, none have been out of addiction long enough to be considered recovered. In Tiggy's case...well, she suspects that her addiction has gone on for a long time, which means, of course, that helping her to acknowledge and overcome it will be very much harder. She had hoped to talk to Dad, but...'

'Does David know what's happened to your mother?' Caspar asked her, concerned about the pain he could see in her eyes.

'Yes, he knows,' Olivia answered quietly. 'Mr Hayes told him this afternoon, but it seems that Dad doesn't...doesn't...'

'Doesn't what?' Caspar waited, not wishing to push her. 'Doesn't care?'

Much as that knowledge must have hurt Olivia, he

wasn't totally surprised. There had been something about them as a couple that somehow hadn't quite rung true, something that despite their apparent togetherness had suggested that they were simply two people who lived under the same roof.

'He's still recovering from his own heart attack, of course, and the doctor has told us that sometimes the shock of that happening, the fear it can generate, can make people behave irrationally and...and selfishly. They're afraid, I suppose, that he could have another heart attack, and so anything that causes him any kind of stress...or soul-searching, has to be avoided.'

In other words, David Crighton was quite happy to let his brother and his daughter take over his responsibilities towards his wife for him.

'That's not all, is it?' Caspar probed gently, 'Something else is bothering you. What is it?'

Olivia gave him a startled look. 'I went to see you at the airport,' she said evasively. 'You were kissing...'

Caspar smiled. So she *had* tried to get in touch with him after all; she *hadn't* simply let him walk away.

'In actual fact,' he explained, '*Hillary* was the one kissing me and she was most certainly not the one I wanted to be kissing me, and that one kiss was as far as it went. Now, tell me what's really bothering you, apart from the fact that there's no way I'm letting you sleep alone tonight or sharing that ridiculous pint-size bed with you, no matter how much your grandfather might disapprove.'

Olivia laughed. 'Gramps won't know,' she teased back. 'He's confined to bed at the moment with his bad leg.'

'Confined to bed. Now that sounds like a very, very good idea,' Caspar began and then stopped.

Olivia saw the look he was giving her and shook her head lightly. 'It's Dad,' she told him simply. 'There's been a...a problem. It's...it's all sorted out now but...'

She knew it was up to her whether or not she chose to tell him. If she did and he didn't approve of the way they had dealt with the problem, then there was a risk that it would lead to a renewed alienation between them, and if she didn't... Well, that wasn't the kind of relationship she wanted with her man, she acknowledged, a relationship where things had to be kept hidden, secret, because they couldn't trust one another's reactions.

She took a deep breath and hoped for the best. 'Dad stole some money from a client. Luckily Aunt Ruth was able to come up with a scheme whereby it could be paid back without Uncle Jon having to report it. I suspect Uncle Jon still thinks that he *should* have reported it, even though it would not have been Dad who would have carried the brunt of any penalties the Law Society might have chosen to impose, but Uncle Jon. Aunt Ruth was very insistent.'

Quickly she told him the whole sorry tale and then stood back searching his face for some indication of his reaction. When she could find none, her stomach muscles started to tighten in knots of tension.

Caspar looked at her.

'So Aunt Ruth was ruthless, was she?' he quipped at last. 'And quite rightly so. What your father did was wrong but Ruth is on the mark when she says that all of you would have been affected if his theft had become public.'

'It still doesn't seem fair that Dad should get away with...with what he did,' Olivia confessed seconds later as she leaned her head in grateful love against Caspar's shoulder. 'Just as he's always got away with things....'

'Perhaps not, but justice, as they say, is blind and sometimes the innocent can be hurt along with the guilty. Oh, by the way,' he added as he turned her gently towards the stairs. 'I almost forgot. I've checked with the university in Manchester and there's a lectureship coming up that I can apply for if I wish. It would mean one or both of us commuting, I suppose, but...'

Olivia stared at him. 'You mean you've actually...you're really prepared... You'd really come back *here* to live and work?' Her voice broke.

'Why not? You're here, aren't you?' Caspar returned lovingly.

'Oh, Caspar!' she cried. 'I love you, I love you so much.'

'Thank you,' he replied simply before adding, 'and never mind "Oh, Caspar". What *I* want to hear and what I fully intend to hear is "Oooh...oooh...ooooh, Caspar".'

Olivia laughed. 'Really. And there was I hoping you wouldn't leave me breath for anything like that....' she managed to say between kisses. She laughed again as he released her and she started to run towards the stairs, knowing perfectly well that he would catch her long before she made it to the comfortable guest bedroom with its cosy double bed.

David smiled at the receptionist.

'You're leaving us?' she asked, frowning. 'But...'

'I have to go,' David told her confidingly. 'My wife isn't very well unfortunately and I'm needed at home.'

'Oh, well, in that case, I suppose...'

David gave her a second smile. He had been planning things all day. No need for him to concern himself with Tiggy any more, thank God. Someone else had that onerous responsibility now. Jack was safe with Jon and Jenny. There was the other matter, of course, but he knew that Jon would find a way of sorting things out. Good old Jon.

It was time *he* was allowed to choose what *he* wanted to do with his own life. High time. Ben would naturally be upset...but he would understand; he always had. Still smiling, David walked out into the darkness.

'He's left...? But *how*...*where*...?' Jon asked the receptionist in exasperation. She had been summoned by the specialist, whom Jon had telephoned when he discovered that David had checked out of the nursing home, to explain exactly what had happened.

'I don't know,' she replied unhelpfully. 'He didn't say. He just said that his wife needed him.'

Jon looked at the specialist, who shook his head. 'I've already checked. I'm afraid they haven't seen or heard from him.'

'But where has he gone?' Jon queried a second time, 'and why?'

Mr Hayes frowned as he looked at him. 'I don't know,' he admitted, 'but what I *do* know is that every year, every day, people do disappear by choice. Some because they see it as their only way out of an impossible situation, and some, because...well...who knows?'

'You think *David* has done that...simply disappeared?'

'*Chosen* to disappear,' the specialist corrected him.

Jon closed his eyes.

'Try not to worry,' the other man advised. 'He may simply have gone to visit friends or...' When he saw the look Jon was giving him, he stopped. 'It happens,' he said, shrugging. 'It does happen.'

As he drove onto the ferry, David was whistling. God but he felt good. This was how life should be lived. How life, his life, was meant to be lived. Freely—unplanned, uncluttered and unencumbered by the needs of others. He was free at last!

'What on earth are we going to tell Ben?' Jon asked Jenny soberly after he told her what had happened.

'Nothing,' Jenny told him crisply. 'Let the doctor tell him. *David* is not your responsibility, Jon,' she reminded her husband. 'He's your *brother*, you are his twin, yes, but he is not your responsibility. Besides, we've got a wedding to plan,' she reminded him.

'And one to attend,' Jon agreed.

Max had telephoned them earlier to announce his engagement just after Olivia and Caspar had left, Olivia having half-shyly asked Jenny if she would help her with her wedding plans.

'I don't want a big fussy affair, just something very traditional and simple....'

'Don't listen to her,' Caspar had warned Jenny. 'I

want the whole works so that I can bore the pants off our grandchildren, talking about it to them.'

'David's made his choice about the way he wants to live his life,' Jenny told Jon gently as she leaned across to kiss him. 'That's *his* right...just as it's *our* right to choose how *we* live *our* lives.'

Lovingly he smiled back at her and then murmured, 'Do you think two ancient people in their forties and fifties would be allowed by their offspring to plead tiredness and go to bed early?'

'*Not* if it's Joss you're trying to convince,' Jenny answered, laughing. 'You promised you'd take him and Jack fishing tonight, remember...?'

Jon groaned and demanded plaintively, 'What does a man have to do in this household to get time on his own with his wife?'

'Put sleeping tablets in everyone else's milk?' Jenny suggested drolly.

'I wish,' was Jon's heartfelt response as Joss came rushing in, demanding to know if his father was ready to leave. 'Oh, I wish!'

shocking pink

THEY WERE ONLY WATCHING...

The mysterious lovers the three girls spied on were engaged in a deadly sexual game no one else was supposed to know about. Especially not Andie and her friends whose curiosity had deepened into a dangerous obsession....

Now fifteen years later, Andie is being watched by someone who won't let her forget the unsolved murder of "Mrs. X" or the sudden disappearance of "Mr. X." And Andie doesn't know who her friends are....

WHAT THEY SAW WAS MURDER.

ERICA SPINDLER

Available in February 1998 at your favorite retail outlet.

The Brightest Stars in Women's Fiction.™

MIRA™

MES415

Coming in March 1998
from *New York Times* bestselling author

Jennifer Blake

**The truth means everything to Kane Benedict.
Telling it could destroy Regina Dalton's son.**

Down in Louisiana, family comes first—that's the rule
the Benedicts live by. So when a beautiful redhead starts
paying a little bit too much attention to his grandfather,
Kane decides to find out what the woman really wants.

But Regina's not about to tell Kane the truth—that she's
being blackmailed and the extortionist wants Kane's
grandfather's business...or that the life of her son is
now at stake.

KANE

Available where books are sold.

**The Brightest Stars
in Women's Fiction.™**

MJB429

From national
bestselling author

SHARON SALA

SWEET BABY

So many secrets...

It happened so long ago that Tory Lancaster can't
recall being the little girl who came home to an
empty house.

A woman now, Tory is trying to leave behind the
scarring emotions of abandonment and sorrow—
desperate to love, but forever afraid to trust. With the
help of a man who claims to love her, Tory is able to
meet the past head-on—a past haunted by images of
a mysterious tattooed man and the doll that was her
only friend. But there are so many secrets, so
little time....

Available in February 1998
at your favorite retail outlet.

 **The Brightest Stars
in Women's Fiction.™**

Look us up on-line at: http://www.romance.net   MSS416